SUSAN,
So grateful for you.
Thank you for carrying us through

Kareen

The

Tsarina's Legacy

You're a blessing
in so many
ways! Thanks
for keeping us
from being
upside down!
ANDREW
MANN

Thanks for
being best
Tsarina in
the world!

Taylor
Upside Down
Conference
2017

ALSO BY JENNIFER LAAM

The Secret Daughter of the Tsar

The
Tsarina's Legacy

JENNIFER LAAM

ST. MARTIN'S GRIFFIN
NEW YORK

THE TSARINA'S LEGACY. Copyright © 2016 by Jennifer Laam. All rights reserved. Printed in the United States of America. For information, address St. Martin's Press, 175 Fifth Avenue, New York, N.Y. 10010.

www.stmartins.com

Library of Congress Cataloging-in-Publication Data

Names: Laam, Jennifer, author.

Title: The tsarina's legacy / Jennifer Laam.

Description: New York : St. Martin's Griffin, 2016.

Identifiers: LCCN 2015045267 | ISBN 9781250091512 (hardcover) | ISBN 9781250068798 (softcover) | ISBN 9781466877344 (ebook)

Subjects: LCSH: Inheritance and succession—Fiction. | Russia—Kings and rulers—Fiction. | Russia—History—Fiction. | BISAC: FICTION / Historical. | FICTION / Sagas. | GSAFD: Historical fiction.

Classification: LCC PS3612.A245 T78 2016 | DDC 813/.6—dc23

LC record available at http://lccn.loc.gov/2015045267

Our books may be purchased in bulk for promotional, educational, or business use. Please contact your local bookseller or the Macmillan Corporate and Premium Sales Department at 1-800-221-7945, extension 5442, or by e-mail at MacmillanSpecialMarkets@macmillan.com.

First Edition: April 2016

10 9 8 7 6 5 4 3 2 1

To Melissa and Lou Ann.
Thanks for getting me started.

The
Tsarina's Legacy

Prologue

A cluttered mind seeks solace in ritual and routine. Grisha reminded himself of this simple truth as he crossed himself and dropped to his knees. How easy it had been to fall away from the world, as though sinking into a bedroll made of the finest down. The monastic order may have resided a short distance from the palace, but it was the difference between heaven and a fatally flawed earth. In this peaceful place, Grisha's melancholy kept a safe distance. The entrancing smoky sweetness of incense mingled with the aroma of birch-wood fires blazing in hearths. All was stillness and bliss.

The flickering tips of tapers and tiny oil lanterns illuminated the face on the icon before him. In the vast heaven of holy images, Grisha sought comfort in the steady gaze of St. Catherine, an eternal beauty in her flowing scarlet robes. He felt the divine presence as a reassuring hand on his shoulder, steadying him while whispering seductively in his ear. Lingering on her visage, he began to wonder how St. Catherine might have looked in life, how her shape might have tempted him. Flushed, he lowered his face to avoid stern looks from the monks gathered for prayers.

As matters stood, the holy brothers barely tolerated Grisha's presence and were particularly vexed when visitors from court disturbed the simple order of this place, their false voices ringing out sharply amid the holy quiet. The women whispered in his ear, giggled while they fiddled with makeshift head coverings, and fussed over his scruffy beard. The monks tried to avoid these preening intruders. They shuffled their feet at a faster pace as they passed his cell, while messages were slipped into the loose folds of Grisha's cassock with delicate, persistent hands.

Grisha accepted the notes reluctantly, reading them by candlelight before the last service of the night. Always the same motif. The empress was distraught and needed him back at court. She was lost without him. Grisha burned the paper in a candle's dancing flame, taking strange joy in the pinpricks of pain as the fire brushed against his skin. The ashes left smudges on his fingers, like those Catholics bore on their foreheads at the commencement of Lent. The women, though charming in their own rights, could not compete with the path he'd chosen. What fool would return to the empty life of court when he'd found sublimity here?

As he lowered his head to prostrate himself before St. Catherine, Grisha's stomach began to rumble. He had grown accustomed to the epicurean delights of the empress's court, whereas the meals of the monastic order were meager even by the stingiest standards. Of course, there were subtle delights for the senses here as well, a blurry haze of hallowed scents, chiming bells, glistening colors, and gold leaf affixed to wood.

Footsteps fell softly behind him. Grisha twisted to see who approached. One of the older monks, Vladimir, his robe in disarray, headed in his direction. Vladimir ducked to avoid a low eave that threatened to topple the black *kamilavka* from his head.

The monks began a low chant. Still on his knees, Grisha scooted to a side shelf and withdrew one of the new prayer books that still smelled of fresh leather and vellum. No doubt Vladimir merely felt out of sorts over some nonsense or other. Perhaps a stray sister from the nearby convent had flirted with a kitchen boy, or possibly Vladimir simply required assistance in dealing with a cat with a lame paw.

"Grigory Alexandrovich, you have another visitor. She appears of a high rank."

Grisha had received a guest only yesterday and wasn't yet in the mood for another, no matter her rank. He shook his head, beard tickling his neck. "After my prayers."

"You should make an allowance for this guest," Vladimir insisted, adjusting his lopsided headwear. "The prayers . . . our Holy Father will understand."

"You know this visitor then?"

"She says her name is Countess Bruce." Vladimir spoke with the weight of newfound self-importance. "Her carriage bears the imperial insignia."

Grisha smiled. The Countess Bruce was one of Catherine's closest friends. It seemed the empress had grown more desperate. "I shall be pleased to see her," he told Vladimir, "once my prayers are complete. She may observe if she wishes." He opened the prayer book and joined the other voices in the singsong liturgy, bobbing his head forward and back in a manner once demonstrated to him by a Talmudic scholar. Vladimir shuffled out of the chamber.

Grisha tried to absorb the power of the moment, to focus on the rise and fall of voices, the rhythm and flow, and so transcend his flawed earthly self. But his mind wandered. He pondered what urgent matter had driven Countess Bruce to the monastery. Likely he would be regaled with tales of collapsed soufflés at the imperial dessert table and the madness of the latest pretentious twits out to win the empress's heart.

Let them try. He had fought to win the enigmatic Catherine's love for years, since the moment he first saw her astride a stallion, wearing the dark green uniform of the Preobrazhensky Regiment, ready to seize her husband's throne on an endless white night. She was regal, radiating power, created to rule. Her gaze had sent lightning searing through his chest. He had been born to worship her. It was his destiny.

But her love? That prize eluded him still.

Grisha sensed a quiet intake of breath as another lowly corporeal presence entered the holy space. Never mind. He had come to the monastery to commune with the celestial. The countess could wait. Yet even as the brothers reached the end of their chant, the visitor remained silent. Grisha found this odd. Countess Bruce had never been a patient soul. He expected her to clear her throat dramatically and tap the dainty heel of her shoe to steal his attention.

Grisha glanced behind him. His visitor had a sable cloak drawn close around her shoulders, her face obscured underneath a velvet hood. Tiny hands in leather gloves clutched a prayer book.

The old wound tore open, piercing his heart. How often had he grasped those dainty hands and begged for a moment of her precious time? How often had he kissed them, declaring his love, heart thumping as Empress Catherine laughed softly in his face?

"I thought I might join you," Catherine said quietly, opening the prayer book. "Forgive the deception, but I did not care to call undue attention to my presence."

"May I stand?"

She nodded and he rose to his feet unsteadily. Taking her arm, Grisha guided her from the chapel to the privacy of a narrow corridor and a shadowy alcove. He drew the thin silken drapes shut.

"Is it wise to cut short your prayers?" Catherine moved closer to him, lowering her hood so that he might see her face in the dim light, her playful features and coy blue eyes. "I should think you of all souls require every last one."

"My heart could not freely return to prayer now, Your Majesty."

"I am surprised to hear it. I think you hide behind God in this place, use God to punish me. You take refuge here, but it is a mere gambit to make me jealous."

Grisha tried not to stare at the empress. He would lose himself if he did. Then he remembered his own face, the scarring in his left eye forever limiting his vision. He had come to peace with the defect, but not around Catherine. For the empress, he needed to be perfect.

Attempting to position himself so she might not notice his disfigurement, he turned his attention heavenward. Through the dusty pane of a high window, he spotted the snowy tips of a birch tree quivering in the wind. This was life. Outside in nature. Inside with God. How much time had he wasted already in chilly palace rooms and overheated barracks?

"I only followed my heart," he told Catherine.

She set the prayer book aside and placed a hand firmly on his arm. "Look at me."

Catherine was his sovereign. He had no choice but to do as she commanded.

"Since you abandoned my court, I am threatened from every side. Even Paul . . ."

She bowed, hiding her face once more in the shadows. Not that it mattered. Grisha had seen the contempt in her expression often enough when she spoke of her feckless son. Paul worried more over his fussy military parades than the qualities of an enlightened empire: culture, art, expansion, tolerance. Catherine, despite a mother's natural inclination to make excuses for her child, was all too aware of his shortcomings.

"Now that he is of age, some would see him rule in my place."

Grisha felt his first defenses slipping. After she had spent ten years on the throne, could Catherine's position be endangered? "Never."

"Paul accused me of trying to kill him. My own son! He claimed

I ordered glass shattered in his favorite pudding. What nonsense. And yet there are those who listen and whisper."

"Some whisper, but none believe."

"Paul must not take the throne . . . not yet," she amended quickly. "He is not ready."

"Anyone can see that," Grisha said.

She stroked the length of his beard. He felt like a pet, like one of her greyhounds, and yet he couldn't help but give in to the comfort of her touch. "You look a fright, my dove," she teased. "Like a sailor trapped too long on an island after a tempest."

He caught the scent of her perfume, floral with a dark hint of musk. "What do you want of me, *matushka*?" he finally asked.

Catherine lowered her voice to a whisper, forcing him to incline his head nearer her body. Her fingers shifted, now lightly resting on his neck. "God would not have gifted you with ambition and a taste for politics unless He intended you to use those talents."

"I am but a humble soul in need of saving. I have found my place here."

"That isn't fair. How can a mere mortal compete with God?"

"You were never a mere mortal," Grisha told her. "You never will be."

"I could command you to return, but I ask it instead. As a gesture of your affection."

"My affection was rejected again and again. How many times did I tell you I loved you? And yet you kept me at a distance."

She removed her hand and looked up at him once more, her bright eyes moistened with tears. He suspected she'd manufactured the tears to toy with his emotions, and yet his heart ached nonetheless.

"I'm sorry you were hurt," she told him. "If you return, everything will change. You will have whatever you desire."

Everything about Catherine left him helpless and besotted,

from the curve of her waist to her intoxicating ambition. Surrounded once again by sensual pleasure, he would change. He would forget the peace he knew here and be at war with himself once more. "I fear for my soul, for what I will become if I return to court."

"You are meant to be a man of this world," she said, eyes flashing. "You are meant to lead armies and build new cities, a new Russia."

"You are surrounded by capable men," he said.

"Who speak only flattery and act only in fear. I have no use for such men. Russia is at a crossroads, on the threshold of greatness. I need someone who will stand up to me and challenge my decisions if they are misguided."

"I am called to a spiritual life. I shall remain here."

"Your motherland needs you. What will become of you if you remain in this place?"

As Catherine spoke, the divine hand slowly lifted from his shoulder. He knew too well what would become of him here. The peace he found so soothing would come to dull his senses until he wasted away. Perhaps God had sent Catherine, not to test his faith, but to show him the right path. A young man with an appetite for life should be of this world—was *meant* to be of this world.

Even so, he would not let her victory come too easily, not after all he had suffered at her hands. "I have found God here."

"God is on my side, Grigory Alexandrovich. He has drawn me here so that you might see your destiny." Catherine tilted his chin gently and forced him to look her in the eyes. "You belong to me."

That evening, Grisha shaved his beard. A thread of guilt wormed its way through his chest as he watched the long strands fall to the floor, but he was no longer willing to turn his back on the life Catherine offered.

The imperial carriage returned him to the Winter Palace, jingle bells ringing on the harnesses of eight white stallions as the runners

cut through the snow lining the ice-encrusted river. Grisha occupied the apartment below the empress, ascending a spiral staircase
to visit her at night. Life meant little without her. It was God's
plan.

One

The sharp smell assaulted his senses immediately. Fortunately, Grisha Potemkin had been warned in advance. He tucked his scroll tighter underneath his arm and withdrew a lavender-scented handkerchief from his pocket. The tight breeches and heavy fabric of his European waistcoat felt thick and burdensome against his bloated stomach. Serving in the south, in his own military encampments, he had grown accustomed to silk robes and loose trousers.

He settled next to a stout cadet in an ill-fitting uniform. The young man gave him a sideways glance and edged slowly away, mopping his broad forehead with a mottled handkerchief. No matter. The opinions of Catherine's courtiers scarcely fazed him anymore. Seventeen years had passed since he left the monastery and returned to this world. He'd long since ceased to care what anyone thought.

Except Catherine. Always Catherine.

Grisha surveyed the crowded salon with his one good eye. Many of the men fidgeted and inched closer to the walls. A few appeared near to forty, while most looked straight out of the Cadet

Corps. Catherine had always surrounded herself with youth. Even the chefs in the kitchen were rosy and slim, their youthful metabolisms impervious to decadent preparations. Amid the fresh faces, Grisha spotted a few men even older than him, bodies stiff in formal uniforms, rusting medals and frayed sashes adorning their fragile chests.

An elderly brigadier, face sun lined and flecked with brown spots, hobbled to a silver samovar and struggled to fill a delicate china cup with hot water.

"Not too strong this time." Catherine's newest favorite, Platon Alexandrovich Zubov, called. He reclined lazily on a richly upholstered chaise longue, long limbs sprawled, nibbling on a wedge of brie. "And don't forget my pot of raspberry jam. Mishka adores it. Let's try to keep him happy. We don't want another accident."

Zubov waved at his pet monkey, its clever face surrounded by a cream-colored ruff of fur. The creature's urine clouded the plush rug, one of many gifts Grisha had presented to Catherine at the close of the first war with the Turks. The rug was woodland green and woven with interlacing curlicues and darkly blossoming roses, a pattern modeled after a concubine's boudoir in Topkapi Palace. He remembered Catherine's breath, warm and gentle in his ear, when she thanked him. *It is as I said. You were meant to be a man of this world.*

The brigadier passed, attempting to balance Zubov's tea and jam in each hand. Tucking his scroll in place under his arm, Grisha extended his hand to take the pot of jam. The old man signaled his gratitude with a weary smile.

Zubov's monkey assessed the room, smacking his lips, small eyes glittering. Grisha flexed his hand and tried not to shudder. He had seen that look before, in the eyes of one of his officers while choosing a man to execute, to break the will of the other prisoners.

At last, the monkey chirped and bounded over to a courtier cringing near the back exit. The creature plucked the freshly powdered silver wig from the man's head and twirled it in his hand, as though preparing for some exotic ball game. He hoisted the wig up in the air, where it caught on the chain of a crystal chandelier.

Sputters of nervous laughter erupted from the corners of the room. Zubov choked on his cheese and coughed, handsome features distorted as he worked the food down his throat and laughed. He took a long swallow of wine. "Priceless! Priceless!"

The men in the room managed a few more chortles. Even the courtier who'd lost his wig tried to smile at his ruined hairpiece. Silver powder scattered on the dark green carpet below.

The monkey scampered up Zubov's arm and hopped onto his shoulder. Zubov ran his hand through the creature's luxuriant fur. Grisha escorted the old man to Zubov's side table, where he placed the pot of jam next to the tea.

"Prince Potemkin!" Zubov cried, catching Grisha's eye. "When did you sneak in?"

The cadet who had been standing next to Grisha suddenly straightened his back. Grisha realized the young man hadn't recognized him at first.

"Your Most Serene Highness," Zubov intoned. "Field Marshal! Grand Admiral of the Black Sea! Have I learned your titles correctly? It seems the empress enjoys frequently adding to their number." He fluttered his large hands at Grisha's medallions and ribbons. "My brain simply cannot keep pace."

"Prince of Tauride," the cadet told Zubov helpfully, using the ancient name for the Crimea.

Zubov glared at the cadet but kept his voice merry, still reclining as though he hadn't a care in this world. "We've been expecting you, Prince. What kept you?" He cocked an eyebrow imperiously. "Fucking one of your officers' wives again?"

Low laughter filled the room, this time genuine.

Grisha needed to appear as though he didn't care—only the laughter had grown so loud he feared Catherine might hear. He felt sure she'd taken to her neighboring study, quill in hand, scribbling her correspondence, one ear inclined to the door for signs of unrest.

But he had no intention of being driven away by Zubov's hollow attempts at wit. The stench of urine cut through the lavender oil in his handkerchief and Grisha stuffed the linen in his pocket.

"And here I thought I was early for our appointment. We were meant to discuss plans for the construction of a mosque in Moscow. I didn't realize you'd planned court entertainment first."

"Yes, yes." Zubov drew to full attention, straightening the ruffles above his ridiculous velvet frock coat. The monkey dug his fingers deep into Zubov's shoulders so as not to fall when his master moved. "But a mosque in the very heart of our land? Wouldn't a church make more sense? We're still a Christian people, are we not?"

Grisha needed to tread carefully. Rumors had reached his ear, even in the faraway southern lands where he had spent the last several months, tales of Zubov's youthful beauty and hold on the empress's affections. He saw it for himself now: Zubov's fine features, broad shoulders, and brilliant eyes, so different from the lumpiness that had spoiled Grisha's own looks as the years passed.

"The empress has taken care to preserve cordial relations with her subjects of the Islamic faith," he said. "I am particularly pleased with this design. It is modeled after a mosque in the old fortress of Ochakov."

"And yet you ran the heathen into the ground in that godforsaken place."

Grisha's hands, slick with perspiration, worked in and out of fists. He had assumed his audience with Zubov merely a formality to make Catherine feel she had taken care with her favorite's pride. He had expected this boy to fuss a bit but ultimately put his stamp of approval on the project, as all of Catherine's other favorites would have done, to curry favor. "The empress's Muslim subjects worship one God, as do we."

"But we have more pressing problems now, what with England rattling a sword in our direction and trying to drive us out of the Black Sea. Your prize, Prince. Should we not ready our forces to teach the dolts a lesson?"

Catherine isn't foolish enough to make needless war, you pretentious twit. "A gesture of goodwill seems all the more appropriate, then," Grisha said. "Surely we don't want the English seducing our old Muslim adversaries with pretty words and promises of petty glory."

Zubov unleashed a dramatic sigh. "Fine. Catherine said I should listen to your plea, so I suppose I don't have a choice in the matter. She has a soft spot for *old* friends. It's one of her many charms." He flapped his hands again, ruffles flopping at his wrists, displacing the monkey. The creature landed awkwardly on the floor but scrambled to his feet quickly. "All the rest of you, go!" Zubov barked. "The prince and I require privacy."

The courtiers shuffled past Grisha to get to the door. Grisha straightened his aching back and sucked in the loose folds of his stomach as best he could manage, ignoring the curious stares as the men strode past. Most of them bowed respectfully in his direction, while others gave him a wide berth, as though fearing contamination.

He didn't move until the last of them, the elderly brigadier, shut the heavy door behind him. Only then did Grisha approach Zubov, the scroll with the plans for the mosque still safely tucked against his side. "The plan is visionary in scope. I think it will please the empress."

"Doubtful." Zubov rose to his feet. "I sometimes fear for Catherine's emotional state. The poor dear has grown so flustered. The last thing she needs is your petty distractions."

Grisha wanted to grab Zubov by the throat and knock his front teeth out. But Catherine wouldn't care to see her current favorite enter the boudoir with his pretty face maimed. Instead he forced his features into a serene expression, preparing to play to the boy's ego. "I would not have troubled you with a whim, Platon Alexandrovich."

"I still fail to understand the point of a mosque. You are a conquering hero, Prince. We were at war with these people. You did what needed to be done."

A voice in his head screamed, fueled by the intense adrenaline of battle, the war cry to Allah as the enemy soldiers rushed toward his men, no matter how futile their efforts. Grisha's voice rose, banishing the bloodthirsty battle cries from his memory. "I am here at the empress's behest. She trusts your opinion on this matter."

"Then I suppose I should at least see this foolishness." He extended his hand. "May I?"

Silently, Grisha handed over the scroll.

Zubov clicked his teeth and unrolled the thin goatskin parchment. He scrunched his black eyebrows together but scarcely looked at the design. Instead, he scrutinized the paper, fingering it and frowning. "What is this? Papyrus? Are you planning to construct pyramids?"

Grisha had commissioned an elderly Tatar to choose the architect himself. "I consulted with a cleric familiar with the needs of the people of this faith."

"A Mohammedan! Oh, that's rich."

Grisha struggled to keep his voice even. "Who else would design a mosque?"

"I understand your whims were given free rein in the imperial treasury in the past, but you've been away too long. Besides, I believe our Tatar friends may already have a mosque or two in our Russian heartland. Catherine will no longer countenance such extravagant waste. I don't care what you've gotten past her before."

Melancholy played tricks with his mind. In an instant, Grisha saw Zubov no longer as a silly boy speaking out of place, but as a powerful man who held the empress in his hand.

"Besides, if you're so in love with these people, why not look to the khans for inspiration?" Zubov assumed a grand academic tone that tore at Grisha's already fractured patience. "They would show far less interest in construction and far more cunning in yielding tribute from their vanquished foes."

"The empress is no khan," Grisha said, "but you would do well to show her deference."

Zubov stepped toward Grisha, lips curving downward and a hint of menace darkening his gaze. As though sensing his master's sudden shift in mood, the monkey emitted high-pitched chatter and covered his eyes with spindly fingers.

"I only meant," Grisha added in a louder voice, so any courtiers with an ear to the door could hear, "the empress should decide such matters for herself. I should like to hear her opinion. I came to you only as a courtesy."

"A courtesy?" Zubov laughed, handing the scroll back to Grisha before sitting back down on the chaise longue. He crossed one long leg over the other and pushed the jam closer to his monkey. The creature dipped his pink tongue into the jar. "You flatter yourself, Prince."

Grisha rerolled the delicate parchment. "Perhaps there is a better time to broach this subject?"

Zubov flashed his white teeth in a youthful smile. His name meant "tooth" after all. Grisha found it irritatingly fitting. "I'll let you in on a secret. I don't care one way or another. Let the poor devils fall on their knees to a golden calf for all I care. But your presumption vexes me. You've been away from St. Petersburg nearly two years. Much has changed while you've been in your new Russia. And you return only to strut into my salon with this scheme at the very time our motherland faces serious new threats."

"I meant no disrespect, Platon Alexandrovich."

"Catherine thought it best I start to make the fiscal decisions. I intend to prove my worth, not throw precious treasure to the wind on your latest fancy. You had Catherine's ear for a long time. I know this must be difficult to hear, but the time for every man to shine comes and goes. It is only now a matter of bowing out with grace."

Despair began to seep through the fragile cracks in Grisha's ego. He wanted nothing more than to retire to bed and bury himself under blankets, taking comfort in hot chocolate, liqueur, and perhaps a warm female body. Better yet, he could call for his horse and force a gallop to Nevsky Monastery. He could grow a long beard and retreat from the world altogether.

Except where would that leave Catherine?

"I have never been asked to leave the empress's side. That is the fate of her young favorites. Her temporary companions."

"Temporary?" Zubov made a mockery of a frown. The monkey crouched at Zubov's foot, nibbling at the toe of his master's boot. "I suppose my position might be temporary. But then again the empress gave me dominion over you."

"I truly doubt that was her intention," Grisha said. "She means for us to work together."

"Why work at all, Prince? At your age most men have fathered many children and look to the darlings for comfort. It must be difficult, having no progeny of your own. Perhaps it explains your meddling."

"I have been called to the empress's side," Grisha told him, gut twisting. "I won't abandon her now."

"I can assure you Catherine's interests are in more than capable hands," Zubov said. "I suggest you find some age-appropriate hobbies. Return to one of the palaces the empress gifted you with. Live your dotage in peace. Give your one good eye a rest." Zubov's gaze shot to Grisha's crotch. "I'm sure your prick could use a rest as well. Godspeed, Prince."

The little valet waited in the gilded corridor outside of Zubov's apartments, struggling to situate himself in a scarlet-cushioned armchair, Grisha's greatcoat slung over one arm. He tapped his new boots against the parquet floor and stared longingly out the massive windows facing the frozen Neva River.

"The boats won't come until April," Grisha told him, "when the ice finally breaks."

At the sound of Grisha's voice, the boy sprang to attention, landing unsteadily in the unfamiliar boots. Grisha's regular valet had grown worn with age. So he'd left the old man at home with his feet elevated and toasting before a fire. In his place, he'd decided to take this boy around with him during the duration of his stay in St. Petersburg. Though he was but thirteen, Anton seemed willing to please.

Anton draped the greatcoat around Grisha's shoulders. "How did you fare, Your Highness? Did the meeting proceed as you hoped?"

The soft sable lining enveloped Grisha in warmth, yet darkness clung to the edges of his mind. "As you predicted, the place reeked."

Anton snorted. "The monkey is in charge then. Just as I heard. Did Platon Alexandrovich approve of the mosque? Did you encounter any trouble?"

Grisha had taught Anton to ask such questions. He enjoyed discussing political affairs with a nimble, if untrained, mind. Grisha wondered if he might bring Anton with him to a state dinner.

Catherine would no doubt think it charming he'd taken a ward. After all, as Zubov had been so quick to point out, Grisha had no children of his own, at least that he knew of.

This evening, however, Grisha desired only solitude and quiet. Even the echo of their boots squeaking on the floor tested his nerves. "I would rather not speak of it," he said shortly.

"I am sorry." Anton had been born a serf and still exuded meekness, as though at any moment his fortunes might reverse and he'd be back tilling a field with the rest of his family.

"No, I am sorry. My head and stomach are in knots."

Grisha gnawed on his red and aching thumbnail. The other favorites he could tolerate. They had known what was expected of them and left quietly when asked, happy with their generous pensions and arranged marriages to comely ladies-in-waiting.

Zubov was different, more like him. Ambitious. Except not like him. Grisha had been many things when he was Zubov's age, but never closed-minded. Catherine was ten years older than Grisha. Even so, to him she would always be that young and vibrant woman who claimed a throne. How could such a woman feel attracted to a shallow boy? He supposed the weight of years on this earth had finally caught up with Catherine, and so Zubov might take advantage and shame her reputation.

"Platon Alexandrovich does not wish to fund the mosque," Grisha said. "I fear he has more sway over the empress than her previous favorites. He seems ready to take on England and Prussia single-handedly. And he believes he speaks for the empress. Someone needs to set affairs back in their proper order."

"I wonder . . ." Anton's eyes gleamed for a moment and Grisha caught a hint of an impish smile. Just as quickly the meekness returned and he bowed his head.

"You wonder?" Grisha didn't want to put too much pressure on his new valet, but he needed all the information he could acquire. "Now is not the time to play the bashful servant."

"They say Platon Alexandrovich is quite handsome," Anton said. "Is this true?"

Must he point out the obvious? As though Grisha could not figure out well enough the source of Zubov's hold on Catherine. "It is true." Grisha loosened the scarf around his throat, itching to rid himself of the confinement of the waistcoat but unwilling to walk through the palace half-clothed. The time when he could get away with such folly had passed. "He is like a statue of a Grecian god come to life."

"And he has captured the empress's heart," Anton said.

"Not her heart," Grisha said, with more conviction than he felt. "But certainly her attention."

Anton threw a surreptitious glance over his shoulder, already wary of palace spies. Grisha steered him farther down the corridor, well out of earshot of Zubov and his fawning admirers.

"Some question the timing of Platon Alexandrovich's first appearance in court," Anton confided.

"What strikes them as odd?"

"It was too perfect," Anton said. "At least that's what I hear people say. The empress's heart was newly broken and she was in need of distraction."

"They say this when they think no one is listening?"

Anton flashed another small smile. "Exactly."

"Do they say anything else?"

"I have thought of something."

"Indulge me."

"Platon Alexandrovich's sponsor at court was Count Nikolai Saltykov."

Grisha chewed his throbbing thumbnail. "You've heard of our disagreements then?"

"And of his closeness with the heir, Grand Duke Paul."

So Zubov wasn't Catherine's plaything alone. He was a marionette, with that fool Saltykov and sniveling Paul pulling the strings.

After all these years, enemies still gathered to remove Catherine from the throne. If Catherine found out her favorite had been thrust before her by another man, rather than coming to her of his own volition, it would crush her. The dark thoughts in Grisha's mind began to lose force, swept away by the storm rising in his chest.

"Is there anything you can do?" Anton asked.

Catherine had never been disposed to ask for help. But when Grisha offered his opinions, she always listened, even if she didn't always follow his lead.

Grisha had made her happy once. A grand passion had ignited. Surely the spark of such a passion remained, even after so many years.

At once the world seemed lighter beneath his feet. Grisha's eyes narrowed. Zubov was nothing more than a silly court jester, a bug to be squashed. Platon Alexandrovich may have cast a temporary spell on Catherine, but he had not counted on Grisha's return.

Grisha started off again down the corridor, beckoning Anton to follow. Soon enough Catherine would want him back in the south, to continue to negotiate the latest peace terms with the Turks. If he were to save her from Zubov, time was of the essence. "You've been practicing your letters? You make a reasonable facsimile of my writing?"

"I do, Your Highness." Anton scrambled in his pockets for the small slate Grisha had advised he carry with him. "You wish me to take dictation?"

"While the words are still fresh in my mind."

Grisha quickened his pace, drawing strength from newfound purpose. Anton readied his stubby pencil and nodded.

"'Your Most Gracious Imperial Majesty,'" Grisha began. "'As I look once again toward the Neva, I am reminded of your beauty so many years ago when you first took our holy throne, that glorious white night when we first met. I fell in rapture then, and I now feel compelled to speak of the rapture I yet experience in your presence.'"

He had returned to the capital, to the center of power. He would convince Catherine she didn't need Zubov. The only person the empress had ever needed was him.

Two

FOR IMMEDIATE RELEASE

ROMANOV HEIRESS TO SEEK HONORARY TITLE
ST. PETERSBURG, RUSSIA

Dmitry Potemkin, spokesman for the Russian Monarchist Society, is proud to reveal the name of the Society's official imperial claimant: Dr. Veronica Herrera. The Society now hopes to validate Dr. Herrera's startling claim to be a direct descendant of the last Romanovs, Nicholas and Alexandra.

LOS ANGELES INTERNATIONAL AIRPORT
PRESENT DAY

"You have items to check?" The ticket agent's sultry Russian accent caressed her words. "There is small charge."

Veronica Herrera tried to summon an answer but only managed a shrug. Her gaze drifted to one of the flat television screens on the far side of the wide terminal. Local newscasters with glossy hair chuckled over a bear cub who had wandered into a backyard pool up near Tahoe.

"Perhaps I do not say well?" A lock of platinum-blond hair fell into the ticket agent's pretty and oh-so-patient face. She tucked it behind a white cap that matched her trim uniform and the stylish dark orange scarf tied around her smooth neck.

"No, no. I mean, yes, I understand." Veronica shifted her heavy new winter coat from one arm to the other. "I don't have anything to check."

The woman nodded at Veronica's modest carry-on bag. "You are brave girl. Big trip for little luggage. I think you are free spirit." She tapped her keyboard and the computer spit out a boarding pass. "Gate eight. Board in ninety minutes. Enjoy stay in Russia." The ticket agent's perfectly manicured hand motioned for her to accept the pass and move aside.

But Veronica couldn't move.

The travelers queued in line behind her began to grumble at the delay. Veronica wanted to take the boarding pass and move like any normal human being, but her heart was pounding. Honestly, what had she been thinking? Everyone would see nothing more than a failed academic with a connection to the Romanovs that was dubious at best. Aside from a few aging monarchists, who cared about her family's story anyway? She should exchange her ticket and go to Costa Rica or the Bahamas. She had always thought it would be romantic to run away. It wasn't too late.

On-screen, the bear cub frolicked in the pool, lapping water with its giant paws and grimacing. The newscasters laughed some more.

The ticket agent maintained her veneer of professional serenity. "Safe travels." She tried once more to hand Veronica her boarding pass.

To Veronica's left, a little girl with curly brown hair ran toward her family, holding a Ziploc bag full of frosted pink and white animal crackers. She tripped over her father's guitar case, dropped the cookies, and began to whimper. Veronica bent down to re-trieve the crumpled plastic bag and handed it to the girl, who gave her a shy smile. A happy child. A happy family. Veronica returned the smile, but her stomach tightened. At times, her own lack of family made her feel as though she was somehow less important than everyone else. And entirely alone.

When Veronica righted herself, the ticket agent still faced her with a patient smile, but her forehead had creased. She was watching the television now. The newscasters' faces had grown somber. The image changed. Flurries of white swirled around the Church of the Savior on Spilled Blood in St. Petersburg and its bubble onion domes of turquoise, gold, and green, some swirling, others in a checkered diamond pattern, all topped by ornate Orthodox crosses.

Veronica's hands felt cold, despite the sunshine streaming through the windows warming the terminal. She knew what images were soon to follow.

The camera zoomed in on a young man standing before one of the church's arches, looking pretty, if slight, with tousled black hair and a scarf strewn carelessly around his neck. He wore a red T-shirt with a dark shadow of a wolf emblazoned on the front. Nikolai "Reb" Volkov had taken on the nickname of "Lone Wolf" since "*volk*" meant "wolf" in Russian. Huddling deeper into his light jacket, he turned to wave his arms at the scene behind him, features animated.

The footage had been taken seven months earlier, when Reb staged an impromptu art exhibit in front of the iconic church. No announcements. No permission granted. The camera followed Reb as he bounced from easel to easel placed along an iron railing overlooking a narrow Petersburg canal. Each of the paintings captured Reb's signature style: an elegantly familiar landmark paired with garish caricatures of contemporary Russians.

The camera focused on Reb's painting depicting Falconet's statue of Peter the Great, *The Bronze Horseman*. The wild-eyed horse reared and Peter looked fearsome as a mythical giant, his massive hand outstretched and flat, long fingers splayed. Behind Peter loomed the golden dome of St. Isaac's Cathedral, shrouded by wispy gray clouds. In the foreground, cartoonish versions of the current Russian president and an Orthodox clergyman, both dressed in the robes of ancient Muscovy, held hands and laughed. Peter's horse stepped on a snake. The president and the cleric stepped on the bodies of two young men locked in an embrace.

The painting was meant to protest the law passed by the Russian Duma banning the distribution of so-called gay propaganda.

Closed captioning scrolled along the bottom of the screen: *Russian artist Reb Volkov sentenced to two years' hard labor at Siberian penal colony for hooliganism.*

"Such a shame," the ticket agent murmured in Russian.

Veronica clutched her coat tighter. "I don't understand. They're sending an artist with an international following to prison? I thought the court planned to dismiss the charges."

"He is brave man," the ticket agent said quietly. She glanced over her shoulder, as though she suspected someone might overhear their conversation. "And for what?" she said in a low voice. "We are supposed to have freedom of speech. Look at Reb. He is never to survive prison."

On-screen, Reb reached his thin, pale hand to his ear and tugged the lobe. She was right. Reb Volkov wouldn't last a week in a *gulag*.

"What to do though?" the ticket agent said. "It is fate. It used to be we all keep thoughts to ourselves and government leave us alone. This is how my parents live. This is how my grandparents live. Maybe it is easier."

Veronica touched the cool bit of silver on her neck: a tiny orthodox cross, the bottom bar slanted down, tarnished from age. It had been a gift from the Dowager Empress Marie to Veronica's Romanov grandmother, before the dowager had sent her away from her family forever when she was still a mere baby. "Someone needs to set things right. Someone needs to help Reb."

"No one help yet."

Veronica caressed the cross on the necklace. One of the tiny bars poked the inside of her thumb. Behind her, she heard the girl who had dropped the cookies whimpering while her mother comforted her by humming the theme to *Raiders of the Lost Ark*.

I need a purpose. That will be my purpose. Veronica wanted to say this out loud but still felt unsure of herself. "If enough people oppose the sentence, the court may reverse its decision."

"I hope you are right, but I am not optimist." She handed Veronica her boarding pass and started to smile. A puffy middle-aged couple in matching USC sweatshirts and carrying dark red Russian passports with the Romanov double-headed eagle stamped on the front sidled up next to her. "Safe travels . . ."

The ticket agent's smile suddenly locked. She glanced at the orthodox cross hanging from the thin chain at the base of Veronica's throat and then regarded Veronica's face more carefully. "Wait." She reached under the counter and withdrew a flimsy, coffee-stained newspaper. She opened the paper and tapped a fuzzy picture. "This is you."

Veronica released the cross, recognizing the picture, a headshot from her former employer. The student photographer had insisted on taking it outside in the bright sunlight and Veronica was squinting like an idiot. Somehow that ridiculous picture had made its way into a Russian newspaper? She gave a brief strangled laugh.

"One of flight attendants bring this paper from St. Petersburg yesterday. I see here. The necklace . . . your grandmother is secret daughter of Tsar Nicholas II. A fifth daughter. They take from Russia because family not want more girls. And then rest killed. It is you, yes?" She thrust the paper in Veronica's face.

Veronica stared at the article, quickly deciphering the Cyrillic alphabet. The article was short and to the point. After nearly one hundred years, the Romanov throne, or at least a ceremonial version of it, might finally be restored.

"You are one? We are to have monarchy as in England?"

She heard the guy behind her whisper: "All of the Romanovs were murdered."

"No, is truth," the ticket agent told him. "This woman is new tsarina." She turned back to Veronica, nodding encouragingly. "It is you who can help Reb. Are you to come to Russia to meet president? The president will like you. He likes pretty ones. He will listen."

"Hey!" she heard someone from the line behind her shout. "No cutting, asshole!"

"It's only for a minute and then I'll go back," a man's voice replied.

Once more, Veronica froze. She knew that voice too well, remembered the deep, rolling pleasure she felt when it whispered in her ear.

"I'm here to escort this woman to Russia," the man announced.

"You're here to do *what*?!"

Veronica abruptly turned to face him, trying to keep her features neutral and fight the unexpected wave of bitterness. Her ex . . . whatever he was, Michael Karstadt, smiled gamely as he jostled past the other passengers and made his way to the front of the line. His height allowed her to see him over the crowd. He looked handsome as ever, his face clever and sweet at once. But his wavy dark hair was dappled with more gray than she remembered, and he looked pinched around the eyes and fuller under the chin.

Even so, he looked good. But he always looked good. No surprise on that front. He wore a dark gray suit, like he thought he was Don Draper and air travel remained the purview of glamorous jet-setters. As she watched him a surge of electricity shot through her chest. Two voices in her head immediately went to war—one wanted to run to him and the other wanted to run away.

She had no idea why he was at the airport.

"What are you doing?" she asked as he approached.

"Oh, hey! Nice to see you, too."

"You're going to Russia? The same day as me?"

"I'll explain in a minute, I promise. Can you keep it down?" he asked the ticket agent as he reached Veronica's side. He paused to catch his breath. "Nothing has been made public yet."

"Not true. This already announced." She tapped the wrinkled fold of the paper. "Who are you? Another American is to help the Romanov?"

"No," Veronica said, a slight edge to her voice.

Michael scratched his head and flashed her a sheepish smile. "Actually, yes." He faced the ticket agent. "Nothing was *supposed* to have been announced yet."

"And you aren't *supposed* to be here," Veronica said.

"You're about to make a claim for the Russian throne," Michael said.

Veronica raised a finger. "An honorary title only. Not an actual claim."

"Even so, I want to help you. Please let me."

The little girl with the cookies looked up at them with wide eyes. "Is she Anastasia?"

"Not Anastasia, but close." Michael lowered his voice to just the right register, dipped his head, and kissed Veronica's hand. "She is the tsarina."

A few people in line started to clap. Veronica pulled her hand away quickly, but her fingertips tingled. Michael leaned toward her and she took in his warm, familiar scent. For a moment, she was back in a hotel room in New York City, buried under soft sheets, stretching her body, luxuriating in the warmth of his skin against hers, stroking his hair, and nuzzling his neck with her lips. And she felt as though she flew high above the earth, immune to the dreariness of everyday life.

Until she came crashing back down, of course.

"Give them a royal wave," he said.

"What?" Veronica curled her fingers, palms damp.

"Do you want to do this thing or not?"

Veronica managed a quick twist of one hand.

The ticket agent stood with her back erect. "Anything else you require, just let us know." She hesitated. "Have you met Prince Harry of England?"

She shook her head. The woman tore a sheet of paper from a notepad and scribbled on it. Michael leaned on the counter to take a look. "If you have a request for the tsarina, you may need to go through the Monarchist Society," he told her. "Make it official and such."

"What?" Veronica eyed him warily.

The ticket agent ignored Michael and handed the paper to Veronica. A few digits had been transcribed along with the woman's name, Lyudmilla, in both Cyrillic and English. "If you meet prince, will you give to him? He comes to St. Petersburg, I can show him around city. He won't regret."

Michael gave Lyudmilla a solemn nod. "That will be her first order of business."

Outside, jumbo jets taxied down the runway, metal husks gleaming in the intense California sunlight. Inside the palm-tree-lined international terminal, Veronica tried to nibble on a pretzel, but it tasted like cardboard. She gave up and fished around in her purse instead. Her hand ran over the thinly embossed golden American eagle on the cover of her passport and the dark ink on her pale Russian tourist visa.

"You still have everything," Michael said, absently turning a page of the *Los Angeles Times*. "You checked five minutes ago."

"It makes me feel better to check."

"Make sure you don't lose Lyudmilla's number in case we run into Prince Harry."

"Ha ha." Veronica zipped her purse shut and fiddled with her phone. A last boarding call barked over the loudspeakers and she jumped in her seat.

"Try to relax, Tsarina," Michael told her.

"This whole situation is strange enough, and now you appear out of nowhere. Why? Seriously, Michael, why?"

"Maybe I was in the mood. I haven't been to Russia in a few years."

"The actual reason."

He set the paper down and raised his hands in defeat. He tried to smile. "Your *abuela* asked me to keep an eye on you."

Veronica's grandmother. She should have known. "But why didn't you let me know you were coming? You know I wouldn't have . . ." Her voice trailed off; she was unsure how to complete her thought.

"It all happened at the last minute. Your grandmother figured I could get a visa quickly since I know the ropes. She kept saying, 'Veronica's going all by herself. What if something happens?'"

"You still could have asked me."

"She was afraid that if I asked, you would say no."

Veronica remembered Abuela's angst when she had told her she was going to Russia, the tissue turning over in her hands. "I told her if something happened she could hire Liam Neeson to find me."

"Sorry to disappoint, but she hired me instead. I was ready to get out of town for a little while anyway." He turned the page of the paper but kept his gaze trained on Veronica. "Your grandmother loves you more than she loves anyone else in the world. She's worried. And I think she's right to be. You should have someone with you, someone who knows you."

Veronica took another tasteless bite of the pretzel. Serving as a bodyguard remained deeply embedded in Michael's genes. He was the grandson of servants sworn to protect Nicholas and Alexandra's secret fifth daughter. His grandmother had helped smuggle Veronica's Romanov grandmother out of Russia as a baby before the Revolution.

"You're obviously stressed," he said. "Talk to me."

They had parted on friendly terms, and honestly, she missed Michael—more than she cared to admit. But he had lied. He'd told her *he* was the heir to throne. Even though he knew Veronica was the descendant of Nicholas and Alexandra, he'd kept the information from her. He thought he'd been doing the right thing and protecting her, but Veronica's resentment still simmered. She wanted to trust him, but she didn't want to get hurt yet again. She didn't think she could take it.

Over the past year, they'd exchanged friendly texts, but she'd kept her distance. She'd even made a halfhearted profile for an online dating site, although she never clicked with anyone else.

Truth be told, deep in the blur of her other emotions, Veronica felt safe with Michael. She wanted to talk to him. It was a relief to have someone around who knew her well. "Do you think the Monarchist Society actually believes my story?"

Michael folded the newspaper and set it down on the table. His hand hovered over hers briefly before falling in his lap. "Don't call it a story. It's your history. The Society invited you to St. Petersburg. They know you're legit."

"I haven't been to Russia in nearly twenty years. I don't even teach Russian history anymore." Since she'd lost her bid for tenure, Veronica's academic days seemed a lifetime away.

"Let me ask you this. What were you doing two nights ago?"

Veronica crumbled the pretzel into pieces in her napkin. Two nights ago, she'd been safely ensconced in her childhood home in Bakersfield, squished in her bed, staring at the ceiling. Traffic from Highway 99 hummed in the distance and trains whistled in the quiet night, as though to emphasize Bakersfield was a stop you made on your way somewhere else. Veronica was a quiet person by nature. She needed an exciting environment so she didn't disappear. "Maybe I went out."

"You brought home takeout from Chili's." She shook her head. "Applebee's?"

"Olive Garden."

"My point is you deserve better. You were meant to be a woman of the world. You have a PhD in Russian history and last time we spoke you were in the admin temp pool at the university in Bakersfield."

"Not anymore."

"Oh. I'm sorry." He tilted his head, appraising her. "Or maybe I'm not sorry."

"It was data entry. Not exactly my dream job." Veronica had spent her days shuffling nonsense around endless spreadsheets. She would stare out the skylight above her cubicle, at patches of blue sky and gauzy clouds, wanting to chew her own foot off to escape. She could never shake the feeling that some phantom version of herself was floating around in the world, enjoying the life she had been meant to lead.

"You're a smart woman," he said. "You should be teaching at the university. You deserve more than the cubicle wasteland."

"I need to support myself somehow."

"You need a purpose. That's why you're going to Russia, right?"

Damn him for knowing her so well. Aside from her *abuela*, all she had of importance was a connection to a long-dead monarchy. Maybe that wasn't much, but she might as well make the most of it. "It's certainly part of the reason."

"You know what? I get it. But this is going to be scary. Americans aren't exactly popular in Russia right now and not everyone will warm to the idea of an American citizen being the new heir of the Romanov family. That's why your grandmother asked me to tag along."

"I wouldn't mind your help. I mean that. But you knew the

truth about my connection to the Romanovs all along and didn't tell me. How can I know you'll be honest with me now, when I'm going to need it the most?"

"I lied because I thought you were in danger. We've been friendly since. I'm surprised you're bringing this up again."

"Michael, you came here without telling me. Were you trying to catch me by surprise? Sweep me off my feet? You don't think we're getting back together, do you? That's done."

The last part came out too quickly. Michael's face remained still. Too still.

"Presumptuous, don't you think?" he said. "Maybe I'm seeing someone."

The comment nicked her feelings, but she pressed on. "If you were seeing someone, you wouldn't be here with me. I only want everything out in the open. Since we're friendly."

He looked down at the paper, but not before Veronica saw him flinch. She wound a strand of hair around her finger, not wanting to hurt him but not sure what else to say. She hesitated and then finally asked, "How are Ariel and Boris and Natasha?"

Michael's expression brightened and he whipped out his phone. "Look." He showed her a picture of his beloved golden chow and two gray and white cats lurking in the background.

"I miss them," she said.

"They're getting spoiled this week by the pet sitter, but I miss them too. You should get a cat or something."

"I think I want a dog."

"You seem like a cat person."

"I am a cat person," she said. "But I want a dog."

He smiled and put the phone back in his pocket. "A big dog?"

"A giant. I want him to growl at anyone who comes near me."

Michael's expression tensed. Veronica's lip twitched. She was about to explain that she didn't mean she wanted a dog to growl at *him* per se but then realized Michael was focused on something behind her. He straightened his back, the loyal bodyguard once more. "Of course," he muttered.

"What's wrong?"

"Nothing, nothing." His shoulders stiffened. "Okay, not nothing. Someone's coming. I think I recognize him."

"Hello!" A baritone voice startled Veronica. The man approached from behind and then moved before her to offer a bow. Veronica recognized his face even though they hadn't formally met: Dmitry Potemkin, the first person from the Russian Monarchist Society to contact her. Dmitry was trim and compact with a strong jaw and an alert look in his gentle eyes. He would have made a perfect all-American action movie hero except for the fair coloring and broad cheekbones that made his features so distinctly Russian.

"I am running late. I apologize. I thought I had time to see Santa Monica Pier this morning before flight. And then I hear news about Reb." His voice grew quiet and he looked away.

Veronica glanced at Michael, who had started to scowl. "I'm sorry, Dmitry. It seems I'm bringing a guest."

Michael made himself taller in his seat before extending his hand. "Michael Karstadt."

"Mikhail." Dmitry shook Michael's hand. "You know Dr. Herrera how?"

"I'm an old friend."

"If that's what you call it," Veronica muttered.

Dmitry looked Michael over. "This is all right?" he asked Veronica, switching briefly to Russian.

"I'm here to help keep her safe," Michael responded pointedly, also in Russian.

"It's unexpected, but if he wants to tag along, it's all right," she said. "My grandmother asked him to do it. She's worried about me."

"Ah!" Dmitry said, eyes widening. "I understand power of grandmothers."

Veronica caught herself staring at Dmitry's face and auburn hair. A portrait from the late eighteenth century came to her mind, a rosy-cheeked and rotund Russian gentleman, also with auburn hair, wearing a military jacket adorned with gleaming medals and a vivid blue sash. "Dmitry is related to Catherine the Great's Potemkin," she told Michael.

Dmitry smiled. "Grigory Potemkin was distant ancestor, great-uncle many times over. I always think of him as 'Grisha.'"

"Yet you don't have a title," Michael said. "Or am I wrong? Should we call you Prince?"

"No titles," Dmitry said. "Grisha Potemkin had numerous titles, of course, but family gave up during Revolution. It seemed diplomatic choice. I am spokesperson for Monarchist Society but not member at present."

"But you're qualified to guide Veronica through this process? Given the tension between the American and Russian governments right now?"

"I understand concern." Dmitry turned to Veronica. "We weren't even sure visa would come through. You are only to stay for week? We will need to be careful with time."

"I just saw the news," Veronica said. "Is it true they're sending Reb Volkov to prison?"

"They are to let him have ten days under house arrest before he leaves for Siberia, to settle affairs and such." Dmitry shook his head sadly. "He provoked government. He used church without permission. I appreciate your willingness to help him. A modern monarch is figurehead, of course, but powerful voice for reform on these matters."

Michael looked at Veronica and then Dmitry. "What do you mean?"

"I discussed Reb's case with Dr. Herrera, even before verdict," Dmitry said. "It is her choice how to play role of tsarina, of course. It is ceremonial only. But I have press conference planned for end of week. This gives her chance to speak out. Reb's case has received some publicity in West, but not enough."

"I didn't realize the Russian Monarchist Society was political," Michael said.

Dmitry blinked rapidly but kept his voice steady. "Not in past. No."

"Why are you involved with Reb's case then?"

"We are to decide now what new Russia will be. We are at a crossroad." He had been speaking in English but veered into Russian as the words grew more complex. "We need to determine who we are: an oppressive or progressive nation. Dr. Herrera is the first modern celebrity Romanov. She can affect how people view such matters as what happened to Reb Volkov. The injustice of it."

"Sure, but once Reb Volkov involved the church he pissed plenty of people off. Is it safe for Veronica to get involved?"

"I'll be fine," Veronica said shortly. Just because Michael needed to play the bodyguard, that didn't mean she needed to accept his services.

"I didn't realize you were being groomed as the tsarina-reformer," he told her.

"You may not be aware, but there is precedent," Dmitry said. "Catherine II was enlightened empress. Alexander II freed serfs."

"And was assassinated right where your friend Mr. Volkov held his exhibit—where the Church of the Savior on Spilled Blood was built."

Dmitry forced a smile. "We can discuss security. Is priority of course."

"We should discuss it now. Our flight leaves soon."

"I will review with Dr. Herrera on plane. We are sitting together, correct?" He compared his boarding pass with Veronica's. "I know you will not mind . . . I am sorry. I forget your name."

Michael nodded a little too quickly. "Michael Karstadt."

"Right!" Dmitry frowned. "Wait. I think I know this name."

"Can't think of why. Excuse me." Michael hopped out of his seat and headed for the counter by the boarding area, where yet another svelte Slavic blonde tapped at a computer keyboard. He smiled and she hunched forward to see his boarding pass and passport.

"Never mind him," Veronica said. "He thinks he's my bodyguard."

"He wants to keep tsarina safe. I understand." Dmitry gave a guarded smile. "Irina Yusupova will join us in Petersburg. She is current head of Society. If your friend has concerns for your safety, he may wish to speak to her."

"Yes," Veronica said, staring at the slinky woman at the ticket counter. And Michael smiling at her.

"If Irina asks anything . . . assertive . . . please do not take offense. Irina simply has her own wishes with regard to position and future of Monarchist Society. On politics, we do not always agree. But she will be strong advocate for you and for your safety."

"Of course." The computer spit out a new boarding pass and the woman exchanged it for Michael's. He headed back in their direction.

"Good news! We're all sitting together." Michael drummed his fingers on the table casually as he addressed Dmitry. "You can tell me all about the security measures you've taken. Veronica told you I made a promise to her grandmother in Los Angeles to keep her safe while she was in Russia. Before that, I made a promise to her Romanov grandmother to keep her safe."

"Romanov grandmother?" Dmitry said. "You knew Grand Duchess Charlotte? The daughter of tsar?"

Michael looked down at his hands for a moment before meeting Dmitry's steady gaze. "Charlotte Marchand, yes. She asked me to look after Veronica, her only grandchild. I was twelve years old. I've kept that promise ever since."

"I understand," Dmitry told Michael, nodding. "As I say, I understand power of grandmothers. All Russians do. I will help you honor this commitment."

Three

Grisha shifted in his seat, wondering how anyone of normal size managed to squeeze into Catherine's petite armchairs. Perhaps his frame had grown a tad larger over the years, but the point remained valid. If he'd had any idea how uncomfortable these chairs made one's arse, he would have sweet-talked Catherine into switching to velvet cushions stacked on the floor, as he had adopted for his military encampments long ago.

Not that he should have been sitting outside of her study at all. She used to hunger for his insights, lust after his ideas. Even when the thrill of their physical relationship ended, she had never made him wait. His time was too valuable. Catherine herself had said as much.

Grisha rose to his feet and paced, the thick soles of his boots squeaking against the parquet floor. Catherine was sure to hear. It was the sort of random sound she detested. But right now, he would do anything to be noticed, even pique her anger.

He had been reduced to behaving like a child. What a laugh. It was never meant to be this way. But then nothing in this earthly life ever lasted.

Catherine had summoned him to her study as soon as she received the letter he'd dictated to Anton. Her reply came in vellum sealed with the imperial sigil. *So you think of the day we first met? I have reflected on that moment myself as of late. What dreams we had, my kitten. I wonder if we are people who can be satisfied. Perhaps we are forever fated to want more.*

The first time Grisha stood in Catherine's presence, he was but twenty-two, the same age as Zubov now. The coup to bring the empress to power was already in motion. Everyone knew of the humiliations her husband, that weasel of a tsar, had heaped on his gifted wife. He abandoned her bed, took to calling her a fool in front of foreign dignitaries, smacked the dogs, terrorized the servants, and held mock trials for palace rats. Before the coup, Peter had tried to send Catherine to a convent so he could marry his drab and slow-witted mistress, a woman better suited to fortifying his fragile ego.

As the force readied before the Winter Palace, it was nearing ten at night, but the sun still hovered low, the white violet of the northern summer. Palace Square hummed with activity, as though for an Easter carnival. No one expected the tsar to put up a fight. Laughing drummers marched while drunken soldiers pushed one another in jest and stripped to their undergarments to shed the stiff uniforms of the hated tsar. Their horses whickered impatiently, stomping hooves on cobblestone and jingling their harnesses. Entire families, from the oldest *babushkas* to babes in swaddling, gathered with baskets of food in hand, hoping to catch a glimpse of the new empress; the scent of fried *pirozhki* and pickled herring hung in the air.

Even before Catherine attempted to consolidate power, Grisha had heard whispers of her bookishness, her unnatural interest in masculine affairs, and her displeasing, assertive nature. He'd never put much stock in such nonsense. Such rumors only intrigued him more.

Catherine had assembled the uniform of the Preobrazhensky

Guard. She wore tall boots, tight trousers, and a fitted dark green coat edged with fine gold embroidering, all of which flattered her shape. She found a hat, a tricornered affair, and set it on her head, adjusting her hair into a long black braid underneath. Captivated, Grisha watched her gather the reins of a massive stallion in her small, capable hands, and he knew he would follow her gladly into battle, into certain death if need be.

Catherine held up a long saber and her delicate black brows furled. It was bare, missing a sword knot. Grisha glanced at his commander, who seemed preoccupied with a spot on his glove. This was his chance. Grisha quickly gave a little click to his faithful gray gelding. On cue, the horse galloped across the busy square and to Catherine's stallion. Grisha unfastened a gold tassel from the hilt of his own sword.

"Most Gracious Imperial Majesty," he said, bowing as best he could while astride, and extending the tassel.

He was nothing, a provincial boy and lowly guardsman. She was about to become empress of all the Russias. Catherine could have swept him aside with a mere brush of her hand. His commanding officer, seeing now what Grisha had done, bellowed his name across the field.

Catherine paused and Grisha thought she would call for her guards. His commander would slap his cheeks and send him to the brig.

And then she winked. His breath caught as she accepted the gold tassel and tied it to her sword. With that simple gesture, he knew she understood his burning ambition and saw it as not a threat but a mirror of her own desires.

"Thank you, soldier." She spoke in Russian, but her German accent made the words oddly charming. "I shall remember this kindness."

Later, Grisha fell asleep with the lilting sound of her voice singing in his head.

Grisha loosened his breeches to breathe more freely and reached into a side pocket to retrieve a collection of tiny rubies and diamonds to massage between his fingers. Such nonsense could occupy a man's time at twenty-two. Nearly thirty years had passed since that fateful night. By now, he should have known better.

So why did his heart still jump in his chest at the thought of seeing her?

A guard stepped out of the empress's study. He wore a long blue coat and a silver helmet adorned with a quivering ostrich feather. His bulging eyes and weak chin looked Hapsburg. Grisha frowned, wondering who had brought him to court. Ambitious diplomats were always placing spies near Catherine's inner circle.

"She'll see you now," the guard said, "but take care to mind her schedule. She is a busy woman."

Grisha transferred one of the little sparkling rubies from hand to hand, recalling a time when a guard would never dare speak to him in such a manner. Perhaps this was another case of Zubov's thorny influence. "And here I thought she had time for a trick of whist."

"No, Your Highness. I've taken the liberty of calling for your valet to return at once."

Grisha had sent Anton to the kitchen to fetch refreshments for the ride home. He'd hoped Anton might bond with some of the other boys or perhaps even sweet-talk a girl into divulging a palace secret or two. "He's running an errand for me."

"I'm sure your boy can attend to it later. The empress is on a strict regimen today. She will see you, but she hasn't much time to spare."

Grisha opened his hand to reveal the jewels: a few tiny rubies and emeralds, but mostly diamonds. He swirled them in his hand and the weak sunlight sent their reflections bouncing off the palace walls like a thousand stars. The guard regarded the reflections with disdain.

"Pity. I'd hoped the empress might indulge me. Must you fetch Anton? I'm feeling peckish. I'd hoped he'd gather some radishes for me."

"As I said, the empress does not have time to play cards or for idle chat today," the guard insisted. "That's why I've sent for your boy."

"That's why," Grisha said. "Of course. Not because Platon Zubov doesn't care for my servants having run of the palace, listening in at doors and what have you."

The guard pressed his misshapen lips together.

"Never mind," Grisha said. "I'm sure you have enough on your hands trying to keep that boy Zubov happy. I only hope I don't slip on monkey feces inside the empress's study." He stepped past, jostling the guard as he made his way through the door.

Inside Catherine's study, Grisha found no monkeys. Zubov's influence had not extended so far yet. Light from crystal chandeliers reflected on the pale blue walls and the room was filled with the warm aroma of strong Turkish coffee. A sleek pair of greyhounds nestled at Catherine's feet and a fat Persian cat dozed on the mantel of the hearth.

He recognized the older of the two greyhounds as one of the canine Thomassin family, a son or grandson perhaps of Catherine's departed Sir Tom Anderson. This Thomassin lifted his head, half-blind now; he and Grisha had that in common. But the dog recognized his old friend's scent and rose to his feet on unsteady legs. He ambled to Grisha, who bent down to stroke his smooth head.

Now that Grisha had been admitted inside, he was reluctant to look at Catherine. He might find himself completely under her power, as he had been when he first handed her the sword knot. He slipped the jewels back into his pocket, gave the dog's head one last pat, and willed himself to face his sovereign.

Catherine sat at her amber-colored *secretaire*, bent over her correspondence, frowning and scribbling. The lines on her face had grown more pronounced. But then again his own face had grown more worn over the years as well. He thought it added character. Her complexion still glowed and her eyes were vibrant as ever.

Grisha dropped to his knees, ignoring the agony of his sore joints.

"I've only just now read the reports from the south, from your Black Sea Fleet." Catherine paused to take a sip of coffee. She wore a *sarafan* in the old Muscovite style, and the wide sleeves nearly knocked over one of the tiny jade frogs she'd assembled in a corner of the desk. Despite her plump figure and white mane of hair, Catherine still exuded a powerful energy. "I do believe Peter the Great himself would have been proud."

He remained on his knees. She hadn't bothered to arrange and powder a wig for this occasion, nor had she applied any rouge. At one time, this neglect would merely have signaled their intimacy. Now he feared she simply didn't care. Grisha didn't expect her to run into his arms. He hadn't expected to scoop her up and take her squealing into the bedroom. But he craved more than this, some echo of their former passion. Perhaps the chemistry would never again be perfect between them. Much as he might try, that first moment when their eyes met could never be replicated. It stood alone and pristine in time.

She began to twirl the feathered quill between her fingers. "When I see the reports, I understand why they call you emperor of the south."

Grisha's pulse quickened. Did she still fear for her hold on power? Surely she did not think he would play the part of a usurper? And yet her new favorite, Zubov, might whisper such nonsense in her ear and then turn her chin so she gazed on his pretty face. Who knew what she might believe then.

"I suppose you were always meant to be a ruler, not a mere prince," she mused.

"If you feel the title of emperor is unwarranted, even in jest," he said carefully, "I will ensure it is not repeated."

She put her pen down, finally looking at him. "Rise to your feet, Prince. It has been too long. I am glad you have returned."

Grisha worked his way upright, pain shooting down the backs of his thighs.

"You look handsome as ever. Hair still the envy of all Europe," she said, smiling.

Grisha touched his unruly mane. He'd powdered it but eschewed a wig, and instead had pulled his own hair back into a ponytail. "Best I could manage on short notice."

"And I understand you have a ward now. You are training him to be a valet."

"He is not my legal ward, but I keep him at my side. He's a sharp boy."

"You know I always encourage the cultivation of young minds." She tapped her finger on a weathered volume of *Candide*. "I should like him to have this."

"He will appreciate your kindness, *matushka*."

"I appreciate your sweet words, but what actually brings you here now, old friend?"

They were old friends, of course, but once they had been so much more. The phrase made him ache, and he wondered if he had come to the point in life where he would rather live with his memories alone. Still, he didn't mince words. Catherine never cared for that. "Platon Alexandrovich."

She sighed. He wished he could have detected annoyance, but it was more the sigh of a smitten schoolgirl feigning disinterest. "Is it his monkey? Did the creature steal one of your wigs? If so, how much do I owe you?"

"You've given Zubov dominion over my new project."

"A man needs dominion over something. Otherwise he is no man."

"I'd rather his dominion stand apart from my interests."

Catherine placed her hands gently on Grisha's shoulders. He no longer saw the light of lust in her eyes, only concern tinged with pity. He bristled.

The corners of her mouth turned down and she backed away from him. She had misinterpreted his reaction. He closed the space between them once more.

"Zubov is still a young man," she said, voice cracking as Grisha drew nearer. "Allow him to find his path. Be patient. Guide him gently, like a father. For me."

He had tried to act as a father figure, as he had with all of her previous favorites. But Platon Alexandrovich wanted more than her favor. He desired influence.

She couldn't see Zubov clearly any more than he could think straight with some nubile lovely whispering in his ear. Men and women both needed to feel vibrant and alive, especially as they aged. The philosophes so treasured by Catherine, even her darling Voltaire, might insist the sexes were different in this respect, but Grisha had never found it so. And he had to remind her of his ability to make her feel thus.

He leaned in to kiss her soft hand and allowed his lips to linger, sensing a shallow spasm in her fingers. Her body still responded to his, even if her heart had been carried elsewhere. "I've missed you, wife."

She pulled her hand away and returned to her desk. The cat on the mantel of the hearth stretched lazily and then opened her eyes, perturbed at the disruption.

"I am grateful you have finally returned to the capital, little dove," she said, gazing up at Grisha. "Only I expect you to be useful rather than creating trouble where none previously existed." She tilted her head. "And much as I enjoyed your sweet words, I wonder if your love note wasn't disingenuous. Who is this one girl

I hear of? Praskovia, is it?" A hint of jealousy sullied her tone. "They say you promoted her husband in the field not based on his talents but so she might be closer to you."

Grisha remained silent. He saw little point in denying his pursuit. Praskovia was but the latest of many, and Catherine had always maintained a high tolerance for games of the heart.

"Perhaps I could try again with Zubov," he said. "I want only what is best for your glory and that of the empire. I will tolerate nothing that stands in the way."

Catherine smiled. "No doubt, old friend." She returned to her letters. "I've never questioned your interests. They have always been with Russia. But much as I trust your wisdom when it comes to negotiating terms with our blood enemies, I'm not convinced encouraging the Muslim faith is the best use of our limited means. Not when we have more important matters at hand."

"You have constructed mosques before."

"Never on such a scale."

"This project will soothe bruised egos, *matushka*."

"You have been away for nearly two years. I fear you may not understand Platon's objections to the project because you do not grasp our current affairs."

"I do not understand because it makes no sense," he said, pushing down a bubble of anger in his chest. "You have always extended goodwill to all subjects, regardless of their faith."

Her voice rose to meet his. "We need to turn our attention outward. The Prussians and the English want us away from the Black Sea region all together. Ochakov back in Turkish hands? How can you of all people bear to give up such a prize?"

A prize. Zubov's words. How could Catherine ever refer to Ochakov in such a callous way? "Mollify Prussia. Let me talk to the English ambassador. You know I've always had a fondness for the people of that little island. I'm sure they're simply in a sour mood over losing their American colonies to a team of crafty republicans."

"What if you're wrong?"

"The English are like vain children, only interested in this 'prize' because it belongs to someone else. Children are to be flattered and outmaneuvered. You don't go to war with them."

Her cheeks flared. "Don't lecture me like a pompous old schoolmaster. I have entrusted you with the care of our new world. Is that not enough for you? You must return to tell me how to run my affairs with the European powers as well? That is my dominion."

"Your dominion or that of your new toy, Platon Alexandrovich?"

"You're acting like a jealous old fool."

Grisha's hands balled into fists. He remembered what Anton had told him of Zubov's connections: his old enemy Saltykov and Catherine's insipid son Paul. He could have sent her running to her boudoir in tears with that choice tidbit. But he could not bear the thought of hurting her. "Zubov and his ilk are trying to goad you into a needless war."

"Do not condescend to me like I'm one of your silly waifs. Remember what the founder of this city, Peter the Great, used to say: delay is death."

"In this case, to delay is simply good common sense. Zubov has gotten to you. That or your damn pride."

"Voltaire says women are the more jealous gender, but I never believed him. You're envious of a younger man. It's not like you. You refuse to acknowledge Platon's talents, and now you seek to degrade my authority."

"I'm trying to stop madness. Our military forces are spread thin. What if the Prussians take a notion to march on St. Petersburg? Do you want an old Germanic toad on your throne?"

"Stop yelling, Prince."

"Damn it, woman, I'll yell as loud as I please until you listen to common sense!"

She rose to her feet. "Prince Potemkin, stop shouting and turn around."

The command in her voice cut through his anger, and he turned. Anton stood at the door, hat in hand, the guardsman with the Hapsburg chin sulking behind him.

"Thank you," Catherine said curtly to the guard. "If the prince's boy is here, it must be time for him to leave. We only need a few more minutes."

As they left, she added, "You talk of this mosque as a legacy project. You have many good years before you, Prince. You might serve me best by negotiating the new terms of peace with the Turks. You are the only man with the talent to do so."

The elderly greyhound, the Thomassin, shifted his weight, ears alert, and growled.

"Tom!" Catherine scolded. "What has gotten into you? The prince is an old friend. You recognized him only a few minutes ago." She looked at Grisha. "Some of the philosophes believe animals are far more perceptive than we understand. Perhaps your words troubled him."

Grisha knew better. They were no longer alone. Catherine's dog had detected an otherworldly presence, the faint change of temperature and electricity in the air. "It's nothing," Grisha muttered. "He's old and grouchy. Aren't we all? I've taken too much of your time."

"Take the book at least," she said gently.

He nodded, snatched *Candide* from her desk, and backed away from the room, determined to bribe the guard outside so he might gain quicker access to the empress next time.

"I'm sorry if I've upset you," he told her. "I only needed to voice my opinion."

"Thank you, husband." She returned to her desk and shuffled a few papers, still not looking up. "But in this case I'd best keep my own counsel. You look tired. Go home and rest."

Her words were like daggers. If he was no longer of use to her, he was no longer of use to this world. "You need me here more than ever. Your legacy in this world is threatened. Your affair with this boy has addled your brain. You need the guidance of a real man."

She rose slowly to her feet, the open sleeves of her gown drooping, her cheeks blazing red. Grisha's heart soared. Perhaps passion lingered between them yet.

"Peter the Great's blood may not run in my veins," she said coldly. "But make no mistake. I am his heir. And you are my subject to do as I command."

She was still the sovereign. She could have ordered him to Siberia had she so wished. For a frightful moment he thought she might. "My apologies, *matushka*," he said quickly. "I suffer from ill digestion and a headache. It sets my nerves on edge."

"See that you get a good night's sleep then."

"Always as you say, *matushka*." He bowed low once more.

"In the meantime, I have work to do." She pointed to the door. "Get out."

Anton scuttled to keep pace with Grisha as they headed down the drafty corridor outside Catherine's study. Grisha gnawed frantically on his thumbnail and nearly tripped on a yowling palace tomcat stalking a mouse.

They were being followed. He knew it. He had known as soon as Catherine's dog started growling, but he would not let Anton notice anything amiss. No need to frighten the boy. Grisha began to hum to himself, a little tune by Herr Mozart that pleased him. He stopped abruptly, reached into his greatcoat, and withdrew Catherine's copy of *Candide*. "A gift from the empress," he said, pushing the book to Anton's chest.

The boy's countenance remained solemn, but his hand shook. "It is too much."

"Nonsense," Grisha said. "A monarch has a divine obligation to educate young minds."

Anton opened the cover and squinted at Voltaire's scrawny signature. "My skills in the French language are too weak for this complicated work."

Grisha glanced at the inscription scribbled in French but couldn't make out the words either. Voltaire had always been too bold by half with Catherine and had no doubt made some lewd comment veiled as wit. Such a reference might shock Anton, but then he was of the age now where he could use a shock or two to ready his path to manhood. "We'll find a French dictionary. Now run and make sure our horses are ready."

Anton nodded and scurried ahead. Grisha waited until the clacking of the boy's shoes against the tile faded. A pair of bonneted laundresses carrying a basket of linen passed. Grisha smiled and bowed, looking up while he did so to wink. The girls giggled, dipped their heads, and shuffled past him.

"When will you speak to me, crusader?" The pasha spoke in the quiet, clever way he did whenever he visited Grisha.

"I will not speak to you here," Grisha said in a low voice. He knew the pasha was merely a figment, conjured from addled memories and imagination, and yet he responded to the apparition as he would to any earthbound man. Grisha feared a random servant might hear and pass word of his lunacy to Catherine. "I require privacy."

"The construction of a mosque in Old Russia was to be a part of your legacy."

Grisha remembered the first time he was briefed on the once-great leader of the Ottomans: Ghazi Hassan-Pasha . . . the so-called Turkish "crocodile" of the sea. He looked much the same now as he did when his earthly life ended, only the sharp lines of his features seemed vague and softer around the edges. Silken robes were draped over his wiry, muscular shoulders and he wore blue pantaloons and a jacket with white sashes crossing his chest, in the mode of the Ottoman court. His high white turban stood proudly atop his head. The pasha's face was still fierce, even though Grisha's campaigns had destroyed him. A tamed lion had followed the man faithfully throughout his life. Grisha hoped the beast rested peacefully now.

"The mosque is the only way Allah will be satisfied when he reviews your crimes." A footman headed toward Catherine's study with a fresh plate of scones on a silver tray. The pasha eyed them with distaste. "Recall what happened to the Roman Empire when shallow luxuries and games took over palaces."

"A weakness for pastries hardly heralds the fall of an empire."

"Your strong woman is softening."

Grisha took care to make sure the footman had disappeared. "She is not my woman. Not anymore."

"And yet she calls you husband," the pasha said. "If the marriage is true, you are as powerful as the sovereign, or at least it should be so."

"You have never understood our ways."

"Do not forget I take as much interest in other religions as you. My own father was of the Orthodox faith. You people refer to your ancient Moscow as the third Rome and yet you run your empire from this swamp? With a woman at the head? And surely you understand my disinclination to support your way of life when you had me poisoned."

"It was your own people. That is the way of your sultans. The barbarous behavior of your empire led to your demise."

"I was poisoned because you would not listen to sense and our peace negotiations were abandoned. After all of the blood you shed."

The shame bore down. "Your men should have seen sense and surrendered those battles."

"Battles? The invasions, you mean. The occupations."

"The Ottoman Empire never acquired a thirst for blood?"

The pasha touched his turban lightly. "Make your woman see sense. Show her the foolishness of that boy she's taken for a lover."

"I have attempted to do so."

"Only in the privacy of a chamber where she can dismiss you too easily. This boy she adores wants to block you? Unveil his presumption and weaknesses publicly."

"It is more complex when trying to woo a woman of such power."

"Because you might offend her? This God of yours is strange. He loved the world so much that he gave his only son? And yet he seems to require no sacrifice from you."

"I do not fear sacrifice," Grisha said, voice rising.

"You make excuses and delay. Have you grown weak in your old age, white demon?"

The pasha was his enemy, had always been his enemy even beyond the bounds of earthly life. He made a roar and lunged at the man, but the pasha dodged and Grisha ran into a thick Grecian pillar in the hallway. A heavy medallion on his chest fell with a clatter to the floor, followed by Grisha.

"Your Highness?"

Anton stared down at him, eyes wide. Grisha's expansive stomach was already sore. A bruise would blossom by morning.

"What happened? You were talking to someone. I heard you."

"It was no one," Grisha muttered, bending to retrieve the medallion and wincing.

"The empress wants you home abed. I need to follow her instructions." His gaze returned to Grisha's form. "Did you fall?"

Grisha started to laugh. His back ached. He looked up at the friezes on the ceiling, doves sailing against a pure blue sky and apostles kneeling to Christ as he exited his tomb.

"A trifling misstep," he told Anton. "I shall take care to make no more of those."

Four

FOR IMMEDIATE RELEASE

The Monarchist Society has interviewed Romanov heirs in the past, including Dr. Herrera's father, Laurent Marchand, but Dr. Herrera's name is the first to have been made public in over twenty years.

EN ROUTE TO RUSSIA
PRESENT DAY

They were rising above the desert, still in California airspace, when Michael started to grill Dmitry for details. "First of all, I thought no announcements would be made about Veronica's connection to the Romanov family until after she arrived in St. Petersburg. Why is she featured in a Russian newspaper?"

"This was mistake," Dmitry said, speaking in English, which he claimed to prefer when in conversation with Americans.

"I suppose you all have decided Veronica should stay in the best hotel in St. Petersburg, where she'll be an easy target to find for anyone with a grudge against the Romanovs."

"Actually, no." Dmitry withdrew an electronic tablet from the seat pocket where he'd stowed it and then shifted in his seat so he could retrieve something. He moved so gracefully he didn't even touch her. "Irina Yusupova has arranged modest accommodation. She thought it best not to draw attention. Not at first."

Veronica had taken the window seat with Dmitry in the middle and Michael on the aisle. Even though she and Michael weren't touching, she felt the weight of his presence. Behind her, the girl who had dropped the cookies earlier was kicking the back of Veronica's seat. "Don't do that to the lady," she heard the father say weakly.

Longest flight ever.

"And transportation?" Michael said. "She needs to move safely from place to place. The Society wasn't supposed to publish pictures before her position was clearly established."

"How do you know this?"

"My grandmother was one of Empress Alexandra's servants. My mother still has connections with the old monarchist groups."

"Your mother. Right." Dmitry's hand tightened in and out of a fist as he waited for his tablet to power up. "I travel with Dr. Herrera and when possible we hire car to avoid metro."

"Have you screened the drivers?"

"I can assure you she is to be well protected."

Finally, the kicking subsided. But two women in the back of the cabin began the loudest Russian conversation Veronica had ever heard, something about a cheating husband caught in the act and a night spent in jail. Right now she didn't need any more drama. Veronica reached for her phone and earbuds. She wanted to close her eyes and disappear into a new wave playlist. She had compiled a soothing soundtrack for the trip, musical comfort food from high school: the Cure, Depeche Mode, and Erasure. So much better than listening to Michael and Dmitry fuss at one another.

"Who do you think leaked the article about Veronica to the newspaper?" Michael asked.

"It could be anyone."

"Anyone in the Monarchist Society? So you don't have control over your own people?"

Veronica was about to press play when she saw Dmitry open his fist, something in his palm twinkling in the high sunlight. "I assure you Dr. Herrera is to be perfectly safe."

"What are you holding?" Veronica asked curiously.

Dmitry opened his hand wider, revealing a tiny red jewel.

"Is that a ruby?"

"It is embarrassing." He smiled sheepishly. "This has been in family for good luck; I get nervous flying. I need it today."

Veronica touched the cross on her necklace and returned his smile. Michael gave her a guarded glance. Did he think she was flirting?

Dmitry deposited the ruby back into his pocket and tapped a few notes on his tablet. He wore khaki trousers and a fresh white button-down shirt that looked strangely crisp for someone who had spent the past few days trotting around the globe. "I hope you will not mind a few difficult questions."

She put the earbuds away.

"I am to serve as your advocate in process. So I need to be sure we are clear on facts. Society wants to present clear narrative to connect your grandmother to Nicholas and Alexandra." He inclined forward to address Michael. "You understand this, of course?"

Michael scratched the back of his neck and reached for a copy of the in-flight magazine from his seat pocket. "Of course. Pretend I'm not even here."

"You say Laurent Marchand is father," Dmitry began.

"Laurent Marchand is her father," Michael answered for her.

Veronica frowned at him, then drew in a breath of the artificial cabin air. "I believe that man is my father, yes."

"Laurent is son of Charlotte Marchand, who claimed to be Grand Duchess Charlotte, secret fifth daughter of the tsar. But you never met Laurent?"

Veronica looked out the window at the red-orange mounds of the desert below them. Her mother had been in one of Laurent's classes, alone and vulnerable in Spain as a foreign exchange student. He never bothered to try to find Veronica. She thought she had formed a thick wall around her heart when it came to anything related to her father, but it still hurt. Wounds heal, but the memory of pain lingers.

When she turned away from the window, she caught Michael's gaze, the corners of his eyes creased with concern.

"Charlotte never made that claim for herself," Veronica said quickly, raising her voice above the chattering Russians. She caught herself clawing the armrests and tried to relax her hands. "We call her Grand Duchess because she was the fifth daughter of Nicholas and Alexandra. But she never used the title."

"This is concern," Dmitry said.

"According to your society's own bylaws and regulations, the claimant's position vis-à-vis a previous claimant or lack thereof doesn't matter," Michael said. "Section three, article five. You have read the bylaws, right?"

Dmitry remained calm. Even being squished into the middle seat didn't seem to faze him. "Of course we attempt to contact Laurent Marchand since he would claim throne before you. But he has been . . . not cooperative."

"He's a hermit. At least that's how I picture him."

"Also, why would any Russian want American on throne?" Dmitry said.

"I'm a Romanov," Veronica said. "I happen to be American by birth."

"What did Romanovs ever do for Russia? The gap between rich and poor was so wide we could not bear it. Royal family did nothing. Is it any wonder they are all murdered?"

The horrific images came rushing back to Veronica's mind: the daughters of Nicholas and Alexandra bleeding to death in the basement, bayonets puncturing their chests when bullets wouldn't work, gunpowder clinging to the stale air, feathers from their pillows drifting to the hard floor. The last violent moments of the family's life had always been vivid and disturbing, almost like a personal memory. Now that she knew those girls had been her great-aunts, the thought of it was even more devastating.

"Is this really necessary?" Michael asked.

"It's okay." Veronica repositioned herself in the narrow seat, hardly a throne, but she tried to project a regal air, even when a bump of turbulence made her stomach pitch.

"If the current Russian government made move to provoke Americans," Dmitry asked her, "whose side would you take?"

She opened her mouth to reply and then snapped it shut again. "Shit."

"We struggle with how you answer question. Just consider."

Veronica raised her hand. "No. I can answer now. I am not a part of either the Russian government or the American government. When I'm in Russia, I follow their laws. When I'm in America, I follow theirs. But I won't be the mouthpiece for either."

"So you remain out of politics?" Dmitry said. "How so? Reb Volkov broke Russian law."

"Hooliganism? That's a ridiculous law. It could mean anything."

"Who are you to say this is ridiculous law? Is not your country."

"I . . . I just know because . . . it isn't right."

Dmitry frowned. "My apologies, but you will need to do better when you discuss Reb. I think you should speak of Russia as adopted homeland. It will sound pleasing to Russian audience."

Michael turned a page in the magazine roughly, ripping it. "I think she did well enough with your trick questions."

Dmitry frowned. "Trick questions? What is this?"

"You were the one who asked her to come to Russia. You knew she was American."

"I only want her prepared for questions journalists will ask. We will ready to make strong case. Otherwise will anything matter?"

Veronica felt as though her heart had dropped to the pit of her stomach. All of this might come to nothing after all. Perhaps this had all been a mistake and she was meant to stay in a cubicle in Bakersfield her entire life. At least it had been a steady paycheck. *Stop it. You are meant to be here.*

Dmitry leaned over to retrieve a canvas messenger bag from under the seat in front of him. "I have everything saved electronically but thought you might want copy of itinerary."

He withdrew a red leather binder with an imperial double-headed eagle embossed on the cover. Heads opposite. Beaks angrily agape. He handed it to her. Veronica traced the outline with her finger. It wasn't so different from the American eagle on her passport.

"I compile schedule, reporters who ask for interview, biographical information—please check accuracy—and background on Society and members."

As Veronica thumbed through the laminated pages, Michael peeked over Dmitry's shoulder. "This looks thorough," he said. "And overwhelming. I'm not sure Veronica's schedule is realistic. Will she even get a chance to sleep?"

That finally drew a scowl from Dmitry. "So where is this you will stay, Mr. Karstadt?"

"The same hotel as me," Veronica said without thinking. "Right?"

"Yes," Michael assured her.

"Actually, I think he should find other accommodations," Dmitry said.

Veronica had a sudden picture in her mind of Michael on a corner of Nevsky Prospect, curled into a sleeping bag while Russian gangsters swaggered past, kicking the cardboard box he used for shelter. "Why?"

Dmitry turned to Michael. "I know now why name familiar. I have seen in our records."

"Your records?" Michael said.

Dmitry shifted his weight. He actually looked uncomfortable, even in his crisp white shirt. "You sought claim on own behalf, were discredited. You are not even Romanov."

Michael's shoulders sagged. "No," he admitted.

"He only registered his claim to keep me safe," Veronica said quickly.

"Even so, Russians lied to for many years by own government. If Mr. Karstadt is exposed as fraud, it could damage your reputation."

"Someone should stay in the hotel with Veronica."

"No worry," Dmitry said. "I've arranged to stay in room on same floor as Dr. Herrera for duration of stay in St. Petersburg."

"How convenient."

"I did not realize Dr. Herrera was to bring guest." Dmitry gestured toward the red binder. "Not part of plan."

"Sorry to have burst your bubble," Michael said.

"What bubble? If you wanted to help, you should have let us know."

An elegant flight attendant approached their row, holding the seats on either side of the aisle to steady herself on her heels. Thank God. Maybe she would offer them all a drink.

"Does this mean you don't want me near Veronica at all?" Michael asked.

"Of course you are still allowed to see her—under my supervision."

"Your supervision?" Michael said. "I told her grandmother I would keep an eye on her. How am I supposed to explain a different hotel?"

The flight attendant stopped at their row, gaze fixed on Veronica.

"I'm not an idiot," Michael said. "I'm not going to do anything stupid."

"I saw picture in paper," the flight attendant said to Veronica. Her voice was gentle, like she had once taught kindergarten. "And Lyudmilla said you would be here. You are Romanov heiress. This is honor."

"Thank you," Veronica said.

The attendant's attention flicked to Michael, then Dmitry, and back to Veronica again. "I am told we have a space for you in our President Class. Would you like to move?"

"Absolutely." Veronica grabbed her purse. Apparently, fame had its perks.

"And your friends . . . ?"

"Oh, don't worry about them," Veronica told her. She stood up and worked her way to the aisle, briskly—if awkwardly—climbing over Dmitry and then Michael.

"Wait . . . what?" Michael said.

The flight attendant smiled and clasped her hands together. "We are moving Romanov heiress to President Class."

Veronica opened the overhead bin. "The three of us are going to spend the next week together in Russia, and I'm already sick of this pissing match." She grabbed her coat and the flight attendant helped her with her suitcase. "Figure it out."

President Class was nearly empty, blissfully silent, and smelled vaguely of a musky floral perfume. Veronica sank back into the enormous seat, her feet in fuzzy slippers, a knitted blanket tucked over her lap, and a glass of Bordeaux on her tray. The flight attendant assured her the seat reclined all the way back, helped her settle in, and then scurried off to find pajamas.

Veronica opened Dmitry's binder. She'd been sent a rough draft of her itinerary via e-mail, and the finalized version looked much the same: interview with Irina, press conference . . . no, wait, they'd added some sort of photo shoot. She flipped past a few more pages to read the first sentence of her bio:

It is with tremendous honor that the Russian Monarchist Society welcomes acclaimed historian Veronica Herrera (Romanov) to St. Petersburg . . .

Acclaimed historian? Try disgraced academic. The biography would need some work.

Veronica turned to the back of the binder, to a list Dmitry had labeled "action items." She found a picture of Reb Volkov grinning roguishly at the camera, his giant ginger-colored cat, Caravaggio, draped around his shoulders, facing the world with a guileless teddy bear face. The same picture had been used in last year's *People*'s "50 Most Beautiful People" issue. She lingered on the page a moment. Reb always brought the pretty.

She flipped the page again and saw a small charcoal drawing of a building with a domed center edged by four slender minarets reaching toward the sky, all topped with tiny crescent moons. Absently she traced its lines. It was a mosque, beautiful in its simplicity.

"Lovely, isn't it?"

Veronica turned in the direction of the perfume and inclined forward to see around the large sides of her seat. The woman who spoke sat in the aisle across from her. She was perhaps five to ten years older than Veronica, with a professional air. Her blond hair was gathered into a side sweep, clipped by an onyx pendant with a picture of a Firebird, eyes glowing, soaring over the Russian countryside like a dragon.

"Has Dmitry mentioned the mosque yet?" the woman asked.

Veronica shook her head, confused.

"I was the one who asked to include it in your itinerary. From what I understand, Moscow is in need of new mosques for guest workers coming to the city. The construction could become a part of your legacy."

"I'm sorry, do I know you?" Veronica finally asked.

The woman extended her hand. A diamond tennis bracelet encircled her slim wrist. Her English was fluent with no trace of a Russian accent, only the affected tone of an American who wished she had been born a Brit. "I'm Irina Yusupova. Pleased to meet you, Dr. Herrera. I'm glad you finally made it up to the front of the plane where you belong."

"Dmitry said you were meeting us in St. Petersburg."

"I wanted to meet with one of our donors in Westwood myself. Don't tell Dmitry. I felt he didn't have the right level of"—she fluttered her hands in the air—"sophistication for this particular gentleman. Fundraising is an art. We need all the support we can muster."

"We didn't even know you were on board."

"Of course not! I always get on right before the gates close. Why would I want to sit on an airplane any longer than necessary?"

Irina kept smiling and nodding. Veronica felt another jolt of turbulence, weaker here than in the back of the cabin, and steadied herself. "So this mosque is important to you?"

"Not just to me but to Russia. It was a pet project of Dmitry's ancestor Prince Potemkin. I think it would be wonderful for you and Dmitry to work together to realize his dream. After all, we are a charitable organization. Our goal is to proudly serve all Russians."

"I appreciate that, I do," Veronica said. "But right now I think there is a more pressing issue—Reb Volkov."

Irina fingered her bracelet and gave a tight smile. "You've let Dmitry influence you. He has let himself get distracted by that boy Nikolai Volkov. The blasphemer artist who calls himself Reb. It's a divisive issue."

Veronica's head was spinning. She tried to remember what Dmitry had told her about Irina Yusupova, the head of the Society. Irina had no claim to the throne herself, though one of her ex-husbands came from a noble and once vastly wealthy family, the Yusupovs, who had a vague connection to Prince Potemkin.

"But never mind all that. This is a momentous occasion! You're a celebrity. I knew they would let you up front. It was only a matter of time." Irina gave Veronica's arm a gentle shake. "It's all about *glamur*. Who has more *glamur* than the heiress to the Romanov throne? You are going to have a marvelous time in Petersburg. We should celebrate." Irina waved at Veronica's binder. "I see you have one of Dmitry's agendas. He's too rigid. If your story is true, you must learn to improvise."

Veronica's heart skipped a beat. "If?"

"I didn't mean it that way," Irina said quickly. "We asked you to come, did we not? Your evidence is compelling. At least Empress Alexandra's letter is compelling enough. Dmitry included a copy on page eight. Alexandra seems to suggest she gave birth to a secret fifth daughter."

"But you don't believe me?"

"I only meant if you want the part, you've got to play the part." Irina frowned suddenly and grabbed ahold of Veronica's hand.

"Hey!" Veronica tried to pull her hand away, but Irina held it fast, examining Veronica's unmanicured fingers and clicking her tongue against her teeth.

"Do you always wear your nails naturally?" Irina said. "We have so much work to do."

"I'm not traveling all this way for a spa day," Veronica said, trying to keep her voice calm and measured. "I want to help Reb Volkov."

Irina released Veronica's hand. "I see. You are a true believer. Perhaps even a patriot of some sort. But you have so much you can accomplish. Let me show you something."

She reached into a sleek tote bag and withdrew a phone in a sparkling pink case. "I've mentioned I've been fund-raising, yes? I know Dmitry tried a bit of that himself, but the poor thing is useless when it comes to monetizing our organization. Thankfully I have a talent." She punched some buttons on her phone. "I met with the owners of a vegetarian Russian restaurant chain based in West Hollywood. They want to expand into Petersburg. Vegetarian! Can you imagine?"

Veronica was beginning to wish she hadn't changed seats, no matter how comfortable the slippers. "Actually, I've been a vegetarian for several months now. It sounds good to me."

"Oh right. The California thing. I suppose you meditate and do yoga too. Well, maybe it's for the best." Irina's hands fluttered some more. "My experience in advertising is limited, but I suppose it's good if you actually believe in the product you're meant to sell."

She turned her phone around to show Veronica a picture. Veronica's face—a different picture than the newspaper had used, a younger version that she used on social media sites—had been Photoshopped above a dress she recognized immediately. It was Catherine the Great's coronation gown: a richly beaded bodice underneath a gold-trimmed cape and metallic double-headed eagles embroidered onto a skirt that stood out stiff and wide at her hips.

Underneath, the copy declared in Cyrillic: "Ekaterina . . . A Royal Feast!" The green and white baroque façade of a building that looked like the Winter Palace hung as backdrop.

"You adore this, right? You recognize the dress? The coronation gown worn by Catherine herself! The greatest woman ever to lead a nation! The enlightened empress!" Irina drew closer and lifted her hair to indicate the back of her slender neck. "Do you smell that? It is a reproduction of Catherine's perfume. I had it commissioned."

Veronica tried to smile. "This restaurant wants me to advertise for them?"

"Not only this restaurant. I've lined up an Argentinian winery and perhaps a Fiat dealer." Irina waved her hand. "It is not a done deal yet, but I have a good feeling. You will have many such opportunities to monetize your brand."

The picture looked creepy, and Veronica hadn't exactly planned to use whatever celebrity cachet Irina thought she might possess to sell crap. Then again she could use the money. She no longer had a job, after all. She looked around the rest of the cabin: an older couple hunched over a movie and a guy with a half-empty glass of red wine snoring in his seat.

"I don't feel like much of a celebrity," Veronica said.

"Surely you've seen some version of *Anastasia* or another. You are a Romanov grand duchess, an heir to Catherine the Great herself. Look like a grand duchess. Act like a grand duchess. And people will be drawn to you. Otherwise none of this matters."

"She is a grand duchess." Michael stood behind them, where a heavy curtain separated the two sections of the cabin. "She doesn't need to put on a show."

The flight attendant was at his side, hands on hips. "He barge past me. I tell captain."

"Just a few minutes," Michael told the attendant, smiling easily, still confident in his charm. "Then I'll go back where I belong."

To Veronica's surprise, the flight attendant looked to her for instruction.

"He's with me," Veronica told her.

The flight attendant stepped back, keeping a suspicious eye on Michael.

"Who is this?" Irina asked as Michael towered over them. Irina ogled him as though he had come in as part of a dessert tray. "You brought a bodyguard of your own?"

"More like he brought himself," Veronica said. "Michael Karstadt."

"Has Dmitry already bored you to tears?" Irina asked him. "You poor dear. That one really should loosen up a little. He is . . . how do Americans say it? A control freak. Grisha Potemkin would be so disappointed in his descendant. Now, the prince? He understood how to enjoy life." Irina slipped her phone with all its sparkles back in her bag and reappraised Michael.

"Mikhail Karstadt. I know that name. You've spent some time in the archives in St. Petersburg, haven't you? Your grandfather was a palace guard, from the North African regiment, no?"

Veronica quickly corrected her. "He left as a member of the Preobrazhensky Guard."

"We're not sure if Dowager Empress Marie was technically authorized to award him this title but we can look into some sort of posthumous honors. I suppose Catherine would have done something similar were she in your place."

"It's the least you can do. His grandfather helped save an heiress to the throne."

Irina smoothed her linen skirt. "You're not tsarina yet, dear. Hold off on giving orders." She looked at Veronica. "Especially to me."

The flight attendant approached once more, presenting Veronica with a cute pair of flannel pajamas, a wing-shaped Russian flag stamped near the right shoulder. But somehow Veronica no longer felt in the mood for a good night's rest.

"We should discuss your personal brand," Irina said. "I think you will find many companies are interested in utilizing your image and voice."

"I think there may have been a misunderstanding. I was under the impression I would be able to speak on . . ." Veronica tried to figure out a way to say it without hurting Irina's feelings but decided to be straightforward. "More important issues. Political issues. Dmitry spoke of this time as a crossroads for Russia."

"You sound like such an academic. We'll need to work on that."

"I'm not interested in being a walking advertisement."

"Not that it would necessarily *hurt* to make a little money," Michael added.

Veronica glared at him.

"I mean if it's convenient . . ." He shrugged and shut up.

Irina leaned back in the enormous cushioned seat, taking in Michael with undisguised admiration. "You seem like a sensible man. And you look like a solid Russian Cossack. I would have loved to put you on television. Too bad you weren't the one."

Michael's cheeks turned pink.

Irina waved at Veronica's pajamas. "You can change, but don't plan to get too much sleep. I've reconsidered. We only have a week together. Maybe you should read that dossier after all, seeing as how Dmitry went to the trouble of putting it together. Best to be well prepared."

"I *am* prepared." Veronica's body gave an involuntary shudder. She tried to cover it by rolling her shoulders back and sitting straighter in her seat.

"Sure you are," Irina told her. "But you should keep Dmitry and this other handsome man nearby, just in case. Now that I've met you, I'm not sure you will be adept at making friends. We'll need to tread more carefully than I thought."

Five

Grisha gnawed on a raw turnip, fighting the temptation to bark an order for the driver to turn around. As he had predicted, a tender bruise spread dark purple and sickly green across his broad stomach where he had smashed into the post trying to lunge at the crafty pasha. Hot chocolate, a little violin music, and his warm canopied bed: that's what he needed now. Not shallow conversations with the pompous twits who populated Catherine's beloved Hermitage.

But Catherine had summoned him for a late supper, an encouraging sign considering she had ordered him out of her presence when he saw her last. Still, traveling to the palace for a public function was a far different matter than a private audience with Catherine. He took another nibble on the turnip, turning the flesh on his tongue, picturing spoiled courtiers sipping lemon- and cherry-infused vodkas, pondering how best to curry Platon Zubov's favor.

His team of six dappled grays trod carefully around spots of slick ice. Grisha drew aside the delicate linens covering the frosted window of his coach. A soft layer of snowfall made even the imposing palaces of the highest nobility seem humble and quaint. Grisha trained his eyes on the less intimidating wooden structures: well-kept apothecaries and simple churches crowned with bell towers, onion domes, and crosses pointing to heaven.

They passed a rumbling wagon filled to the brim with vegetables and tubers bound for market, the man at the front bravely tightening his modest brown coat against the cold. Grisha caught a whiff and remembered his childhood in the countryside, the soothing scent of onions frying for a simple pierogi supper.

This was why Russia had gone to war and then to war again. He and Catherine may have shared the dreams of expansionists, but it had all been to preserve and protect the simplicity of this life. They could not let it all fall to pieces in service of Zubov's vain desire for glory.

Anton sat across from him in the coach, swinging his legs back and forth, engrossed in his dog-eared copy of *Candide*. Whenever they hit a bump, the boy grasped the sides of his seat and the book dropped into his lap. Grisha caught a glimpse of the notes Anton had scribbled to himself along the edges of the page. He dusted a speck of lint from his greatcoat, trying not to smile.

He should use this short journey to instruct the boy. He could tell him of Catherine's moment of victory, the people of St. Petersburg lining the streets, cheering and falling to their knees as they watched Catherine astride her stallion, ready to seize power as an empress of the Enlightenment, saving her adopted homeland from a backward and insipid tsar. Or he could speak of more frightening tales, how in the deepest dungeons of his great fortress, Catherine's hero, Peter the Great, had his own son tortured and beaten to death.

But Grisha just peered out the window. Dim lanterns, redolent of the coarse scent of hempseed oil, provided pale illumination for the bridges, and he tried to make out the golden spire of Peter and Paul Cathedral across the water. He smiled at Anton but remained silent. The picturesque scenery put him in a contemplative mood. He didn't want to meditate on games of power. Anton would find his path in this world, as they all did. He might find a woman to love and they would raise fat, happy children together. Perhaps he would find happiness in a normal life of routine and habit, the kind of happiness that had always eluded Grisha.

The Winter Palace was alive with candlelight and the bombast of a full orchestra strumming a popular waltz. By the time Grisha and Anton alighted from their carriage and pushed their way inside, a sea of swaggering courtiers and giggling ladies-in-waiting had already crowded into the receiving area, rife with the sensual fragrances of jasmine and citrus blooms, expensive French colognes, and freshly applied pomade. When the doors of the ballroom opened to admit a new group inside, Anton rose to his tiptoes to catch a glimpse of the fantasia of waltzing couples in silver wigs.

Grisha tried to take it all in stride, to revel in the youthful energy and joy. In truth, this quirky lightness only made him feel obsolete. He could see himself in the crowd, as though observing a stranger at a distance. Even as he smiled, dark clouds gathered inside of him.

"They say Zubov's monkey has his own bedtime routine, like a child," Anton said, scurrying behind as Grisha led them through the palace halls to the empress's Little Hermitage. Once they reached a cloakroom, Anton withdrew a brush with fine hog's-hair bristles from his bag to dust the snow from Grisha's heavy greatcoat. "Each night, Zubov forces a courtier to read the beast a fairy tale. The story of Father Frost and the Snow Maiden is his favorite."

Grisha touched his chest to feel the diamond-studded medallion with Catherine's portrait in the center, worn near his heart. "Perhaps the courtiers are only looking for an excuse to avoid

Zubov. Wouldn't you rather read to the monkey than listen to his master prattle?"

Anton snorted and hung Grisha's coat from a hook. The other guests had not been as fastidious. Melted snow clung to the wool of the coats, creating a damp and dank odor in the receiving hall, despite the vanilla potpourri and candles burning in sconces along the walls. Anton withdrew the plans for the mosque, sheathed in a silk wrap, from his bag and moved them to the coat's pocket so that Grisha might easily access them.

"Be sure my horses are stabled in a timely fashion," Grisha said, moving slowly now, forcing himself to push through the dark clouds in his head. "Mind the new driver and the horse master. I don't trust either. Ask for the horses again within two hours. I don't intend to linger."

Anton regarded him with such a lack of guile that Grisha had a sudden pang of nostalgia to be a boy again "Have you considered using the information about Zubov's connections to Saltykov's household and Grand Duke Paul?"

"Catherine thinks she's in love with the handsome fool. It would hurt her too much." *And I would never hurt my wife.* Grisha bit his tongue to keep those words silent. Who knew what spies lurked, ready to use any word against him?

Anton nodded obediently before he withdrew from the alcove. Grisha strode toward Catherine's private dining room, passing colorful Renaissance paintings, busts of Catherine's precious philosophes, and shelves stuffed with thick folios. He tried to pretend a confidence he didn't feel, that he experienced less and less of late.

A guard of the North African regiment waited at the door, jewel-encrusted turban dipping as he bowed his head. Grisha recognized the guard and recalled a long night they'd spent discussing his plans for the mosque, as the man had mentioned he was of the Muslim faith. Grisha would have liked to ask him to join his household, where he would have greater responsibilities than opening doors for drunken courtiers. But he was in no position to vex Catherine by stealing her staff.

Grisha adjusted his tight scarlet waistcoat, trying to ignore his bulging stomach and the throbbing bruise.

The guard opened the thick door and Grisha stepped inside.

There was a time when the entrance of Prince Potemkin would have been an occasion for pomp and ceremony. Once his foot stepped over the threshold, he would have been accosted with stiff words of congratulation and welcome from generals, ambassadors, and even Catherine's latest young favorite.

The reverence lingered yet among the select group of ten dining with the empress this evening, along with the unsubtle stares and curiosity he always attracted in the gossip-minded capital. When he entered, the string quartet in the corner of the room played a tired tune ten years out of fashion. Catherine had never had a good ear for music, as she freely admitted. She still needed his advice on so many matters. The thought cheered him.

A young lady in a finely spun silver wig caught his eye. Her delicate fingers caressed an open locket with Grisha's portrait hanging from a copper chain. He'd heard such items were in fashion among the women of the service nobility and merchant classes, to celebrate Grisha's military successes. The young woman looked him over with a sly smile. Grisha was not delusional enough to suppose his oversized self cut a particularly appealing figure to women these days. Still, he liked to think he'd earned a fine enough reputation to attract one or two. He returned the smile as subtly as possible. No need to give Zubov any reason to start wagging his tongue.

Grisha had no wish to join the clan of older courtiers, with their empty gossip and jests they all deemed so funny in one another's company. Success bred jealousy and jealousy bred contempt. He made his bows and then found a spot toward the end of the table, across from the woman with a far more youthful version of his face on her chain. As he took a seat, he gestured toward the trinket. "Handsome chap."

The young lady chattered about her father's service and his admiration of Grisha's military and diplomatic prowess while Grisha took a sip of sparkling wine from a crystal flute. A few of the other latecomers scribbled their preferences on slates, while already an array of delights was being rolled to the table on large platters tiered on portable shelves.

Catherine sat at the head of the table in traditional Russian dress, a loose-fitting vermilion gown with deeply cut sleeves and ermine trim. He watched her laugh along with a burly and aged ambassador who was no doubt relating some humorous vulgarity or another. She dipped a chunk of bread into a steaming beef broth. The movement was so familiar, so delicate and perfect, that for a moment, Grisha forgot himself, overcome with fondness.

Catherine smiled and laughed, but devoted more energy to the roasted pheasant sprawled across her Sèvres plate than to catching the eyes of those around her. Grisha took in the other delicacies before them on glittering golden platters: English mutton and game hen, French duck in orange sauce, and puffy cream pastries from Vienna. He thought of the wild mushrooms and strawberries he'd known as a boy. He wondered why he and his countrymen now considered the European forever superior to the homegrown.

Zubov, in his usual ridiculous velvet frock coat, had been seated away from the empress and pouted like a neglected puppy. The boy noticed Grisha and raised his voice over the vapid conversations and the chirping monkey on his shoulder. "Prince Potemkin! I thought a supper held at this late an hour would find you at home abed."

Even as the laughter swelled around him, the jest rang false, as though Zubov had hired some professional wit to pen it for him. Grisha seldom retired before dawn. Still, the melancholia began its descent. If it settled in his soul, it would become a parasite intent on devouring him from the inside.

But he had learned to disguise his own distress well enough. Grisha arched his eyebrows and turned his gaze to the rules of polite behavior Catherine had posted to the cream-colored wall. Her Little Hermitage was meant to be a place of affection: a noble goal, if unrealistic. "How kind of you to tolerate me despite my advanced years, Platon Alexandrovich."

Catherine hadn't joined in the laughter. Despite a profusion of rouge, shadows hovered under her eyes. She had always been abed by ten, even in her younger years. The empress forced herself to remain up late for Zubov's sake, but keeping pace with her young lover had taken a toll. Age had caught up with her, as it often did for mere mortals.

"Prince!" she said, squinting in his direction, her weak eyes getting the better of her.

Grisha stood, dipping into a bow, as deep as his knees and back would allow.

"Not in here." She touched a linen napkin to her lips. "This is but an informal supper."

"Even so, I recognize how fortunate I am to have the great pleasure to dine with Your Majesty and your current favorite."

The term "favorite" had long since lost its sting, but Grisha took care to emphasize the word "current." He doubted his meaning was lost on anyone. Zubov's pretty lips wrinkled.

Catherine picked up the gold-enameled base of her fan and twirled it. "It has been too long since we dined together. I wish us to remain family and rise above our petty squabbles."

The laughter began to die and the last vestiges of it had a nervous ring. Perhaps the courtiers fretted over the empress's changeable moods and the affection she might reserve for her old adviser and lover. Perhaps Catherine had finally grown bored of Zubov.

The quartet struck up a new tune, the overture from Herr Mozart's latest, *Così fan tutte*.

The title made him smile. *Women are like that*, he translated silently. He began to hum, hoping to retain her attention.

Catherine touched her white hair, which was immaculately dressed, and beckoned him with a tilt of her chin. Grisha felt a wave inside, a sudden rush of energy. He strode to her side, light on his feet despite his girth.

"Ah! How you used to make me laugh," Catherine said. "How I miss it." She turned to the ambassador seated next to her. "Our prince is a fine impersonator." Catherine turned again to Grisha. "Make me laugh. Please."

"You seem to be enjoying yourself as it is, Your Majesty."

"Come. Pretend I'm someone important and you must do as I command." She caught the fan in her hand and opened it, fluttering the silk gauze as the ambassador attempted to conceal his boredom.

Grisha repeated the first impersonation he had ever performed for her. "Someone important? *L'etat c'est moi.* The state demands amusement." He raised his voice to a higher pitch and hit the words with a distinctive German accent to mark his target not as a native speaker but merely an apt learner. "Make me laugh, Grisha. Say something funny, my kitten."

He heard a sputtering from the lips forced shut around him. He dared not draw his gaze away from Catherine's face. But her laughter came easily enough. And then there was laughter all around and a hard slap on his back from the ambassador.

"Exactly so," Catherine kept saying. But there was no special warmth to her tone, only the formal admiration she might express for any amusing acquaintance. "I treasure you as a friend, Prince. With such wicked wit, I would hate to have you as an enemy."

Never an enemy. He forced himself to concentrate on the clink of silver on porcelain and the obnoxious slurping sound as the ambassador polished off his fish soup.

"Yes, quite amusing." Zubov draped an arm over the back of his chair. "Now that you honor us with your presence, do you plan to regale us with tales of this Mohammedan monstrosity?"

"If you're so eager to be apprised of my work, we should arrange for an evening of whist and chatter. Perhaps my secretary might contact yours," Grisha added, knowing Zubov had no secretary.

Zubov reddened and Grisha heard a few low chuckles, momentarily drowning out the rapid notes of *Così fan tutti*.

But the boy recovered quickly enough. "Why wait? We all want to hear of your newfound desire to defile Catherine's Christian empire. Or is it even Catherine's land anymore? Are you not emperor of the south?"

The laughter stopped. Grisha still heard crunching and slurping as some of the older courtiers focused on their meals rather than the unfolding political game.

Grisha bowed again, not as deeply. "As I've told Her Imperial Majesty, that title is nonsense and I've asked its use be stopped even in jest. Empress Catherine is still in charge here, is she not?"

"Of course," Zubov sputtered. "It's treason to suggest otherwise."

Zubov's monkey emitted what sounded like a taunting bray and Zubov shooed him away. The creature retired to a corner where water and peanuts awaited him in sparkling china dishes. Once Zubov was banished, Grisha would make the monkey a pet for one of his niece's children.

"I would be happy to share the plans," Grisha said, "if it pleases the empress."

Grisha had staged such performances before and always she'd rewarded him with a smile and a gleam in her eye. When he held Catherine's attention, Grisha held the world. He turned to her, confident once more in his own charisma.

But she was focused on Zubov, the smooth lines of his face, his broad shoulders and biceps shown to full advantage under the velvet. Grisha knew he couldn't divert her romantic attentions easily and yet he'd hoped she would find him a more powerful distraction.

"I would like to hear Prince Potemkin's plans," she told her favorite. "How clever of you, teasing to coax him to speak. I believe I've employed similar tactics over the years. Our two minds are as one."

She wanted to help Zubov save face. Grisha tried to stuff the jealousy down his throat. At what point would she wake from her dream, as Titania had in Shakespeare's comedy, and see the boy for the jackass he was?

Catherine sat back in her seat and twirled the fan to the side, addressing Grisha once more. "Please speak, *giaour.*"

The word was one of Catherine's favorite endearments, a term for a non-Muslim. He had heard the phrase many times campaigning in the south, and not in the loving manner with which Catherine bestowed it now.

Grisha's waistcoat pinched his stomach and his head began to hurt. He withdrew a lavender-scented handkerchief from his pocket and patted his forehead. He'd planned to retrieve the scroll from his greatcoat and speak of the mosque. But Zubov would likely make a fuss, and then Catherine would make yet another pallid attempt to preserve the boy's reputation.

So he changed tactics. "Our long conflicts with the Turks have expanded our empire and brought us great glory and riches."

"Yes, we all owe you," Zubov said. "We owe you palaces and furs and jewels."

Catherine had awarded Grisha those prizes. He imagined Saltykov on the other side of a wall, cup pressed to his ear to better eavesdrop, cringing at his protégé's misstep.

"We cannot expect to hold these lands in peace without proper development," Grisha said. "Her Imperial Majesty has been clear on this point."

Catherine waved a hand in vague acknowledgment.

"What drivel," Zubov said. "How much of the imperial treasury has already been poured into these developments? Besides, weren't you the one who wanted to chase the Muslims out of Europe alto-gether? Take Constantinople itself back and claim the city for our holy faith?"

Grisha bit his lip hard to keep from chewing his thumbnail; it already smarted from previous abuse.

"Although you were a younger man then, I suppose," Zubov added, regarding a small wine stain on his cravat and readjusting the ruffled linen folds so the stain wouldn't show. "With greater energy."

"Our attentions to a mosque would help smooth our peace ne-gotiations and mend our relations with the people of this faith, particularly were it located in Moscow."

"I suppose it would not hurt to see your plans. It might make for lively discussion this evening." Catherine waited. Grisha did nothing. "Well?" she said.

"Unfortunately, when the plan was presented to your charge, it was roundly dismissed."

"Surely you are here now to fix that error."

"I was told in no uncertain terms that the funds for such a proj-ect were not available in the imperial treasury." Grisha drew in a deep breath, felt the pressure of his waistcoat loosen. "And he made it equally clear he was empowered to speak for you." Grisha turned to Zubov and smiled. "Perhaps you have now styled your-self emperor of the north."

Zubov threw a linen napkin down on his plate and rose to his feet. Catherine's cheeks flushed and Grisha's spirits rose. How he longed to see passion once more in her eyes.

"If Your Majesty feels differently," he said, "I welcome your opinion but would prefer to speak to you directly. Platon Alexandrovich has no authority to make such decisions, pleasant though you may find his companionship in other respects."

Grisha raised a crystal flute and tilted it in Zubov's direction before enjoying a long sip of the sweet champagne.

"Thank you, Prince," Catherine said dryly. "I shall take your words under advisement."

"I look forward to a more intimate conversation, Your Majesty." Grisha returned to his seat. Though he hadn't found time to write down his order, a bowl of lobster bisque had been placed near his plate. He drew in its rich scent and gathered a spoon in hand, finding he suddenly had a great appetite.

After another hour, when the conversation had sufficiently dwindled to drunken blather, Grisha felt ready to have Anton call for his horses. Outside, the chill in the air had turned bracing. Grisha buttoned his fur-lined greatcoat and crunched through the layer of snow. Ice-flecked marble statuary of glaring tritons and serene Roman maidens kept watch over the courtyard. The wind whistled past his ears but didn't drown out the music and merry laughter of waltzing guests inside the palace. His horses were taking too long. He supposed other guests might have left early, eager to head home before the snowfall transformed to a full-blown storm. He'd interrupted Anton's study of *Candide* and sent him to investigate the delay.

Grisha's gloved fingers flexed in the cold. The night had gone well, all things considered, even if he had departed from supper early enough to arouse curiosity. He wondered if the pasha would appear here in the courtyard. He was more likely to pay a visit when Grisha felt ridden with guilt, but he would have enjoyed his company now.

Instead, he heard Catherine's firm voice and the crunch of her small boots following his in the snow. "That wasn't a fair trick."

Grisha eyed the ground. If he went down at a sloppy angle he'd be sure to injure himself sliding on some hidden patch of ice. Nevertheless, he prepared to drop to his knees.

"Don't."

He struggled upright, wondering if he had miscalculated by challenging Zubov so soon.

"It is just you and me here now, husband. I invited you to the palace for supper, not as a performer in one of those circus sideshows that so enrapture the English."

"It was necessary," Grisha replied.

"You wanted to embarrass a rival. You should have spoken to me privately."

"I tried. You would not listen," he said. "You are too indulgent of your new pet."

Catherine's diamond earbobs swung as she stepped forward. "I never interfered in your trysts, even when they broke my heart."

He refused to be distracted. Not with an old argument. He had never engaged in any trysts until his heart had already been broken again and again by the widening gulf between an empress and a prince. No matter the long-buried scrap of paper that confirmed they were husband and wife. They had never been equals. "When the tryst involves you, it's a different matter than those that involve me."

"Because I am a woman?"

"You know me better, *matushka*. You are an empress. Your choice of companion has consequences for us all. I have never interfered before. I've taken care with your favorites, taken them under my wing, just as you asked. This is no mere jealousy. It's heartfelt concern."

"So that is all," she said flatly. "You merely play the adviser?"

"I have always freely offered my honest opinion, as you asked of me."

"You're obligated to tell me Platon Zubov is a preening fool giddy with power."

"Don't attempt sarcasm when you speak plain truth."

To his relief, she laughed. Her laugh hadn't changed. She used to turn to her pillow and make that sound when he'd joked at some poor courtier's expense. And then she would turn back to him, ready to open herself to him, body and soul. "You don't see Platon as I do. His gifts."

Grisha couldn't defeat Zubov by sniping behind his back. "As you say."

A gust of wind blew her white hair back from her face. She had neglected to bring a hat.

She drew her sable stole tighter around her shoulders, shivering in the cold, tired and drawn around the eyes. Catherine's appearance was far from perfect, not anymore. But then what dullard sought perfection in a woman when complexity was far more alluring?

"Perhaps I hoped there was more to it," she said, "that your heart was involved. I dared to hope you had grown tired of chasing other women and were jealous at last."

Grisha leaned in close. The scent of fresh leather on her gloves mingled with the rose-scented cream she used to soften her hands. "You make it difficult to speak the truth when you employ hypotheticals. Speak plainly, woman."

"Don't expect me to share my heart freely. Not after all we've endured. I have an ego, husband. Surely you've taken note of it."

He took her hand gently. When she didn't withdraw it, he lifted the flap at the edge of her glove and planted a light kiss on her wrist. Catherine's gaze lingered on the spot where his lips had pressed her skin. He thought she might ask for more time with him, but her gaze shifted and she extracted her hand from his. "No . . . that was only wishful thinking on my part. After our affair ended, you were never possessive. I could take a hundred lovers and you would only assume they all pale in comparison to you."

"Do they?"

She tapped him lightly on the chest with her fan. Bells jingled as his carriage approached. His geldings held their snouts back to avoid the strong gusts of wind.

"I will not make your poor horses wait in this weather. We will speak again soon." She lifted her skirts and ascended the stairs. Two of her chevalier guards waited outside the door, dependable as always in their silver and blue.

Behind them, in the blink of his one good eye, he caught a glimpse of the pasha, turban in hand, still dressed in pantaloons as though for the Ottoman court. The pasha lifted his chin, the regal gesture echoing Catherine's. The memory of the last failed attempt to negotiate flooded Grisha's mind, shaming him.

"And the mosque," he called after Catherine. "You'll consider it?"

Catherine turned to him once more, frowning. "Always business, Prince?"

Her cheeks flushed red from the cold. It reminded him of their time together seventeen years earlier, after he had returned from the monastery. They would meet in one of the *banyas* deep in the basement of the Winter Palace to discuss the latest court intrigues, their skin pink and glowing in the steamy air, until they tired of chatter and the snap of birch twigs and fell into one another's arms.

"Business and pleasure together," he said. "As always."

Catherine let out an exaggerated sigh, likely for the benefit of the guards.

"What did I do wrong?" he asked. "How have I displeased you?"

"You're toying with me to get what you want. I see it in your eyes. You drifted off to another world. No doubt to another woman or perhaps countless others."

He shook his head. "I am not toying with you. How could I even think of another woman when I'm in your presence? You eclipse them all."

She lifted her small hand. "Leave your sweet words at your bedside and don't trouble me with them again. My heart cannot bear it."

She regarded him one last time before gathering her skirts and ascending the steps two at a time, returning to Zubov. If she wouldn't back away from her young lover, then Grisha needed to take a direct route, to convince Zubov that he might entertain Catherine, but affairs of state were to be left with Grisha.

"I will never hurt you again, wife," he murmured. "And I will never let anyone else hurt you either."

Six

FOR IMMEDIATE RELEASE

Dr. Herrera will spend a week in St. Petersburg as a guest of the Monarchist Society and will make herself available for interviews as time allows.

ST. PETERSBURG
PRESENT DAY

"Reb Volkov is a blasphemer!" A disembodied Russian voice shouted over the static of the radio. "He broke the law. The deviant is getting what he deserves."

Veronica rubbed her forehead, fighting the urge to tell the driver to forget all this, to turn around and head back to the airport. Her eyelids kept drooping. Irina had sped off from the airport in a hired car, so Veronica was now squished between Michael and Dmitry in the back of the taxi. The three of them had spoken little during the ride, only Dmitry's curt directions and the driver's grunts of reply. Veronica tried not to mind the stale tobacco and gasoline stink.

"But an archaic law, wouldn't you say?" a calmer, more cultured voice asked.

"Who cares? Let him rot in the *gulag*."

Veronica could only see the back of the driver's massive blond head, but it shook at the word "gulag." He tapped his gloved fingers on the steering wheel and veered to dodge one of the other smoggy little cars crowding the boulevard.

"Hooliganism," another voice chimed in, "is hardly an archaic law. The government is within its bounds to protect citizens from dangerous influences."

The driver's shoulders tensed but his gaze remained fixed on the road. Veronica opened a map of St. Petersburg and spread it on her lap, forcing herself to focus and appreciate Peter the Great's city. Golden streetlights, trios of round bulbs, flickered on, softening the gloom of storm clouds to gently illuminate baroque palaces, cathedrals, and snow-dusted bridges over canals. St. Petersburg rivaled Venice, an imperial city as elegant as any in Europe. Across the Neva River, she spotted the svelte spire of Peter and Paul Cathedral glimmering under the fading light in the pale sky. The remains of Nicholas and Alexandra and three of their children, the last Romanovs, were buried inside.

She wondered if her Romanov grandmother, the secret grand duchess Charlotte, would ever be buried with them, if she would even want to be buried with a family she had never known. Unfortunately, Veronica hadn't met Charlotte's son—her father. So Veronica would never know what Charlotte wanted.

They passed a neoclassical opera house painted pastel green with white Grecian columns adorning the entrance and a red, white, and blue Russian flag flapping in the wind. Slender birch trees lined the streets, branches naked and vulnerable. Veronica looked down at her lap again. Her hands shook. She'd fiddled nervously with the map of the city too long and her fingers had frayed the edges.

Michael put his hand tentatively on her knee, covered by the thick winter coat she had purchased for this trip. When she didn't pull away, he let his hand rest there. "You okay?"

"I'm okay," she said. "This will be okay."

But by the time they arrived at their hotel, Veronica was ready to collapse in a heap.

Dmitry had made preemptive apologies for the quality of the hotel, a Soviet-era concrete block. The lobby downstairs seemed pleasant enough, bland but welcoming, with staff who politely greeted them at the front desk and reproductions of paintings from the Hermitage Museum hanging on the walls. After a dicey ride in the shaking cage of an elevator, they arrived on her floor and the decor dramatically changed. Mildew stained the ceiling, cigarette burns pocked the threadbare carpet, and the ammonia stench of cat urine clung to the overheated air.

Michael kicked at something. Veronica cringed, hoping it was only a dust tumbleweed. "Was the roach motel booked?" he asked Dmitry.

"Irina claims this was best we could manage." Dmitry put a subtle emphasis on the word "claims." "She says Peter the Great disguise himself as common soldier and sleep with troops in barracks and tsarina should do same."

"So much for *glamur*," Veronica muttered.

Dmitry shrugged. "I will upgrade as possible."

A *babushka* in a shapeless gray dress sat sentry near the elevator, staring at an old laptop propped precariously on a filing cabinet behind a crumbling fortress of a desk. In Soviet times, older women were hired to serve as floor attendants who doubled as "minders" to spy on foreign guests and prevent them from seeing anything they weren't supposed to see. Apparently, at least here, the practice had survived the transition to capitalism and beyond.

Veronica approached the attendant with the registration card she had received downstairs. "Hello." Veronica used English by mistake instead of a friendly Russian *preevyet*.

"*Shto?*" the old woman asked grumpily.

"You know perfectly well what," Dmitry shot out in Russian. "The key."

"Why not get in lobby?"

"When we asked for the key, they said you would help us up here."

She crossed her arms in front of her ample chest and turned to Veronica. "You have two husbands per woman in America?"

"They're not my husbands." Veronica wanted to say something wittier, but she was so tired she could barely think in English let alone Russian.

Michael smiled and cute little creases appeared at the corners of his eyes. Either he had managed to snag a nap on the plane or magical powers protected him from sleep deprivation. He leaned forward on the desk. The thin plywood made an ominous cracking sound.

"Room twelve thirty-eight," he said in proper Russian. "At your convenience."

Veronica knew the monotony of a desk job only too well. If she was sitting at her desk and Michael walked into her life, gifting her with that smile, she would have done anything he asked. The *babushka* appeared far less impressed. She frowned and waved a wrinkled finger in his direction. "You look familiar."

"You mean she does?" He gestured toward Veronica.

"You." She squinted. "I have seen you somewhere." She didn't make it sound positive.

Veronica heard a familiar snippet of music and craned her neck to see the video playing on the laptop. The attendant was watching Veronica's favorite *telenovela*, *La Familia Rosa*, with Russian badly dubbed over the Spanish. "You don't watch the Russian *novelas*?" she asked.

The woman's eyes widened a little when she heard Veronica speak in Russian. "Not as good." The woman nodded her round chin at the laptop. "My grandson showed me how to find the ones I like best."

Veronica imagined her grandmother back home, trying to sew and twisting thread in her hands, fretting. Abuela would watch *La Familia Rosa* on her own this evening and then afterward, she would force herself to watch all the latest bad news: Reb's verdict, Russian incursions into Ukrainian territory, economic sanctions. Veronica had given up a boring but comfortable space in the world to travel to Russia. Surely a room and a decent night's sleep weren't too much to ask in return. If that meant she had to charm her way past this *babushka*, then that is what she would do.

"Have they revealed Ana's secret lover yet?"

The attendant still glowered but shook her head.

"Will you let me know when they do? I haven't had time to watch."

"Neither have I," the woman said, focusing on the screen and recrossing her arms.

"It's my grandmother's favorite show. We watch it together back home. I miss her."

When Veronica said the word "grandmother," the attendant's lip twitched. She opened her creaking desk door, fumbled around, and withdrew a large silver key with a gold tassel. She handed the key to Veronica.

"*Cpacebo*," Veronica said, thanking her, and headed down the hall, rolling her luggage behind her.

"That's my girl," Michael said in a low voice, following Veronica. He stopped her and took the luggage handle. "Let's get breakfast tomorrow before your meeting with Irina." He turned to Dmitry, who was trailing just behind them, and gave a sarcastic little bow. "If that's okay with you. I'm sure you'll want to supervise us and all that."

"You need not ask permission, Mr. Karstadt. Breakfast is served promptly at nine."

"And you?" Michael turned to Veronica. "You're okay with breakfast?"

"Sure. A giant, greasy hotel meal. No vegetarian options. Looking forward to it."

Out of the corner of her eye, she saw Dmitry frown and tap on his phone.

"I meant are you okay with me joining you."

"Of course," she said, suddenly realizing she meant it. Perhaps it was good to have a familiar face around. "Do you know where you'll stay tonight?"

"Oh," Michael said. "The Ambassador."

Veronica jerked her head. "You bastard." The Ambassador was posh. Definitely a few steps above her accommodations. "How did you manage that?"

"Well . . . Irina knows someone there. She may have hooked me up."

"Oh, right," Veronica said, her tone flat. "Let me guess. She's staying there too."

"Irina has apartment in city." Dmitry put his phone back in his pocket. "In addition to her *dacha* in the countryside near Moscow." He hesitated. "Of course, her apartment is near Ambassador."

"Of course," Veronica said. "And why shouldn't I stay in Hotel Soviet Dump if it means the handsome American gets the finest treatment?"

Michael ducked an exposed, flickering bulb hanging from the ceiling. Veronica didn't see any smoke detectors. She imagined the cheap wood of the hotel walls burning.

"You sound nervous," he said. "Everything will be okay. If I didn't think so, I wouldn't have let you come."

"You wouldn't have *let* me?" Veronica said. "Wow. You are such a feminist."

"You know what I mean," he said playfully. She smelled the damp wool in his coat, his leather gloves, and fresh shaving cream.

Perhaps Abuela hadn't been completely wrong to have him tag along. "I'm going to head back to the elevator. I'll see you in the morning."

Veronica nodded, too emphatically, and twisted her fingers in her hand. Michael could have tried to kiss her cheek or hug her or something else but he only hovered awkwardly for a moment. She didn't know what she expected, but she knew she wanted . . . more. Some reminder of the passion they once shared.

Maybe the past was all they had.

In the end they parted with nothing more than a nod. The elevator doors rattled shut.

"We meet in lobby tomorrow?" Dmitry asked. "I am to stay on other end of the floor. Room 1203."

Veronica redirected her gaze from the elevator to Dmitry. "Okay. Sleep well."

"With permission, I want to escort you to room and make sure is all right." He headed down the hall, transferring his room key from hand to hand.

"Did Michael ask you to do that?" Veronica followed him, hitching her purse higher on one shoulder and dragging her luggage behind her once more.

Dmitry gave a mischievous smile. For a moment, he was the spitting image of his ancestor Grigory Potemkin. "My idea. But yes, Mikhail did mention. We had much time to talk on plane." Dmitry's gaze took in every nook and cranny in the hallway. Veronica wondered if he was checking for bugs, and not the kind Michael had been kicking on the carpet a few minutes earlier. She assumed none of the old guard from the KGB would bother to listen in on them, but someone might make use of all the old gadgets.

"So you and Michael are friends now? Will you talk about me behind my back every time I step into the ladies' room?"

"We only want to see room is secure." Dmitry thrust his hands deep in his pockets. "When someone assumes power, even cere-monial power, they attract enemies. Unfortunate, I suppose, but is natural. You are to speak out against Reb's sentence? Some people feel Reb only get what he deserve. You hear on radio. You may make an enemy or two." Dmitry shook his head, as though trying to free it of negativity. "This, I should not have said. It is only when I think about Reb . . . I suppose now I think worst. I am cautious."

Veronica hesitated. "You care so much about his situation. Even though you think it's dangerous to help him. Why?"

"You have only recently learned your tie to Romanov past. This is all new. For me, restoring monarchy life's work." He switched to Russian. "I can't let what I have worked for my whole life be in service to ancient prejudices and oppressive laws. The monarchy might be a traditional institution, but Russia must be a modern nation. Otherwise what is the point of anything we are doing here? I want to be on the right side of history. I want to help people like Reb who are hurt by oppressive laws."

The words were complicated, and it took Veronica a few min-utes to process them. But she finally said, "I understand." When they reached her door, she turned the heavy key in the lock. "Are you going to check inside the room?"

Dmitry's frown became a sheepish grin. It changed the whole impression of his face, made him seem more like a nervous col-lege student. He spoke in English once more. "I step in only for moment."

She opened the door. "Knock yourself out."

"Knock? Why?"

"No . . . I mean go on inside," she said. "I don't mind. But then I want to sleep."

Veronica felt the steady gaze of the attendant at the other end of the hall.

"Don't forget to let me know if Fernando proposes to Ana," Veronica said. "Maybe then she'll give up her affair on the side."

"Fernando will never propose, the jackass," the attendant replied grumpily. "No wonder she keeps a secret lover."

Breakfast the next morning was served in a conference room that struck Veronica as strangely spacious and modern given the wreck of the guest floors. Judging from the digital billboard flashing in the lobby, the hotel hosted groups and delegations from all around the world. This included a group of American men in stiff, ill-fitting plaid shirts, jabbering in grating Upper Midwestern accents, checking out every woman who passed their table.

Dmitry and Michael waited at the end of the line for the buffet, Michael smiling broadly, Dmitry checking his phone. Conversations floated around her in Russian, English, Mandarin, and Farsi. She thought of the way she had spent most of her mornings for the past three months, wolfing down a veggie burrito on her way to work, spilling hot sauce, and then frantically scrubbing the stain off the front of her dress. She perpetually ran late and rushed to her desk murmuring apologies, only to stare at another dull spreadsheet.

Yet today, despite jet lag and getting less than five hours of sleep last night, she had popped out of bed wide awake. Veronica felt a little bounce in her step as she approached the buffet. Something was going on inside of her, a sensation she had almost forgotten.

She felt *alive*.

"So, my body is ten hours behind," she said, joining Dmitry and Michael, "and thinks I should have dinner. But I guess I can make this work." She tapped the red leather binder with her itinerary. "I'm meeting with Irina later this morning, right? Might as well get off to a good start."

Dmitry stepped back and gave the international gesture for "after you." She eyed the breakfast spread and smiled: soft cheeses in tinfoil, potatoes, little puffy dumplings, fresh fruit, and eggs scrambled with red pepper in sparkling metal platters.

"Happy?" Dmitry asked, eyes twinkling. "I ask favor to make menu to your taste."

Michael spun around. "You got the hotel to change the menu for Veronica?"

Dmitry gave a perfect Russian shrug. "And why not? This is healthier, yes?"

Veronica remembered the picture of her face Photoshopped on Catherine's coronation portrait. "Did the food come from Ekaterina Restaurant? Irina mentioned they were expanding to St. Petersburg."

"Well, yes," Dmitry admitted. "They delivered and hoped you might like."

"I guess we'll find out." Veronica tucked her binder under her arm.

After going through the line, they elbowed their way through the crowded dining area, plates piled high with food. Music played low over the speakers, electronic Russian-language Eurovision-type pop. Across the room, four women in full makeup, short skirts, and slinky accents had joined the American men in the awful shirts.

"Did you know Irina wants me to be a walking ad campaign?" she asked wryly.

Michael's expression remained calm, except his eyes crinkled. "What?"

"She has different ideas about what it means to be a royal than I do." They slipped into their chairs. The table was covered with a lacy cloth the color of sea foam. Beautiful goblets and linen napkins had been set out for them, along with an assortment of mineral waters and juices. "But first I want to discuss these potential 'enemies' of mine," Veronica said to Dmitry.

"Enemies?" Michael asked.

"I was tired when I say this. I apologize."

"Can you at least elaborate?"

Dmitry looked over his shoulder. "Some people may not want Dr. Herrera—an American—to interfere with Reb. This is all I mean. We will take care. She will be safe."

"Uh-huh." Michael took his phone out of his pocket. He tapped a few buttons and then turned it around. On the main Russian news website, Reb's pretty face dominated the first screen, along with a screaming Russian headline: "Reb Volkov under house arrest. Speaks for first time on impending prison sentence."

"He made a YouTube video that posted last night," Michael said. "Have you seen it? He's calling out the government, the church, even foreign nationals who pump money into the Russian economy while all of this crap is happening. He doesn't strike me as a happy-go-lucky kind of guy. I find it hard to believe he wants to associate with a new tsarina. Doesn't he like to talk about his grandfather who served in the Red Army?"

Michael let the video play and the image switched briefly to Reb at his trial, looking pretty and defiant behind the bars of the cage used for defendants in Russian courtrooms.

Dmitry's hands balled into fists on either side of his plate. "Reb is passionate man but not judgmental."

"So you know him well?" Michael said.

Dmitry looked at his eggs. He hadn't eaten a bite. "I do. I am sure you understand is more to this than free speech. Or do you?"

"The art exhibit was a pretext," Veronica said. "Reb was arrested because he is gay."

"You knew?" Dmitry asked.

"He came out a few years ago, didn't he? Around the same time the Duma began spewing antigay rhetoric and passing laws against gay 'propaganda'—whatever that means. And he helped organize Pride Parades here and in Moscow."

Dmitry nodded. "Yes. He is activist, as Americans say. Reb is grandson of Red Army in best way. He feels responsibility to new Russia."

"The whole situation is ridiculous," Veronica said. "Peter the Great founded this city and some historians think he was bisexual. And Tchaikovsky? He was gay no matter what Russian movies want people to believe."

A few other diners turned to look at her.

"And Reb is not type to be bullied," Dmitry said.

Veronica knew what it felt like to be bullied. She also knew what it felt like to be powerless, as though your voice meant nothing and could be ignored or easily cast aside. If she had an opportunity to speak, she would not let it go to waste.

"Why didn't they arrest Reb using the propaganda law?" Michael asked.

"Reb is smart. He use careful language. He does not carry political materials on his person. He spoke through his art. He thought this safe. I tried to warn him . . ." Dmitry's phone started to buzz. He checked the number and frowned. "This is Irina. Excuse me for moment." He got up, moving away from their table to take the call.

Veronica glanced at Michael and popped a fried potato in her mouth. "I doubt Irina will have any objections to you tagging along to our meeting this morning."

Michael pushed his dumplings around on his plate. "Do I detect a hint of jealousy?"

"Ha!" Veronica tried to smile, tried not to picture Irina pouncing on Michael as soon as she saw him. "More like concern. I need her help, but I don't trust her."

"So this is just friendly advice?"

Veronica wasn't about to start complaining about Irina like a harpy. "Do as you please."

"Maybe I hoped you were jealous."

She saw a wistfulness in his eyes. Something lingered there, even with the distance between them. Even if he had only come because her *abuela* asked him to tag along. She wondered what would have happened if they had met under different circumstances, if they would have found happiness in a normal life of children, day jobs, and mutual friends. She had the sinking feeling that kind of blissful domesticity would always elude her.

Michael reached for her hand. "Never mind," he told her, squeezing briefly before letting go. "That was just wishful thinking on my part. It's all right. I know what you're doing here. I know it's important. We should focus on that. I only want to make sure you're safe."

She knew he was right. But his touch lingered on her skin long after he let go.

"Please," Dmitry told her, gesturing broadly at the heavy furniture as he led them inside the office of the Russian Monarchist Society. "Have seat."

The office was located in a converted palace. The walls and floor were painted light gold and two electronic chandeliers hung from the center of the ceiling. Behind a large cherrywood desk, floor-to-ceiling picture windows looked out at the dark river and the gentle northern sun poking through the clouds. Small patches of ice speckled the granite embankment.

Veronica took a seat in the leather office chair behind the desk, running her fingers along the smooth padded armrests. She could imagine either Catherine the Great or Nikita Khrushchev sitting here. Catherine dipping a feather-tipped pen into an inkwell before signing her name on a letter to Voltaire. Red-faced Khrushchev pounding a shoe on his desk as he yelled at Kennedy over the phone. She wondered which ghosts haunted the rooms more frequently, those of the tsars or their neo-imperialistic successors, the Soviets.

Michael paced the room, hands clasped behind his back, examining framed documents and gold-plated certificates in lavish Cyrillic, and then moving on to drawings of St. Petersburg from the early eighteenth century, when it had still been a quaint maritime port. Russians in plain trousers pointed at the Neva River and the simple bridges and buildings beyond the water.

Portraits of Russian aristocrats hung on the wall to Veronica's left. The older pictures were rudimentary, men with sharp features, long hair, and wild eyes. That led into more refined portraiture and then black and white photographs of early-twentieth-century Romanovs. Along the back wall, opposite the desk, a glass-fronted set of mahogany shelves and display cases housed worn eighteenth-century medallions and ribbons, including a frayed tassel tied to the hilt of a rusting sword that hung next to the shelves. Above that, official portraits of Potemkin and Catherine were majestically lodged in ornate silver frames. They were depicted later in life, stout but still regal. Prince Potemkin had a mischievous glint in his eye that reminded her of Dmitry.

"This wasn't one of his palaces, was it?" Veronica pointed at Potemkin. "I thought this place was built in the eighteen hundreds."

"Irina purchase mementos and move them to office," Dmitry told her. "The Yusupovs were proud of their connection to Prince Potemkin and Irina is obsessed with Catherine. I think she tolerates me only because I am related to Grisha."

An array of knickknack animals perched on a corner of the desk: puckering angelfish and tiny frogs made of jade, a silver and gray owl in a gilded cage, a polar bear made of rock crystal. Dmitry chose a crouching carnelian rabbit with tiny diamonds for eyes and began to transfer the trinket from hand to hand. "However, some people think this building was originally *banya* in eighteenth century, perhaps space for rendezvous. Some say Grisha wanders halls, naked except for towel, nibbling on radish or turnip, looking for Catherine."

"Let me guess," Michael said, swinging around. "When they try to talk to him he walks through a wall and disappears."

"Exactly," Dmitry said, smiling.

Veronica felt sure the ghosts of Catherine and Potemkin were here, huddled together over some document or decree. She shivered.

"What's this? A mosque?" Michael approached a charcoal drawing. Veronica recognized the sketch from the dossier Dmitry had given her. She looked more closely and saw a curved, bell-shaped entrance adorned with abstractly flowered tiles and curling arabesques.

"It is," Dmitry said. "Prince Potemkin's plan and a testament to his attempts to live in peace with Catherine's Muslim subjects. It was meant to stand in Moscow."

"Was it never built?" Michael asked.

Veronica heard tapping heels and a high female voice with a hint of a faux British accent. "You arrived right on time. I should have known with Dmitry at the helm."

Irina entered the room in black pumps, blond hair swept neatly to the side. She wore a white skirt and crisp matching jacket trimmed in black piping. A man followed her, young and tall, rugged and handsome in an inoffensive way, with a hint of a scruffy beard. He wore a ribbon with a Russian flag and a double-headed Romanov eagle on his lapel.

"*Matushka.*" Sarcasm colored Dmitry's baritone.

"Spare me." Irina held her hand up in Dmitry's direction and turned to Veronica. "I see you've made yourself comfortable." Irina sank into the chair on the other side of the desk, opposite Veronica, and then gestured fondly at the young man who had followed her inside. "This is Alexander Yusupov, the son of my second husband, the late and honorable Ivan Yusupov. We lived together in San Francisco for a time."

"Hi," the young man said in laid-back English. "Please call me Sasha." He extended a hand, the businesslike American despite his Russian nickname.

"So you're also from California?" Veronica said.

"Sasha lives in Mill Valley," Irina answered for him. Her features shifted when she looked up at Sasha, genuine affection softening the set of her lips and relaxing her high cheekbones. "He is here to visit. I'm sure you're familiar with his ancestor Felix Yusupov." Irina nodded at one of the pictures, a black and white photo of a pretty and slender aristocrat with bright eyes, posed with his dark-haired wife, also named Irina Yusupova.

"Of course," Veronica said. "Felix murdered Rasputin."

"Whoa." Sasha held his hands up. "The guy was only doing what he thought was right."

"Your poor great-grandmother Empress Alexandra wasn't as strong as Catherine the Great." Irina looked as though she feared some of Alexandra's weakness had manifested in Veronica. "She let Rasputin get ahold of her. Felix did what needed to be done. After all, he was a descendant of Prince Grigory Potemkin as well."

"Do you speak Russian?" Veronica asked Sasha.

"Uh . . . *un peu.*"

Michael had circled in on their conversation. He looked over Veronica's shoulder to address Sasha. "That's French."

"Oh right!" Sasha said. "So yeah, I guess not. Everyone has been really nice here, though. They all speak English, or most anyway, and I've made plenty of friends."

"You see," Irina said, gloating. "Americans are more than welcome here, despite what you might have heard on your sensationalist news stations."

Veronica's forehead creased thoughtfully as she wondered why someone like Sasha, who seemed more suited for a Silicon Valley start-up, had come here. And then she looked again at his ancestor Felix. "The Yusupovs were extraordinarily wealthy before the Revolution."

"So I hear." Sasha had the smile of a handsome man, like nothing bad had ever happened to him.

"There's talk of restoring wealth to some of the old families."

"That would be pretty sweet," Sasha told her.

Veronica looked at Sasha's pleasant, open, oh-so-very Northern Californian face. He seemed harmless enough, but he also seemed very happy to be in Russia. Too happy. She wondered what his stepmother had promised him. Veronica turned to Irina. "One of the goals of the Society is restoration of property that was taken away by the Communists. Reparations."

"It is," Michael chimed in. "It's in the bylaws. I looked."

Irina smoothed her skirt. "I'm so glad you were able to come, Mr. Karstadt. What *would* she do without you?"

"Your stepson is set to benefit from those reparations?" Veronica said.

Irina shrugged mildly. "All of that is a long way off, I'm sure. Who knows what the future will bring? In the meantime, we must do what we can to raise money for our organization today. Otherwise, what use is any of this?" She reached into her leather handbag and pulled out her sparkly phone and an oval locket with a little insignia of the Romanov double eagle.

Veronica rocked in her seat, still slightly off balance from jet lag and lack of sleep. Dmitry put a hand on her arm to steady her, leaving it there longer than necessary. Out of the corner of her eye, she saw Michael watch them, frowning.

Irina opened the locket and Veronica saw the same picture of her own face transposed onto a body wearing Catherine's coronation gown that Irina had shown her on the plane.

"Again . . . this is just a rough mock-up," Irina said. "But as you see, there are a number of uses for such a remarkable image. That's why we're fitting you for a reproduction of Catherine's gown. It's all in Dmitry's schedule I'm sure. You will be the epitome of *glamur.*"

"Do you really think this sort of trinket is necessary?"

"Trinket! It's more than that. We want your royal persona firmly planted in the public's mind. People seek meaning in their lives. We wish to return to a more cultured and beautiful existence, just as we enjoyed prior to the Bolshevik Revolution."

Most Russian people had led anything but a beautiful life prior to the Revolution, but Veronica decided it would be undiplomatic to mention that right now.

"Try to embrace this idea. Think of the possibilities! We are already looking into restaurants willing to put your name to dishes and drinks . . . of course, it is such an unwieldy name . . . Veronica . . ." Irina frowned and tapped her fingers on the desk thoughtfully. "When we use the Roman alphabet let's spell it with a 'k.' And we need to start calling you Nika."

"Nika! I like that," Michael said.

"Thank you, Mikhail. I'm glad one of you understands. I think it will remind people of poor Tsar Nicholas." Irina crossed herself in a haphazard fashion and then began typing notes into her phone. "I see the press conference is scheduled for the day after tomorrow at five. That's when we will announce Nika is the Society's official claimant. The honorary tsarina."

Veronica exchanged glances with Dmitry. They had already made plans for the press conference. Different plans. Nothing to do with reparations.

"The tsarina should be graceful," Irina said. "She should be elegant. And yet she should also prove herself a woman of the people. By the way, what did you think of Hotel Krasny?"

Sasha exhaled. "You're making them stay at that dump?"

"The Red Hotel. This was a little test," Irina said. "I like to think I have some sway around this city and I wanted to try the princess and the pea, although I admit I wanted slightly different results. The perks of monarchy shouldn't go to your head. We want you to be relatable after all. Glamorous, yes, but also someone everyday Russians can trust. Be humble, but be regal. This is the monarch's art. This is how you gain trust."

"But we're all Americans," Veronica said. "We're all liberal

Californians for that matter. You don't think that will bother any-one?"

"Well, yes, but then what does anyone expect?" Irina said. "The nobility were all killed or kicked out of the country in 1917."

"You have an even bigger problem the way I see it," Michael said. "As your stepson says, restitution of property to old families would be 'pretty sweet' for him. But I doubt most Russians will support it. I have family here. I've spent time here. Russians don't want more oligarchs."

Irina stood up and walked toward Michael with a coy smile. "A solid Russian Cossack."

He shifted his weight, but his voice remained steady: "I promised Veronica's grandmother I would take care of her the best I could."

"Ever the loyal servant." She appraised Michael. "Perhaps we might commission a reproduction of the Preobrazhensky Guard uniform so you can participate in the photo shoot with Nika. A masculine presence is always welcome." She rested her hands on his shoulders, looking at him closely. "Yes, you'll do. You'll do quite nicely."

As she watched Irina tilt forward, closer to Michael, the heel of Veronica's boot started clacking against the smoothly polished floor. She tried to summon a sarcastic remark, but before anything came to mind, her thoughts were disrupted by a harsh shout from outside, only slightly muffled by the double-paned windows. "Tsa-rina!"

"What was that?" Michael asked, removing himself from Irina.

"Oh!" Irina said innocently. "Have they arrived already?"

Dmitry strode past Michael, unlatching one of the large win-dows facing the Moika River and the courtyard below. When he opened it, a blast of icy air made Veronica shiver.

"What is this?" Dmitry demanded, pointing outside.

Irina regarded one of her manicured fingernails. "You would

think they could keep it down out there. After all they are here only at our invitation. Sasha?"

Sasha peeped out the window. "Oh sweet! Let me see who came." He headed downstairs.

"I guess you can't blame them for being excited," Irina said. "It is a historic occasion."

"Who?" Veronica said. "Who's here? Who's excited?"

"I think you know them best by Italian name," Dmitry told her. "Paparazzi."

Veronica made her way down the flight of steps to the courtyard, hand gripping the cold iron railing, Michael and Dmitry flanking her. Ominous silver clouds rolled across the slate-gray horizon. Her fingers trembled as she buttoned up her new winter coat, stiff in the elbows and chest, against the sharp wind and pulled a pair of gloves from her pocket. Dmitry hunched into his thick raincoat and squinted out at the road. He said he had ordered a car service but Veronica only saw buses and taxis zipping past bedraggled private vehicles. The stench of diesel fuel competed with a musty scent of dying flowers.

When Dmitry had said "paparazzi," she expected a horde of screaming men with giant flashbulbs. But the courtyard outside seemed perfectly quiet. She felt a little disappointed.

"We should have car by now." Dmitry checked his watch and frowned. "I will check to see what happened."

"*Pazhulsta!* Tsarina!"

A round white face popped into Veronica's view and a flashbulb winked. For a few moments, the world consisted only of splotchy brown dots. Once Veronica's vision cleared, she saw four more reporters circled around her, pale, doughy men pressing buttons on their smartphones, the sort of guys who lived in their grandmother's basements and played lots of geeky Russian video games. Of course, she lived with her grandmother as well . . .

Dmitry ran up to them. "Wait!" he called in Russian. "Direct your questions to me and I will translate for Nika."

"I can speak to them in Russian," Veronica said.

"This will give you few extra minutes to consider question."

"I've got this." Veronica smiled. And then she held the smile even though it felt fake. More flashes went off, winking in the gray light. Someone held a large television camera. Her heart raced, but in a good way. The reporters began to shout questions, mostly in Russian, but some in accented English.

"Have you made plans for the coronation ceremony?"

"Are you planning to investigate the disappearance of the Romanov jewels?"

Veronica bobbed her head like an idiot, breathing deeply and drawing in the frosty moisture in the air. She noticed a woman in the back, holding her phone high but not shouting questions at Veronica. She wore a fitted fuchsia raincoat over her slender figure and a matching *hijab* framed her delicate features. When she looked at Veronica, her eyes came into intense focus behind the lenses of cat's-eye glasses with thick frames.

"Is it true you plan to host a dinner party with William and Kate at the Winter Palace?" another reporter asked.

"What?" Veronica threw him a puzzled look. Unfortunately, he chose that exact moment to take a photo and she cringed. She must have looked exactly how she felt right now, awkward and out of her league. She shook her head, blinking away the spots.

"Hey!" Michael told the guy. "Can you at least warn her first?"

"Dr. Herrera, my name is Anya and I write for the *Moscow Review*." The woman in the fuchsia raincoat and head scarf spoke in clear Russian. "Is it true you are related to Nicholas II?"

Veronica almost said, "That is the story," but then she glanced at Michael and remembered what he had told her back in Los Angeles. It wasn't a story. It was her history. "Yes."

"Do you plan to make a claim for the Romanov throne?"

Veronica was trying to think of a more sophisticated way to answer "yes and no" when Dmitry stepped in front of her.

"Dr. Herrera appears to be a Romanov relation. That's all we are prepared to say at this time. And her title would be strictly ceremonial."

The reporter, Anya, gave Dmitry a half-smile and a wink. She tapped a few notes on her phone. "A Potemkin at her side. I suppose this is a tradition."

"Hello, Anya," he said quietly.

Anya adjusted her glasses and her full, rosy lips parted in a smile. "I came all the way from Moscow. When do I get my interview?"

"Not now." Dmitry motioned toward the street and began to descend the staircase once more. Veronica and Michael followed.

"Can you at least tell me whether or not she will help Reb?" Anya said. "I think he'll agree to meet with her at least."

Veronica stopped. "I could meet with Reb Volkov?"

Anya nodded. "As long as you agree to give me your first one-on-one interview."

Dmitry turned to face Anya. "That is supposed to go through me."

Veronica tried to listen to what they were saying, but a wiry male reporter had sidled in close to her. Veronica prepared to smile and pose for another picture. But then she realized he wasn't looking at her. He raised his phone and tapped Michael's back.

"Mikhail Karstadt?" The reporter took a picture and then lowered his phone to smooth back a few strands of greasy blond hair from his waxy forehead. The reporter held his phone closer to Michael's face. "You are the imposter? The one who claimed to be the heir?"

Michael stopped short.

"Is this another scam?" the reporter asked. "Do you have a comment?"

"No. No comment. No."

"It is not small thing to impersonate member of royal family. Why are you here with latest Romanov heiress?"

Michael turned to Veronica. "I'm sorry."

So that was why the floor attendant back at the hotel recognized Michael. Michael had lied, but only because he thought it would protect her. Veronica hadn't realized this would come back to haunt him once they were in Russia. She had a sudden flashback to Michael's home in Los Angeles, how good it had felt to curl up with him on the couch, his chow panting at their feet. She couldn't bear to see him hurt because of her.

"Leave him alone," she snapped at the reporter. "You don't know the whole story."

"Would you like to tell it to me?"

Dmitry leaned in to pick up on the conversation. He put a hand on Veronica's arm and shook his head. "No, she would not."

"You don't need to defend me," Michael told her. "I'll be fine."

He walked down the steps, hands stuffed in the pockets of his own new wool coat. He had forgotten to cut off one of the tags and it hung loose from his sleeve.

"I will never let anyone hurt you," she said quietly, though she knew Michael could no longer hear her. "And I'll try not to either."

Seven

"You've lived in the capital for years now," Grisha said, "and this is the first you've seen of this magnificent monument?"

Anton glanced behind at the horses standing patiently in front of Grisha's carriage while the driver took a quick sip from a cheap leather flask. Anton ran his hands up and down his arms. The tip of his nose was pink and he shivered in the frigid evening mist. Grisha made a mental note to ensure the boy had a heavier coat by morning.

"I have heard of the monument, Your Highness. But I've avoided it until now. It's too frightening."

"Frightening?" Grisha chomped on an apple he'd found in the pocket of his greatcoat. The vast square around them remained strangely quiet, save for a woman with a bright red muslin scarf wrapped around her neck who passed them, trudging through the snow, pulling a whimpering hound dog in a sled behind her. Grisha smiled at the woman and raised his apple in greeting, but she passed without so much as a hello.

"I heard an old man say the horse comes to life at night and chases people."

Grisha laughed and tossed the apple core into the snow. He wished he could show the boy more of the city. He wanted to tell Anton not to believe any nonsense about a ghostly horse, but then the pasha's face appeared in his mind, a mere apparition and yet very real. Such a fragile line existed between this world and the next. The imaginations of St. Petersburg's drunkards were notoriously grand, but for all Grisha knew, the tale of a phantom horse had merit. Considering the number of men who had died to forge the new capital from the marsh, he could well imagine their anger forcing bronze to life. A poet was sure to write of it one day.

"Even so, perhaps you might take a moment to savor the sight," Grisha said. "One of your empress's greatest accomplishments. This is our new Russia. Grandeur and enlightenment. Fearless expansion and unparalleled beauty."

Reluctantly, Anton threw his head back to take in the wild-eyed, rearing steed and then the grim countenance of Peter the Great. His long arm stretched forward, pointing to the marshland on the other side of the river, where his capital would first rise forth despite everyone's objections. They had told him it was all wrong: the northerly location, the rampant disease, the abysmal weather.

Grisha regarded Peter's head atop the statue, his familiar mustache and the garland of laurels meant to make him a true "caesar." Peter had stayed firm in his choice. And so here they stood, a short distance from the shores of Europe but far from the central heart of their own country. Grisha agreed with the naysayers. He thought it a mistake to locate the capital away from the core of the Russian soul—Moscow. Nonetheless, he admired Peter's resolve. Peter was quite the bon vivant in his time, despite the stern military bearing. He'd been fond of good food, intrigue, clever inventions, lovely women, and perhaps even a lovely young man or two if palace whispers were to be believed.

He wondered if he might share the story of the horse coming

to life with Catherine. Of course, if he caught her in a foul mood, the image might rub her the wrong way. *What are you really trying to say? Do my own people fear me?*

"And why would the horse bother to chase anyone?" Grisha asked, chewing on his thumbnail.

"They say the souls of those who died making the city reanimate the beast."

Grisha forced his hand into the pocket of his greatcoat. His thumbnail was inflamed and aching. He located a few random jewels, as well as a radish for later. He rolled a small ruby between his thumb and forefinger to keep his mind from its darker impulses. The words of the ghostly pasha rolled through his mind. White demon. *Giaour.* Revenge had reanimated his old foe as well. Only the construction of a Russian mosque would soothe the restless pasha's spirit.

"Any further word on Zubov since we were last at the palace?" Grisha asked. "Any rumors making their way round the kitchen? Other women in his life?"

Anton lowered his face and kicked at a pile of dirty snow. "None that are spoken of, Your Highness. But I did hear he has been seen with the Grand Duke Paul."

"Any word on what they say?"

Anton shook his head. "I suppose that is for us to consider and guess."

"Yes, I suppose it is." Grisha caught the eye of his carriage driver, who quickly capped his flask and took the reins of the horses.

"May I ask a question, Your Highness?" Anton stepped closer. "What's different about Zubov? Why is he so vexing? You've gotten along well with the empress's previous favorites."

Grisha thought back to the man who had captured Catherine's heart earlier in her reign: her great favorite, the handsome Grigory Orlov. He and his brothers had bothered Grisha, but of course he hadn't said anything. He still couldn't. The Orlovs had brought Catherine to her throne. The men who followed Grisha into Catherine's bed later in her life had all been young, sweet faced, even-tempered, and willing to learn, to treat Grisha as a father figure as the empress wished. They would never have objected to any project of his.

"Platon Alexandrovich is overly ambitious," he told Anton.

"You are ambitious. So is the empress. You taught me ambition isn't a bad thing."

"It's not his ambition, but the potential fruit of that ambition. He is vain, superficial."

"The empress cannot see this in Zubov herself?"

"The empress is aging. As we age our vision clouds. We rely on the help of others to see the truth." Without thinking, Grisha reached up to the space in his breast pocket, under his greatcoat, where he had placed a few of Catherine's old letters, bound together with a velvet ribbon.

"We should be on our way to your appointment, then. You said you would pull the 'tooth' once and for all, remember?" Anton chuckled.

"Yes, yes." The laughter that had come so easily a few minutes before now felt a lifetime away. He was sinking. A voice rang in his head: *"Still planning a march to Constantinople, crusader? Is that why you delay?"*

Grisha spun around, expecting to see the pasha. But the voice died in the wind like a candle snuffed between two fingers. He rubbed his forehead and felt a trace of perspiration.

Anton touched Grisha's sleeve. "I'm sure Zubov would not mind if you waited to see him."

"I am quite sure he would not mind at all," Grisha said, suddenly cold and wanting back inside the waiting carriage. "That is why I must go now."

. . .

"I'm surprised you showed your face here again after the stunt you pulled at Catherine's supper the other night," Zubov told him. "I was certain she'd have you barred from the palace. Or at least sent back to your negotiations with the Turkish devils."

"It seems I can still make it past the guards," Grisha said. "Perhaps they are not so selective when it comes to admitting visitors to see you."

Grisha nibbled on a bitter radish. It kept him from his thumbnail and besides, he liked the effect the spectacle might have on Zubov. Sure enough, he caught Zubov giving him a look of thinly veiled disgust. Grisha wondered if the boy's monkey would try to steal the radish, and then realized the creature wasn't in the room. He hoped Catherine had not turned into a simian caretaker. She had far more important things to do with her time.

"Besides, I only spoke the truth to the empress," Grisha added.

Zubov adjusted the cravat at his neck. He smelled of too much cologne and hair powder. "Catherine never can stay angry with you for long. I wouldn't have bothered to take a meeting with you at all except if I refuse you will tattle."

Grisha rolled his head to take stock of the room. Zubov may have agreed to see Grisha only to avoid Catherine's tears, but he had insisted on meeting in not his own study but a coldly elaborate receiving room: marble floors, mosaicked ceiling, and long mirrors around the walls reflecting their images in multiplicity. He supposed the boy thought this ostentatious display reinforced his power, that he could receive in such a majestic setting, as though he were a consort rather than a mere favorite. Likewise, Zubov wore a diamond-seamed coat with silver braiding and red boots that cut off at his ankles, showing off his fine silk leggings and the bulging muscles in his calves.

Grisha may have had a diamond or two sewn into his own coat.

Nonetheless, he thought it all a tad desperate. "You dismissed my project without the empress's knowledge," he said. "You acted as a ruler rather than a subject. If you feel confident in this role, why shouldn't it be known? I believe in transparency."

Zubov took a seat and leaned back in the chair, tapping his fingers on his knee. "Transparency? I find that difficult to swallow."

Grisha bit into the radish with aggression but smiled placidly. "How so?"

"After your little display at Catherine's supper, I did some asking around about you."

"I am well-known enough. Had you no interest in politics before securing your apartments in the Winter Palace?"

"People say you're not known for your plain truths. Take Catherine's grand tour of your precious southern provinces, for example."

Grisha knew what was to come. His free hand curled in and out of a fist.

"We have all heard the stories. You created happy villages out of cheap plywood, paying peasants to wave and smile when the empress rode past them with her entourage." Zubov did a quick imitation that made him look like a marionette in a vulgar French comedy. "You took advantage of poor Catherine's bad eyes. And what of when she left? Crumbling stacks of nothing. But I did not realize there is actually a name for your creations: Potemkin villages."

Would these rumors never pass? One of his old foes had commissioned tracts to circulate behind the empress's back, illustrated with caricatures. Grisha, bloated and covered in furs, the preening Cyclops with devil's horns on his head, rested his hand on Catherine's back while she squinted desperately at two-dimensional structures, doors with nothing behind. Someone must have told Zubov this was a particularly sour point. "All lies."

Zubov tossed his hair, black powdered with silver. A few

strands fell into his eyes, making him seem even prettier and more useless. Grisha wouldn't have thought it possible.

"This mosque of yours will be the same. All smoke and mirrors. Nothing of substance."

Grisha tried not to shiver. He wished he had not left his cloak with Anton, for the room still held a strong chill. The pasha hid in the room somewhere, he was sure, frowning and disapproving of this conversation. Silently, Grisha implored the pasha to be patient. "It is still the empress's decision to make. You overstepped your boundaries."

"I am not the one who styles myself emperor of the south."

"Your style"—Grisha looked the boy's outfit up and down and waved the radish in his direction—"leaves much to be desired."

"I don't expect a man of your age to know the latest fashion," Zubov said. "I've heard it said a man prefers the style of the era in which he felt most vibrant. Perhaps fifteen years ago in your case?"

"I've never heard the empress complain about my manner of dress."

"She never complains about much when it comes to you, does she? Her anger flashes and then disappears. Is it true she pays your debts? Such a strain on the treasury. But then the old dear clearly has a soft spot in her heart for a friend. Still, I believe I will speak to her of it."

The smugness of the boy's tone aggravated him and Grisha hated to hear even the suggestion he might have to concern himself with the pedestrian matter of his own bills. But Zubov's lower lip trembled. He wasn't as confident of his position as he wanted everyone to think. This could be useful. Grisha stepped forward, ready to finish this once and for all.

"Listen to me," Grisha said. "And listen well."

Zubov made a snorting sound but didn't budge.

"I know you warm the empress's bed." Grisha remained alert to the slightest creak at the door, the possibility of a servant on the other side. He waited until the silence in the room was absolute. "And I know she can't see straight as long as you excel at that particular task."

"Once Catherine knows you've spread filthy rumors—"

"Please, boy. Do you really think your talents in the boudoir are a state secret? Your whimpering will accomplish nothing, only lower your manhood in her eyes. And that is something you can ill afford."

Zubov's tongue moved flaccidly under his lips. This reaction pleased Grisha, and yet he began to feel light-headed, the room wobbling around him.

"I'm sure you do a fine job on that front," Grisha continued. "I also know the empress is a jealous woman nearly forty years your senior."

"The empress is ageless," Zubov declared.

Anton may not have heard anything about another woman in Zubov's life, but Grisha felt the time had come to make a gamble. "I find it hard, appealing as the great woman is, to believe you don't have . . . shall we say, another affair of the heart to occupy your time?"

Zubov gave a stiff laugh, so Grisha knew he was onto something. He continued to play his hunch. "I doubt any young woman loves you so much she would turn down the money I could offer her to talk in detail about how you seduced her behind the empress's back."

"No woman would be so foolish. Catherine would send her to Siberia."

"The empress is not the sort to turn on her own sex over a man."

Zubov fished an enameled ruble out of a crystal dish of coins on the desk and began flipping it in his hand. The sight made Grisha dizzier. "Catherine might have my head, but she would have the other woman's as well. Who would risk that only to help a deviant like you?"

"The empress would be furious at the man who caused such a travesty, no matter how nimble his performance in the bedroom. Particularly if she were given to believe his heart hadn't carried him to her, but rather his lust for power. "

Zubov caught the ruble in his hand. "You are one to talk!" he snapped. "All you have ever desired is power."

"From the beginning of my relationship with the empress, I was clear as a summer day about my ambition. You have not been so forthright."

"You're bluffing. She no longer trusts your word."

"If I had tried this with every man who made his way to her bedchamber it wouldn't work, or at least it would no longer work," Grisha said. "But I choose my battles wisely."

"I assume there's an 'unless' in this tiresome monologue?"

"The mosque," Grisha said, "as first requested. Stop blocking its path."

Zubov gave another sputtering laugh, only now it sounded more like a girlish giggle. "That can't be all you want. They say you are an Asiatic now, what with your robes and jewels and harems in your ungodly palaces in the south. Still, I doubt you converted to the religion of our cohabitants. Why is this project of such importance to you?"

The temperature changed abruptly, and the room grew suddenly warm. Grisha felt beads of perspiration gather behind his ears and the oppressive heavy fabric of his European uniform pulled tightly over his flesh. "It is a symbol of our new Russia: an orthodox power, a Christian empire, but a land of tolerance as well."

"Drivel," Zubov muttered.

"In addition, you will cease to meddle in my future plans and projects," Grisha said. "Those affairs are between myself and the empress only. You have no place in them."

"Well," Zubov said, exhaling slowly. "This is quite the passionate soliloquy, Prince. I shall have to consider all you have said."

"You will consider it this moment. And you will give me your answer now."

"Such a rush! Off to gamble? Bed a woman of low confidence?"

Grisha managed a smile. "As you are so quick to point out, I am but a fading old man. Time is not on my side."

Zubov may have been a pompous ass, but his instinct for self-preservation was well honed. He twisted his lips and again regarded Grisha's face. "I still disagree with you on the endeavor's merit, but I suppose there is more than one way to look at such a project. I might suffer a concession to our Mohammedan cohabitants in the interest of a stronger peace."

Zubov looked far too pleased with himself. Grisha nibbled on the radish once more to soothe his troubled stomach, unable to fully savor the moment. "I'm glad you see it my way at last."

"Can you at least put that damned vegetable away? I feel as though I've been bested by a rabbit."

Grisha shrugged, snapped off one last bite, and wiped his hands. "I'm finished anyway."

"You know, Prince," Zubov added slyly, "you have been through so much in your life. Your mind is quite impressive. Everyone said this was so. I confess I had anticipated your advanced age would have dulled you somewhat."

Grisha thrust his hands behind his back, rocking unsteadily on his feet. He had to keep his hands entrapped or he would end up throttling the boy.

"Take your dead eye." Zubov stood and began to stroll the perimeter of the room as though taking a constitutional through the empress's gardens. "The Orlovs are responsible for the injury?"

Grisha squeezed his hands so tightly he thought the pressure might make them burst. In truth, the Orlov brothers had nothing to do with the damage to his eye. It was an inflammation that would have resolved on its own, only he had been young and impatient and trusted a surgeon with a faulty knowledge of herbs and folk remedies. But Grisha far preferred the tale of the Orlov brothers beating him to a pulp to try to keep him away from the empress. He relished the image of himself, young and handsome, emerging from the ordeal damaged and bloody but triumphant, for it was he who would eventually win Catherine's love.

"You go through life, thrive even, with this affliction. And I see your wits are about you, sharp as ever." Zubov's voice altered slightly. The mockery was gone, although Grisha wouldn't have gone so far as to describe the boy's tone as sincere. "We should consider some sort of alliance."

"You and I?" Grisha asked innocently.

"My God, man, were we to work together . . . think of the possibilities. Surely we can find some project on which we both agree. Something far more lucrative than a heathen shrine. Why, I understand your New Russia has untold riches in silk and vineyards."

Grisha remembered what Anton had told him of Zubov's involvement with Paul. He decided to play a hunch once more. "You and I and Grand Duke Paul? Would we three work together?"

Zubov fingered a delicate gemstone vase. Grisha imagined the look of fright in Catherine's eyes had she been there, her motherly fussing and her small hand steering Zubov away from the vase. "Paul? Oh, you mean the empress's son?"

"The same," Grisha replied. "The tsarevich. The one who hates his mother. The one who blames her for his father's death. The one who thinks she tried to have him killed by having glass smashed in his pudding. Are you proposing some new triple alliance?"

"Paul is not the cleverest, nor the most stable fellow, but he *is* heir to the throne. I can't say I think the grand duke's talents particularly profound. Still, he has his partisans." Zubov made a show of examining his fingernails. "What do you think of him?"

"I give no second thought to Grand Duke Paul," Grisha lied. He had in fact given quite a deal of thought to Paul over the years, wondering how he might convince Catherine to pass over the sap and instead name her young grandson Alexander the heir.

"You must wonder how our worlds will change with Paul as tsar."

Grisha reached for his lavender-scented handkerchief. "Someday he will be tsar. Until then, my attention is focused on my Catherine."

"Your Catherine." Zubov made a little snort. "Priceless! How easily you fool yourself into thinking your relationship is what it once was. You are not my father, Prince Potemkin, no matter how much poor Catherine would like to see you behave in such a role. If you wish to believe I have some sort of special connection with the tsarevich I doubt anything I say could change your mind anyway."

Grisha was impressed with the boy's adroit answer. He had an eye for merit, even in enemies. He wondered now if this wasn't more a fault than a strength.

"You never know about the grand duke, though," Zubov continued. "Perhaps with the proper mentorship he might fill his mother's shoes."

He had been wrong to give Zubov any credit for having a brain, but surely the boy could not be this stupid. "I assume you mean once the empress has passed."

"Of course!" Zubov exclaimed. "Good God, man, what else could I have meant? Even so, are you sure you have no desire to meet with Paul yourself? Who knows, perhaps he might surprise the both of us and show a singular flair for leadership."

Grisha attempted a smile, but the thought of Russia under Tsar Paul left his stomach feeling weighted with stones. "I have no desire to work with you and even less desire to meet with Paul."

"I shouldn't have imagined it should be of interest, but then we never know, do we? I had to be sure of your loyalties. Some in court prize the grand duke's favor. Perhaps you are among their number."

Zubov's reflections swirled all around Grisha's in the room's mirrors, taunting him. Did the boy really think he could be played this easily? Would this day not end? "Glad to have saved you the trouble."

"No trouble at all, Prince," Zubov said. "Only take care with your words as you make your way around this palace."

"And why should I? To avoid your spies?"

Zubov inclined forward, a languid smile plastered on his face. "You may act the pasha with your harem at your encampments. But here you are merely a subject of your great sovereign, as are we all."

"I am well aware of my relationship to the empress."

"I meant don't overstep your boundaries."

"Between the empress and myself few boundaries exist."

"So you say. Nonetheless, I would watch my back were I you."

"I have always done so among the empress's courtiers," Grisha said.

"Yes, but now the empress herself might turn on you if she feels her power threatened. I only tell you this as a newfound ally."

"Of course," Grisha muttered.

"Now that we are in agreement, I believe we should see the empress together and united on this point only, for now at any rate." Zubov extended a hand. "Your shrine in the south, Prince Potemkin. So be it. We will work together as one happy family."

Eight

Once her claim has been confirmed the honorary tsarina will be available for public appearances for a reasonable fee, which can be arranged through the number listed below.

ST. PETERSBURG
PRESENT DAY

Veronica ducked into a corner alcove. Someone had left a business card on a cheap plastic flower stand, under a vase filled with synthetic daisies. Residue from stolen cigarette breaks clung to the cheap silk petals. A brown tabby perched on the windowsill, tail twitching, watching a pair of doves on a balcony opposite the hotel. Cars backed up on the flat length of the street below, and the gold cupola of a nearby cathedral peeped through the morning mist of rain and gloomy storm clouds. St. Petersburg was not a city of skyscrapers and industry. It was a city of low rooftops and church domes and ornate architectural flourishes, of history and operas and palaces and ballets.

And Romanov heiresses.

Veronica pressed call on her phone and waited for her *abuela* to answer.

"What happened?" her grandmother asked frantically, without so much as a hello. "Have you been arrested?"

Veronica picked up the business card and started tapping it against the stand. The tabby glanced over its shoulder, annoyed.

"I'm fine," Veronica said. "But I had quite the surprise at the airport."

"Oh?"

"You asked Michael to come with me?"

"He's such a lovely man," Abuela gushed. "And he knows Russian."

"I studied Russian for six years!" Veronica paused, counting to three in English, Spanish, and Russian in her head. "I just wish you had asked me first," she added calmly.

"What if you had said no?"

Veronica looked down at the card and a sexy picture of a woman in a low-cut dress smiled up at her. The card was for an escort service. She wrinkled her nose and dropped it back on the flower stand.

"There is so much happening in Russia right now." Abuela's voice faltered. "On the news tonight they said the government might ban European airliners from Russian airspace. What if you're stuck there? What will you do?"

"I can practically walk to Finland from here, or at least walk to the ferry." Veronica thought of the story of Michael's grandparents, the servants Lena and Pavel, rescuing the Grand Duchess Charlotte, Veronica's other grandmother. They had spirited her away from the palace at Peterhof and across the Gulf of Finland a century earlier.

Not a story, she reminded herself. *My history.*

"I only thought it would be good for you to have someone

around who understands visas and passports and immigration law," Abuela said. "And Michael was more than happy to come and keep you company. Be nice to him."

"I am being nice to him. Why wouldn't I be nice to him?"

"One more thing." Abuela hesitated. Veronica heard the television blaring in the background. "You received a phone call today. From Laurent Marchand. I don't know him. I only know what your mother told me . . ."

The rain gathered force, beating now against the pipes on the outside of the building. The cat hopped off the windowsill and Veronica peered down at the street below. Morning commuters, men in trench coats and women in black tights and sophisticated ankle boots, opened up brightly colored umbrellas as they shuffled into a metro station.

"Well, he only waited thirty-nine years to get in touch with me," she muttered.

"I know this is difficult, but, *mija*, listen. I talked to him for a bit. His English is weak, but his Spanish is beautiful. What else would you expect from a professor of literature? So elegant. And he seems like a gentleman. We managed. I think you would like him."

Veronica knew her grandmother was trying to keep it together for her sake, but the last thing she wanted to hear about right now was her long-lost father and his perfect Spanish. She grabbed the business card and tore it to pieces. "Too little, too late."

"He's an old man now," Abuela said. "He would be what . . . in his seventies?"

"What did he want?"

"He wanted to know if it was true you were going to St. Petersburg. Apparently, he follows the news in Russia closely. He saw your picture. He sounded worried."

"What I do is none of that man's business."

"You know how much I resented him for what he did to your

mother. Leaving her alone with a baby. But he lived in Spain under Franco for most of his life. It couldn't have been easy. And so much happened to his family during the war."

"He's never even reached out to me."

"I know."

"Then why are you humoring him?"

"You can't blame him for being cautious." Veronica heard her grandmother sigh. "But I feel as though the two of you would see eye to eye. I think maybe you should talk to him. Can I give him your cell number?"

"No."

"You might regret not seeing him."

"No." Veronica felt pressure at the back of her eyes. "He's never reached out to me and now that I'm here in Russia, finally exploring this side of my family's history, he decides to make an appearance? Maybe he wants to pursue the claim himself."

"He never expressed an interest in that before."

"He never expressed an interest in me before either."

"I won't force you into something you don't want to do."

Veronica drew in a deep breath. The cat twitched its tail and hopped back on the sill, staring at the plump raindrops. "How many times did I want to see him? How many times did I ask about him when I was growing up?"

"I know, I know." Abuela softened her voice. "I'm sorry, *mija*. I should have realized how much this would bother you. Forget I mentioned it. Only take care of yourself. And try to let Michael take care of you too."

A few hours later, Veronica was still thinking about her long-lost father, Laurent Marchand, and his mysterious phone call to her *abuela*. She stood before a full-length oval mirror encircled by a gilt frame ornamented with rusted miniature cherubs blowing horns. The overall effect was meant to be charming, but the cherubs' faces looked misshapen and smug. Veronica wanted to throw a drape over the mirror.

"Is only reproduction." The seamstress, Elena, had fire-engine-red hair that gleamed under the lights of the chandelier, a stark contrast to her black sheath dress. She hardly looked a day over eighteen, young enough to be Veronica's daughter, at least in a *Gilmore Girls* sort of way, and had asked if they might speak in English. She was studying for a language certification and wanted to get some practice. Elena smoothed the material around Veronica's hips and adjusted the thick cape around her shoulders. "What is it you think?"

Veronica focused on her own face now, her wide brown eyes outlined in deep black. Her straight dark hair normally grazed her shoulders but now stood full and glossy around her head like a crown. The expertly applied cosmetics were far too heavy for her taste and made her face feel strangely waxen. Still, all of that was familiar enough. The rest of what she saw in the mirror took time to process.

"You are happy?"

Veronica touched the glossy gown, a reproduction of Catherine's coronation dress, impressed at its resemblance to the original. The snug bodice glinted in the light dancing from the electronic chandeliers, as though it were made of spun gold. Tiny double-headed eagles were embroidered into the silver satin, and the dress spread into an exaggerated width around her waist. She stood taller and felt stronger.

She looked like an empress.

She was supposed to be here.

Veronica gathered the long gown in her hands so she could walk without tripping as she made her way to the sink in the washroom adjacent to the office. Irina had reserved the Monarchist Society's office for the fitting. She had also given Veronica a key card and said she should feel "free to use the space" at any time while she was in St. Petersburg; as she was a tsarina, this was her "rightful place." Veronica's gaze flickered over the drawings of old St. Petersburg, the musty sword tassel, and the official portraits of Potemkin and Catherine.

The heavy dress dragged against the carpet. Veronica threw the cape, lined in what she had been assured was faux fur, back over her shoulders so it wouldn't get wet. She turned on the water and reached for one of Irina's monogrammed towels.

"Careful! Careful!" Elena hopped over and grabbed a larger towel, wrapping it around Veronica's throat and shoulders. "You do not want to damage dress."

Veronica moistened the face towel and began to rub her cheeks.

"What is this you do now?" Elena asked.

"I'm not used to wearing so much blush."

"You look pretty!"

"I look pretty without it."

"Pretty but too pale."

Veronica held her wrist up to Elena's, comparing her own olive skin with Elena's pale Slavic tones.

"All right, maybe this is point," Elena conceded. "But I still think you look pretty in makeup, like Disney princess!"

"Which one? Which princess?"

Elena shrugged. "Any of them. All of them. That is how you should look, Tsarina!"

"Ceremonial tsarina," Veronica said, using her towel to remove some of the glittery silver shadow from her eyelids. "Not exactly the same."

Elena rustled around in a cosmetics pouch she had tied on a belt around her waist and grabbed a fluffy brush. "Maybe you let me work on your face more and see what you think."

"What's the point of being a princess if people don't take you seriously?"

"You can look pretty and be taken serious," Elena said.

Veronica turned back toward the hanging rod Elena had set up for her in the office: sophisticated skirts and sweaters and blouses Irina deemed suitable for various events. She frowned, wondering how much money she might owe Irina by the end of this trip. "You send a message with clothes and makeup. I want to send the right message."

"Yulia Tymoshenko always wore pretty makeup and pretty clothes. That braid! And she was prime minister of Ukraine. How many women have been American president?"

Veronica spun around, cape swishing. "All right," she admitted. "Not a terrible point."

Elena zipped her cosmetics bag shut. "Maybe remember me when you need to dress again for important events, Tsarina Nika."

Someone rapped on the door. Before Veronica could manage a "come in," Irina entered, wearing a flawless cream-colored pantsuit that flattered her trim figure. Irina stopped short and looked at Veronica.

"You've done well enough," she told Elena. "But I think we need some nips and tucks to make sure the gown fits perfectly. After all, this is our inspiration."

Irina held a copy of the portrait of Catherine the Great, looking rosy and clever, at the time of her coronation. The imperial crown sat heavy on her head. It must have weighed a ton, but you would never tell from her serene expression. Veronica imagined Catherine posing, stately and magnificent, for the portrait, and then screaming afterward for her minions to get that thing off of her head.

Two long dark braids spilled over Catherine's creamy shoulders. Irina tapped those. "Your hair isn't long enough for the braids." She set the picture back down on the little stool in front of the mirror and fluffed Veronica's hair. The dark floral scent of Catherine the Great's perfume on Irina's neck wafted around them. "But I like what they've done. I only wish you would let someone work on your poor fingernails. And then there is this . . ." She pointed to the orb Catherine clutched close to her waist and the scepter she held daintily in the other hand. "We thought that might be a little much, but we do have some props that might work." She turned to Elena. "What do you think?"

"We could try," Elena said. "I brought props. I will go get."

As Elena left, Irina stared at Veronica's reflection. "You look wonderful, Nika. Majestic. Dmitry told me you did very well with the reporters yesterday. You are meant for this."

Veronica started to fiddle with a pincushion Elena had left behind. It was soft and shaped like a little tomato. She imagined it growing heavy in her hands, transforming into a royal orb.

"Think of Catherine for inspiration." Irina gestured at the dress. "Catherine began her life baptized as Sophia, a little German girl. She wasn't a Romanov at all except by marriage."

"I know. I know." Veronica set the pincushion back on the counter and stared at the gown, wondering if some of Catherine's power might reside within, even in a reproduction.

"Catherine was renamed. She fashioned her own image. Her own *glamur*. She made herself the true heir of the tsars and changed her world." Irina stepped back, once again taking stock of Veronica in the dress. "Our donors will be thrilled. The opportunities you will have to make a name for yourself, to be a true tsarina, will be endless."

Veronica remembered the video of Reb Volkov on YouTube. Perhaps Irina had decided it was appropriate for Veronica to assume a political role after all. "I hope so."

"This is not the time to hope. This is the time to act." Irina began typing something on her phone. "I want to take a picture of you in the gown and see what Sasha thinks. One of our donors asked if he might see a picture of you in Catherine's regalia. You should talk with him . . . I think he might fund a tour of the country for you if he gets access to your image. Of course if you promote the Ekaterina Restaurant as a spokesperson, they may want exclusive rights. Sasha's the branding expert so I'll ask him."

"I don't want to be a company logo."

Irina smoothed the gown around Veronica's hips. "Your decision, but I hope you will take advantage of such opportunities. You will find we have friends in the Duma as well. I believe they are going to make great things happen for us and help restore the nobility to its former glory. You can do very well for yourself here. I wonder if you might consider making Russia your permanent residence. Of course Petersburg is hardly Russia at all. It is a special place in and of itself."

"St. Petersburg is beautiful," Veronica said, "but I'm American. I want to make my home in the United States. In California, near my family."

"You no longer have a job in California, from what I understand."

The dress suddenly felt too tight. "I'll manage."

Irina fussed with a lacy ruffle at Veronica's elbow. "Your friend Mr. Karstadt seems to be enjoying his room at the Ambassador. I understand he received free room service last night."

"What?" Veronica spun around.

"Food. Dinner. Room service. I have sources in the hotel keeping tabs on him and this is what they tell me."

"Oh." She should have known Irina would find a way to circle the conversation back to Michael and mess with her head. "I'm not surprised. He has a way about him."

"But he is also an imposter," Irina said. "Some people call him the False Mikhail. Dmitry told me a reporter approached him. He pretended to be the heir. He faked a lineage. Faked it! It sounds as though that unfortunate little story has gotten out. This could reflect poorly on our organization at the very time when we hope to accomplish wonderful things. I mean, take Prince Potemkin's mosque for example." Irina gestured to the sketch on the other side of the room, the four minarets capped by crescent moons. "Think of what it might mean to construct such a place. It would demonstrate you are an enlightened tsarina. It would go a long way toward building goodwill between the Society and our Muslim friends."

Although she agreed with what Irina was saying, Veronica sensed a false note in Irina's voice when she spoke of the mosque, like it was more of a distraction than a genuine passion. Nonetheless, she still needed Irina's help if she was to have validity as tsarina. She didn't want to challenge her. Not yet. "I understand why you find it so appealing," she told Irina mildly. "I think it would be a wonderful project to add to my agenda."

"And you wouldn't want to ruin any opportunities. If it becomes widely known you are associating with the 'False Mikhail,' it might damage your reputation."

Veronica's stomach clenched. "Michael is only here to help me."

"I spoke to him earlier. He claims he was trying to protect you and that's why he lied to you about his identity. But now he's poking around again?"

Veronica tried to emulate Irina's demeanor, to pretend she was Nordic and blond and emotionally detached, even though she was about as far from any of those things as a person could possibly be.

"I wonder what Mikhail really wants," Irina mused. "Charming men can always get away with more than everyone else. I will be honest, Nika. You will need advisers and I don't know about him. Are you sure you trust him?"

"My grandmother asked him to come," Veronica said. "I called her and she confirmed."

"So you don't trust him." Irina narrowed her eyes. "Otherwise, why would you need to call your grandmother?"

Veronica managed an indifferent shrug. She didn't want to let Irina know she still didn't completely trust Michael.

"Not that I blame you," Irina said. "He lied for so long. And now he is your number one supporter? If we're not careful, the press could have a field day with this."

"He led me to believe something that wasn't true," Veronica said carefully. "But he had good reasons to do so. He acted in good faith."

"You are no longer with him? Romantically, I mean."

Veronica felt a tingle of a blush. "We're friends."

"Just be careful," Irina said. "As long as you are in Russia you are a celebrity and you will be watched. Try to act accordingly."

After Veronica's dress was hemmed, Irina decided they should take a look at backdrops for her first photo session. When they stepped into the dimly lit corridor outside the office, Veronica caught the dry taste of cigarette smoke in the air.

Irina tapped her hips. "What hooligan has snuck in here?" She turned around. "Who are you?" she demanded.

Veronica turned to look. The reporter she'd met yesterday, Anya, took a drag on a slim brown cigarette. When she saw Veronica and Irina, she quickly stamped the cigarette out in a potted plant and began waving her hands frantically in front of her face and dark violet *hijab*. "I know, I know," she said quickly in Russian. "This is not supposed to happen. It's disrespectful. But old habits die hard."

"We don't want the smell lingering on Catherine's dress." Even as she said this, Irina cast a covetous look at the cigarette.

"I meant disrespectful to my lungs and my beliefs, but sure." Anya turned to Veronica. "Dmitry said you would be here and that you would be willing to answer a few questions. He let me inside. May I have a moment of your time?"

Irina crossed her arms. "Dmitry should have cleared any interview with Nika through me first."

"I promise to respect Nika." Anya smiled and widened her already large eyes. "And no more cigarettes."

"Which paper do you work for?"

"The *Moscow Review*."

"A Muscovite." Irina rolled her eyes. "Of course."

"I think I'm ready for a short interview," Veronica said.

"You look fabulous," Anya said. "And I only want to ask a few questions."

"Fine," Irina said, before Veronica had a chance to answer. "But be quick about it. Nika needs to get ready for a party tonight."

Veronica thought back to Dmitry's itinerary for the week. "At the Hermitage?"

"Yes. Important members of the Society will attend. VIPs, as you say. So I want you at your best."

"What do you think I'm going to do to her?" Anya asked.

"I don't know." Irina took a step back and appraised Anya, gaze lingering on the fringed tassels edging her head scarf. "Just don't monopolize Nika's time. We have work to do."

Anya adjusted her glasses on her nose as Irina walked away, heels tapping on the tiled floor. "You do look lovely," Anya said, "but Dmitry gave me the impression you hadn't come to Russia for this." She waved at Catherine's gown.

"This just sort of happened."

"I really only have one question," Anya said to Veronica. "Why are you doing this? Why are you agreeing to work with the Monarchist Society?"

"It's my birthright."

"Did someone tell you to say that?"

Veronica had no idea why she had said that. It sounded like something Irina, Michael, or Dmitry would say, not her. "No. But I don't feel like I have an easy answer."

"I'm not looking for an easy answer. Tell me the truth."

How good that sounded, at least in theory, to tell the truth and not worry about appearances. Something about Anya's straightforward questions, the earnest look in her eyes, and even her lapse with the cigarette made Veronica want to confide in her. "Before I came here, I felt lost."

Anya nodded. "Dmitry told me you quit your job to come. You must feel pressure. I'm sure Irina's ideas for commercializing your image are tempting."

"It's that. But it's not only that. I've felt lost for a long time. I never really felt like I fit in where I grew up. I love my family, but I never wanted to stay in my hometown. It's too conservative. Too quiet. Does that make any sense at all?"

Anya gave a little smile. "I come from a small town. I left to come to university in Moscow when I was eighteen. Yes, this makes sense."

"I moved to Los Angeles to pursue my graduate degree. And that was good. That worked for me for a while. But then I was engaged . . . and that failed. And I never had children. That makes me feel like I need to make something of my life. Otherwise what's the point? What will I leave behind after I'm gone?"

"I see." Anya started to smile. "Dmitry said you were a passionate woman and you would be a strong advocate for Reb. I see this in you as well." She reached into her bag and withdrew a phone. "I will record the remainder of our conversation, with your permission."

Veronica nodded and tried to look comfortable in the massive dress.

"Many people have claimed to be a grand duchess but then were proven imposters . . ."

Veronica played with a loose fold on the gown and tried not to think about Michael and the way the reporter had hassled him yesterday.

". . . and other Romanovs have made claims, but their connection to the last imperial family was distant. You're different, a direct link to the last family. This will give you emotional sway. How do you picture your role?"

"In the modern world, a monarch is nothing more than a figurehead. But that's the point. A monarch is apart from politics and free to champion just causes."

"Do you have any specific causes in mind?" Anya nodded vaguely at the phone, as though Veronica needed a reminder she was being recorded.

"Irina mentioned a mosque she wants built . . ."

Anya's eyes widened. "I've heard rumors about this. So it's true. That would be wonderful. I have connections to imams in Moscow who may wish to speak to you about this." She pressed the button once more to go off the record. "At least this woman Irina and I agree on one thing." She pressed the button again and the red light went back on. "But of course I am curious about what other causes you wish to support."

"Reb Volkov," Veronica said. "I think his sentence should be dismissed."

"If you speak for Reb's release, won't you be in direct defiance of the government? Isn't that political?"

"A Russian court made the decision. A terrible decision."

Anya nodded thoughtfully and pressed something on her phone.

"We're off the record again, I take it," Veronica said.

"I think you are a brave woman."

"I may be a Romanov, but I'm also an American citizen. I can get away with speaking out more, or at least I think I can."

"I still say you are a brave woman." She inclined her head. "I understand what you say about purpose. I do. Americans are like this, looking for something more. Reb always said this. He enjoyed visiting America so much. He wanted to live there. I wish I had encouraged him to do so. He would be safe now."

"So you know Reb?"

"Dmitry didn't tell you? Reb is my little brother."

"Oh!" Veronica said. "I didn't know."

"We have different fathers," she said. "Mine was a journalist from Afghanistan originally. Reb's father was a member of the Old Guard. Would have made it to the Politburo if the USSR lasted long enough."

"Can I meet Reb?" Veronica asked.

She leaned forward. "Are you sure you want to do this? Reb is no monarchist. I can't guarantee he will be friendly."

"I'd still like to meet him."

Anya lifted her palms. "All right. I think he will do it. He's stuck at home anyway. Who knows? Perhaps the two of you will get along."

"I thought Reb was under arrest," Michael said. "How are you going to meet him?"

"House arrest. For the moment." Veronica struggled with her umbrella against the wind. The wet pavement was uneven and she trod lightly in her unfamiliar rain boots, making her way through a group of young men in heavy rain slickers. An Australian tourist bus had just parked on the other side of the street, and the men were braving the cold rain to shout into bullhorns about discounted tours of Tsarskoye Selo.

"They slapped him with an ankle bracelet like he's Lindsay Lohan," she added. "So Reb can't get very far regardless."

"I thought they wanted to make an example of him."

"The government wanted to give him time to get his affairs in order, make it appear as though due process is being followed before they send him off to the *gulag*."

"They're not really using that term anymore, are they?"

"They might as well be," she said.

"What if they find a reason to slap an ankle bracelet on you and send you to the *gulag*?"

"Then they'll have to deal with our government."

"Forget our government." He smiled. "They'll have to deal with your *abuela*."

Veronica laughed softly. When she drew in her breath, she caught a strong taste of the gasoline pollution that clung to the cold air, along with the faint scent of forest and river.

"I know you're worried about me," she said. "But it's bad, Michael. It's really bad. I know this is a long shot, but maybe if I say the right thing at the right time it could make a difference. I have to try."

"At least let me come with you to see Reb," Michael said.

Veronica shook her head. "Anya said he would only see me. And frankly, even that sounds iffy."

"If anything happens to you, your *abuela* will kill me."

"That's probably true," Veronica said.

Most of the souvenir stands had shut down for the season, but they approached a lemon-yellow kiosk in the tree-lined square, where a middle-aged man in a bulging white jacket sold newspapers and mineral water. Next to the kiosk, a large canopy sheltered a folding table lined with doe-eyed nesting dolls, T-shirts featuring brash images of the Russian president, and flaming Firebirds painted on wooden *balalaikas*.

"Look." Michael pointed to a Soviet-style movie poster for Sergei Eisenstein's *Battleship Potemkin*, a defiant sailor holding a red flag. "I wonder what Dmitry's ancestor Grisha would have made of that?"

"From what I've read, Prince Potemkin was full of himself." Veronica put her umbrella down to dip under the canopy and take a look for herself. "I'm sure he wouldn't mind. He'd probably find it flattering. A ship was named after him on *Star Trek* too. The *Potemkin*."

Michael gave her a sidelong glance, playful and sarcastic, just as she remembered.

"I'm a nerd," she said. "You already knew that. I thought you liked that about me."

"I still like that about you."

The rain began to fall harder, pounding against the canopy over the table. It felt good to talk to him this way again, but she didn't know what to say. Veronica rifled through miniature icons of John the Baptist and amber pendants dangling from cheap chains. She spotted an entire chess set with Romanov and Bolshevik figurines facing off and scowling at each other. Nicholas II and Lenin were the kings.

At the end of the table a postcard of the last imperial family caught her eye. Fairly standard, except someone had drawn an extra Romanov, a redhead with features similar to Grand Duchess Tatiana. The fifth daughter stood to the side, gazing wistfully at the rest of her family.

"Is that supposed to be Grand Duchess Charlotte?" Veronica asked the man behind the kiosk, pointing to the postcard. "Who drew this picture?"

"You like our secret grand duchess?" In his bulging white jacket, he resembled a snowman.

"How much?" she asked.

"For you, eighty rubles, or two dollars." He spoke in heavily accented English. He must have detected her American accent. "Should buy now. Price goes higher tomorrow."

The wind gusted, stinging Veronica's ears. "This is my grand-mother."

"This secret Romanov?"

Michael peered over Veronica's shoulder at the postcard. "I met Charlotte once. She was older when I met her, but whoever drew this got her right."

Veronica fumbled in her purse for her crumpled wad of ruble notes and handed them over. Then she tucked the postcard in the side pocket of her purse and started walking again, still struggling with her umbrella. She would just as soon have spent the chilly afternoon inside the Hermitage or another museum, but Michael wanted to see *The Bronze Horseman*.

The little yellow flowers encircling the statue wilted under the rain. Above them, Peter's hand was extended forward while his horse reared up on its hind legs. Personally, Veronica didn't much care for the statue. She had always thought Peter looked awkward and too stiff.

"I can't believe you've never seen him," Veronica said.

Michael kicked a pebble. "When I was a little boy, my mother read Pushkin's poem to me. A statue coming to life? A wild horse? I had nightmares for weeks."

Veronica laughed. "So what do you think? Afraid he'll come chasing after you? Drive you crazy and you'll jump in the river?"

Michael's expression remained calm, but his brow furrowed as he gazed up at Peter's stern face. "I can see why Pushkin thought he might come to life."

Raindrops pounded down on her umbrella and she shivered in her coat. Veronica thought of Reb's painting that featured *The Bronze Horseman* and the exhibit that had gotten him in so much trouble in the first place. "Michael, has my *abuela* been in touch with you?"

He frowned. "About what?"

"My father."

He drew in a deep breath and watched a trio of soldiers in dark green uniforms pass, all holding paper cups of gelato despite the cold. Michael exhaled, his breath misting in the cold air, and finally met her eyes. "What about him?"

"He wants to talk to me."

Michael tilted his head. "After all these years? Now?"

"Exactly. I wonder if he regrets not claiming the title for himself."

"He had his chance. From what I gathered, he never wanted anything to do with it."

"I know. That's what's I don't understand." A bulbous street lamp hanging from a thick metal hook flickered on for the evening. Veronica stared at the writing on a small metal trash bin. In the glow she could just make out the Cyrillic letters and roughly translate them in her head.

All gay men should burn.

Veronica felt like someone had put a knife to her throat. "Do you see that?"

Michael turned around to read the graffiti. "God," he said under his breath.

Veronica had grown interested in Russian history after the collapse of the Soviet Union. She remembered that time: freedom, openness, democracy. "Irina is conservative in so many ways, but she also seems desperate to have me emulate Catherine the Great. What do you think Catherine would do if she were around today?"

"She had her issues, but she was an enlightened empress," Michael said. "I don't think she would care for this." He paused. "Veronica, about your father . . ." Michael stared at the buttery-yellow classical façade of the Senate and Synod Building, half-cloaked in the drizzle. "I don't have any right to tell you what to do. This is your decision."

"No, go ahead. What do you think?"

Michael leaned forward and dipped his head to look up at her, the way he used to do. "I know you have issues with your father," he said.

"He's my father in name only."

"But you decide to come to Russia and then out of the blue he tries to get in touch with you? I don't know. I think we should find out what he wants."

Abuela had said something similar, that she should give her father a break or at least a chance. "Your mother still has connections. You said so on the plane. Will you try to find out what he wants?"

Veronica felt something warm in her hands. Without thinking, she had taken Michael's hand, her fingers folding over his. Her heart raced and she found herself babbling. "I'll consider talking to Laurent, but I just need to know why he chose to reach out now."

Michael raised her hand, still resting in his, and lifted the edge of her glove. He kissed the inside of her wrist. She felt the slow melting inside, her desire still so close to the surface.

"I'll do whatever you need me to do," he told her. "I'm here for you."

"And I'm glad . . ." She couldn't manage more and began fussing with her umbrella. Michael didn't say anything further. The figure of Peter and his horse loomed above them, not exactly in judgment, but killing the mood—at least for her. She had her own goals to accomplish in a week here and all the time in the world to worry about her feelings.

Nine

"So now we find ourselves in agreement, Your Majesty." Zubov paused to take another shot of cherry-flavored vodka. "And couldn't wait to share the good news."

"I see," Catherine said flatly. She slapped a Jack of Clubs in the center of the table and rearranged the cards remaining in her hand. "Prince Potemkin is that convincing, is he?"

"Most persuasive." Zubov sat directly across from Grisha and gave one of his languid smiles before fanning his cards out and choosing one to play. He looked to the monkey perched on his shoulder for approval.

Grisha took another bite of his radish. Despite this show of affability, he sensed Zubov merely tolerated the game, another of Grisha's tricks to be endured and laughed at later behind his back. He had not expected to see Catherine again so soon, but apparently there had been an opening in her daily routine when the envoy from England took ill with the grippe, or so Zubov claimed. Why didn't they all gather in Her Majesty's Hermitage for a few friendly tricks of whist? He couldn't shake the feeling that the boy had anticipated this entire adventure, even before Grisha had approached him yesterday.

That suspicion was lent greater weight whenever Grisha stole a glance to his right, at Catherine's partner for the game: her own son, the Grand Duke Paul.

For the most part, Paul remained silent. Grisha supposed this was a blessing and he did not wish to question it. Paul's squishy face and low sloping brow underneath his powdered wig were offensive enough. Worse yet, he had insisted on joining them dressed in full military regalia: dark jacket, gold braiding around his waist, bright blue sash draped over his chest, the color seemingly chosen for its ability to reflect the gold medals affixed to his coat, medals Paul had so generously awarded himself.

"You even convinced the prince to play as your partner this evening!" Catherine returned the cards to their original places in her hand. "Now, that truly is a miracle."

"A convenience only, *matushka*." Grisha tried to wink, a useless gesture with only one good eye, but he made a diligent effort. "You know I play to win."

The monkey let out an approving bray and then clasped his little hands together and looked all around the room. Grisha patted his head, hoping his wig, so carelessly tossed atop his head this morning, was safe around the beast.

Catherine lowered her cards, her blue eyes sparkling in the candlelight. "So, what is your secret, Prince? How did you find the right words to turn my stingiest adviser into such a spendthrift? I assume he has not become a convert to Islam."

Grisha managed a small smile and eased back into his uncomfortable chair. Catherine's dog, the old Thomassin, had risen from his favorite spot by the hearth to greet him, placing his silky smooth head in his lap.

"Can we get to it?" Paul asked in a voice that reminded Grisha how much the impatient child the grand duke still was, even at midlife. Paul tossed a card on the table without even looking at his hand and Catherine scowled. "I told you, Mother, I'm to review the troops in an hour."

"Tell me of the mosque," Catherine said to Grisha, ignoring her son. "Platon Alexandrovich can now speak of nothing else." She set a gentle hand on Zubov's arm and Grisha tried not to wince. "He claims it will be a sight to behold, that it will put the mosques I commissioned to shame and rival the most elaborate shrines to Allah in the Arab world. Surely that can't be true, Prince. And yet . . ." She gestured toward the scarf around his neck. It had been a gift from the grateful wife of a Tatar khan, once Grisha assured the woman's husband of a high appointment in the New Russian administration. "Has your heart been so enraptured by the place that you fashion yourself a pasha?"

"I believe it's the pasha's turn." Zubov fed his monkey a peanut. "Perhaps he could play a card and then tell us of his grand vision."

"But be quick about it," Paul added. "This whole Mohammedan project strikes me as odd anyway after your triumph in Ochakov." Paul's voice changed at the mention of Ochakov, suddenly drenched with admiration. "You are a hero from folklore to the troops after that siege. I often hear my soldiers speak of it."

Despite the fire crackling in the hearth, Grisha felt chilled. Zubov's monkey began to bray again, only now a high-pitched wail. The creature's teeth chattered and he hopped from Zubov's shoulders to Paul's, where he immediately began to pick at a brilliant medal shaped like a sunburst on Paul's chest.

"Can't you control this beast?" Paul sniped.

"He does as he pleases," Zubov said, taking another swig of vodka. "Don't you appreciate a fiery spirit, Grand Duke? Life isn't all military parades and sword rattling."

"But a mosque in Moscow is a most singular project, Your Highness," Paul blathered on, squinting at Grisha while batting his fat little hand at the monkey. "I understand you refuse the care of physicians, but perhaps you might consider a consultation."

Despite the shivering, Grisha assumed the blasé tone he always took with Paul. "And why would I want to visit some quack?"

"Why, because some would say you must be out of your mind! Staking so much importance on this project, testing my mother's patience."

Zubov managed a halfhearted laugh, but Catherine glared at her son. Grisha made a mental note to speak with enthusiasm of her grandson Alexander next time he saw Catherine alone. With some luck, she would finally tire of her son altogether and name Alexander her successor, leaving Paul to permanently wallow in his own fussiness. Grisha fumbled in his pocket, past the little rubies he carried for luck and a few of Catherine's old letters, until he located a handkerchief. He patted the linen on his face, breathing in the calming fragrance.

Grand Duke Paul pursed his pouty lips. "I agree with Platon Alexandrovich's first decision on the matter. Why expend your energies on this nonsense? We need to prepare for war, not dither with phony idols. England and Prussia want to challenge us? Let them try."

Zubov shuffled his cards aimlessly. "And hesitation is death . . . didn't you say something to this effect, my darling?"

Catherine was still looking at Grisha, barely paying any attention to her cards. "It was Peter the Great's maxim," she said, "but I trust it has merit."

"For God's sake, Prince, your delay at Ochakov is infamous," Paul jabbered. "Look what happened once you acted. Triumph! Why delay again when we face enemies from the West?"

One of the wax candles on the table went out, as though caught in a sudden breeze. Under the table, the greyhound emitted a low growl.

Grisha could scarcely see the cards in front of his face. He struggled to catch his breath. He heard the sounds of battle, as though in a distant dream and yet right here, in the room, pounding in his ears. The sick squelching sound of a sword running through a man's chest. The strangled animal screams.

Beads of perspiration slipped down the sides of his face. He was fat and out of breath and now he was perspiring in front of Catherine. He wanted to sink into a hole and disappear.

"Besides, you don't seem quite yourself," Paul continued, "so perhaps your recommendations are suspect. Wouldn't you agree, Platon Alexandrovich?"

Zubov, engaged with his neckpiece, looked up and shrugged.

"Not that I know much about the troubles of older men," Paul said. "As you know my father was taken from me while I was still a boy."

"We all know," Catherine said with a crisp slap of her cards to the table. "You have mentioned it often enough."

Zubov clicked his teeth and made an attempt to cross himself and fiddle with his cravat at the same time. "Such a tragedy."

"Some would argue otherwise," Grisha muttered.

"What was that, Prince?" Paul said. "I'm sorry, but you see I am accustomed to my soldiers answering in full voices like good honest men."

Grisha waved a card in front of his face to get some air, wondering how he might best ask the empress to open a window without worrying her. "I understand you take a whip to your men when they displease you," he told Paul. "You truly are your father's son after all. And the way you treat them, I wouldn't be surprised if you miss much whispering behind your back."

"How dare you!" Paul rose to his feet. He was slight of stature and far from intimidating, but out of habit Grisha worked his large frame to his feet as well.

"Oh no," Zubov said disinterestedly, searching his pocket for another peanut for the monkey. "What have you done now, Prince?"

"Enough!" Catherine barked. "Paul, stop nagging the prince and take a seat. And you . . ." She turned to Grisha, stared at his broad and heaving chest as he towered over the table. "Stop teasing him, little kitten. You don't look well. You don't need the agitation."

The Thomassin greyhound snapped at Grisha's boots as he sat back down.

"And you're upsetting my dog," Catherine added. "The last thing I need is a nipped finger tonight." She peeked under the table. "I know he has turned into something of a grouch in his dotage, but honestly, I don't understand what is wrong with him sometimes."

The Thomassin skulked into a corner, but his cloudy gaze remained fixed on the pasha. The old warrior had appeared on the opposite side of the room sitting straight-backed on the large Turkish divan, arms folded, turban carefully propped on his knee.

"I don't know." Even as Grisha spoke, he was staring at the pasha's pet lion, seated faithfully at his master's feet. The lion's giant pink tongue shot out of his mouth and he licked his chops. Grisha caught a glimpse of the lion's pointed teeth set back in his wide jaws, the twitch of his ears. No wonder the dog and the monkey were so upset.

"Mother thinks you've lost your courage," Paul said, "when it comes to taking on England and their Prussian allies over the jewels of New Russia."

"Those were not my exact words. I only suggested the prince no longer seeks battles."

"You have won," the pasha told Grisha. "She wants to help you. And as she is so fond of repeating, delay is death."

Grisha looked around the table. Paul was now grappling with the monkey, who had finally ripped the medal from his sash. He tried to extract it from the animal's greedy hands. Zubov smothered laughter, while Catherine stared even more intently at her cards. It was as though they were in another world entirely, which of course they were.

"Your powerful woman will build the mosque. It is the slightest token after what you did to our cities. You are a conqueror and you can have your conqueror's guilt assuaged. You should be celebrating. Why are you still upset?"

"I am not upset." Grisha spoke harshly and out loud without meaning to do so. Catherine looked up from her cards. "So I don't know why the dog would be," he added quickly.

"Thank her and return to the south," the pasha said. "This is the will of Allah."

The room around him seemed to dissolve, except for the pasha and his lion, still sitting, waiting patiently for his reply.

The heat of the southern summers could be unbearable. Grisha never spoke of it in front of his men, instead praising the blue skies and healthy atmosphere, particularly after the frozen horrors of winter campaigns. Secretly he longed for frigid nights and droplets of snow clinging to pine trees.

But when the winter came at last to Ochakov, the supplies for his men began to dwindle. If they were cut off entirely, the men would freeze to death. They would starve. The camp already stank of bowels loosened by dysentery. They could not withstand another winter. Grisha received new missives from St. Petersburg, from the other generals, even from Catherine herself. Why wouldn't he take action? Why wouldn't he begin the siege? *Delay is death.*

Grisha grew careless. One day he marched onto the field in full uniform, daring their enemies to kill him and take his head as a prize. That's when the rumors began. He had a death wish, or so it had been whispered around the encampment when his junior officers thought he couldn't hear. But Grisha only assumed God would will his fate, as he always had.

Others under his command had not been so favored by providence. After Russian prisoners were taken, they all waited, knowing the faces of the prisoners would reappear. Hours later they did, bodies missing but eyes wide open, mouths twisted in agony. Heads strung along the walls outside the fortressed city.

Grisha remembered the men as they had been in life, laughing, wrestling with each other over tobacco, full of themselves. Proud men, foolish men, arrogant men, but valiant Russian men nonetheless. And to be reduced to this . . . He saw the heads when he closed his eyes, when he attempted to pray or to sleep. Images of those same men in life haunted him, tortured him: happy, drinking, slapping one another on the back, galloping on their horses. Honorable combatants in war. Precious souls in the eyes of God.

Men of his tribe, his people.

Tears pinched the corners of his eyes.

The pasha dipped his head and rubbed his brow as though he knew Grisha's thoughts. The lion placed its chin on the pasha's lap, much as the Thomassin had with Grisha.

There hadn't been a choice. No other way. He had to storm Ochakov. He'd kept telling himself that over and over. If he had waited any longer more of his men would have died: from cold, from exposure, from lack of nourishment. The raiding bands continued to swipe soldiers in the middle of the night and display their heads on pikes the next morning, vibrant young men now refashioned into the macabre.

"I had no choice," Grisha said.

The room came back into focus. Catherine, Zubov, and Paul all stared at him.

He quickly chose a card and tossed it to the center of the table. "No choice at all." He managed a smile. The pasha and his lion had disappeared.

Catherine's features tightened. There had been a time when he craved her matronly concern nearly as much as he craved their time alone in the bedroom. He let her fawn over him.

"Are you not well?"

Grisha wiped away the perspiration and returned his handkerchief to his pocket. "Only fatigued, *matushka*."

"Speak the truth. What is wrong?" Catherine's gentle hand shook his shoulder, soft as rose petals. "It is the return of malarial fever? You must see a doctor."

Grand Duke Paul drummed his fingers on the tabletop. "Really, Mother, such a fuss over this man. Call a nursemaid to care for your husband, if you must."

Paul had spoken rapidly; the last part came under his breath. But as soon as the grand duke said "husband," Zubov's features grew dour and his skin pale as snow. Only a moment before, Zubov had seemed so smug, but that confidence had been as false as people claimed Grisha's villages in the south had been. He gave the impression now of a death mask.

Still, Grisha didn't care to talk about the marriage in front of Zubov. "I do not need a doctor," Grisha told Catherine. "Only a good night's sleep."

The room started to roll beneath him, as they said the earth had moved in Lisbon so many years ago. Grisha prayed he could make it to his feet. He wondered how far Anton had wandered from this room and how quickly he could get inside a carriage. He longed to scream Anton's name, to summon him to his side.

"Perhaps I should save this discussion for another time," Grisha said wearily. He stumbled to his feet and gave the Thomassin one last reassuring pat on the head.

"I've never known you to abandon whist," Catherine said, frowning. "I hope it is nothing worse than what you say. I still need you, as ever. We still have peace terms to negotiate with our old foes the Turks. I trust you will handle them."

"Either way, it seems rest would be just the ticket," Zubov said, shaking off the death mask and returning to his former tone of merriment. Sensing the change in Zubov's mood, the monkey clapped his tiny hands together and emitted a whooping sound of delight.

"Now that your plans for the Mohammedans are in order, you can lie abed."

Grisha forced sharp words for Zubov back down his throat. He bowed and reached for Catherine's hand. He would kiss it. He would declare his love for her, just as he had when he was still a boy and she newly crowned. Their bodies as one body and their minds as one mind. But his vision failed him. Where there should have been one hand for him to grasp, he saw several. It was no use. He could not manage it.

He needed to show her he was still the man she loved, the man who could take her side as she led, support her as she needed. "I am pleased with your decision regarding the mosque, *matushka*. A celebration is in order! I plan to honor your triumphs with a ball."

Zubov withdrew a peanut from the pocket of his jacket and waved it in the direction of his monkey, who had returned to cowering in a corner. "That sounds like so much work for a man of your age."

Grisha expected Catherine to defend him. Instead she added, "And your condition."

Zubov curled his large hand around Catherine's, looking pleased with himself.

Grisha stared at their hands. He had been fooling himself after all. Zubov was the man she loved now. He had a higher mountain to climb than he had anticipated. He wasn't sure he had the strength. He wanted out of this place now.

"Please take quinine, *giaour*," Catherine said. "And see a doctor."

"Yes, yes, take care." Paul checked his gold pocket watch.

Grisha nodded and headed for the door. Catherine's gaze followed him, her eyes brimming with concern.

As Grisha left, he heard Zubov say, "Malaria? Is that what ails him? Poor man, having to deal with such an affliction at his age. He should be encouraged to rest more often."

"Don't worry about Prince Potemkin. He's like a clever cat. He always lands on his feet." But Catherine didn't sound as confident in her words as Grisha might have hoped.

"A ball?" Anton exclaimed. " That sounds like so much work."

Grisha rubbed his head. Hadn't Zubov just plagued him with those very words? "If you tell me it is a task beyond my years, I might rethink your place in my household."

The boy didn't even flinch. "It is only that you don't seem yourself."

They had returned to his newest palace, on the outskirts of the capital, built in the neoclassical style that had so enraptured Catherine, after the ruins uncovered in the ancient city of Pompeii. He had only recently taken up residence and the massive structure still felt unfamiliar. Anton held a candelabra aloft to lead Grisha through the central hall. It was lined with towering pillars that diminished their forms, calling to mind the grandeur of the ancient world. Their boots echoed in the ghostly emptiness. Grisha tried to imagine the palace made golden with reflected candlelight from scores of chandeliers, halls filled with courtiers and commoners alike, long tables heaped with delicacies and main courses from across the empire and beyond. He had heard maize from the Americas could be a colorful addition to a festivity but he didn't think it was the right time of year for it. And the winter garden needed work. Hopefully, diplomatic difficulties with England wouldn't hinder finding a fellow from that land to help him.

Grisha stopped short, dizzy, and grasped one of the pillars for support, the marble cold underneath the thick flesh of his palm. From where he stood, he could see into one of the side rooms, a library from the looks of it, with no door to hinder his view. A boy of about the same age as Anton sprawled across a fine silken chaise longue, muddy boots propped on an embroidered pillow. He chewed on a loaf of black bread, smacking his lips as he perused one of the volumes Grisha thought he had hidden, a folio of illustrations based on a short work by a prisoner locked up in France. The marquis had managed to smuggle copies of the work to a privileged few outside of France, something about a young woman named Justine. Grisha had spent an enjoyable night with the folio himself.

The boy turned the folio, appraising the pictures from different angles.

"Ho there!" Anton thrust the candelabra forward. "What do you think you're doing?"

The servant snapped to attention, kicking his feet out from the pillow, tossing the book to the side and then gathering it back onto the chaise so it didn't hit the floor. He managed a bow in Grisha's direction.

Grisha looked at Anton. "Impressive."

"I'm sorry, that was your prerogative, Your Highness. Only he shouldn't take advantage when you're away." Anton caught a glimpse of one the drawings that accompanied the story and his cheeks turned beet red.

"What is your name?" Grisha asked.

The boy had lanky yellow hair that fell to his shoulders. He gave Grisha a sheepish shrug. "Oleg Ivanovich, Your Highness."

"Oleg Ivanovich, I don't mind if you borrow volumes from my collection, only please mind your shoes stay away from a spot where I might want to rest my head. Understand?"

"I do."

Grisha turned to Anton. "I believe that settles the matter."

Anton scowled but led Grisha out of the library. Catching the boy with the folio had raised Grisha's mood somewhat, but he knew this evening was hopeless. Usually when his mind felt lost, he would call for his carriage and go out to play faro. None of that tonight. He'd had enough cards for one evening, watching Zubov's smug face as he tossed another card on the table and his monkey chattered like an idiot. Grisha planned only to bathe, change into his ermine robe, and sleep until he felt himself again.

His body was vulnerable to both melancholy and malarial fever. He wasn't sure which attacked him now. Perhaps both. Either way, he'd found the best defense: a combination of rest and sensual pleasure. He would try to focus on a picture on the wall or a particularly lovely piece of music he'd commissioned from his orchestra. And then he would steer his mind to a peaceful place, perhaps accompanied by a religious chant his friend Jacob Zeitlin had taught him, in the manner of the devout Orthodox Jews.

He would have his cook prepare hot chocolate with amaretto or some other such delight. And then he would lie on his back and relax and put Platon Alexandrovich Zubov as far from his mind as possible. He refused to think of the besotted look on Catherine's face when she gazed at the boy. It made him sick inside.

He gave instructions to Anton to relay to the chef. Once Anton had gone, he entered his bedroom. It felt overly warm. He had expected the chill of the pasha in the master bedroom, tormenting him with further memories of Ochakov. Grisha did not think he could tolerate any more visions.

But the person waiting for him tonight was no mere apparition. The finely sculpted face, dark eyes, and soft curves were all too real.

Praskovia lounged lazily on his Turkish divan, leaning nearer the fire in the hearth to warm herself, casually thumbing through a political tract from Poland—a dry piece of work that had been quite effective in helping him get to sleep the last few nights. Seeing her now, when his attentions were so focused on Catherine, seemed incongruous, like a spring lily sprouting from its bulb in the middle of winter: lovely in its own right, but strangely disruptive.

"Grig!" The same endearment his family used for him. It caught him off guard. In the instant before her presence fully registered in his mind, he was suddenly transported back to his family's home in the provinces. He was a boy lying on his back under the broad blue sky, nibbling on an apple, as golden blades of grass swayed in the wind.

Praskovia tossed the tract carelessly on the lush carpet and rushed to him. Grisha thought she might throw herself into his arms and feared if she did his muscles would fail and he would drop her to the floor. But she stopped short and raised her chin so she could look into his eyes, regarding him with a distinct mix of admiration and desire. His ego's weakest points.

"Why are you here?" He saw no need for an overture.

"The officers told me you had changed your plans and that you were staying longer in St. Petersburg. They didn't know when you would be back, and I had to see you."

"I thought we agreed you were to return to your husband."

"That was a foolish idea." Her chest was heaving and for a moment he had the strange notion that perhaps she had run a great distance only to be with him for a night. "How could I possibly stay away from you for so long? What was I thinking?"

She stepped back, but her gaze still held his in a most provocative fashion. A low, throbbing hum began in his head and then slowly coursed through the rest of his body. "Who let you in?" he asked, only because he could think of nothing else to say.

"Your servants seemed to expect me," Praskovia purred. "They didn't think it unusual for a woman to call on you without warning."

A dull pain thudded in the back of Grisha's head, warring with the stirring hum. He thought he had expressed his intentions from the beginning. It was true he had promoted her talentless husband so they might have more time together. But he had also made it abundantly clear that their arrangement was to be temporary.

"I explained I had business with Prince Potemkin and they did not question me. It seems I belong here." She lowered her face but then regarded him again behind her long lashes in a most appealing manner, as though he were the center of the world. "I always suspected as much."

"You do not belong here." Grisha's voice was both gentle and firm, although already her nearness provided a welcome respite from the images of Zubov and Catherine. He began to wonder if Praskovia had developed feelings for him beyond physical passion. And in that moment further wondered if he might appreciate a young and simple woman as a companion during his declining years.

A fire blazed in the hearth, but she still wore her sable coat. This seemed odd to Grisha but he soon found the scent of the citrus perfume she dabbed on the back of her ears robbed him of all sensible thought.

Once he had spoiled her with an outfit in the Turkish manner, of the finest silk and in a rich shade of turquoise. At first it had been a shock to see a woman in trousers, even the loose ones favored by the Turkish women, but then he had fondly remembered Catherine in her tight-fitting guardsman trousers.

Praskovia had been thrilled with the ensemble, though it took her time to get used to exposing her trim and pale stomach. But she delighted in the gold bangles running up her arms, the charms tinkling around her ankles, and the thin veil she seductively tied behind her ears so that Grisha could only see her eyes.

It might not be so bad to live out his days indulging in such fantasies.

Now she slid her hand to the top of the coat and slowly drew it open at the chest. She wore nothing underneath.

"I don't expect anything," she said. "I only desire the comfort of your presence for the evening. And I understand you are staying in tonight. Please don't turn me away."

She caressed his face. He thought he caught her glancing at the tracts once more, but then her finger trailed over his cheek and her gaze met his and he knew he would never order a woman he desired out of his bedroom.

Ten

FOR IMMEDIATE RELEASE

Dr. Herrera's first notable public appearance will be the opening of the "Treasures of the Romanovs" exhibit at the Hermitage Museum, where she will be available to answer questions for members of the Monarchist Society and others in attendance.

THE WINTER PALACE AND HERMITAGE
PRESENT DAY

Veronica's hand lightly rested on the cold, gray-white marble. The Jordan Staircase towered before her. Golden ornamentation curled around the high windows and alcoves and up the creamy walls. Glowing light fixtures illuminated classical statuary with firm torsos, solemn expressions, and gracefully curved arms. The Romanovs had descended this staircase every year in January for the Blessing of the Neva River to honor the baptism of Jesus on the Jordan. Catherine the Great had done it, no doubt magnificent in her elaborate eighteenth-century apparel. Veronica's great-grandmother had done it as well, nervous and shy Alexandra. Veronica imagined Alexandra taking care to remain a few steps behind her beloved husband, Nicholas.

"It is impressive, yes?" Dmitry offered his hand as they ascended a scarlet runner on the massive staircase. "And now you are here. The Romanov heiress. You will be enlightened empress for our time . . . as Catherine once was. This is fate."

Veronica threw her head back to take in a painting of gods and winged angels floating on dark gauzy clouds. Would she be asked to bless the waters of the river Neva as well? She was from Bakersfield, for God's sake. She reached for her heart, fierce underneath the thin purple silk of the blouse Irina had suggested she wear this evening. The air didn't feel right. She detected an artificial undertone of vanilla.

Dmitry put his hand on her arm. "Are you well?"

She hated to admit it, but she wished Michael had come. After his encounter with the reporter, they had agreed it was best if he didn't attend the reception tonight, if he kept his distance at public events. In some ways Veronica felt relieved. She had enough on her mind without him around. But she would have liked to talk to him now, to have the reassurance of his hand on her back.

Veronica closed her eyes, trying to push the anxieties out of her head, focusing instead on the background noise, the murmur of voices and sound of shoes thumping as tourists began to tramp down the stairs. She opened her eyes and saw a family descending the staircase, a little girl with long black hair in pink ribbons carefully following her mother's footsteps. How nice it would be to join them, to lose herself in the crowd, to be only a dazed tourist like any other, showing paintings to a wide-eyed child.

She thought then of the cold tile on her cheek, the twisting pain in her middle, and the pounding on the bathroom door. The dark lumps of blood clotting in the toilet and the sudden collapse of a dream she hadn't even known she desired. The end of a pregnancy and soon the end of her engagement and the life she thought she would have back when she was still in Los Angeles, still in graduate school. A lump caught in her throat.

"Try to enjoy." Dmitry's even voice summoned her back to the present. "This is informal event. Have fun. And look who is waiting." He nodded his chin.

"Hey! You made it. Sweet!"

Sasha Yusupov stood at the top of the staircase, before a pair of high granite columns. He smiled down at her, jawline adorably scruffy, monarchist ribbon affixed to his lapel. Two girls stood to his side, a willowy blonde and voluptuous brunette, in jewel-toned cocktail gowns and stiletto heels that made them almost as tall as Sasha. No wonder he seemed happy all the time. As Sasha spoke, the girls appraised Veronica with their heavily lined eyes. She had the sense they found her a tepid heiress to the Romanov throne.

Irina stood on the other side of Sasha in a low-cut, off-the-shoulder blue gown that flattered her creamy skin and blond hair and made her seem almost as young as Sasha's leggy girlfriends. "Borya and Zenaida will be here tonight," she told Veronica, not bothering with niceties. She tapped her hip, as though she longed for a cigarette.

"Who?" Veronica said.

Irina cocked her head and looked at Dmitry, her eyes wide. "You didn't tell her about Borya and Zenaida?"

"Not yet," Dmitry said.

"It is imperative you talk to them. Borya's brother is in the Duma, and you are the representative of the Romanov family this evening."

Veronica tried to nod, but her hands had suddenly grown cold. The State Duma was the lower house of the Russian parliament.

"Avoid anything controversial," Irina said. "If you want to talk politics, bring up Prince Potemkin's mosque. Not Reb Volkov. Borya's brother has spoken in favor of property restoration for the nobility. Reparations. You need to be charming."

"Reparations," Veronica said. "For the nobility." This wasn't exactly a cause for which she felt undying passion, but she supposed she could play nicely enough with Irina's friends. "I was hoping to see some paintings."

Irina swept her arm grandly. "The reception won't begin for a little while still. You have time to visit a gallery or two in the Hermitage. One of my late husband's ancestors helped Catherine acquire paintings for her collection. Now that I think about it, a show of good faith with reparations is the least this country can do to express gratitude." Irina lifted her hand up and let it rest on Sasha's shoulder. "You agree, don't you, darling?"

"It's not like I would complain. Oh, and hey . . ." Sasha moved forward, so the girls were left slightly behind. "I'm in charge of social media for the Society. So I set up a Twitter account. You're on Twitter, right?"

The last time Veronica had tweeted, she'd still been an adjunct professor. She'd mentioned an article on Alexandra and no one responded. Another Veronica Herrera triumph. "Yeah . . ."

Sasha steered Veronica away from Irina. "Live-tweet this party. Tell everyone it's awesome. I mean, it helps the brand, but it also makes us more visible for everything. Anything you want to do—politics or whatever. Make sure to get selfies with some of the guys. They'll love it." He whipped out his phone. "Are we following each other?"

Veronica fumbled for the phone in her purse and pressed her Twitter app. She saw the new follower and followed back. "@RussMonarch. Yeah, I got it."

"I'll retweet you so people get used to you without really shoving you down their throats, you know?" Sasha said.

"Nice image," Veronica told him.

"Exactly!" Sasha said. "It's all about image." He glanced over his shoulder and lowered his voice. "And if you want to tweet something about Reb, I say go for it." He winked.

She smiled up at him. "Thanks."

He patted her back. "Try to have fun."

"I'll try." Veronica looked around, wondering how much time Catherine and her Potemkin had spent in the palace. Maybe she would find their ghosts in the Hermitage, roaming the halls, examining the rich oil paintings in one of the museum's brightly painted galleries. She wondered what they would have made of an American woman, tottering on unfamiliar heels, ready to convince a roomful of fading ersatz Russian nobility that she was the proper representative for the Romanov throne.

No doubt Grisha Potemkin would have been a social media pro. He would have tweeted something witty about Veronica's upcoming appearance. And then he would have laughed and laughed and told her to have fun.

"This is a perfect opportunity to mingle," Dmitry said. "Many members of the Monarchist Society also support the Hermitage Museum."

The word "mingle" made her cringe, but Veronica didn't want to let Dmitry down. As they approached the foyer of the Hermitage Theater, she saw a poster board propped on an easel, a picture of Nicholas II, placid and affable as ever, surrounded by images of jeweled Fabergé eggs, ruby medallions, and a diamond-encrusted signet ring featuring a portrait of Catherine's grandson Tsar Alexander I.

"Smile," he whispered.

"No, don't do that," she groaned. "Never tell a woman to smile."

Dmitry seemed confused. "It is party. You are to have fun."

Given the situation, Veronica supposed she shouldn't default to her normal resting bitch face. She tried to fix her features into a smile.

Dmitry nodded a little too quickly. "Maybe think of something happy and let face do what will."

Still smiling like a fool, Veronica bent over her phone and typed:

Amazing party at Hermitage tonight! Thank you @RussMonarch!
Brilliant.

"Okay." She heard a Tchaikovsky concerto tinkling, the music coming from the other side of cream-colored doors laced with gilded curlicues. Dmitry touched her elbow, opened the doors, and gently steered her into the foyer. Under the light of crystal chandeliers, Veronica felt as though she had entered a rococo fairy tale. The room had been decorated with miniature pine trees trimmed in red, white, and blue bows seamed with tiny Romanov insignias, the double-headed eagle. Silver-haired couples circulated near small round tables set at a height made for drinks, canapés, and small talk. In one corner of the room, a man in a tuxedo played a grand piano. Long picture windows looked out over the dark and churning canal waters, waves tipped with beads of ice.

She heard a soft laugh with a sarcastic edge to it and abruptly turned her head. She realized, with a little jolt of annoyance, that she had expected to see Michael, had wanted to see him. But it was only an elderly gentleman at one of the tables, happily biting into a puff pastry topped with smoked salmon.

A waiter in a stiff white shirt came by with a tray of drinks and little cups of black caviar. Veronica accepted champagne and clutched the delicate flute as tightly as she dared.

"Several people from Society are here." Dmitry pointed to one of the couples lounging against a pastel-blue wall. They were both in their sixties, a red-faced man with a full head of pure white hair and a woman with perfect oval eyes but thin lips. "That is Borya and wife, Zenaida. His family has influence in city back to time of Peter the Great."

Veronica took a quick sip of the dry champagne and tried to look calm and approachable. The couple wore the same ribbon as Sasha. As her gaze traveled around the room, she noticed it on other guests as well. "What is that?" She gestured to her chest, where she might have pinned one herself.

"Oh. Back in vogue now," Dmitry said. "Is meant to show loyalty to monarch. To you. Please chat with Borya and Zenaida." He caught the eye of a woman on the other side of the room and waved in her direction. "Remember Borya's brother is in Duma."

"How could I forget? Irina wants me to charm him so he'll convince his brother to vote for reparations."

"Maybe he can do something for Reb as well." Dmitry looked her square in the eye. "You understand this."

"Irina has her ideas about the new Russia. I have mine."

"Excellent. I will check in with you soon." Dmitry gave a quick bow and headed to the other side of the room, stepping lightly across the slick floor. The pianist concluded the concerto and now the room echoed with animated conversations: skeptical Russian, precise English, and melodic French.

Borya and Zenaida seemed to take Dmitry's leaving as their cue to approach. Veronica rolled her shoulders back. Borya smiled widely at her, but Zenaida only took another sip of champagne. "Hello, Dr. Herrera!" Borya said in Russian. "Such a pleasure to meet you."

"Lovely," Zenaida added, a flat, unenthusiastic note to her voice.

Veronica extended her hand. Borya kissed it rather than shook it. There was a time when that might have surprised her, but not anymore. Borya then took a step back, while Zenaida took another drink and looked elsewhere. She smelled strongly of a rose perfume that reminded Veronica of her *abuela*.

"A secret daughter of Tsar Nicholas II," Borya said. "Who would have thought?"

"All of the other claimants to the throne have been distant relatives," Zenaida said. "No one took them seriously. Certainly no one took reparations seriously. But your grandmother claims she was Nicholas and Alexandra's daughter. And the Society vetted the evidence?"

Veronica took a moment to translate the last sentence in her mind. Zenaida didn't sound convinced. And had the Society vetted the evidence? A waiter, looking crisp and indifferent, passed by and Veronica set her empty champagne flute down on his tray. "Grand Duchess Charlotte was my grandmother."

"Another woman on the throne," Borya said, as delighted as Zenaida was skeptical. "The first since Catherine."

Veronica nodded as though this would make the conversation speed along.

"We never thought we would see the day." Zenaida focused on Veronica now. "You're so different than we expected."

"Really?" Veronica touched her hair. Michael had once told her she looked like Alexandra, only she couldn't see it. *Stop thinking about Michael.*

"We weren't sure what to expect," Borya added diplomatically.

"Who are your parents again?" Zenaida asked.

"My father was—is—Laurent Marchand, Charlotte's only son." Veronica tried to swallow down the hurt the name summoned. "My mother met him while she was an exchange student. He was a literature professor."

"Of course," Zenaida said. "And you were raised in California but speak fluent Russian."

"I was a historian," Veronica said. "I learned the language in graduate school so I could work with primary documents."

"Such a coincidence!" Borya said.

They didn't believe her. Panic descended and she started to babble. "I know it seems like a coincidence. But I was always drawn to Alexandra and Nicholas. My other grandmother had books about the Romanovs lying around the house when I was growing up. That part isn't a coincidence."

"So your mother knew your father's history?" Borya asked.

"She had an idea," Veronica said. "She didn't know everything, but apparently my father had hinted about his background. When she came home to California, she grew interested in Russian history, particularly the last Romanovs. And then after my mother died . . . my *abuela*—my other grandmother—took an interest in it as well. I think it was a way for her to stay close to my mother even after she passed away."

"But now you know," Zenaida said. "And you have grand plans."

"I don't know about 'grand plans.'"

"A strange situation," Zenaida said. "I didn't expect the Romanov heiress to be . . ."

Veronica shook her head. "What?"

"You don't look like we expected a Romanov to look." Borya cleared his throat in warning, but Zenaida would not be deterred. "No, no, you are very lovely. Only different than what I expected a Romanov would look like, that's all."

"What do you mean?" Veronica had a bad feeling she already knew what Zenaida meant.

Zenaida gave a dismissive shrug. "I think many of our members have been raised on the tale of the Snow Maiden and other traditions. You don't look Russian."

A rough knot chafed the back of Veronica's throat, as likely to turn into angry words as tears. Zenaida hadn't really said anything wrong. But wasn't that always how it worked? No one said anything overtly offensive—*you're a little brown for a Romanov, aren't you?*—only offensive enough to make you feel uncomfortable and awkward. In many ways that was worse. She wished she was the type to put it all out there, hashtag Russian racism on Twitter. Instead she wanted nothing more than to escape.

"Excuse me." Veronica slunk away.

As she looked around the room once more, it dawned on her how silly the couples looked with their outdated gowns and little ribbons, prancing around as though they still lived in the world of the tsars. These people were racist, homophobic liars. They only wanted to use her to sell their stupid restaurants and wine and key chains and whatever other nonsense they invented to make a buck, to get their family's property back and make even more money.

Forget it. She wasn't helping them. She wanted out of this place now.

She spotted Dmitry on the other side of the room, head bobbing as he spoke with a petite older woman.

Veronica was heading in Dmitry's direction when she bumped into a man with close-cropped gray hair, a thick black turtleneck sweater, and a deep tan. He was so tall she had to look up to see his face. He didn't wear the monarchist ribbon. He did wear small glasses with what looked like transition lenses. Veronica assumed he was a museum curator or an artist.

"Excuse me." She had no quarrel with the curators, but she didn't want to talk to anyone right now.

"You are the guest of honor," he said in Russian. "Where are you going?"

"To see my friend."

"You are Veronica Herrera, the heiress apparent?" His eyes, barely visible under the lenses, flickered with interest. His sonorous voice sounded familiar. "You are here to celebrate the exhibit? This is only appropriate."

"Yes," she said. "But I'm on my way out . . . I . . . I have another engagement."

"Can I have a picture at least?"

"Of course." Veronica only wanted out of there as quickly as possible. The man extended his arm and held his phone in front of them. She smiled.

He held the phone so she could see the picture and she nodded. It wasn't the greatest shot, but at least her eyes were open. "That's fine."

He started typing on his phone. "I will be the envy of all my friends."

"Okay." Dmitry was now sampling bruschetta and chatting with the server. She approached, tapped his back, and he jumped before he could take one.

"I need to go," she said.

"You are not having fun?" He said it like an accusation.

"I'm not feeling well. I think I need some air."

"What is wrong?"

She shook her head, feeling the pressure behind her eyes.

"We go somewhere else," he said, more gently now. "I know a place. Maybe relaxation is what you need tonight."

Veronica sat close to Dmitry behind the crowded bar. On a low stage, a raven-haired woman in a tight red dress sang a folk melody, mournful and frenetic at once. Veronica couldn't follow all the words but caught something about a *troika* lost in the snow. A bald man with intense eyes accompanied her on a *balalaika*. Every so often, he left the stage to serenade a table of laughing young women.

She had been skeptical when Dmitry suggested they head to Dumskaya Street. Despite the elegant arches, the nearby metro reminded her of Sunset Boulevard on a Saturday night: leggy blondes with spray tans, tight dresses, and outlandish heels that looked like ankle fractures waiting to happen. She had been afraid they might end up in one of the seedy karaoke bars, already crowded with drunken teens.

Instead, Dmitry led her to a café that reminded her of the little coffee shops and bars tucked away in Hollywood. Framed photographs of St. Petersburg landmarks were priced for sale on the forest-green walls. Patrons in the back of the café lounged on oversized armchairs with coffee and wine, sketch pads, laptops, and textbooks. Strings of orange lights like tiny fireflies looped along the walls.

Dmitry had loosened up a bit, removing his jacket and draping it carefully over the back of his chair before he sat down. He had unbuttoned the top of his shirt, perhaps one button too many, showing off a thick gold chain and a cross inscribed with Old Church Slavonic. On most Russian men, it would have seemed tacky, even thuggish. But on Dmitry she found it strangely charming. She had to admit she felt more relaxed now, although the vision of boarding a plane back to California, Michael in tow, still ran through her mind periodically.

"Are you religious?" she asked, gesturing to the cross after the singer had finished the last song in the set and the applause died.

"I am a believer."

"Reb's art—the way he portrays the church—doesn't bother you?"

Dmitry's jaw went rigid. "I do not believe everything Reb creates is respectful of church, but I defend his right to express freely. Besides, you and I agree government's issues with Reb have more to do with his . . . sexuality." He stumbled on the last word. "You know laws that Duma passed. Banning gay 'propaganda.' They want to make example of him."

Veronica adjusted her position so she could take a bite of her sweet cheese *blini* without jostling the man on her other side, huddled over his phone. "And what about Anya. The reporter? It seems as though the two of you might know one another."

Dmitry didn't answer, instead picking up a chopstick and poking at his plate of pink sushi. It looked dubious, but she had to admire the eclectic nature of Russian menus.

"Is there some history between you?" Veronica asked. "Does that make sense?"

He regarded her with a coy smile. "We have something far more important to discuss. What happened at Hermitage?"

Veronica took a sip of the wild strawberry soup she had ordered with her blini. The guy with the *balalaika* strummed the instrument again, warming up for the next set. He caught Veronica's gaze with his crazy eyes and she lifted her shot glass in his direction. The food was delicious and the vodka had loosened her tongue. She told Dmitry about her conversation with Borya and Zenaida.

When she finished, Dmitry remained silent for a moment, poking at his salmon roll. "I am sorry," he said at last. "I didn't realize they would say this, but I am not surprised either."

"I don't get it, Dmitry. I really don't. Alexander Pushkin is Russia's greatest poet, right? Beloved of all Russians."

Dmitry straightened his back. "Of course!"

"And Pushkin was proud of his African heritage. He spoke of it all the time."

"And he was admirer of my ancestor Grisha Potemkin," Dmitry added.

"Sure." Veronica raised her glass again. Now that she had gotten the incident with Borya and Zenaida out in the open she felt chatty, her mind buzzing and thoughts flowing. "So why is this country so damn racist and homophobic? I mean, these old, ultraconservative, überorthodox, xenophobic mentalities still abound."

"I am not sure what all of this means." Dmitry frowned.

"It seems like people have medieval attitudes," Veronica said.

"Not in Petersburg."

"In St. Petersburg too. I've seen the graffiti. I hate it."

"But I am Russian and even Christian. Do you think I am racist?"

"No, but that doesn't mean—"

"Do you think that I am . . . against gay people?"

"Obviously not when you're doing so much for Reb. But I feel as though these attitudes are so prevalent here that anything I do to try to change people's minds is pointless."

"Is not pointless. You will encounter people who think these ways, certainly within the Society. And for that . . ." He put a hand over his heart. "I am truly sorry. But you can do good here, provide strong voice. People will appreciate."

"Not Irina."

"Irina does have great influence, it is true. She knows enough people in Petersburg to help her acquire things she desires. But she needs money. And for money? For true security? She needs support from conservative Duma."

"Wait." Veronica narrowed her eyes. "What do you mean she *needs* money?"

"The way she lives. It is not like she has ever had real job. This is why she is wanting you to be advertisement for companies. But Irina does not represent us all."

The music began again, the strumming *balalaika*.

"I talk to Anya. You meet with Reb tomorrow morning, do you not? Eleven a.m.?" Dmitry reached in his front shirt pocket. She caught a glimpse of his little ruby, the Potemkin family talisman. "You know his reputation. Reb is great talent. This is privilege."

"I guess. But I'm nervous, Dmitry. Growing up in Bakersfield didn't exactly prepare me for this role. Being an academic certainly didn't, although I guess both professors and monarchs are guaranteed a job for life."

"You have people to help."

"I have a Potemkin at my side," Veronica said, smiling. "Only please don't erect any fake villages with cardboard peasants for my benefit. I'm as nearsighted as Catherine the Great, but I put my contact lenses in every day. You'll have a hard time fooling me."

"Now, you are historian, are you not?" Dmitry's baritone added silk to his voice. Then again it may have been the vodka playing tricks on her. "Surely you know the prince had enemies at court who spread rumors about so-called Potemkin villages."

"Do you have enemies?"

"As I say before, support for Reb will make enemies, I think."

The music grew louder and he raised his voice. "What about your friend Mikhail? How do you see his role? Once you are tsarina."

"I think he will make a good adviser."

"That's all there is? When I see him look at you, I think there is more."

"We were together."

Dmitry gave a short laugh. "You mean you were lovers?"

"Well, yes. What's so funny?"

"Americans are reluctant to say things as they are. Say what you mean."

"Fine. We were lovers."

"And now?"

"I'm not sure." Veronica took another shot of vodka and felt the slow burn in her throat. She tapped the glass back down on the counter. "Maybe I want a relationship like that, like what I had with Michael, to stay in my head, where it can be perfect. If it's real, something can go wrong. This way, I don't get hurt again."

Dmitry looked at the vodka and tilted his head curiously. The portrait of Prince Potemkin flashed in her mind. Dmitry leaned forward, cross on his chain dangling. His head hovered over her shoulder and his smooth baritone whispered in her ear. "Nika, give him another chance."

"Tsarina!" she heard. "Nika!"

Something bright flashed in her eyes. For a moment, she was blinded by blinking gray spots. When she could see again, she made out the startled look on Dmitry's face, and then the figure of a man who had been sitting next to her scurrying off the bar stool, clutching a camera, and hurrying out of the bar and out to the cold street.

Eleven

Mornings were difficult under the best of circumstances, when his mind played its queer tricks. Perhaps the soul desired to remain forever wrapped in pleasant dreams.

Grisha shielded his eye from the muted light streaming in through the high windows of the master bedroom. All of his muscles were spent. He had hoped to rest his hand on the softness of a feminine hip, or perhaps in a nest of sweet-smelling hair. He lifted himself, wincing at the pain in his shoulders. The silken sheets and pillowcases were still damp. The sable was gone, the fire in the hearth extinguished. He pulled the blankets tighter.

Praskovia had snuck out in the middle of the night. Some women were like men in that respect, good for a quick cuddle but then they disappeared, afraid of opening their carefully guarded hearts. But Praskovia had stayed through the night always; he often awoke to pry her lovely arms from his neck for fear of suffocation. Endless tears spilled as she spoke of the differences between Grisha and her husband, how he made her feel so much better about herself.

He wasn't interested in someone who loved him for how he made her feel. He wanted someone who loved him for his soul.

Grisha grabbed a lavender sachet from the basket stored near his bed and draped the linen over his eye. His thoughts raced so quickly they pained him. With Praskovia gone so soon, in a manner so unlike her, she must have had more in mind last night than simple sensual release. Grisha ran his hands through his hair, perspiration beading on his forehead. Perhaps pleasure remained part of the equation, but Praskovia had a keen and quietly ambitious mind. She had wanted something.

When he first returned to St. Petersburg, he had hoped to once again warm Catherine's bed. Now that seemed a faraway dream. He was old, broken, and Catherine was done with him in that way. She saw him only as an aging friend in need of small physical comforts. For all he knew, Catherine had sent Praskovia to him.

Grisha could not summon the name of one person who still loved him for who he was and not what he could do for them. How agreeable it must feel, to be loved for oneself and not for what one might offer to others, to have a family of one's own. But it seemed it was a happiness not meant for him.

He tugged on the top layer of bedding, a quilt Catherine had embroidered for him, with a makeshift design of curving arabesques in honor of his victories in the south. She had found the pattern during her tour of New Russia, in one of the old Islamic cities where they sat still to listen to the long musical call to prayer.

An image of Catherine astride her stallion flashed. Her shining eyes met his before she tied the gold tassel to the hilt of her sword. He had remembered that day when he read her letters insisting he take Ochakov. *Delay is death.*

After the siege, after his men had run the place into the ground, the leader still refused to surrender. He should have surrendered beforehand, should have known what was to come and set his pride to the side. That part was between the man and Allah. Grisha had delayed as long as possible, despite all good military sense. He could not lose his men to starvation and disease in the unrelenting winter. The death and destruction were the fault of the Ottoman leaders. Grisha had convinced himself of this truth and told the captured vizier as much.

Not a trace of guilt marred the vizier's expression as he bowed before him and praised his superior leadership. Gray wisps of hair encircled a round patch of baldness at the center of his head. This was no great leader before him but a broken old man. In an instant, he saw how easily their places might have been switched. Grisha may not have surrendered either. He wouldn't have wanted to look weak in Catherine's eyes. He'd ordered a pair of his officers to search for the man's jeweled turban among the rubble of his palace. He wanted to allow the man that small measure of dignity at least.

"And my lion," the pasha said softly. "Bring him for me, *giaour*."

Grisha made him repeat it, unsure he had heard correctly. He seemed to rise above himself for a moment and no longer saw the vizier at Ochakov, but Ghazi Hassan-Pasha himself. His mind was playing tricks on him again and the waking dream continued undeterred.

He saw the lion, lean and mangy with age, but still fierce as his master. The animal's golden eyes locked on Grisha's one good eye. One of the soldiers lifted his rifle.

"Halt!" Grisha had shouted. And the man turned, confused. Grisha strode over to him and lowered the rifle himself. "Have a damn heart," he'd muttered.

Grisha approached the lion. The beast sat back on its haunches, like one of the wolfhounds back at his own camp. A gold chain attached to its collar served as a leash. He thought the beast might pounce and avenge his master's humiliation by tearing him to pieces. Grisha hesitated and then tentatively grabbed the rope knotted at the end of the chain. The animal let out a sharp growl from the back of its throat. Grisha snatched his hand back. He tried again, more gingerly this time, and then they walked back to the pasha together. The lion tried to avoid stepping on bodies, but they were too thick and the bones crunched under paw and foot.

Grisha fingered the embroidered arabesques. His stomach turned violently and he feared he would be sick.

The point of war was to conquer in the name of their enlightened empress. He tried to focus on the cities he had constructed, the plans for the botanical gardens and concert halls and universities. Instead, he visualized the minarets of a mosque, crescent moons alongside the crosses of Moscow churches. Perhaps that would begin to make things right between himself and God. And Allah. And the pasha. Perhaps then the man would know some peace. Would cease visiting this world and be content in the next.

Grisha felt the sachet move and then damp roughness and the bracing impact of cold water on his hot skin as Anton pressed a cloth to his forehead. Anton had forgotten never to approach him from that side, where his vision was compromised and he could not see when someone was coming at him.

"What did you hear?"

Anton's boyish face entered his field of vision. Lines of concern marred his youthful expression and his eyes seemed watchful. Grisha saw fear in them as well. Anton had never observed the worst of either the malaria or the melancholy.

"That is not my concern, Your Highness," Anton said. "I sleep deeply."

Grisha laughed gently and let his hands rest on his stomach, as though he were a sarcophagus. "I meant after Praskovia left. I take it you did not watch us make love?"

Anton's gaze focused intently on the taffeta curtains and crystal candelabra, anywhere but the bed. Grisha thought that he needed to have his room redecorated completely, to reflect a simpler life of contemplation. Perhaps an icon of St. George slaying his dragon and a cross or two above the headboard.

"I only meant my dreams are often unpleasant," Grisha told him.

"You're delirious," Anton said weakly.

"I fear I may have shouted something disturbing."

"The illness is back. The servants say your visions of the past are at their worst then."

"You heard something that bothered you. I can tell."

"It sounds as though the last campaign was horrifying." Anton lowered the towel into the basin near the bed stand once more and then patted it on the sides of Grisha's face until his ears tickled. "I pray I never see war."

"I pray the same."

Grisha started to shake. It was a terrifying thing to shake so hard, helpless as an infant. Anton held him down gently until the tremors passed. "We should call a doctor."

The chill was an illusion, a mere fancy, same as the visions of the pasha and his lion, a reaction to his body's elevated temperature. And yet he craved warmth. Grisha pulled Catherine's quilt tighter over his shoulders. "A doctor can do nothing I can't do for myself."

"With all respect, I don't believe this is so, Your Highness."

Grisha tried to remain stern, but he was proud of the boy for daring to contradict him. "Doctors do more harm than good with their potions and talk. A doctor ruined my eye."

"I thought the Orlov brothers caused the injury."

"When Grigory Orlov realized I had won the empress's heart, he threw a punch or two in my direction, but those were mere scratches." Grisha tapped underneath his dead eye. "A quack did this. Afterward, I vowed always to be master of my own fate."

Melancholy began its descent. To fend off the darkness, he indulged in an image of Zubov manacled and marched off in chains. He couldn't think of anyone who would weep if the empress turned on her new favorite. Catherine might spend a night or two crying over the boy, but plenty of handsome men came to her court.

"Only last night you mentioned your ball. A masquerade. You seemed so happy. I hate to see you stuck abed now."

He remembered. He had spoken to the empress of a ball in her honor. He repositioned the sachet on his forehead. "Perhaps some music might help." The pace of his voice quickened. "I brought in new sheets of music for the orchestra. Perhaps we can hire a few of them to play here. I might like a tune or two, before I face the day. Summon the musicians to the hall."

Anton scuttled off and returned within a quarter of an hour. Grisha's orchestra had assembled in the hall. Their sheet music rustled and then he heard the notes he had found so charming at Catherine's supper, the overture to *Così fan tutti*.

The notes soared, punctuated with grand flourishes so lovely and visceral they took shape around him. Grisha lost himself in the music. His thoughts floated alongside the notes, bright strokes of energy. He envisioned streams and fountains meant to call to mind Catherine's cities in the south, a life-size statue of her, wall hangings of great female leaders of the past, perhaps a giant elephant.

Through the exquisite musical notes, a bell tolled to announce a visitor. Grisha could not wait for a servant to announce the guest. He grabbed a thrashed silk dressing gown and a long pink scarf from the floor, shooing Anton with his other hand. "See who it is. I have much to do."

Anton stepped back. "You need to rest."

"Go see, boy! Time is of the essence."

He watched as though through a gauzy curtain as Anton left the room. Grisha's heart raced in time to the music. Catherine had come. She wanted to see how he fared through the illness. She wanted to speak to him of the ball. Perhaps she had ideas of her own she wished him to incorporate. Her mind was not as completely occupied with Zubov as he thought. A renewed sense of purpose invigorated him, as though he might conquer the world once more.

Anton returned a few minutes later, muttering to himself like an old man. He kneeled at the side of the bed, voice low. "Platon Alexandrovich is here. Should I send him away?"

Grisha's joy collapsed in on him like a flimsy tent. Catherine had not come after all. And his palace was too far afield for Zubov to have stopped by for a casual visit. "I can see him. It's not the first time I've received in a dressing gown." Grisha used his elbows to heave his body upright. "Let him in . . ."

Zubov was already approaching Grisha's room, working his way through the musicians, glaring as they continued to play. He wore a greatcoat and clutched a walking stick with a gilded eagle attached to the end of it, as though taking a stroll through the palace.

"The prince is following doctor's orders?" Zubov asked Anton. "He looks a fright."

Anton ignored Zubov and bowed his head in Grisha's direction. "Your Highness, I asked him to wait at the door. I am sorry."

"The empress of all the Russias is sick with worry over her old friend." Zubov glanced at Anton with no more concern than a cat might give a small bug before crushing it. "She wanted me to see the prince with my own eyes."

"I'm fine," Grisha said, gesturing impatiently. "Come. Come. Only don't take too much of my time. We have much to accomplish. Anton, tell the musicians they may take a break."

"Yes, the prince and I require privacy," Zubov said, raising his thin and haughty voice to be heard above the music.

"It's all right. I trust Platon Alexandrovich will not see anything shocking. Perhaps he might even report back to the empress if he finds anything under the robe noteworthy." Grisha gave a slight laugh.

"I suppose if Platon Alexandrovich need not wear a wig to call on us, you need not bother to dress," Anton said.

"What?" Zubov snapped.

The fierce loyalty in Anton's eyes touched Grisha's heart. He couldn't have been prouder if Anton had been his own son. He let his next laugh ring out heartily. The boy nodded and backed out of the room.

Zubov waited until the musicians had moved and their footfalls were no longer audible. Then he tossed his pretty black hair out of his face and began to remove his coat, revealing a velvet frock underneath. Grisha slipped the silk dressing gown over his shoulders, fussing with it. He should have asked Anton to help him. The effort hardly seemed worth the time. He let the robe fall carelessly to his sides.

"Is it true you are married?" Zubov asked.

So he had heard Grand Duke Paul muttering after all. Their long-kept secret was out. Perhaps it had never been much of a secret in the first place. Grisha thought back to the modest ceremony over candles so many years before. They had been entirely enraptured with one another. Such love had filled Catherine's eyes. But he could not bear for anyone to think him an indulged pet and Catherine was not one to share her hold on power, even if a slip of paper made Grisha co-regent. They had promised never to speak of their union to others.

Now the truth was known. Still, it needn't be a weapon for Zubov to yield. Grisha fumbled with his robe again, playing the invalid, and then drew the silk around his shoulders as he rose from bed, feet only slightly unsteady. He didn't bother with slippers, nor to gather and tie the dressing gown around his expansive stomach. He found a few jewels in a small crystal dish on the nightstand. He gathered them in hand and began shifting them from palm to palm. "If I had a wife, she would hardly allow you to see me this way."

"You understand my meaning. Don't pretend otherwise. You and the empress. Are you married? I understand legal documents exist but are buried."

"If the papers are buried, surely a marriage is no longer valid.

This seems just as good as one of the pagan divorces the Anglicans obtain when the mood strikes them."

"No one wants it known the empress is an adulteress, even if the one wearing cuckold's horns is a worn-down, overweight, pompous ass whose time has long since passed."

The insult had been calculated to prick Grisha's ego in tender spots, but the boy's rage was clearly born of fear. Zubov tried to retain a passive exterior, but Grisha noted the twitch in his pretty lips and his fingers curling. Grisha almost felt sorry for him. He sank back on his plump pillows. "You heard Grand Duke Paul speak of this alleged marriage?"

"You still evade the question? Fine. If I withhold information, I know you will only send your spies hunting." Zubov took a seat on the same large Turkish divan Praskovia had lounged on the night before. "I have no legal papers in hand, no proof such a marriage exists. But yes, I heard Paul. And we discussed this topic last night, Catherine and I. Truth be told, we quarreled. She called you husband. It slipped. So now I ask you plainly."

He imagined Zubov and Catherine whispering in the dark over silk pillows. Perhaps Zubov had mounted some tepid insult in his direction, trying to confirm the veracity of what Paul had said. Catherine would have tapped Zubov on his broad shoulder and insisted he not make remarks about her "dear old friend and husband."

Grisha let the jewels sift through his fingers and back into the dish with a clatter. "If the empress wishes to tell you she will. I am at her command."

"If it is true, why not press a claim to the throne?" Zubov spoke so slowly, so carefully, it grated on Grisha's skin. "The empress has made her share of enemies. If you are the legal consort, it would be easy enough for you to gain favor. You might have ascended to power."

"I do not wish it."

"All men do. You styled yourself an emperor in the south. Even this so-called casual dress you wear . . . that Oriental robe and outlandish scarf. You look the pasha. All you need is a turban and a few more diamond rings to complete the masquerade."

"I am no emperor. I am a servant under the empress's command."

"It's not as though you lack ambition. You and I share that distinction from Catherine's other favorites." He leaned in close with a smug smile, voice lazy and measured. "Reconsider our previous conversation. We would make a powerful team were we to work together rather than indulging in these petty squabbles. Perhaps we might view your mosque as the first of many fruitful collaborations."

"You don't know me as well as you presume," Grisha said. "Ambition is a fleeting pleasure and I treat it as such. I nearly pursued a life in the service of God. Perhaps I still might."

"That is merely a different type of ambition. Now speak freely. Why have you left the throne to her alone when it might have been yours as well?"

"The truth? I loved Catherine. The throne is everything to her. Why would I try to take it? Why would I betray her that way? What does it all matter in the end?"

"Do you love her still?"

Grisha remembered Catherine's soft hand on his shoulder, the scent of her perfume. She was older now, but still beautiful as a sunset. When he had loved Catherine there were no dark days. Perhaps it was that memory he loved, and yet he saw no point in hiding this part of himself from Zubov. In truth, he wanted to see the boy squirm with jealousy. "Yes."

"And so you must hate me."

"I do not hate you. But Catherine's life, her command, and her legacy are all I have left in this world. Otherwise I merely linger uselessly in this life until God calls me to the next. You will understand when you are older."

"And you hold a special place in her heart even now," Zubov said.

The words pleased him, but Grisha merely shrugged.

"It is the truth. I should be a fool not to see it. I think you might destroy the empire and she would only say Prince Potemkin set the stage for the next incarnation of Rome. I could tie you to every woman in the capital and she would only praise your prowess."

Zubov must have sent Praskovia. But it would take far more to turn Catherine against him. Their relationship had moved past the shallow jealousies that plagued its infancy. Then again, that all might have been part of an elaborate act, her masquerade as all-powerful empress. Who could rise above such jealousy?

But Catherine had been born to play that role. The masquerade was her true self.

"Why won't you see me as a friend? What do you think I will do?" Zubov said. "Why must you stand so steadfastly against me?"

"I believe you are in league with Grand Duke Paul to undermine the empress's power. If I'm right, end it. End it all now. He is not worth your time. Only Catherine is worth your time. She is a great empress who has made history. He is a pimple. Hundreds of years from now people will speak her name with reverence and they will laugh at his, the same way they laugh now at his pathetic father."

"Why tell me all this, Prince? Is this part of an even grander plan? Perhaps you're not content to be emperor of the south alone. Are you looking for a crown in Poland?"

Grisha turned so that Zubov could see his face full on, even his dead eye. He remembered Praskovia in the instant before she registered his presence in the room, perusing the tracts. He had made plans to seek refuge and title in Poland in the event Catherine should perish before him without naming Alexander as her successor. He knew there would be no place for him in Russia under a Tsar Paul. "I look to preserve the empire and Catherine's legacy. That is all."

"Then why not support her in confronting those English fools? She could redirect troops from the south. Surely we do not need so many there anymore. We'll withdraw and let them run matters on their own. Aren't you supposed to negotiate peace with the barbarians? Hasn't the empress ordered you to return to your true place in the south?"

"The English will back down. We should wait it out and let them. A war on multiple fronts will destroy the Russian military."

"Grand Duke Paul supports war."

"The grand duke is a fool."

"I've seen his plans and they are well thought out. He's always had a special passion for military maneuvers. I don't think he's the fool you take him to be."

"That's because you never knew his father."

Zubov snorted. "Of course! Poor befuddled Tsar Peter III. Catherine's late and not lamented first husband. No, I did not have the pleasure. Died of hemorrhoids, did he? I suppose the Orlov brothers just happened to be in the same room when the attack struck."

Grisha willed himself not to chew on his fingernails. It was an open secret that the Orlovs murdered Peter and the story of hemorrhoidal colic had been an inelegant cover at best. Now Paul thought he could conjure his father's murdered ghost, as if he were some sort of modern-day Hamlet. And Zubov no doubt took tea with the grand duke and listened to his sob stories, lips twisted into phony concern.

"I'm not old enough to have known Paul's father, unlike . . ." Zubov pointed his hand in Grisha's direction. "But I do not think the two are anything alike at all. I understand the man was a petty and cruel sort of creature, no matter how Paul might sanctify his memory. No, I am no fan of the late tsar. Yet I think Paul is his mother's son, not his father's."

Grisha stumbled to his feet. "You wouldn't dare put Paul's priorities before those of the empress."

"Really, Prince." Zubov bowed his head. "Surely even the Asiatics you adore so much would feel some shame in the presence of other men."

His robe had fallen open, revealing his hairy chest, his bloated stomach, and parts farther south. He gathered it around his belly once more and adjusted the sash.

"You still insist on holding this ball in honor of yourself?" Zubov asked.

"Not in honor of myself. In honor of the empress's military triumphs."

Zubov rose to his feet. "I take it you will secure the empress's safety. Who knows what fellow, sick in mind, might take it upon himself to jump out of some shadowy corner and try to stick a knife in the empress over some drivel."

The image left Grisha so horrified that for a long moment he could not respond. "Every precaution will be taken."

"It is only that you are so clearly a man of another time, and I am a man of this age. I wonder sometimes if you consider the dangers that lurk in this new world. Honor is no longer in fashion."

"I will not jeopardize the safety of the empress."

Zubov nodded. "Consider coming aboard with us. We should make our own triple alliance, you, Paul, and me."

"You no longer consider such an alliance treason?"

Zubov twirled his walking stick, making it spin like a top on the floor. "I see now that the empress needs us united."

"The empress needs to avoid another war," Grisha said. "And take care around her son. He is more dangerous than you think, even if he is a fool."

"Every fool has his day. But then that day ends soon enough, I suppose." Zubov gestured in Grisha's direction. "I came here to see if you were indeed the empress's true husband or if that was merely another trick. I see now that it matters not one whit. You are ill and weak enough to sleep with a silly girl if she looks at you with big eyes. I was wrong to fear you might have some hold on the empress. She has affection yet but sees you only as an old friend with a damaged ego in need of her attention."

Grisha tried to straighten his back, but even as he did the weight of the boy's words sat heavy on his chest, paralyzing him. As Zubov took his leave, Grisha glanced back longingly at the quilt on his bed, wishing to sink back down under the covers once more.

He heard the patter of feet and Anton appeared at the door. "If he had not left of his own volition I would have escorted him to the door on his arse, Your Highness."

Grisha laughed, but ended up coughing. Anton frowned.

"I need paper," he said between hacks. "And a fresh pot of ink."

"If it's a letter you need, I can write that for you," Anton said. "My handwriting now mirrors your own."

"This one must be written by my own hand," Grisha said, glancing at the arabesques on the quilt. "It is to be in a code of my own devising and I will deliver it personally to the empress."

Twelve

FOR IMMEDIATE RELEASE

PRESS CONFERENCE SCHEDULED FOR ROMANOV HEIRESS
ST. PETERSBURG, RUSSIA

Dmitry Potemkin, spokesman for the Russian Monarchist Society, is delighted to confirm that Dr. Veronica Herrera will speak with reporters later this week to make an official statement regarding her ceremonial title and her role in Russian culture and politics.

ST. PETERSBURG
PRESENT DAY

Veronica punched her pillow and told herself she was being paranoid. The picture the reporter had taken of her with Dmitry Potemkin wouldn't make the papers. And if it did, why should she care? A surprisingly calm voice in her head whispered, *You don't want Michael to see it. You don't want him to think you're getting too close to Dmitry.*

Should she tell Michael what happened? Risk hurting him needlessly? She may not have kissed Dmitry but they had shared an intimate moment that could easily be misconstrued. Or maybe it didn't matter; perhaps it was too late anyway. Maybe she had blown it at the airport when she told Michael they weren't getting back together. She thought she had meant it. But if it was true, then why was she so restless now, so worried about what Michael might think?

Giving up on sleep, she reached for her phone, texting Dmitry:

I'M GOING TO GET BREAKFAST ON MY OWN TODAY. AND THEN HEAD OVER TO SEE REB. I PROMISE I'LL GET TO ANYA EXACTLY WHEN I'M SUPPOSED TO MEET HER.

And then, before she could change her mind, she texted Michael.

WILL YOU MEET ME AT THE HOTEL AT 8 A.M.? LET'S TALK.

To her surprise, he wrote back immediately:

I WANTED TO TALK TO YOU LAST NIGHT. I WANT TO HEAR ALL ABOUT THE RECEPTION.

She replied:

I KNOW. I WAS OUT LATER THAN I EXPECTED.

For ten minutes, he didn't respond. Veronica knew it was ten minutes because she stared at the faded red digital numbers on the cheap alarm clock facing her bed, which blinked three a.m., and then slowly counted out the minutes past three. A wedding party had gathered at a restaurant across the street from her side of the hotel and she heard them pouring out of the banquet hall, loud drunken voices over rushing gusts of wind and the blare of a car alarm.

Finally, she heard the ping of a text and grabbed her phone.

SURE. SEE YOU IN A FEW HOURS.

Veronica rose from bed, got dressed, and then paced for a short while before turning on the television. Someone on the other side of the wall banged furiously. She turned the volume down, missing home and Abuela's little couch, missing Abuela's hugs. She reached for her phone and earbuds and found her new-wave playlist. As the music played, her mind still raced, but at least she could lose herself in the lyrics.

At a quarter to eight, exhausted and loopy, Veronica headed to the elevator and pressed the down button. She gave a friendly nod to the floor attendant, glad when the doors sealed her inside, even if it still felt like a cage. She needed a few moments to gather her thoughts.

When she stepped into the crowded lobby, she spotted Michael at once. He was in the front of the dining room reading a newspaper and frowning. Behind Michael, service people in white hats loaded platters of steaming food into the silver trays of the breakfast buffet. It smelled delicious, but she had no appetite.

As she passed the front desk, a man checking in caught her eye. He wore all black and had a shaved head with a tattoo of an eight-pointed star on the back of his neck. He looked her up and down as though he recognized her. Dipping his head, he addressed her in a voice hoarse with old smoke. "You are on our side after all, little brown one."

Veronica's head shot up, but the man was now talking to a woman behind the counter.

She looked to see if Michael had noticed. He had one tense eye on her, but once the man moved away from Veronica, he returned to the paper. Any number of intriguing items could have been in that newspaper and Michael was a curious guy. Even so, a seeping sense of dread accompanied her every step.

She approached, heart galloping, and waved, but he didn't acknowledge her until she was right on top of him. Without even a hello, he opened the paper and held the page up to her eye level.

Veronica knew how weak the words sounded, how trite, and yet she could not stop herself: "It's not what you think."

"And what exactly do I think?" He spoke in the same droll tone she liked, but with a hard edge she hadn't heard before.

Two pictures. Michael's hand blocked one of them. She was in the picture she could see, forcing a smile next to the man who had asked for a selfie with her at the reception last night.

"I don't understand," Veronica said. "Why would anyone care about that picture?"

"You don't recognize him?"

Veronica shook her head. "He looked artsy. He was one of the Hermitage curators, wasn't he?"

Michael lowered his voice. "Vasily Turgekov. Does that name ring a bell? Haven't you seen any of his movies?"

That's why he sounded familiar. Veronica remembered an animated movie she'd watched in one of her Russian language classes in graduate school. Vasily Turgekov had played a sassy turtle. And then just as quickly an alarm went off in her head. "Oh!"

Vasily Turgekov was a self-described Russian nationalist, monarchist, and Slavophile, a devout Orthodox Christian, and a close friend of the Russian president. He had also recently told a journal in Moscow that all gay men should be "liquidated." The *Moscow Review*—Anya's newspaper.

"I didn't know," she said, horrified, shaking her head. "I didn't know."

"Veronica, now I'm afraid," he said. "Really afraid. I saw that thug in line. Now he thinks you're a homophobe. How will people like him react when you support Reb Volkov?"

"I'll be fine. It'll all be okay." Veronica wished she actually believed it.

"And what about this?" Michael moved his hand so she could see the other picture.

Veronica snatched the paper. Dmitry Potemkin's head was inclined toward hers. Veronica's eyes were closed and she had a serene smile on her face, as though she were waiting for her lover to give her a kiss.

She surveyed the article and got the gist quickly enough. The woman who said she was the Romanov heiress. Russia's newest celebrity playgirl. A helpful adviser named Potemkin. No doubt she had taken him as a lover, emulating her famous ancestor Catherine the Great.

She heard herself say again: "It's not what you think."

"Veronica, don't try to spare my feelings or anything pathetic like that," Michael said. "I need to know what's going on. I deserve to know. Don't lie, and I won't be upset."

Don't lie. Ah, the irony. He had lied. Everyone lied, didn't they? Massaging the truth was a self-protective instinct, one she should cultivate more.

"You're not the only one who was hurt in the past," he said. "You got screwed over by your fiancé. I got screwed over by my ex-wife. I know what you told me at the airport . . . that I shouldn't expect we would get back together . . . but I thought we were growing close again, that we were working past everything. I thought because we had both been hurt in the past, and understood each other's anger, maybe . . . maybe we were meant to be together."

She thought he would dip his head the way he used to do, so that he was looking up at her. Instead he took a step back, lips pressed in a tight line.

"But maybe it doesn't work that way. Maybe both of us are too broken." He ran his hand back through his hair and scratched his head. "Did you kiss him?"

At that moment, as far as Veronica was concerned, it didn't matter whether she had kissed Dmitry Potemkin or not. She had been attracted to him. Michael must have sensed this as well. Otherwise he wouldn't have been reacting so strongly. Guilt clouded her thoughts and she was tempted to confess. But a self-protective instinct still winked faintly inside of her. "No."

"You look as though you were thinking about it."

Her first impulse was to tell him fine. To hell with him. Who needed him anyway? But she knew she would regret it later and she was tired of living with regrets. "I'm not interested in Dmitry. Do you know what we were talking about when that photo was taken? You. Michael, it always comes back to you. Don't you understand that by now?"

Michael's features softened momentarily before returning to stone, his emotional walls as carefully guarded as hers. Her heart sank.

"Even if that is the case, you've compromised your position," he told her slowly. "The Society is ready to accept you and your claim. But this makes it look suspicious, like Dmitry might have a special interest in you and pushed you forward because of your relationship."

"I told you! There is no relationship! Who would even care about this picture?"

Michael nodded his chin. Slowly, Veronica took stock of the lobby. No one was touching her, yet she felt violated all the same. The American men she had seen at breakfast earlier in the week held copies of the newspaper, and they were all looking intently at the paper and then at her. She took a deep breath, forcing herself to remain calm. "I didn't say it wouldn't attract interest, only that it won't matter."

"They're interested," Michael said. "And considering what you want to do, getting involved with Reb, interest could be dangerous. That's the point."

"I hoped you would . . . I want . . ." She hesitated. She wanted to make sure she really understood what she wanted before she said anything further.

"What?" He looked away from her, moistening his upper lip with the tip of his tongue. "If you have something to say to me maybe now is the time to say it."

Veronica closed her eyes and drew in a deep breath. "Look, back at the airport, I shouldn't have told you I was done. It wasn't true." She opened her eyes once more. "Because right now I don't care about what they think. I don't care about the potential danger. All I care about is what you think. You."

She thought she saw a bit of the old magic in his eyes. "What are you trying to say?" he asked carefully.

I miss you. I miss how it feels when you touch me. I miss the smell of your hair. I just . . . I miss you.

"I want . . . I want us to do this together," she said.

"Come with me today then," he said, his tone urgent. "I'm going to talk to Irina about your grandmother's mysterious phone call from Laurent."

"Thank you." She put her hand on his arm. "But I need to meet Anya. She's taking me to Reb Volkov."

He threw his hands up in frustration. "How can you be so casual about all of this? You're going to see Reb? You understand where we are, right? In Russia?"

Veronica winced. He may have been trying to make a point to protect her, but he didn't need to act like a flippant jerk in the process. She had already put herself out there. She shouldn't have to tell him he was hurting her feelings. Thinking back to her conversation with Dmitry the previous night, she took another tactic. "You're overreacting. Besides, we're in St. Petersburg. Things are different here."

"Really? What about the graffiti by *The Bronze Horseman*?" He looked around self-consciously and lowered his voice. "You remember that?"

She shook her head. "I still think you're overreacting."

"Maybe you don't care if you're in danger, but I do. Your grandmother does too."

"It's not that I don't care," she said, defenses rising. "But it's why I'm here. To meet with Reb. To help him. I'm not going to abandon that now."

They looked at one another a moment more, but to her disappointment, Michael dropped his gaze first. She stared at his dark lashes and the curve of his forehead, wishing he would just hug her. Something. Anything to show the distance between them was closing.

"I'm not standing in your way," he said. "But at least be careful. For my sake if not for your own."

"But how could you not recognize Vasily Turgekov? He is one of our most famous public figures!" Anya's tiny car, a shaky product of some Eastern European factory, pulled into a narrow alley lined with a jumble of buildings, showing their age but newly painted in cheerful pastel hues of blue, green, and pink to counter the dull gray sky. "Don't you watch movies?"

"It's just been so long since I've seen him," Veronica said.

"He is a monarchist, you know. Is he funding the Society? Is he a friend of Irina who gets special treatment? A major donor?"

"I didn't know. I mean, I don't know if Irina knows him."

"You don't know. You don't know. But I know! I interviewed him. Me! I was so excited. I admired his early work. I wanted to think the best of him."

"I know. I know." Veronica put her head in her hands, trying to concentrate on the rattle of Slavic pop music coming from Anya's car radio. As they made their way down the narrow alley, Veronica peeped through splayed fingers. The last remnants of flowers and ferns clung to pots clustered haphazardly on balconies with intricate iron railings.

"But the things he says in the interview! And he *knows*." Anya pounded the steering wheel with one closed fist. "He knows Reb is my brother. He knows Reb is gay. And still he would say these things to me. Liquidated! Can you imagine?"

"I am so sorry, Anya," Veronica said. "I will make this right. I promise."

At the end of the street, a group of approximately ten young men and women had gathered with picket signs. The men sported hipster beards and the women had dyed their hair turquoise and violet. Veronica translated their Cyrillic signs in her head: "Free the Wolf," "Gay Rights Are Human Rights," and "I stand with Reb Volkov."

"Wow!" Veronica said, switching to English without thinking. "This is awesome."

Anya glared at her.

Veronica returned to Russian. "I only mean I didn't realize Reb's fans were so devoted. Have they been out here long?"

"Since the announcement of Reb's sentencing. It is nice of them to come, but it would be far nicer if the press covered their protest. Or if there were more of them." Anya leaned back in her seat and pressed her voluminous head scarf down so she could look over her shoulder as she made her first attempt to navigate a tricky parallel-parking space.

"The protesters come to his flat every day?"

"There may not be many of them, but yes, they are fiercely loyal, so they are here every day. Unfortunately, as you can see, this isn't a highly visible street. Not many people see them. Their online presence is much stronger. At least for now."

Anya made a sharp turn and squeezed her car into the space between a delivery truck and a long sedan with tinted windows.

When she pulled forward, Veronica was jolted in her seat as the car bumped the delivery van. The bump didn't faze Anya.

When they exited the car, the group of protesters approached, more curious than aggressive. A few faces paled as though they thought Anya and Veronica were part of the government's security force, ready to whisk Reb away to prison camp. Veronica waved at them and received blank looks in return. Had she really expected them to recognize her? To call her Nika? Tsarina? Not everyone followed celebrity gossip like that. *Get over yourself.*

"Nice building," Veronica commented once they were inside the lobby. They passed a set of crumbling metal mailboxes and trudged up precarious stairs that creaked under their weight.

Anya looked pointedly at the exposed circuit breaker and electrical wires dangling from sickly green wallpaper.

"I wasn't being sarcastic. I like the ambiance. This place would fit in San Francisco or North Hollywood." Veronica pulled her coat tighter around her chest, shivering. "Maybe Chicago or New York."

"Aesthetically, perhaps, but the truth is we might as well live in a separate universe."

"What do you mean?"

They reached the second floor and stopped at Reb's door. Anya raised a gloved finger to press the bell. "I would rather we stuck to our old Soviet concrete blocks if we had control over who we love."

The door opened abruptly. They were greeted by the beautiful face of Reb Volkov, all angles and dark hair and piercing blue eyes. He stood barely taller than Veronica and wore a white V-neck shirt with a wolf imprinted on it.

"This is her?" Reb said in Russian, indicating Veronica with a grand sweep of his hand. A giant orange cat perched across his shoulders and appraised Veronica with steady golden eyes, tail twitching. "The long-lost Romanov heiress? Our tsarina? Our grand hope?"

"She is the one," Anya said.

Reb eyed Veronica up and down. She returned the favor and took note of the black Velcro band around his lower leg and the slight bulge at his ankle.

"Oh, you noticed," he said, tapping his ankle. "Yes, this is what has become of me. Trapped like an animal!"

"Remember what they said," Anya cut in gently. "A two-kilometer radius around your apartment. Now, will you let us in?"

"Fine." Reb opened the door and beckoned them inside. The room smelled strongly of oil paint with an undercurrent of healthy male perspiration. A sultry male French voice, Serge Gainsbourg, Veronica thought, sang from an iPhone propped in a deck with speakers. Reb strode across the room, the cat still lodged on his shoulders.

"And another thing," Reb said, as though continuing a previous conversation with Anya. "What will happen to Caravaggio? I can't take him with me."

"If it comes to that, I'll take him in." Anya offered her hand to the cat and let him sniff and nibble at her fingers. She moved a few canisters of bushy-tipped paintbrushes out of her way so she could place her purse on a low bench in the corner of the room. She kept her phone in her hand. "But it won't come to that. You're not going anywhere."

"What if I do? He can't handle being away from me. Look at him! This is how he has spent his days since he was a kitten." Reb looked at Veronica, his voice still hostile, as though she were personally to blame for the animal's plight. "I found him curled up under *The Lute Player*. Just a ball of orange fluff who found his way into the gallery."

"He's a Hermitage cat. He's feisty. *He* will be fine." Anya adjusted her glasses so they sat farther back on her nose and then righted her *hijab*. "I'm not worried about Caravaggio. I'm worried about you."

Reb dropped down onto a low sofa that looked like it had come straight from a garage sale back in Bakersfield—a garage sale in the seventies. Canvases of Russian landmarks were tacked to the walls, left half-done on easels, drying near an electric fan with a blaring motor that almost drowned out Serge Gainsbourg. Red and black Soviet propaganda posters covered the back of the door and random paper balls hung from the ceiling. It looked as though Reb had either purchased the balls from a discount party store or made them himself out of papier-mâché. On the humming refrigerator, she spotted a large magnet with a reproduction of Caravaggio's *Lute Player*, the sad young musician, mouth half-open, gently cradling a rounded lute in his elegant fingers.

On the opposite side of the room, clinging inconspicuously to an easel, Veronica saw one of the paintings that had gotten Reb into so much trouble in the first place. She pointed to it. "They didn't confiscate your work?"

Reb stroked the back of Caravaggio's furry neck. "I managed to smuggle this one out by bribing a guard." He swept his hand in its direction. "What do you think?"

Veronica moved closer to the painting. Reb had painted the iconic swirling onion domes of St. Basil's Cathedral in Red Square. The cathedral was lovingly rendered, tilted at a dramatic angle so it appeared as though you were lying on the ground and looking up at the structure. Clouds billowed behind it, stark white against a cobalt sky, adding further drama to the scene. Part of the reason Reb had become so popular in the first place was his obvious love for Russian culture and the Russian soul.

Apart from the church, however, the rest of the painting was cartoonish. The Russian president stood in front of St. Basil's, chest puffed like an angry bear. He wore the robes of ancient Muscovy and a long beard. Anyone with even a passing knowledge of Russian history would think he looked like Ivan the Terrible. Behind this figure lurked two Siberian wolves, licking their chops. But they weren't eyeing the president. They were looking directly at Veronica, as though they intended to gobble her up for dinner and then spit out the bones.

Another figure in the background was clearly meant to represent an Orthodox clergyman in a high hat and vestments. He was masturbating.

"What's the matter?" Reb said. "You want to say something?"

Veronica knew nothing about art. And the painting was weird. One minute she liked looking at it, and the next minute she wanted to turn her head. She preferred the softness of *The Lute Player*. She resorted to the mantra of the graduate student who hadn't read an assignment: "It makes you think."

"Spare me the platitude. I want to know *what* you think."

"The way you've portrayed the church and the sky makes me wonder what it's like to be in your head. You must see the world in such a beautiful light."

"And the rest of it?" Reb asked.

"You've taken a sacred place," Veronica said, "and you've made it ugly. I mean, I get what you're trying to say. The oppression and absurdity. But I can see why some people were upset."

"Reb did nothing wrong!" Anya cried.

"Oh no, please, let the royalist speak," Reb cut in. "We know what a long history the Americans have of treating sacred spaces as such. Please, Ms. Bourgeois Capitalist Autocrat, render *your* judgment."

"I'm not saying you did anything wrong. I'm only saying that since it is such a sacred place and since you have the patriarch or metropolitan or whoever he is"—Veronica gestured toward the painting, struggling for a way to express it in Russian—"taking care of himself, perhaps an apology is in order."

"The church is a joke!" Reb said, pointing an accusing finger first at the painting and then at her. Miraculously, Caravaggio remained on his shoulders.

"The Society wants me to serve as the official representative of the House of Romanov. That means I'll work intimately with the church. I knew that before I came here. So I can't agree that the entire church is a joke."

"Oh! Well! Forgive me, Your Holy Majesty! Should I kiss your toes? Why didn't you just say that when you came in! I'll say I'm sorry and all will be absolved." He crossed himself carelessly, in the Orthodox fashion, from right to left.

"Why are you so angry at me?"

"You defend the precious Orthodox Church. You know what they think of me? Of gay men? Of gay women for that matter? They want us burned alive. You heard me correctly. And you know what? The other religious groups aren't any better. Not in Russia. Islamic clerics?" He glared at Anya's *hijab*. "Same thing!"

Anya sighed. "I don't think that way."

"A few extremists are making disturbing comments," Veronica said.

"More than a few! Religion encourages them to think that way. They say we're satanic. I say they're a joke. This is exactly what my great-grandfather in the Red Army fought against. But oh, I forgot." He ducked toward Veronica again. "These people are your friends."

She shook her head. His eyes grew wide. "So innocent." He grabbed his phone and tapped a few buttons. Caravaggio hopped down, shaking himself off and giving his leg a few quick licks. "I never should have listened to Dmitry. Me! Working with the Romanov heiress! Nobles are pigs. My great-grandparents fought with the Reds in the Civil War. The Romanovs were ignorant xenophobes who thought of nothing but their own pleasure. For all I know my great-grandfather might have had your great-grandmother, your precious Alexandra, arrested."

Veronica followed most of Reb's tirade but had trouble formulating a response in Russian. "I mean . . . obviously . . . that was a hundred years ago."

"You say you support me. Dmitry insists you can help and bring attention to what is happening to gays in Russia to the West and tells me all of the wonderful things you can do to help me. But how do you explain this?"

He thrust the phone in Veronica's face. She saw the two pictures from the newspaper that Michael had shown her earlier: Vasily Turgekov and Dmitry Potemkin.

"I told you there had to have been some mistake," Anya said, bending down to pet Caravaggio as he rubbed against her legs. "She says she didn't know who he was."

Reb held the phone up again and pointed an accusing finger at the phone. "Vasily Turgekov. How could you not know?"

"I am sorry," Veronica said. "I truly had no idea. I haven't slept much. Everything happened so fast last night."

"Oh, I can see that." Reb swiped the phone with his finger and showed her the other picture. "And this? You are in love with Dmitry Potemkin now?"

"What?" Anya grabbed the phone from Reb.

"I'm sorry, no. No. I . . . it's not what it looks like," Veronica told Anya.

"Again with the idiocy. You think Anya is in love with Dmitry?"

Veronica shook her head uncertainly.

"Heteronormative and bourgeois. I should have known." Reb swiped the phone again and showed Veronica another picture. In this one, Reb held Dmitry in front of St. Basil's Cathedral as they gazed into each other's eyes.

It took Veronica a few seconds. Reb was right. She was heteronormative. "Oh!"

"I told Dmitry he should come out." Reb shoved his phone

back in his pocket. "He thinks he can help better this way. But now I wake up to this? To these idiots in the Russian media declaring the love of my life has fallen for a woman? An American woman? A noble?"

"He has not. My God, Reb. Ever since I met that man he has done nothing but talk about you. You're right. I was looking at the world like a stupid straight girl. If you were a woman I would have figured it out immediately. He is desperately in love with you."

Reb bent to stroke Caravaggio. "The people I love most in this world—Anya, Dmitry—tell me to trust you. But a royalist can never be trusted."

"I'm not a royalist," Veronica said. "Tsarina is only a ceremonial title. I want to use it to help you in any way I can."

"Why? I hear the Society is interested in reparations for the noble pigs. The rich get richer. Why should I believe you want to help me?"

Veronica raised her hands helplessly. "Because this is all I have left. The Romanovs haven't held the crown in nearly a hundred years. And maybe this is just a ceremonial title, and maybe it's silly, but this is it. This is what I have in my life. And I want to make a difference. I know that sounds dramatic, but it's how I feel."

Reb arched his beautiful black eyebrows in a wonderfully skeptical manner. Veronica realized Russians were the last people in the world who would worry about being "dramatic."

"I want to do what's right," she said. "At some point I have to say I'm in charge of my life, not my doubts."

Reb folded his arms in front of his chest, appraising her.

"I am going to do this. I am going to help you."

"Let's pretend I believe you. Let's say Dmitry and my sister are right." He gestured to Anya. "But I am not going to apologize. Can you deal with that?"

"At one point an apology might have been worthwhile," Anya said, resting a steadying hand on Reb's shoulder. "But it has come too far for that now. This sentencing must be opposed completely. Nothing but complete absolution will do now. No apologies."

"But it might save him from prison," Veronica said.

"I'm willing to make some statement saying we have the right to worship as we see fit, blah, blah, blah. The Soviets wouldn't let us worship. I get that. I have no issue with the flock per se. Dmitry seems to get something out of the services. But their leaders spread hate."

"Unchristian hate," Veronica offered.

"Perhaps," Reb said. "But the church is infested. I won't apologize for ridiculing that. And when the flock goes along with what the leaders say? To hell with them."

"I see," Veronica said. "I think we can work with the statement you want to make."

"Work it as you will," he said. "Just beware." Reb took a step forward, eyes flashing. "I caught you on TV the other night. You were avoiding the reporters but I saw your two men."

That had made it onto television? "They're not my men."

"Dmitry can take care of himself. He gets that from his imperialist ancestor. But what about your other man? The tall one that came poking about pretending to be a Romanov pig. Can he take care of himself?"

"I think so." *Take care of himself? What the hell does that mean?*

"Aha!" Reb said. "That is the one. You were in love with him; at least Dmitry thinks so. Do you love him still?"

Anya raised her delicate black eyebrows, looking much like her brother now, and watched for Veronica's answer.

"I . . . maybe . . ." Veronica stumbled over the words. "It was a while ago."

"Not that it matters. But perhaps you do understand love. That will help." Reb stepped forward. "This is what I want you to do. Dmitry had an idea. I think it is a good one. We are organizing a boycott of Russian vodka in bars across Europe and even one or two in your country, from what I understand. This will be a coordinated protest starting with your press conference. A show of solidarity against the anti–gay propaganda law. But understand that our government will not be pleased." He clapped his hands and his cat darted under a chair. "They might arrest you. That is what they do. That is the risk you will take."

Anya held her phone up a little higher. Veronica suspected she was about to record her. "Will you do it? You'll support this protest for our new Russia?"

Veronica hesitated, her heart loudly thumping in her chest. She didn't even know what was happening inside to hold her back; only some deep and as yet unspoken fear blocked her words. And then the tattoo of the eight-pointed star, the hoarse voice of the man at the hotel came back to her: *You are on our side after all, little brown one.* Now Reb was asking if Michael could handle himself.

But when she realized Reb was still looking at her, she said: "I'll do it."

Reb scowled. He didn't believe her. He saw that she was scared. And she was. Of course she was. She might be forced to stay in the country under some pretense or another and then who knew what would happen to her. But that didn't mean she wouldn't do it. She only needed to figure out how to convince Reb she meant what she said.

Thirteen

ST. PETERSBURG

APRIL 1791

"Are you certain this can't wait even another day?" Anton frowned and gave the wig another pummeling with the brush. "You're still not recovered."

"On the contrary, I have never felt better." After the frenzy of the last several days of preparations for the ball, Grisha's body was worn to exhaustion, but his mind still raced.

"I'm sure the empress won't mind if you delay your visit." Anton's gaze wandered to Grisha's desk, where possible designs for the theater stage Grisha planned to erect in a back room were scattered about, alongside discarded drafts of letters he intended for Catherine but lacked the focus to complete. "And perhaps the ball could wait as well."

"I have no desire left in this world but to see the empress and tell her I love her. It is why God has called me here. It is my purpose on this earth."

The music had stopped. Why had it stopped? Grisha strode toward the bedroom door and stuck his head out in the hall. His musicians were shuffling through their sheets. "*Marriage of Figaro*," he said, clapping his hands. "You've put me in the mood for Herr Mozart. Surely you have it on hand."

Grisha turned back to the mirror, frantically humming the opening notes of the overture. He affixed the medallion of Catherine to his coat, near his heart, and then stepped back to evaluate the effect. Though he would never admit it to Anton, the ashen pallor of his face worried him and he was having trouble focusing his good eye.

He imagined Zubov whispering to Grand Duke Paul: surely Grisha's mind was impaired by his illness and his judgment suspect. And then the fuss the tsarevich would make in front of his mother. He had seen enough of Paul's bitterness, his harshness with his soldiers, and his rudeness to Catherine. He was more than a troublesome fool. He was dangerous.

And then there was the matter of Praskovia. He felt poorly about what had happened, but not so poorly that he was willing to throw away Catherine's heart as penance. "Have you learned the whereabouts of my guest from the other night?"

Anton lowered his head, cheeks flushed pink. "She has left the city."

"Without as much as another word to me?"

"Apparently."

Grisha leaned against his bureau, hoping Anton wouldn't notice he couldn't stand of his own volition. The boy might get cheeky and tell Catherine something was wrong. So be it. If need be he would fight them both, but he was getting to Catherine one way or another.

Anton took another tack, his voice wheedling and tender as he stepped on a footstool and placed the wig on Grisha's head. "You've been rushing around occupied with plans for the ball. Everything is proceeding marvelously! What will another day or so matter?"

Grisha's head felt as though it were ready to implode. "What is it you fear then, little man? You think I see too many ghosts? That the horseman will chase me through the streets?"

"Perhaps another few days' rest will do you good."

"Do you imagine you are somehow in charge because I've been lenient?"

Anton winced. "I thought nothing of the sort, Your Highness."

The music restarted, quick and vibrant. Perspiration collected underneath the wig, making his hair sticky. As soon as he was out of Anton's sight, he would rid himself of the damn nuisance. Except he couldn't imagine how he would make it to the door, let alone into his carriage, for the ground kept undulating like waves of a great sea beneath his feet. He tried to hum along to the music but had to stop abruptly when his breath caught in his throat and a fit of coughing wracked his chest. He imagined Catherine fretting over his condition and Zubov stroking that damn chattering monkey while mentally calculating how many weeks Grisha had left in him.

"The empress will send you right back here. And she'll blame your folly on me."

Grisha chuckled. "Ah! So you're afraid of the woman now, are you? At last we get to the true heart of the problem. I assure you all blame will lie squarely at my own feet, as always."

Anton stepped lightly off of the cushioned footstool and straightened his new waistcoat over his chest. Grisha smiled at him fondly. This is what it would have been like to have a son. What an amazing child he and Catherine would have had, an heir or heiress to the empire eminently more worthy than Paul. How wonderful it would be to see the reflection of his own features mingled with Catherine's in a boy's face, Grisha's auburn hair and Catherine's blue eyes.

"The empress adores you." Anton paused in a dramatic fashion that refocused Grisha's wandering thoughts. "Even if Zubov fights with you. At least let me come with you. I'll see to the horses and driver myself."

"Fine." Grisha tried to sound grumpy about it, but in truth he was grateful for Anton's presence. He might give Grisha exactly the amount of vigor he needed to face Catherine and speak his mind plainly, with no further games between them.

"You've heard the news then! My agents abroad inform me England has backed down." Catherine stood at the door of her study, twirling her fan. "It seems the people of that land are not willing to send their men to war over the faraway Black Sea. And the leaders must cave to the will of their people. Perhaps there is something to be said for a democratic form of government after all."

"This is wonderful, *matushka*," he murmured.

"And Prussia will back down now as well, the cowardly toads."

"I knew they would not dare cross you."

"You were right not to pursue a policy of war. This will teach me to pay more attention when you speak." She tapped Grisha lightly on the shoulder with the enameled base of her fan and he tried to smile, but even such a light touch smarted in his feverish state.

"I did not ask to see you merely to collect accolades." He tried to say more, but his throat felt rough and he bent over in a spasm of coughing, chest seizing at the effort. When he worked his way upright again, he saw Catherine's brows had pinched and she'd paled underneath her rouge.

She swept him immediately into her study, past the sniveling guard with the Hapsburg chin. "You should be under a doctor's care."

Grisha wasn't above playing on her sympathy. He missed her mothering. It made him feel worthy of love. He allowed his composure to crumple as he lowered himself into a bow. She guided him to an oversized settee, so different from the fragile and un-comfortable chairs normally reserved for her guests, and he let his limbs sprawl. "I am sorry if my appearance frightens you, *matushka*." He had abandoned his wig. He withdrew a linen from the pocket of his jacket and patted the perspiration from his brow. "Only I needed to see you."

"You look a fright. Why can't you rest and be at peace?" Her tone was scolding yet still throaty and desirable. "Now I hear you run yourself ragged over this masquerade. These are the golden years when you should relax."

"One could say the same of you, wife."

"You forget that I was born in a Germanic land. Work is my enjoyment."

"I may not share your Teutonic heritage, but it is the same for me. You know that."

She continued twirling her fan, shifting it from one small hand to the other. He thought no other woman who walked this earth had ever managed to look so regal and sensual at once. He doubted even Elizabeth of England, with her red hair and clever little face, had achieved a majestic aura as perfect as Catherine's. "The recurrence of this illness will be the death of you."

"I have inhabited this earth over fifty years. When the time comes, I intend to accept God's will without complaint."

Catherine tapped her slippered foot on the floor. She had always found God an unwelcome competitor for his affection. "How can you be so casual? Your life may be a small thing to you, Prince, but it is not so in my eyes. Do I not need you?"

"It gives me great pleasure, wife," he told her, "to learn you still care. I thought your affections had dimmed."

"Both of our affections dimmed," she shot back. "Yet I manage to care for myself and not let this world slip from my hands. Why won't you go to a doctor?"

"I went to a doctor with a damaged eye." Grisha lowered his head, hiding his dead eye from her view. "And you see how well that turned out."

"Be grateful your affliction never impeded your work. And you still have so much more work ahead of you in your New Russia. You must finish the peace negotiations."

He shook his head, at a loss for how to explain that it didn't seem worth it to visit a doctor and yet at the same time he was not ready to stop clinging to life. "After your little friend Zubov came to see me I grew worried."

That stopped her in her tracks. "I did not know he had come to see you."

"He has grown close to Paul."

The light of affection that had glistened in Catherine's eyes a moment before went out. Catherine rose to her feet, her calm face hovering above him. "Let me worry about Paul."

"They sent Praskovia to spy on me."

"That silly girl is no spy." Catherine pressed her hand to Grisha's forehead, summoning memories of her hands on him in moments of passion. "But they shouldn't have sent her. She has worn you ragged, I suppose. Is she to blame for your state? Look at me."

The need to obey her wishes overpowered the humiliation of his dead eye and bloated body. He looked into her face, gazing with the adoration that in truth had always been part pretense. And yet there had always been genuine affection as well, even after the passion had mostly died. A whisper of it always remained. He saw the brightness still in her eyes and the traces of wrinkles, in spite of all her luxuriant creams, marring the symmetry of her face but adding character to it as well.

"I love you, wife," he said simply. "I have always loved you and I always will. I only wanted you to know, to hear me say it plainly. I am composing a letter to you to express my feelings but could not wait until the words had been perfected."

She leaned into him and pressed her lips against his. Even in his lowest moments, Grisha had never rejected pleasure. He had always thought pleasure God's means of counteracting the miseries faced every day.

But Catherine's kiss did not inspire passion, only affectionate nostalgia.

"You tell me you love me, and yet I feel you are a stranger to me," she said, pulling away. "How could we have let ourselves come to this? Weren't we meant for more?"

"We agreed our ambitions were best kept separate," he said quietly.

"Couldn't we determine a way we could tolerate one another? Why do you make my life such a trial?"

"I wish to make your life a joy every day."

"Then why will you not become friends with Platon Alexandrovich? It has worked so well for us in the past, the families we created together, and the contentment."

"I don't begrudge you the other men. Truly. I have always thought no one could replace me. But I miss the intimacy between us."

"I have thought the same, husband. I thought I could handle other women as long as I still held a special place in your heart. But the women were so young and beautiful. Praskovia might be one and twenty if she is a day. How could I compete?"

"You have always held the only true affection in my heart." He extended his hand tentatively but could not quite bring himself to caress her.

"We should never have come to this place. We should only have relied on one another as every other man and wife."

"I may be like other men, but you are unlike any other woman who has walked this earth. And I have loved you since the moment I saw you."

Grisha took her wrists in his hands and drew her close, pulling her on top of him in the settee. She softened at once in his arms and he felt her tiny heartbeat fierce against his chest. He pressed his lips to hers, parted them gently, and kissed her as ardently as when they were first together, after she had convinced him to return and pursue a life with her. When he had been willing to forsake everything else if only he could feel her tremble in his arms and know she belonged to him as he belonged to her.

Tears stained the powder on her cheeks as she pulled away. "Tell me you are not here for my patronage. Tell me you are here only for me."

Grisha still held her wrists tightly in his hands. It would have been so easy to deny that one had anything to do with the other. Where was his shrewdness? His impulse for self-protection? Candor had always been of the utmost importance to him, and in this moment he hesitated.

As quickly as she had come into his arms, she withdrew, freeing herself from his grip and straightening her long gown. He felt the chill in the air. The pasha was in the room. Perhaps he had been there all along. But he could not see him. There was only Catherine.

"I love you," he told her. "I have always loved you."

"Is it truly the only reason you make love to me now?"

Grisha felt as though he were being suffocated and he wished she would open all of the windows, let the cool air in, anything to calm him and allow him to breathe freely once more.

The words slipped. "Now that Zubov has agreed, will you allow me this last wish for the mosque? I've heard nothing further of it. When will construction commence?"

Sighing, she rose and took a seat behind her desk, still in close proximity to the settee, but it might as well have been on the opposite end of the empire. "Can you no longer speak of love without requesting a token to cement your own glory?"

"This is no mere token. It is for the good of our empire. It does not diminish my feelings for you."

"And what of Poland? Of your ambitions there?" She began to finger a carnelian rabbit, one of the trinkets on her desk. "Do you wish to be king of that land?"

Grisha reached into his pocket, but he had forgotten to bring his jewels, or even a bit of radish or turnip. He gnawed on his thumbnail. "What has Platon Alexandrovich told you?"

"He fears your ambitions have grown twisted and you truly believe you share power with me. I have eyes and ears. I know you wish to make your power known in Poland."

Though it seemed less and less likely of late, Catherine might leave this earth before he did. All he wanted was a safe haven should Paul ascend to the throne. But he didn't dare explain his reasons, to articulate even the possibility of her death. "Only in your name, *matushka*."

"Aren't you happy with your New Russia? Must you encroach into my domain as well?"

Perhaps Cleopatra and Mark Antony had the right idea, to end their lives willingly before matters came to a head, before the final humiliations. He imagined Zubov and Paul in another corner, staring at him as he struggled for breath.

"You are trying to have it all," she said. "As you always have. You want my affections but need more. You behave as any man toward a woman. Only looking to feed your own precarious ego. It isn't enough merely to satiate your whim. We must also pretend— no, believe—that your whim is our greatest desire."

"Do not compare me to your other men. My ego has never required such attention."

"Exactly my point," she said. "You show yourself as a mere delicate man at last."

"And what about you?" He gathered his energy and rushed toward the desk, so close to her that she stood and took a step back. "Will you speak of me as the grand love of your life while Platon Alexandrovich shares your bed?"

He thought she might slap him. He was no stranger to slaps from women, but Catherine would not stoop so low. "You presume to tell me with whom I can and cannot share my bed? After all the women you have seduced?"

"We are husband and wife," he shouted, no longer caring who might overhear.

"Husbands may take a wife and then as many mistresses as they please. But a wife must remain faithful no matter how far her husband strays? I never took you for such a prude. I think you wish to change the parameters of our singular arrangement not because of any great change in your feelings for me, but only because you grow selfish in your old age."

"Your silliness with Zubov is a whim. Discard him for me. Be with me . . ." His voice trailed off. He gripped the desk for support. He felt tears slipping down his cheeks. His thoughts returned to the monastery, the rhythm of the liturgy and the smoky-sweet incense. The icons in a blur of color around him and the birch trees outside the high windows.

Catherine moved away, but her gaze lingered on him still. "I forgive you for your harsh words because it is clear you require rest. I wish you a safe journey home, Prince."

He waited. He felt her hand on his shoulder. But that was all. Pity. That was all she had left for him.

Grisha limped down the marble staircase, arm draped around Anton's shoulders. His steps felt unsteady, even underneath the thick soles of his boots, and he found it increasingly difficult to hide his shivering. Perhaps the ghostly horseman would chase him all the way home. He shouldn't have tempted fate by mentioning it earlier in the day.

"You can't make me leave." He knew he was ranting but could not stop himself. "I only require a few more moments. The shouting was only our passion."

"She asked me to take you to the court doctor."

"I am your master. You will take me home."

Anton's voice was not unkind, but it remained firm. "First of all, you're not my master. You saw to that yourself. I am no serf bound to you by law. Not anymore. Secondly, even if you were my master, your orders would not outrank those given by the empress." He paled. "She said she would flay me alive if I didn't get you to a doctor. I told you she would blame me for letting you out."

Grisha had to stop and chuckle, but the laughter soon changed to coughing as his body rebelled at the effort. "She said that, did she? And she would attend to the matter herself rather than set her guards on you with one of the vicious rawhide knouts they so enjoy wielding."

"That's right." Catherine came bounding down the stairs, skirts flouncing, a greyhound nipping at her ankles, relishing this unexpected bout of play. "And I would hold true to that promise except obviously you have given this boy more trouble than I anticipated. Really, Prince. Will you force us to carry you all the way to a doctor?"

Anton tried to bow to Catherine but couldn't do so without releasing Grisha and having him tumble down the stairs. At least Catherine's playfulness had returned. The quarrel between them wasn't as dire as he'd feared. But he detected distress in her voice when she lowered it to speak to Anton. "I will help you get him to his carriage. I've never seen the attacks this bad before. Something is wrong."

"My lady, I must beg you not to do that." Zubov now rushed down the stairs behind them. Had he been hiding in the shadows? Listening in on the most intimate moments of their interaction? Grisha wished he had enough fight left in him to challenge Zubov to pistols at first light, as the French and English gentlemen were so fond of doing when they felt their honor under siege. But fatalistic as Grisha felt, he had no desire to risk losing his other eye.

"The prince makes his own poor decisions," Zubov blathered. "He conquers the Turks, crushes them underfoot, and then wails for a mosque. He earns glory on the battlefield and then urges restraint when younger men might earn similar glory. He demands too much of your time and treasure."

"Oh hush," Catherine said under her breath, and Grisha thought she sounded as though she were talking to a child rather than a lover. Or perhaps one of her dogs.

"He is manipulating your affection to further glorify himself and his morbid designs for greater power," Zubov insisted, oblivious to Catherine's mounting annoyance. "I hear that he has his sights set on becoming king of Poland now. As though the south were not enough for him. I wouldn't doubt this sudden spell is a farce to distract you from his dalliances. He has used you and betrayed your tender feelings. That is treason, I think."

"I have served the empress well." Anton reached for his head again with a damp cloth, but Grisha batted his hand away. "Despite your interferences."

Catherine raised a gloved hand, still moving quickly to the front door. "Enough! If I want to see fighters tear into one another, I'll purchase bantam cocks. Not one more word. I'll make sure Prince Potemkin is attended to properly. Then I will return and we shall discuss this no further."

She nodded to two figures by the door. Her guards, a pale Cossack in embroidered gold and a North African in a fez and scarlet waistcoat. They opened the door, and Grisha blanched at the blast of chilly evening air. Farther out, he spotted his coach and six dappled geldings.

"I must see the prince home," Catherine said. "Get him into his carriage."

The guards appraised Grisha's large frame and the pale one winced.

"I will accompany him myself," Catherine added.

"You can't do this," Zubov began to sputter. "It is unseemly. Even if he is your husband, you must not treat him like a cherished pet."

Zubov seemed to know he had gone too far. He couldn't look Catherine in the eye.

She marched toward him. "I supposed it would get out sooner or later. Your manly virtue is offended? It seems I've made an adulterer of you. But then perhaps you don't mind so much seeing as how you have put the cuckold's horns on the prince. Isn't that what you truly want, love? To humiliate your rival? Shame on you."

With that, the guards at the door hoisted Grisha onto the padded cushions inside his carriage. Catherine shooed away the hands the guards offered to help her. She lifted her long skirt and made her way to his side. "And no arguments from you either," she told him as Anton climbed in behind her. "The last thing I ever wanted to become was an old woman bickering with my doddering husband."

When the carriage shot off, she tucked a thick fur blanket around his lap while Anton held him upright, hands shaking, no doubt due to being in such close quarters with his sovereign.

The horses jolted over bumps and potholes in the cobblestone road. Grisha tried to focus on Catherine's face as his body slowly relented to pain. "I told you we needed to pay better attention to the infrastructure of this city. Hasn't Zubov attended to any of it?"

"Why do you begrudge me this happiness?"

"I am not asking you to abandon happiness." The chills wracked his body and he started to shake. "I believe with all my heart that your true happiness in this world is with me."

Catherine moved her hand to Grisha's forehead, her touch cool and light on his feverish skin. "Voltaire told me once he thought a female ruler might be rid of such distractions. I never had the heart to tell him he was wrong. We are all enslaved to our bodies, men and women."

"You were never enslaved. You only made a poor judgment or two."

"You have always helped me avoid poor judgments."

"You will rid yourself of Zubov then?" he asked, heart soaring. "So that we might be together again, as we were meant to be?"

"Care for yourself first, so that you might be of greater use to me now and in the future. I expect you to be around for a long time. I require it."

She had avoided his question, but he hadn't yet abandoned hope. Only the fever was growing worse and his eyelids had started to droop. Her voice still sounded in his ear, but she seemed to be speaking to him from much farther away than the confines of the carriage.

"He's slipping again," he heard Anton say.

"But you cannot do this," Catherine insisted, imperious once more. "How can you leave this earth without finishing your work, your great projects in our New Russia? You are to negotiate a lasting peace with the Turks. It is your duty, Prince. Don't shirk destiny."

The carriage came to an abrupt halt, shaking him back into the moment. The driver opened the door, allowing a blast of cold air into the coach.

"Your guards," the driver told her. "They must speak to you now."

Catherine scowled. A minute later, her personal guards were at either side of the carriage, astride their white stallions.

"Forgive us," the one nearest her said, removing his tall, feathered hat. "But we wouldn't have stopped you unless absolutely necessary. You're needed back at the palace. Platon Alexandrovich is raising a terrible ruckus. He won't stop. He demands you return."

"Oh dear Lord," Catherine muttered.

"We can ensure the prince gets to the doctor."

Catherine cast a regretful look at Grisha. "I'm afraid to let you out of my sight. Who knows where you might end up this evening?"

"I'll see to him," Anton told the empress. Grisha detected a quiver in the boy's voice as he addressed Catherine, but otherwise he remained strong and Grisha flushed with pride. "I'll make sure he gets the medical attention he needs."

"You won't let him drag you to a brothel or a faro table instead?"

Anton reddened. He attempted to answer, but Grisha watched his lips move as he stumbled on his attempt at words.

"I can assure you I'm in no condition to do anything of that kind," Grisha told her.

Catherine rested her hand on his shoulder again. "Very well. But I am holding you to this." She slanted her fan at Anton. "Once I've attended to this nonsense, I will check on you."

The guard opened the door, hand extended, ready to escort Catherine to a waiting horse. Grisha wished he could have been the one to offer her a hand and help her out, a service he had offered many times in the past. But then, Catherine was never the sort of woman to need help anyway. She managed well on her own. It was the quality he loved most about her.

"You will see me at my palace and at the ball in your honor," he said weakly. "To celebrate your triumphs against the Turks, the English, and the Prussians."

Catherine turned around and cupped Grisha's face in her gentle hands. "I suppose there's no point in trying to convince you otherwise. Very well, Prince. Perhaps this ball will be just the thing to bring you back to this world." She kissed him lightly and smoothed his hair back away from his face. "I love you, husband. With all my soul."

Fourteen

FOR IMMEDIATE RELEASE

*Dr. Herrera will speak on at least one issue confronting the coun-
try: the arrest and conviction of Nikolai "Reb" Volkov on charges
of hooliganism.*

ST. PETERSBURG
PRESENT DAY

Irina insisted on a final fitting before the photo shoot for Ekaterina Restaurant. Again Veronica tried to summon Catherine's
power, to think of how she might have behaved in Russia today, to
draw strength from it. But the gown no longer looked authentic,
only tacky and cheaply made. Perhaps it was the poor light, the
grayness outside as another storm gathered force and inside as one
of the chandeliers malfunctioned and flickered out. The creepy
cherubs hovering on the mirror's gilded frame sneered. *Who do you
think you are?*

Veronica put her head in her hands and rubbed her temples.
Elena had a few pins stuck in her mouth as she adjusted the hem
of the gown. She removed the pins and gazed up at Veronica,
pursing her pink lips. "You are not happy. Skirt is still too long?"

"It's not that." Veronica scrutinized her reflection. It made no sense to see her own face hovering above that gown. In some ways, it seemed even more surreal than the Photoshopped version Irina had shown her on the plane. A part of her felt ridiculous, like suddenly she'd been enlisted to play Glinda the Good Witch in *The Wizard of Oz* but didn't know any of her lines. "It just doesn't feel the same today."

"Is there anything I can do?"

"I don't think so. It's not the gown. It's me."

She watched Elena's reflection as she stood upright and tried to fluff Veronica's straight hair. "It is most important you are comfortable, Tsarina Nika. You must take good care of yourself so you can help others."

Elena patted her shoulder, a bare spot underneath the cape. *This is what it would have been like to have a daughter. She would have loved having a daughter.* She smiled at Elena in the mirror, liking the feeling, the twinge of sadness underneath soon forgotten as her thoughts turned to Laurent. She had received only one text from Michael since she'd seen him yesterday at the hotel:

IRINA DOESN'T KNOW ANYTHING ABOUT LAURENT, SO I CALLED YOUR ABUELA. LAURENT SENT HER AN E-MAIL SAYING HE IS COMING TO ST. PETERSBURG. I CONFIRMED WITH MY MOTHER. LAURENT WANTS TO MEET WITH YOU. HE'S WORRIED ABOUT WHAT YOU'RE DOING. HE'S WORRIED ABOUT THE IMPLICATIONS. WILL YOU TALK TO HIM?

The thought of the message still made her angry. First, her long-lost father, suddenly appearing out of nowhere to inject himself in her life. That took some nerve. And then Michael's tone. All business. She didn't know what exactly she had expected from him, but the stiff formality of the message made her want to throw her phone across the room.

After another ten minutes had passed—and she hadn't responded—she received another text from Michael:

I'M SORRY I GOT UPSET EARLIER. ONLY PLEASE REMEMBER I'M WORRIED ABOUT YOU. I PROMISED YOUR GRANDMOTHER I WOULD KEEP YOU SAFE. THAT'S WHY I'M HERE.

"Not too much makes sense to me right now," she told Elena.

Irina clamored into the office on heels. Sasha trailed after her, smiling and affable as ever. Another man followed Irina as well, short and dark haired in a pressed shirt and slacks, head shyly bent, carrying a long garment bag.

"Now that you are set for the photo shoot, we need to think about the press conference. As I suspected"—Irina waved her hand contemptuously at Veronica's open suitcase and the clothes hanging from a rack—"this looks like the wardrobe of a second-rate office manager."

"Gee, thanks," Veronica said.

"Not to worry. This only makes the fairy tale all the better. We've found something of which even Catherine herself would approve, were she living today of course."

The man handed Sasha the garment bag and retreated into a dark corner near the washroom. Sasha unzipped the bag, revealing an elegant lilac skirt and matching blazer trimmed in silver: exactly the sort of thing Irina would wear, but in Veronica's size. "What do you think?"

"You shouldn't have."

Irina regarded her with cool judgment. "You don't like it? I prefer neutrals, but we thought the color suitable. Purple is the color of royalty, after all." She took the blazer and held it next to Veronica. "Are you afraid you've gained weight and it won't fit? Elena can easily make a few tucks here and there."

Elena huffed at that and Veronica gritted her teeth. "I meant you shouldn't have bought this for me because I can't pay for it."

"Oh, is that all?" Irina shrugged.

Veronica glanced at Elena. "What do you think?"

Elena ran her hand over the silky fabric approvingly. "I can see Yulia Tymoshenko wearing something like this."

"I don't know that you need to be so generous." Veronica tried to summon a diplomatic way to tell Irina she didn't want to be obligated to either the Society in general or Irina in particular. "I'm sure something I brought will be appropriate for the press conference."

"It's nothing," Sasha offered. "You're going to help us bring in so much money."

Veronica wheeled around to face Sasha, narrowing her eyes. "Really? That's the main reason I'm here then?"

Sasha was still smiling but hunched his shoulders. She'd rattled him, at least a little. He even looked slightly abashed. "I didn't mean it like that."

"What did you mean?"

"He doesn't mean anything," Irina said, tossing her hair back and glaring at Sasha.

"Do you mean I'll have more 'branding' opportunities?" Veronica realized then how much she hated the word "branding." It made her feel like a prize cow. "More photo shoots?"

"He didn't mean you personally. He didn't even mean 'us' in terms of the Society, but 'us' in terms of Russia. Tourism. Celebrity. Promotions. The possibilities are endless."

Sasha gave Irina an apologetic shrug and her gaze became tender once more.

"You should look your best regardless," Irina told Veronica. "And we are in a position to help you. Let us do that."

The man who had entered with Irina and Sasha emerged from

the shadows, head still low, so Veronica couldn't see his face. He approached her, clicking his tongue between his teeth at something on the dress. At last he met her gaze and in a low voice said: "For what it is worth, I think this suits Your Majesty."

Veronica stiffened. She would have recognized his blue eyes anywhere.

"May I have a few minutes," she said slowly, taking care with her voice, so she wouldn't give away her guest's identity when he was so clearly trying to hide it, "to try on the outfit?"

"Fine. Good idea." Irina took Sasha by the upper arm and practically dragged him out of the room, saying: "I told you not to mention money. It upsets her." She didn't notice that the man with the garment bag hadn't followed them out.

After Sasha shut the door behind them, Elena looked up, surprised, and asked, "Reb Volkov? I thought you were under house arrest."

Veronica waved her arms to indicate Elena should keep her voice down.

"How come they did not see you?" Elena added, gesturing in Irina and Sasha's direction.

"The noble is concerned only with herself and the handsome man lives in his own world." He turned to Veronica. "We need to talk."

"I'm supposed to take pictures."

Reb eyed the gown with obvious distaste. "This is why you came to Russia? To become a trinket? A tool for the noble pigs and their capitalist masters?"

"She looks lovely!" Elena cried.

"Why don't you wear the dress then?"

"I am not the tsarina."

"The selfish nobles only want a pretty face to help their cause. Yours will do as well as any other. They don't care about this one's connections to the Romanov oppressors."

"This is not true," Elena said. "They care about Nika's family."

"Do they?"

Veronica was thinking about everything that had happened since she arrived in St. Petersburg. Had Irina even once asked her to take a DNA test? To talk further about her family? To have the letter from Empress Alexandra speaking of her secret daughter authenticated? It seemed like all she cared about was having someone who fit the gown well enough, who seemed like enough of a Romanov. Veronica looked in the mirror again. Maybe Catherine would finally make her presence known.

Veronica felt nothing, only knew she was over Irina and her self-aggrandizing fluff.

"To hell with this." Veronica unhooked the clasp and slipped the cape off her shoulders.

"What are you doing?" Elena cried. "What am I supposed to do?"

"Tell Irina I'm not doing the photo shoot," Veronica said. "But I will be here for the press conference. I'd tell her myself, but I want to make sure Reb gets back to his flat safely and I don't trust Irina."

Reb tapped his ankle. "I'll make sure this won't betray me. I've stayed within two kilometers of my flat. We'll remain nearby. But you? Little Miss Romanov Heiress? Dmitry and I want a word."

Reb wore a jacket too light for the weather. The cold rain had dissolved into a wet and heavy mist with traces of snowflakes. Frustration chilled his voice. "Imperialist scum."

Veronica scrutinized the monument before them, set on rounded steps like the curved seating in an amphitheater, swamped in a slushy mix of mud and ice. Atop the pedestal, Catherine the Great stared straight ahead, not deigning to look down at her loyal subjects. Catherine was encircled by her most prominent advisers. The tranquil Princess Dashkova read a book, representing her position as the head of the Russian Academy. Among the men, Veronica recognized Prince Potemkin, his boot resting atop a limp turban. Her gaze lingered on his proud expression, and yet somehow she thought if the statue could move, he would lift his foot.

Reb gestured toward the sad little turban. "A conqueror. Disgusting."

"This is supposed to help?" Veronica asked, switching to English as she turned to face Dmitry. "This is your big pep talk?"

"Pep talk?" Dmitry said.

"You brought me here to see Catherine, to inspire me, and then I have to listen to this."

Dmitry cast a warning glance in Reb's direction.

"Fine." Scowling, Reb reached into a leather bag he'd brought with him and withdrew a thick notepad and a stubby charcoal pencil. Catherine and Potemkin may have been imperialists, but that didn't stop him from sketching the lines of the statue in broad strokes.

"I'm going to help. I told both of you already."

"We only want to remind you we are here and to see if there is anything else we could do to support you. Even Catherine had advisers."

"Advisers! Dima is so modest." Reb looked up from his sketch. "He orchestrated everything. Otherwise you would remain the tool of that silly noblewoman."

"Irina's focus has always been money," Dmitry admitted. "It is starting to worry me. That is not what you want though. I know this. I told Reb you would abandon the photo shoot with only little nudge. And I was right."

"Yes, yes." Reb waved his hand in the air and continued his sketch.

"People in the West do not fully understand what happens in Russia," Dmitry said. "I think you are right person to speak. You can draw attention we need."

"I'll speak at the press conference," Veronica said. "I'll speak out against the propaganda law and other civil rights violations. I'll support the vodka boycott."

"Look." Dmitry motioned behind them. Veronica turned around. Two long rows of benches faced one another in the square. They seemed innocuous enough. Veronica shook her head and shrugged. Dmitry motioned again and she looked closer. On the side of the bench nearest them, she read a tiny graffiti message in Cyrillic.

Burn the gays in ovens.

Veronica shivered. "I saw something similar by *The Bronze Horseman*."

"That tag has been here two weeks," Reb said. "The police will not remove it."

"The problem is not only laws," Dmitry said. "It is violence, lynchings, and everything between private companies and government."

"Russian bureaucracy," she said. "I understand."

"Do you understand the extent of it? If a bank makes a loan to gay couple . . . closed. If a university accepts gay faculty member . . . no funding. If landlord rents to gay person . . . suddenly building does not meet codes. This is how they go about it. They want us out of country."

"Out of Holy Russia," Reb added bitterly.

Veronica couldn't look at the graffiti any longer. Instead, she looked up at Catherine.

"What do you think she would have done?" Dmitry asked.

In truth? Veronica now realized she had no idea. This was the historian's curse. She wanted to be transported to an age where beauty and manners and honor were highly prized. It sounded appealing and sexy. The late eighteenth century had been the age of enlightenment. And yet how did the eighteenth century look from modern eyes? Sexist, despite empresses like Catherine of Russia and Maria Theresa in Austria. Racist. The conquered turban beneath Potemkin's foot spoke to that well enough. Certainly homophobic.

On the other hand, people who lived in the present liked to believe that if they lived in the past they would have done things differently than their ancestors. Catherine and her prince were conquerors and expansionists, but they were also intellectually curious, cosmopolitan, open to debate, and tolerant of other religions, remarkably so.

Maybe it was wishful thinking, but she believed Catherine and Potemkin would hate what was happening in this new Russia.

Veronica turned to Dmitry. He had taken Reb's hand. Reb scowled but otherwise looked as though he could have been purring. If she had been able to catch Prince Potemkin staring at Catherine, she would have seen the same look in his eyes. Dmitry gazed wistfully at Reb and Veronica knew he wanted to kiss him. But he didn't dare. Not in public.

Guilt barbed Veronica's thoughts as she realized she had violated an intimate moment between them. She remembered Caravaggio's brokenhearted lute player, his lips gently parted and his gaze so tender.

"I'll do whatever I can to help you," she told them quietly. "I promise."

At least it was a small event. Veronica was glad for that much. Irina had only asked ten reporters from various Russian news agencies and popular blogs to attend and now they crowded into the foyer of the Hermitage Theater, where Veronica's disturbing conversation with Borya and Zenaida had taken place. The reporters were seated in folding chairs, tacky and anachronistically modern in the rococo fairy tale. A podium was centered in front of one of the windows looking out to the canal and the gray morning.

Sasha hung a banner with the Russian red, white, and blue flag and the Romanov double-headed eagle in front of the podium. In Cyrillic, it declared: "Welcome, Tsarina Nika." Sasha took a step back and then glanced at Veronica, who was waiting in a corner wearing the suit Irina had chosen for her. "I'm so stoked! I can't wait to hear what you have to say."

He gave her a thumbs-up and a big smile.

Veronica remembered what he had told her at the party, that she could tweet about Reb. She tried to return the optimistic gesture but even her thumb felt nervous.

Irina stood nearby, trying to smile but looking more like a hyena baring her teeth. Her shoulders kept rising and falling dramatically and her perfume made Veronica's head hurt. She had barely spoken two words since Veronica had bailed on the photo shoot.

"Don't blow this," Irina said in a low voice. "Don't try to cross me again. Remember why you are here. You don't have anything waiting for you back in California. Get this right."

Veronica drew in a deep breath, remembering to count to three in English, Spanish, and Russian to calm herself. One of the windows had been left slightly ajar and she heard a bird trill outside. Veronica wondered again what Grigory Potemkin would have made of all of this: the spectacle of a woman from a foreign land staking a claim in Russia. He'd seen it before, of course. A German girl who changed her name to Catherine and ruled an empire, becoming a woman he had loved for so many years. She thought Grigory Potemkin must have been watching her from somewhere, one of the ghosts of the Winter Palace, of St. Petersburg, of all the lost Romanovs and their courts.

Sasha pressed something on his phone and the first grandly thundering notes of Tchaikovsky's Piano Concerto No. 1 filled the room. This was one of Veronica's favorite pieces of classical music, one she had known as a child when she first read *Nicholas and Alexandra* and started to dream of palaces dusted with snow.

At the majestic sound of the music, the reporters who had been invited to meet her all swung their heads to look. Veronica followed Irina to the podium as calmly as she could manage, trying not to scramble in her purse for her notes. The reporters snapped pictures as she nodded, trying to look pleasant and approachable and yet fully in charge of the situation.

Irina was slated to speak first and introduce Veronica. As they waited for the murmuring to die down, Veronica scanned the room. She spotted Anya in the back row and then, to her great pleasure, Elena's fiery hair. Elena stood against the back wall and wiggled her fingers at Veronica, who smiled in return. Other than that, everyone's faces seemed fuzzy.

She looked around the room one more time but didn't see Michael. Her heart sank.

Veronica adjusted her purse at her side, feeling stiff and stuffy in the lilac skirt and blazer. Her phone buzzed and she reached inside to peek, hoping it was Michael. It was a voice message from her *abuela* but she didn't have time to listen. She put the phone back.

Dmitry cleared his throat and the reporters' murmuring died down. Sasha pressed his phone again and Tchaikovsky's epic concerto came to an abrupt halt.

"Thank you for joining us," Irina said, trim and self-assured in an ivory-colored pantsuit. "This is truly a momentous occasion, a day for celebration. As most of you know, the Monarchist Society has been engaged in the most important project in our history. We searched a hundred years for an heir to the Romanov family and have been disappointed time and time again. But now . . ." She paused for dramatic effect. "Our prayers have been answered."

Veronica shifted her weight, thinking of Reb's painting. She saw Dmitry reach for something near his collar and caught a quick glimpse of his cross.

She touched her own cross, at the base of her throat, a gift from the Dowager Empress Marie to Grand Duchess Charlotte.

"The woman before you now is the true heir and representative of the House of Romanov," Irina continued, her affected British accent growing more pronounced even though she spoke in elegant Russian. "The granddaughter of a grand duchess, a secret fifth daughter of the tsar, removed from Russia by the saintly Dowager Empress Marie Feodorovna before the Bolsheviks came to power."

Veronica rolled her neck. Marie had removed her granddaughter from Russia before the Revolution. But Irina made it sound like a heroic act, as though somehow Marie had foreseen a revolution fifteen years later and had known that if the girl remained in the country, she would be murdered along with the rest of her family. In truth, Marie had merely been trying to protect her son's throne from the political fallout of yet again failing to produce an heir.

"This true grand duchess, named Charlotte, took the married name Marchand. The fifth daughter of the tsar, unrevealed for nearly a century. We are proud to introduce her granddaughter and Nicholas and Alexandra's great-granddaughter, the woman who is the true claimant to the Russian throne, Dr. Veronica Herrera. Our honorary tsarina. Nika."

Veronica hadn't expected excited applause. Or had she? An obligatory smattering of claps acknowledged it was her turn to speak.

She traded places with Irina and scanned the notes before her on the podium. For such a simple piece of furniture, the podium was intimidating. "Thank you," she said in Russian. "Thank you all for coming." Her voice was high and she made a conscious effort to lower her register. "I am not pursuing an official title, of course, but I am honored to accept this symbolic position with the Society."

Someone cleared their throat. Anya crossed her legs.

"I have always believed a ceremonial monarch can effect positive change in the modern world." Veronica struggled to convey complex ideas in Russian. "A monarch can act as a force for good in a country and a cultural diplomat to other nations. I am honored to serve." She straightened her back, tried to seem regal. Had she really just said all of that? At her first press conference? She scanned the crowd. Some of the reporters were looking at her with a fixed and almost hostile lack of interest. Others typed furiously on their electronic tablets.

"If it's what the people want, that is," she added quickly. "I hope it's something people might be open to considering. I understand people probably have mixed feelings. It's complicated."

She looked again at the paper, imagining Dmitry and Irina huddling over the speech, diagramming every last word. And yet those words felt so artificial right now, so canned. More branding of Tsarina Nika. Veronica steadied her trembling hands. She crumpled the paper, folded her palms on top of one another, and looked directly at the reporters.

"I think having another voice in Russian politics is a good thing. These are troubled times. I know, times are always troubled. And I can't say that I am in the mood to celebrate, given what is happening in this country. The suppression of free expression."

Veronica could just kill the time with platitudes: national unity, pride, good works, and blah, blah, blah. The reporters would jot down a few notes. It would be good enough. Russia was scary. The leaders of this country had proven they would do whatever they needed to do to shut down dissent. They didn't care who got hurt. They didn't care if they offended other countries. They still had all of the old Soviet weaponry at their disposal. Why should they care?

And she was about to piss them off.

But she had promised Reb and Dmitry. She had promised herself. She would never be able to live with herself if she backed down. Now was the time to fight.

"I wish to address the arrest and conviction of Reb Volkov. I was immensely sorry to hear of it."

"So what of the picture with Vasily Turgekov?" a reporter called out. "Vasily says Reb is getting exactly what he deserves."

That stopped Veronica, but only for a second.

"I am sorry to have inadvertently posed for a picture with a man, a celebrity, who has expressed social views I find repugnant. Vasily is a fine actor but he is a homophobe."

"You didn't recognize him when you took the picture?" Anya clarified.

"I did not," Veronica said, voice still clear and even authoritative. "That was a mistake. I want to focus on Reb's situation now. I know some people think because I'm an American I should stay out of Russian affairs. But I understand many Russians feel Reb's punishment was inappropriate. I intend to start a petition to reverse his sentence and ask the Duma to reconsider the so-called gay propaganda legislation. It is discriminatory. It is hateful. It must stop."

A pin could have dropped. So when the door handle turned with a loud squeak, everyone heard. Michael came in as quietly and unobtrusively as he could, but he was so tall he couldn't help but draw attention. He caught Veronica's eye and once again she thought of the sad-eyed lute player from the picture. She and Michael kept hurting one another. They were breaking each other's hearts. What was the point? She wanted him at her side. She didn't want to turn him away any longer.

Veronica removed her blazer. Underneath she wore a T-shirt with a Siberian wolf on it. The same image that Reb used on his website. "I stand with Reb Volkov. But I also stand with the communities in this country who have been marginalized at the hands of the current leadership." The reporters' faces were a blur, but Veronica caught Dmitry's eye. "As a show of support, I understand that bars in several cities around the world are declining to purchase or serve Russian vodka. I call on the bars to stick to this boycott until Reb's sentence is reversed."

A flurry of Russian questions from the audience, all at the same time, impossible to distinguish and understand. Anya was beaming. Dmitry stepped up to the podium and blurted: "Wait! Please! One question at a time. Once we can hear you, then we will take the questions in a fair order. We'll get to as many as we can."

Head spinning, Veronica looked once more to the back of the room. Michael's features were serious, but he nodded and then flashed a smile.

Irina made a dash for the podium, sidestepping Dmitry. "Actually, your questions will need to wait. We will reschedule questions for another time. Thank you."

The questions died, but one of the reporters in the back, a small man with a bowl-shaped haircut and intense expression, approached Veronica. "Do you have a moment now?"

"She does." Dmitry took one of Veronica's arms gently and quickly steered her to the door, away from Irina.

"What are you planning to do next? Once the protest is made, are you going to deliver the petition of signatures directly to the Kremlin?" the reporter asked.

Veronica realized she hadn't thought this out yet. "This is under consideration."

"I have sources that say the government is considering reversing the decision. This could be a tipping point."

Veronica heard the clomping of heels. Irina approached, the sides of her neck flushed red. "The tsarina will move along now," she said, cutting between Veronica and the reporter.

"I only want to answer his question."

"It's done," Irina told the reporter. "Go." He scuttled off, joining the rest of the hive.

"What is your problem?" Veronica cried.

"You're making a fool of yourself," Irina hissed, "and worse yet, you're making a mockery of the Society and everything we have stood for all these years."

"This is my prerogative," Veronica said, louder than she intended.

Irina tapped her hips. "We discussed Reb Volkov. I made my feelings clear."

"You made your opinion clear," Veronica said. "But I don't share your opinion and this is my platform. I get to decide who and what I support."

"Your actions have implications beyond yourself. Reb Volkov is a homosexual. We need the church to support our cause. To support you. We need parliament."

"Not at that price," Veronica said. "And the law the Duma passed is wrong."

"What you think doesn't matter," Irina said. "This is Russia, not California. There is a way of behaving here, a yearning for traditional life. We are not going to legalize marriages between homosexuals or celebrate their lifestyle."

"You're going to let thugs 'liquidate' gay men and women?"

"We have a certain image to protect and keep sacred."

Out of the corner of her eye, Veronica saw Michael approach. Irina didn't respond in her normally flirtatious way but kept her arms crossed in front of her chest as though daring anyone to break her tough exterior.

"That was really exciting," Michael said, trying to sound cheery. "But I think we've given the reporters what they need for now."

"Agreed." She glared at Irina. "We can discuss this later."

"Why bother?" Irina shot back. "You ruined everything. I had great plans. You never would have had to return to another dull office. You would have been in charge of your own fate. You would have been financially secure for life."

"There is a big difference between financial security and happiness."

"You know perfectly well you crossed a line here."

Veronica took a step forward. Irina flinched.

"I'm not backing down," she said. "Live with it."

She allowed Michael to take her hand and lead her out of the room. Once they reached the door, he loosened his grip but didn't let go. "I'm proud of you. Worried, but proud."

Veronica squeezed his hand reassuringly and then they clasped their fingers together. "I have a voice mail from my *abuela* to check. Maybe she heard from Laurent."

"Give her a call," Michael said. "But first I want to take you out to Palace Square. Something has started out there and I think you should see it."

Veronica breathed in the chilly air and trod carefully on damp cobblestones flecked with snow. A mass of people had gathered around the granite Alexander Column, towering high above the Winter Palace and Hermitage and into the slate-gray sky. The crowd looked similar to the hipster protesters in front of Reb's flat. But there were fifty or sixty of them, brandishing signs and wearing the same shirts with the image of a wolf. Several waved giant rainbow flags back and forth and someone held a picture of the Russian president. In the picture, makeup had been artificially imposed on his face—rouge, lipstick, and mascara—and the word "Tsarina" was printed above him in Cyrillic. One protester banged on drums. Another strummed a *balalaika* and sang a Free the Wolf anthem.

"Did you know about this?" Michael asked, surveying the crowd.

"I had no idea," Veronica said, heart thumping. "I bet Reb organized it."

"His timing is perfect."

As Michael spoke, the reporters rushed past them, readying

their phones to take pictures. "You get it now, right?" she said to Michael.

"I 'got it' before," he told her. "But I was worried. You understand."

He looked around and then directly at her, his eyes wide and his expression tender. "I'm proud of you. I'm glad I can be part of this."

"You helped make it happen," she said. "You helped me. You told me who I was in the first place. You protected me. You did so much for me . . ." Her voice started to crack, her armor breaking down. She stood on her tiptoes and kissed him lightly.

Shock registered. He stared at her for a second. Her heart raced. That kiss had been innocent enough, but perhaps she had misread him.

"It feels right being here," he said. "Being together."

She felt the same way. But how to begin? Veronica knew how she wanted to respond but hesitated.

From the farthest corner of Palace Square, a dozen policemen amassed in two lines. They were clad in puffy dark gray jackets with fur-lined collars and the double-headed eagle, the Romanov emblem, embroidered on arm patches. Instead of fur hats, the policemen wore helmets and visors over their faces. They approached the Alexander Column and the protesters.

"Michael . . ." She nodded her head at the police.

He turned to look and his brow creased. "What are they doing?"

Veronica had a bad feeling she knew the answer. The policeman in front held up a loudspeaker and barked: "Leave the premises immediately."

A few of the protesters looked at one another. The one who had the drums shook his head and the rest of them nodded in apparent agreement. They dropped to the ground, legs crossed in front of them.

"Free the Wolf," one of them shouted.

The boy with the drums had taken a space at the head of the protesters. "That's right," he proclaimed loudly, waving his pale hands. "Free the Wolf."

"Leave or you will be forcibly ejected," the policeman yelled.

The boy let out a large "*Nyet*." The others joined in until the sound resonated.

The policeman reached his arm over his shoulder, grabbed a black canister from his belt, and aimed it at the protesters.

Veronica knew what was going to happen. It happened all too often in the United States as well, police, nervous and agitated, pitting themselves against protesters instead of offering protection. Her gut twisted into a knot. The protesters may have been speaking for Reb, but they had gathered in this particular place because of her press conference. This was her fault. She hadn't meant for anyone to get hurt.

She rushed toward them, screaming in Russian: "Please. They aren't doing anything."

The policeman with the pepper spray pointed at a boy paused, confused. He looked at her blankly and then at the reporters on the other side of the protesters.

"That's the new tsarina," the boy with the drums said. "You will listen to her, won't you?"

"Tsarina?" the policeman said. "Now she is giving orders?"

"I'm not ordering," Veronica said, raising her hands. "I'm asking."

"You are part of this?" The policeman waved dismissively at the protesters.

"Yes," Veronica said. "Yes, I am." She braced herself for the chill in the air and then unbuttoned her jacket. She let the policeman see her "Free the Wolf" T-shirt. And then she lowered herself to the ground next to the boy with the drums. It was hard to cross her legs in a skirt, but she did the best she could and felt only a little awkward as she hit the cold, hard ground. The reporters swarmed, holding their phones up to take pictures.

"We have orders." The policeman looked at the boy with the drums and then raised his visor to scratch his ear. He was young as well; he could have been one of Veronica's former students, with clear skin and rosy cheeks and an uncertain look in his light blue eyes.

"These are just kids," she said.

"What did this guy Reb do that was so bad anyway?" the policeman said, backing away.

"Thank you." She stood upright again, her words met with a round of applause by the protesters. "Thank you."

"I liked the last painting he showed. The church does have its dick in its hands right now." The policeman raised his hand and his group retreated. Veronica smiled and walked back to Michael.

Except Michael wasn't there.

She looked all around the square, hands shaking, a bitter taste clinging to her tongue.

She finally saw him, smaller in the distance, on the opposite side of the massive square.

Veronica pushed her way past the protesters and tried to follow Michael. She lost sight of him but then she saw the policeman's helmet, bobbing through the crowd, and Michael next to him, hands cuffed.

Her throat felt raw but she shouted his name and kept running. "Wait for me," she cried.

Michael turned to face her. They tried to tug him along, but he stood firm. His features remained calm, except right in the eyes, where he looked pinched, as though he were about to cry. He saw Veronica and when she opened her mouth to speak, he gave the slightest shake of his head. She moved forward, and he shook his head again. That stopped her in her tracks. She didn't dare make things worse for him. The policeman tugged on his arm and he allowed himself to be turned around and pulled along. And so she stood, cowardly and insignificant, as they lowered his head into the backseat of an unmarked black car that quickly sped away.

Fifteen

Grisha leaned against one of the Grecian columns painted a blinding white, braving the sudden rain shower so he might greet Catherine as soon as she arrived. His heart raced, but then again that may merely have been a side effect of the laudanum Anton had procured from the apothecary. It had a most pleasurable effect on his mood, even more so than the stronger opiates he had sampled abroad.

Guests already stampeded through the wide hall behind him, invited to partake of his largesse per tradition. They roved the palace in packs, laughing and dancing to orchestral music, some in formal dress and others in colorful imitations of Venetian carnival masques or hastily assembled cloaks and hats. Servants heaped delicacies on fine china platters: oysters, sturgeon, caviar, citrus fruits, fresh figs, rice flavored with ginger, roasted legs of lamb, and delightful French pastries, all accompanied by copious amounts of wine made from grapes cultivated in Crimean vineyards. He had not been able to procure the maize he had heard of from the New World, but so be it. When he glanced behind him, he caught someone thrusting a mutton drumstick into his pocket, along with a handful of sweets. Someone's family would eat well tonight.

Servants liveried in blue, yellow, and silver surrounded Grisha, candelabras in hand, ready to light a path for the empress. The boy he had caught reading the Marquis de Sade in the library, Oleg, stood among them, rigid in the unfamiliar uniform. As atonement, Grisha had assigned Oleg a special task. Rather than a candelabra, the boy held Grisha's enormous, jewel-encrusted hat and his shoulders sagged under the weight of it. If Grisha had placed the heavy ornament on his head, the damned thing might have killed him.

"Well done!" Anton cheeped as he saw the other boy. Anton wore his own blue and yellow uniform, complete with a special sash and a fresh pair of boots for the occasion.

Oleg scowled at Anton and then at the guests stuffing food in their pockets. "Do you want me to say something to the rabble, Your Highness?"

Grisha took another sip from his gold-plated mug. He preferred simple fare this evening, a light cabbage soup, similar to that he'd had when he fell ill as a boy. It kept his mind and stomach somewhat settled. "Let them be. This is part of the fun. Besides, if you leave, who will hold my hat?"

Oleg attempted to stand straighter but mumbled something under his breath. Grisha decided to let it pass, but Anton shouted, "Show some respect!"

At the sound of the boys fussing at one another, Grisha's head began to throb. Catherine's carriage arrived not a moment too soon, drawn by ten horses in feathered harnesses lined with tinkling bells. Gilded leaves and cherubs ornamented the windows and a double-headed eagle insignia was embossed on the door. A bead of perspiration trickled into Grisha's good eye, clouding his vision. He patted his forehead with a fresh linen infused with lavender. He couldn't let Catherine see he was still ill. She might call a halt to this whole affair and have her guards escort him to some quack.

"And if you say anything further," Anton was telling Oleg, "we'll have words."

"Don't you have a show to manage?" Grisha told Anton. It wouldn't do to have him scuffle with the other boy in front of Catherine. Besides, he didn't want his expensive hat to get soiled with mud. "I will see you inside later."

As Anton scurried off, Catherine stepped down onto a velvet footstool, dressed in a rich amethyst brocade gown that fit snugly around her chest and opened into a wide circle at the bottom. The long sleeves gaped open in a triangular cut at the wrist, making her already tiny hands seem even smaller. Her white hair was gathered under a high *kokoshnik* covered with precious stones that winked in the blazing candlelight. She had gone a bit heavy with the rouge, but she held her chin high and moved quickly, gracefully holding her dress off her ankles to navigate puddles. Laughing gaily with her crowd of courtiers, she seemed as energetic as a woman half her age. He hadn't seen her so magnificent since her coronation.

"Prince! How fine and bright your palace looks tonight! I knew I had not made a mistake gifting it to you, despite what my stingiest advisers would have me believe."

Grisha adjusted one of the gold buttons on his red coat and patted his chest to ensure his medallion with her portrait hung straight. The uniform fit tightly around his wide stomach, but he knew she would be pleased with the effect, the diamonds and medals emblazoned across his chest. He took one last swig of the sour cabbage soup, chewed on a sprig of mint, and then thrust the mug at a nearby page. The boy had a difficult time balancing his candelabra and the mug but found a way to manage both.

Grisha strode forward and swept low before Catherine, heart dropping to his stomach.

"Rise, Prince," she said pleasantly, motioning to the grand entranceway and the main hall of the palace behind him.

He worked himself upright, adrenaline and laudanum pulsing through his system. He had worn one of his fur-lined silk robes for the better part of the week as he fussed around the palace, making sure the last preparations were in order, and his breeches felt tight. He took her hand as she shooed her courtiers away.

Grisha turned his head quickly to the right and left. He waited for his men to form a path for the empress with their candelabras. "So I will not have the pleasure of Platon Alexandrovich's company this evening?"

Catherine squinted to see ahead of her. "I'm afraid we've had a bit of a squabble."

"Squabble?" Grisha said.

"A trifle. I thought it best if we traveled separately this evening so as not to wear on one another's last nerve. But never fear." She eyed Grisha playfully. "He will be here later. He said he would not miss it for all the world."

"As long as he understands his monkey is not welcome." Grisha pressed her hand, now determined to find Anton and have him ask questions among Catherine's entourage. Once they had imbibed, their tongues might loosen and he could learn the true state of affairs between Catherine and Zubov. "I spent my last ruble on our entertainments for this evening," he added. "How would I manage the cleaning bill?"

Catherine laughed and patted Grisha's arm. "There he is! There's the prince I know. And you do look better than when I saw you last."

The high voices of the chorale Grisha had summoned sang for Catherine as she entered the main hall. Guests still milled about, piling their plates high with food, but paused, recognizing the empress. How could they not when she was dressed so extraordinarily? Despite all the effort he had put into security for the evening, the eyes he had charged with watching from all corners of the palace, Grisha's fists clenched. Any of the guests might have held a grudge against the empress. Any one of them might have held the assassin's knife. He thought of Zubov's comment, so casual and yet so calculated to strike fear in his heart. Perhaps Zubov was right. Perhaps Grisha was a man of the old world and ill-prepared for the new.

But he saw no signs of discontent this evening, only loyal subjects falling to their knees and murmuring "*matushka.*"

"Tonight is for celebration. Please." Catherine gestured toward the roasted meats and pastries arranged on tiered china platters, long sleeves billowing. "Prince Potemkin has been most generous."

"Mother," a high voice brayed from the other side of the hallway. "I wasn't sure if you would make it this evening. Weren't you expected nearly an hour ago?"

As they passed a blazing rendition of Catherine's insignia on a thick tapestry, Catherine tightened her grip on his hand. Grand Duke Paul lingered near one of the organs, where a nervous musician attempted to play an original tune in honor of the empress. Paul had insisted on dressing in one of his Prussian military uniforms, a gaudy sash strapped around a chest already gleaming with medals. At least his pale wife had kept to the tone of the festivities. She was dressed in a modest white gown and diadem like the Snow Maiden from the fairy tale.

"Paul," Catherine said stiffly. "You look well."

"It's difficult to be anything but merry among such opulence," Paul said. "It seems the prince has spared no expense." He glanced at the guests gathered around the food, scarcely hiding his distaste. "Not the best choice when we may be so close to war."

"Oh, you haven't heard," Grisha said casually, intending to savor every moment.

"Has my mother come to a decision then?" Paul said, ignoring Catherine as she scowled beside Grisha. "Has she put an end to her womanly dithering?"

"We have it on good authority that the English prime minister gave quite a convincing speech to avoid war," Grisha said. "We should have official word soon enough."

Catherine smiled up at him. "It seems Prince Potemkin's counsel was correct. The English are backing down."

Paul's cheeks blazed redder than his mother's rouge.

"We are here to enjoy ourselves this evening and I understand"— she glanced sympathetically at her daughter-in-law, hovering at Paul's side—"that one of the entertainments this evening features two of my favorite people in this world, your two sweet sons, my dear."

Grisha led Catherine by the hand through the long central hall, past immense columns disguised as palm trees and other exotic plants, black crystal chandeliers aglow, and marble statuary half-hidden in shadow. Excited as a schoolboy, he steered her to the lush and tropical Winter Garden, enclosed in walls of glass, to the pedestal he had constructed for her.

The children proceeded in two elegant configurations. Catherine reclined on one of the thick Persian carpets that lined the platform and gasped with delight. The beaded trimming of her *kokoshnik* swung to and fro, framing her face. She pointed at one of the dancers as they took their positions. "Monsieur Alexander!" She tried to wave, like the proud grandmother she was.

Grisha smiled and clapped his hands. At once, the young grand duke took a spot at the front, dressed all in black with an elaborate hat on his head, in the Spanish manner, pom-poms dangling jauntily over the brim. Alexander began to perform a solo, punctuated with a complicated series of *jetés,* choreographed to showcase his finesse with intricate footwork. By the end, Catherine dabbed tears from her eyes. "So precious," she said.

"He carries himself well," Grisha commented. "Already in a regal manner some might say. I imagine him twenty years hence, tall and proud. Perhaps he will face some menace from the outside. He will be tested."

"You now have a gift for seeing into the future, Prince? Like a roadside Gypsy?"

Grisha allowed himself a small shrug and looked at Catherine full on, eye twinkling. "I would not presume such talent. But I believe I have moments when the second sight comes to me. It is because I'm from the heart of this country, *matushka*. I see Alexander as tsar, tall and lean on a proud stallion, at the head of a cavalry, and his foot soldiers standing loyally behind him. I see snow pounding in drifts, opposing armies shivering and flailing in it. And I see more than that as well. I see Alexander ruling an expansive, secure, enlightened, tolerant empire. I see him ensuring your legacy."

"Indeed," Catherine agreed, eying Grisha slyly. "What a grand vision, Prince. Nevertheless the heir to the throne remains my son Paul. For now."

"Of course!" Grisha said with sarcastic emphasis.

"What else can I do?" She shrugged. "Dear Lord, what would Paul do if he were passed over? He already has the formation of his regiments taking an aggressive Prussian style."

Grisha fought the temptation to gnaw at his thumbnail. Paul was excessively cruel with his soldiers, just as Peter had been, taking a whip to them for the slightest offense. Not exactly a way to cultivate the loyalty he would so desperately need when he ascended to the throne.

"You have something further to say?" Catherine gave him another sideways glance.

"Paul is the heir," Grisha said simply. God help them all if the empire faced a formidable threat under his watch.

"The boy would throw himself off a balcony if I passed him

over." Catherine squinted at Alexander, who was chatting with other boys now. Her eyes misted over fondly when she looked at her grandson, in a way they never did when she gazed at her son. "But you never know. Perhaps Paul will surprise us."

"You have a generous spirit, *matushka*."

When the evening meal was served, Grisha stood behind Catherine. As each dish was brought into the room, he lifted the silver top from the plate and offered it for inspection and approval. She smiled coyly and allowed him to serve her. He thought he did rather a fine job, all things considered, and wondered if he might have a future as a servant below the stairs. Or perhaps it was as those of an Eastern philosophical bent believed and he had lived a past life as a servant in one of the courts of old Muscovy.

And yet even in this moment of triumph, the floor seemed to move uncertainly beneath his feet thanks to his illness. Nevertheless, he held his ground. He had planned this triumph for too long.

After the final dish was served, and Catherine had her fill of the spun sugars and candied fruits he had ordered, he would find a deserted nook and ingest more laudanum. Grisha had no use for doctors. But their potions were sometimes worthy of his attention.

He spotted Zubov on the other end of the table. He had arrived late, as Catherine had predicted, and yet just in time for the midnight supper, a *gauche* gesture in Grisha's opinion. Zubov wore a long frock coat made of dark blue velvet, lined with fur, and a new pink cravat. The ensemble looked uncomfortable for a room so warmed by candles, but Zubov struck Grisha as someone who cared far more for appearances than comfort. Frankly, it was one of the few qualities he didn't begrudge in the boy.

Each time Catherine smiled at a dish and offered words of wonder—how delicious it tasted, how far Grisha's servants must have traveled to find such a rare treat, how clever the presentation—

Zubov pouted and Grisha smirked in his direction. Grisha's place was at his empress's side, just as it always had been. There wasn't a damn thing Zubov could do about it.

After supper, one of the servants announced they would gather in a different room. Catherine couldn't quite conceal a yawn behind her napkin. For a moment, Grisha worried she would declare she was ready to retire to the Winter Palace for the evening. But once she stifled her yawn, Catherine turned to one of her ladies-in-waiting and nodded. Following her cue, the other guests left their linen napkins—embroidered with an elaborate "G" and "P" just in case they still had any doubt as to who was responsible for their revelries this evening—on their plates. They followed the empress to the room where the remaining performances were scheduled to begin.

Elaborate woven tapestries portraying biblical stories draped the walls. Grisha had a particular fondness for the Book of Esther and had commissioned the tapestries to take a prominent place in the artistic vision of the room. He was even more particular about the artist's portrayal of Queen Esther herself. His Jewish adviser, Jacob Zeitlin, had once spoke of a girl who had performed the role of Esther in a play staged to commemorate their holiday of Purim. Grisha had listened carefully to his description of this adored young woman. She had been re-created in the center of the back panel, a gorgeous and raven-haired Esther dramatically lifting her hand to point an accusing finger at her king's disloyal adviser Haman.

"You are already prepared for the merriment," Catherine said in her low voice, sidling up to Grisha and placing her hand on his arm once more. Grisha took a moment to take in the feminine scent of her, the perfume and powder from her newly freshened face.

"What is life if not merriment and love and learning," Grisha replied. He shifted his attention, somewhat reluctantly, from the lovely lines of Esther's face to those of her enemy, the adviser Haman. "Take the story of Esther, a fine example of love and loyalty triumphing over those who would do wrong to their sworn leaders."

"And do you have anyone in mind? Someone who would do wrong to a sworn leader?"

His gaze traveled pointedly to Zubov. The boy appeared out of sorts without his damn monkey perched on his shoulder. Grisha almost felt sorry for him.

"You have something up your sleeve, Prince," Catherine said merrily as Grisha guided Catherine into a makeshift throne beneath the tapestry of Queen Esther. "I can always tell."

Grisha rolled his sleeves up and bared his forearms for Catherine, who laughed. He clapped his hands. The curtains at the other end of the room rose, revealing the full-size stage Grisha had commissioned for the occasion. Catherine gasped. Grisha had not bothered to inform the empress of the latest addition to his palace, but he knew she would be pleased with the effect.

Onstage, a line of the dancers from the ballet joined Grisha's own servants, all dressed to represent the many peoples of the empress's empire, from the colorfully kerchiefed peasants of old Muscovy to the Sami people from the far north in thick wool capes and fur-lined boots. And of course, the Muslims of the south were represented as well, pashas in high turbans and bodyguards brandishing scimitars.

Catherine watched the tableau for several minutes, squinting, enraptured. Grisha smiled to himself.

"It is a fine display," she told him softly.

"It is your legacy, *matushka*," Grisha bent low to whisper in her ear. "God is smiling in heaven at the thought of it. Once wars are over and an empire is safe . . . is this not the true purpose of our religion . . . peace on earth? Or at least on the part of it for which we are responsible."

When she gazed at him, Grisha saw love glimmering in her eyes. The old passion that had never truly died.

"Thank you, husband," she whispered back. "Thank you."

The tableau gave way to a theater troupe Grisha had hired to perform a pair of popular French comedies. The actors mimed outrageously and strutted about the stage in the manner so beloved of European audiences. Personally, Grisha had little taste for such nonsense. Amid the raucous laughter, he slipped out and found an alcove, praying some pair of lovers had not sought out the same space before him.

Sweating profusely, Grisha sank into the folds of the silk covering the divan, swearing under his breath at the stains he was no doubt leaving on the fine material. He fished in his breast pocket for the vial of laudanum he had stashed there earlier in the evening. He hadn't realized until now how much of his energy had been expended keeping up appearances for Catherine. In truth, the preparations had turned him into one of the walking dead, alternating between the brink of tears and the sensation of flying.

"Abandoning the empress so soon, Prince? Why, I would think you'd want to remain at her side all evening, distracting her with your homemade bread and circuses."

Grisha rubbed his hand against his head, maneuvering away from the vial. God help him if Zubov caught a glimpse of it. By the break of dawn, he would have the entire capital believing Grisha a hopeless addict.

He bowed his head slightly, not caring for Zubov to see the ruin of his eye. "Lonely without your monkey? Are you so desperate for company you seek mine?"

"You don't look well. I worry for your health, believe it or not. For Catherine's sake, if not my own."

Grisha looked up at last, trying not to think about his desperate need for the laudanum he had slipped beneath him and out of

Zubov's line of vision. "Your concern for your benefactress is touching."

Zubov's smooth forehead wrinkled. "You really believe that is all she is to me?"

"Don't worry." Grisha waved his hand, hoping the gesture would encourage Zubov to go away. "I'm sure you'll be well provided for one way or another. I'll see to it myself if need be."

Zubov snorted. "Never mind, Prince. I only sought you out because I want you to know how grand this entire sham appears." Zubov stepped forward, ducking so he wouldn't bump his elegant head against the alcove's low entranceway. "Yet another sad artifice constructed by Prince Potemkin to fool the poor shortsighted empress. Another Potemkin village."

"I don't follow," Grisha said.

"I suppose we should all be used to such nonsense by now. But I wanted to tell you personally, Prince, since you were so hell-bent on ruining me, I thought I would return the favor. This whole miserable enterprise is a failure."

"The empress seems well pleased, as do the other guests. Is envy really your best play right now?"

"In the moment the empress is pleased, perhaps," Zubov said, examining his cuticles, rearranging his ridiculous pink cravat, and trying to match the lazy note in Grisha's voice. "But in the end, I believe you have played into her worst fear."

"You presume to understand the empress so well. What is her worst fear?"

"You."

Grisha's stomach tightened. "The empress knows I am her truest friend."

"It was not enough to be a friend," Zubov snapped, "you had to be her lover. It was not enough to be her lover, you had to be her husband. You forget your place. You fashion yourself an emperor. No, not even an emperor. A pasha. You only dress in the Western style for show this evening. We all know that any other night you can be found lounging abed in your robes with a hookah pipe, concubines in harem pants dancing about. You wish to be pasha in the south. You wish to be king of Poland. You desire too much and you are a threat. And if she did not see it before, how could she help but see it tonight with all this showy fuss." Zubov retrieved a handkerchief from his pocket and waved his hand. "Your time is over. You have ruined yourself."

The entire evening had been designed to celebrate Catherine, but he supposed with a few clever tweaks and whispered words his intent might be misconstrued. "And you are the man to be at her side from now on."

"Not only me," Zubov said, lowering himself, squatting before Grisha. "I have powerful friends on my side. Grand Duke Paul for example. These symptoms you display now? Catherine says it is a recurrence of the malarial fever. The tsarevich has a different theory."

"Pray tell."

Zubov reached over and wiped perspiration from Grisha's brow. Grisha shuddered, understanding how a woman must feel when subject to the unwanted grope of a lecherous man. He grabbed the boy's slender wrist, but Zubov was more powerful than his lithe frame suggested and easily broke from his grip.

"Grand Duke Paul thinks your prick has finally got the best of you." Zubov stuffed his handkerchief back in his pocket and stood upright once more. "Could this not be the tertiary stage of syphilis? In its last stage, syphilis attacks the brain, fills one with all manner of delusions of pomp and glory. It explains your physical ailments, your moodiness, and your grandiose dreams of power. In a way, it is the only logical explanation for the spectacle you have made of yourself these past months. And all these years . . . married to the empress but sharing a bed with any woman who would have you? Such behavior would catch up with you. This is your fault."

Grisha's hands shook so badly he feared the vial might fall and clatter onto the floor. He tried to tell himself Zubov didn't know what he was doing, didn't know the implications of what he was saying, what this vile rumor would do to Catherine. It was Grisha's fault, for testing the boy and for making light of Paul. He had underestimated them both. He had failed Catherine.

"You know the last stage of this dreadful venereal illness, Prince?" Zubov stroked the folds of his cravat. "Death. It's only a matter of time. Anyone can see that. You look as though you have one foot in your grave already."

"The empress may sense death near me," Grisha said in a low voice. "And may feel more apt to grant my wishes so that I might leave a legacy."

"But then what if it is syphilis, Prince? Your paranoia. Your grandiosity. All symptoms of a brain addled by the disease in its final stages. The empress may pity you, but she can hardly wish to indulge the insane wishes of a barren old fool intent on usurping her power."

He lunged at the boy, but Zubov was quicker and backed away in time. Grisha fell to the floor, winded and coughing, feeling cowardly and impotent.

"Nice try, Prince," Zubov told him. "If you can't struggle to your feet, I'll be happy to accompany the empress to her carriage and back to the Winter Palace."

Sixteen

Dr. Herrera has made plans to participate in St. Petersburg's Pride Parade and other organized efforts to oppose both Reb's prison sentence and the so-called propaganda law.

PALACE SQUARE

PRESENT DAY

Veronica stood alone, panting from the sudden sprint, watching the black sedan pull away from the curb and maneuver past tour buses. Everything around her—the heavily clouded steel sky, the protesters chanting, even the black iron double-headed eagles on the railings—seemed to close in on her. Despite the cold, she felt overheated and sick to her stomach. Gasping for breath, she stared up at the stormy sky, at the angel on the column towering above— built to commemorate the victory of Catherine's grandson Alexander over Napoleon in 1812—and the grim line of statues atop the long façade of the palace. She felt insignificant, useless. She needed to pull herself together. She needed to get to the American consulate and talk to an ambassador, a diplomat, anyone who could find Michael. Dmitry would help. She would figure out a way to get Irina's help as well. Hadn't Dmitry told her Irina had influence in St. Petersburg?

But why did Michael shake his head? Like a warning.

She ran back across the square, tripping on stones slick now with streaks of icy snow, flinging her arms to her sides for balance. As she righted herself, she ran smack into Irina, bundled into a long silvery fur coat and scowling as someone squawked on her phone. Anya stood next to her in a thick red head scarf and matching wool coat.

"Michael is gone," Veronica cried, shuddering as she tried to control her mounting panic. "They took him. Did you see?"

Anya looked lost in her own thoughts. Her breath formed a cloud of frost in the air as she spoke. "I saw."

"Why would the police take him? He hasn't done anything!"

Anya's voice remained calm. "It was the same with Reb. We didn't find out why he was arrested until much later. We will figure out what happened. I promise."

"Where is Dmitry?"

"He had to go to Reb," Anya said in a low voice. "Once you made your announcement, Reb received a death threat. It's not the first one, but Dmitry needs to be with him."

The protesters still chanted at the top of their lungs, but now the police stood to the side, averting their eyes. One of them even laughed. Veronica wondered if she should approach them for help. Michael's tourist visa was only good for thirty days. What would they do if that expired? Could the American consulate get them a new one? Maybe one of the police officers would know what to do.

And then she turned to Irina, still on her phone. Veronica's eyes narrowed. She suspected Irina would be more useful than any police officers. Irina likely knew the right people or at least could direct Veronica to the right people.

"I'll call you back," Irina said, pressing a button on her phone.

Veronica bit her lip. She could barely manage the words. "The police took Michael."

Irina ran her hand through her silky blond hair. "I know. I just spoke to Sasha. He will investigate."

"How?" Sasha looked as though he would feel far more comfortable surfing on a beach somewhere or hiking through redwood groves than busting an American out of a foreign prison. She couldn't stand the thought of Michael's fate resting in his hands. "He doesn't even speak Russian."

Irina pulled her fur tighter around her pale neck. "Sasha does well here. He has plenty of friends."

"Female friends?"

"Besides the bimbos. The Yusupov name opens doors. Besides, you never know when those women might be helpful."

The Yusupov name. All of that money before the Revolution. "These 'friends' think he will clean up if the family fortune is restored."

"It's his family's money. Everyone has a right to their proper inheritance. You should know this better than anyone."

Irina swept her hair to one side with her fingers, trying to keep it from getting mussed in the wind. Her phone rang again and she scrambled to answer it. Veronica heard Sasha's deep American squawking and fought an impulse to snatch the phone from her hands.

"I see . . ." Irina's voice trailed off. "Very well then. I'll tell her."

"Tell me what? What's happening?"

Irina dropped the phone back in her purse abruptly. Then she fumbled around until she located the Firebird pendant to pin her hair in place. "Your friend, Mr. Karstadt, he is an attorney? Immigration law?"

Veronica thought her heart might burst. "Yes."

"You would think he'd know better then. Apparently he was

carrying something on him he shouldn't have been. Sasha doesn't know the details yet, but Mr. Karstadt has been taken to a holding facility in the center of the city."

Veronica swallowed, throat suddenly hoarse. "A holding facility?"

"He's American," Irina said. "They won't keep him in a common jail with Russian pickpockets and Gypsies. This is a more serious matter."

"Michael hasn't done anything wrong."

"Not that you know of," Irina said. "But how much do any of us really know? We have strong authorities here. They keep us safe. Besides, you're the one who made this mess. I told you. I told Dmitry. Stay out of this. Keep the Society out of politics. You're to blame."

Veronica took a step toward Irina but felt Anya's steadying hand on her shoulder. "You think the arrest of Nika's friend is related to Reb's case?" Anya asked.

"Of course it's related," Irina said. "They want to send a message and this is the best way they know how. They will hurt someone close to the new tsarina. But that doesn't mean your precious False Mikhail is blameless. The police must have had some reason or another for taking him into custody."

"No," Veronica said, shaking her head. "He hasn't done anything."

"Either way, the solution is simple," Irina told her. "Back down. Stop talking about Reb Volkov and this silly vodka boycott. I guarantee things will look much better for Mr. Karstadt."

The guard took his time inspecting Veronica's paperwork, running fat fingers over the form, her tourist visa, and her passport. Veronica wondered if he would find fault with some detail and turn her away. But after another minute, his features relaxed. He adjusted his brown jacket and made a little bow as he returned Veronica's papers. "Everything looks to be in order, Nika." He nodded toward the hat resting on the station before him, the gold double-headed eagle medallion, and winked.

So he knew her. Veronica found herself leaning in close to him, not exactly flirting but taking him into her confidence. "How is he doing?" she asked in Russian.

"Mikhail? He is managing well enough."

She would have preferred the guard sounded annoyed when she asked about Michael. Instead he seemed sorry for him.

The guard gestured for her to follow. The sound of his boots on the tile floor echoed off the walls around them. The facility was not the darkly lit stone-walled dungeon she'd imagined, but rather pristinely white. Narrow hallways fanned out from the central booking area in neat lines and the strong scent of bleach almost overpowered the decay in the air. She'd feared Michael would be taken to a place where he would be dumped and forgotten. This seemed like a place prisoners were taken to be shot. It would be easy to clean blood from the walls. She fought off another chill. She needed to get Michael out of here now.

No. They had let her in to see him. The situation couldn't be that bad.

Unless whoever had taken Michael saw her as no threat at all.

The guard led her down one of the hallways to a steel door and swiped a key card over a magnetic strip. On the other side of the door, five cells were lined up side by side. The tiny cells only had room for a cot and a basin. As they continued forward, she saw they were all empty except for the cell nearest them at the end of the hall, which was occupied by a skinny, pale adolescent. His head was shorn and on the right side of his skull he had a bluish tattoo of a spider enmeshed in a web. He curled his arms around his legs and rocked back and forth on top of the narrow cot, muttering to himself. Veronica quickened her pace.

The guard directed her to the last cell in the row. Veronica ran the final few steps and then stopped and gripped the bars. Michael was lying on his back, arm draped over his eyes. He shifted and dropped his arm, squinting at her. A dark purplish discoloration tinged with red swelled under his left eye.

"Oh my God!" she cried. "What are they doing to you?"

Michael stood quickly and grasped her fingers. "It's okay," he said. "Just a little misunderstanding, but I'm okay. I promise. Don't panic."

She drew a deep breath, taking in the terrible bleach smell and trying not to stare at his eye. She couldn't let the panic consume her, no matter how hard her heart thudded in her chest. But she didn't believe him. He wasn't okay. He was here because of her. This had happened to him because of her. She turned to the guard, pressing her lips together until she could speak in lucid, proper Russian. "May we have a few minutes of privacy?"

The guard tipped his hat. Eyes wide, Michael watched him retreat to the other end of the corridor. "I don't think he's supposed to leave you alone with me. I thought he was going to bark at you and tell you we only had two minutes. I'm surprised he's giving us even this much space."

"He called me Nika. I think he might want the Romanovs back."

"Ah!" Michael grinned. She was glad to see him in good spirits at least. His fingers felt comforting against her skin. "Royalty has its perks."

"Maybe he has some noble bloodline in his family and a lost fortune he wants to recover." She leaned forward. "Irina says I'm turning conservative members of the Duma against the Society. She says you're in jail as some sort of retaliation, that someone is trying to get to me through you." Without thinking, Veronica turned her hand sideways to slide it between the narrow bars, gently touching Michael's bruised cheek. He flinched and she lowered her hand. "What happened? What did they do?"

Michael glanced at the guard and lowered his voice until it sounded gravelly. "I lost my temper for a minute and didn't think before I said something stupid. Trust me. It won't happen again."

She was afraid to touch his face again so she squeezed his fingers. "I'm getting you out of here. I have a call in to the American consulate. They'll help. And I'll talk to this guard. There must be something I can do."

"I don't want you to do anything, Veronica. Look, the guard notified the consulate for me already. Let's wait and see what happens."

"What are they saying you did?"

He scratched his head.

"You didn't do anything . . . did you?"

He shrugged.

"What did you do?"

"They found something on me."

"What? Drugs?"

"Veronica, come on. No. It was a pamphlet for an LGBT advocacy group. They found several in my coat pocket. I was arrested under the gay propaganda law."

Her chest felt like ice. "Oh my God."

"Not that I'm offended or anything, but, Veronica, the pamphlets weren't mine. Someone planted them in my coat. And when I tried to explain, no one listened."

"You were set up." She rocked back and forth now, sliding her hand out and holding on to the bars to steady herself. A hooting sound came from one of the other cells, the boy with the spider tattoo. She couldn't let Michael stay in here one more second.

"And then they asked for my visa and said it was the wrong kind. I guess because of the pamphlets they think I'm here for political reasons and the tourist visa isn't valid."

"That's crazy. I'm going to sort it out."

"Let the people in the consulate do their job," Michael said.

"I don't know who set me up, but the Americans aren't going to let anything happen to me."

"My apologies, Tsarina Nika," the guard called from the end of the hall. "But there will be more men coming. I must ask you to leave now."

"One more minute."

"Please, Veronica. Do what he says. I don't want you to end up in a women's ward somewhere. Help Reb. Don't let this intimidate you. I'll be fine."

Veronica took his hand again and grasped his fingers tighter. "I miss you. I wanted to say it before . . . I miss you." She touched his face gently, steering clear of the bruise. "I love you."

He smiled sadly. "I love you too. I've always loved you. But I think you know that."

"Just a little while longer," she told him. "I'm getting you out of here."

By eight that evening, Veronica still hadn't heard back from the consulate and she didn't want to return to her hotel. It was too cold to wander the streets aimlessly, and besides, it didn't feel safe. Dmitry had asked her not to come to Reb's flat. He thought it might make matters worse for everyone, at least until they learned more about Michael's arrest and the threats to Reb. And she still hadn't returned the call to her *abuela*. She couldn't bear to tell her Michael was in jail. Abuela would order her home immediately.

So she ended up back at the office of the Monarchist Society, staring out the window at the twinkling streetlights lining the courtyard. The white curve of a half-moon flickered into view between the bare limbs of the trees outside, casting shadows on the aristocratic portraits and mementos lining the walls. She stared blankly at the itinerary Dmitry had prepared for her and all of Irina's notes neatly placed underneath a blotter on the desk.

Michael was paying for her ambition. The thought made her

stomach turn. The more time she spent by herself, turning over worst-case scenarios in her mind, the more she was convinced coming to Russia had been a huge mistake. She'd had a secure job; she was rebuilding her relationship with her grandmother. She could have gone to Los Angeles to see Michael. When she reviewed the way her life was taking shape, she wasn't sure her head had done her many favors. She should have listened to her heart.

Her phone pinged and a text message from Dmitry popped up on the screen.

I'M STILL AT REB'S APARTMENT. TURN ON THE TV.

Veronica didn't have access to a television, but she stayed on her phone, searching for the latest news to come out of Russia, anything connected to Reb.

She soon found the footage. She recognized the front steps and the same crowd of protesters she had seen in Palace Square earlier in the day. Rainbow flags unfurled and she spotted the picture of the Russian president with makeup. A few black-clad policemen lingered toward the back of the crowd. Reb descended the staircase with Dmitry two steps behind him and the crowd cheered. He waved and looked as though he were about to speak.

Before he got the chance, the camera jostled, suddenly focusing in on something happening toward the back of the crowd. Two protesters—a boy and a girl no older than eighteen—had gotten into a scuffle with a policeman. Except this didn't look like an ordinary policeman, at least not the ones Veronica had seen earlier. The man who confronted the boy and girl wore a fur hat and a gray-green tunic coat with red military epaulettes. Veronica realized he was one of the so-called neo-Cossacks who had started engaging in military and civilian patrols. The camera focused on something that was in his hand, a gleaming piece of metal with long, snaking, rawhide tendrils attached to it.

A knout.

The Cossack pushed the protesters. When the boy made a move, he lashed the whip at them until they were huddled on the ground, feebly struggling to protect their faces from the blows. The Cossack turned toward the camera, looking very young. Too young. He raised his hand, raised the knout. The camera phone fell to the ground and the last few seconds were just shaky footage of shoes.

All of this had happened far enough away from the crowd that only a few people toward the back caught what was happening and recorded videos with their phones.

Veronica stopped the video. She couldn't take it anymore. She had always been prone to anxiety, but nothing like this. A wave of panic sat heavily on her chest, paralyzing her.

As she struggled to catch her breath, her gaze shifted to the drawings of St. Petersburg in its early years. What a quaint little city it seemed back then, and yet she knew the history. How many thousands of men had died forging a city in the swamp? St. Petersburg was nothing more than artifice, a pretty façade covering a history of leaders willing to build legacies on the massive suffering of other human beings.

Veronica shivered, chilled to the bone. She felt a presence draw near, not to speak with her but to judge her somehow. Slowly, she lifted her hand to massage her forehead. The muted gold of the frayed sword knot caught her eye. It hung precariously from a hook near the portrait of Potemkin. At that same moment, a truck rumbled by outside. The vibration shook the tassel from its place and it hit the floor.

A light chill skipped across her shoulders.

Veronica stared at the portrait of Catherine the Great. Maybe what Dmitry said was true and ghosts still haunted the building, looking for the old *banya*.

"Okay, I don't know if I even believe in any of this stuff at all," she whispered. "But if you're still around here somewhere, please. I could use your help now. I could use some advice." She looked at Catherine again, right in her steely blue eyes. "What would you do?"

She waited, but nothing happened. And she couldn't just stay in this office like an ass feeling sorry for herself and talking to imaginary spirits.

She turned to the portrait of the auburn-haired Prince Grigory Potemkin, Dmitry's ancestor. Catherine had been a strong woman, confident and self-assured. But Potemkin? One minute he was moody and ready to take on the world, and the next he withdrew from it completely. Veronica realized that for all her admiration of Catherine, she identified far more with her prince. Her eyes glazed over, imagining how he might respond to what was happening in contemporary Russia. She blinked quickly, trying to focus, and then found herself looking at the sketch of the mosque. The frame hung at an awkward angle. Veronica walked over to the drawing and tried to right the frame. When her fingers moved underneath the wood, she felt something dry and crumpling, poking out of the backing. Dust spotted her fingers.

Veronica heard a murmur of a voice in the hallway. She pressed as gently as she could on the paper and it began to slip out from its hiding place behind the frame. It looked like a letter, yellowing and smelling of must, so brittle with age she was afraid it might tear apart in her hands. The crumpled Cyrillic handwriting in the first part of the letter was shaky and her heart thumped wildly as she tried to make it out.

Matushka,

I can't believe we are separated this one final time, especially when I feel the end is so near. I want to be near to hold your little hand and help you with the hundreds of small tasks that occupy your day. But this time, darling wife, even from afar, I must ask you to grant me one last favor to make our legacy to this great empire complete.

The voice in the hallway grew stronger, headed her way. Veronica looked all around the room, her gaze coming to rest once more on the itinerary Dmitry had prepared for her. Hands shaking, she placed the delicate paper between two of the plastic leaves for safe-keeping. Then she went to the door to listen.

It was Irina, deep in conversation with someone on the other end of the phone. Veronica got as close to the door as she dared and strained to hear.

"Homosexual propaganda!" Irina was saying in Russian. "That makes him a clear and present danger to this country."

There was some kind of fuss on the other end of the line. Veronica braved a quick look through the narrow space between the door and the wall. Pale moonlight streamed into the hallway through high windows. Irina paced, twirling her blond hair in one hand.

"We knew the Americans would harp, but you assured me you could take care of that."

Veronica put a hand on her chest, certain Irina could hear her heart beating.

"Let him stay in there as long as we see fit. I need more time with her. Let her get more scared of what might happen to him."

She knew it. She knew there was something off about that woman. Veronica wanted to shove into the hallway, grab Irina's phone, hurl it away, and then punch her smug face. But first she wanted more information.

"I don't know how long. How should I know?" Irina cried. "They're only allowed to be in the country another few weeks anyway. I'm sure the silly American girl will behave by then. She doesn't want to see her handsome boyfriend rot in jail. Have another guard mess up more of his face. We'll make sure she sees it. That should be enough to convince her."

Veronica's hands balled into fists. She pushed on the door and stepped into the hall. When Irina saw her, she fumbled with her phone and almost dropped it.

"Tell me again," she said. "How do you want this silly American girl to behave?"

Seventeen

Grisha stumbled out of the alcove, still reeling, touching his pocket to make sure the vial of laudanum was situated deep within and would not slip. Candles blazed, dripping wax, making the hallway so hot he didn't know how much longer he could bear it. He grasped one of the pillars the designers had fashioned as an exotic palm tree to celebrate his triumphs in the south. His time in St. Petersburg had passed. His time as a force in this world had passed. But then hadn't he known that from the beginning, from the moment he first stepped into Zubov's makeshift salon of fawning courtiers? The darkness unleashed venom in his mind. Zubov was the future. Grisha was useless. He was nothing. He should have retired years ago to the monastery.

Zubov touched his arm. "What say you, Prince?"

Grisha shook the boy's hand off. Having secured the vial, he moved his hand to a lower pocket where he kept a few spare rubies. Grisha rubbed the tiny jewels, trying to will the floor not to spin so quickly at his feet. He ran his toe along the design of a lily of the field on one of the thick floor runners he'd had Anton order last week. How he wished the boy was at his side now, rather than managing the vulgar French comedy. How satisfying the courtiers would have found this performance. Grigory Potemkin's final fight and bested by a dandy. He laughed softly.

"Have I said something amusing?" Zubov swung his long arms behind his back.

"Nothing at all, I can assure you. I can't recollect a time when you've said anything I found even remotely humorous."

"I should think you'd be more upset. For all your talk of empire and legacies, when it comes down to it, all you care about is your own fortune and reputation."

"And what do you think I should do if you insist on starting this rumor?"

"I suppose you might try to convince Catherine I'm wrong. She might believe you. But then she may not have the energy to deal with your foolishness any longer either."

He had raised Catherine's hopes, and his own hope as well, for a new life together. And all for naught. The pain of it made him sick to his stomach. He would hurt her again. But he could not let her pay such a high price for his own thwarted ambitions.

"Personally, I think the empress will be relieved to see you go," Zubov said, his voice tearing through the shadows in Grisha's heart. "She has grown so flustered these past few weeks. She believes the two of you work best when you are apart, even if you are man and wife. You will do her a favor by leaving. Some might see it as your duty to the motherland."

"Perhaps so, perhaps not. But I cannot go to the empress because I intend to sap this rumor of its strength here and now."

Zubov looked supremely proud of himself. "As I anticipated."

Grisha rose to his full height and moved forward. The boy reeled, as though Grisha might strike him. But then, just as quickly, he extended a tentative hand, like he wanted to catch Grisha should he fall.

"I will leave the capital, as you request," Grisha said. "But if either you or that dimwit Paul lets this falsehood carry any farther than your two ridiculous minds, I assure you I will return as quickly as the finest horse can fly, find you in the dead of night, and slit your throats myself."

Zubov raised one of his pale hands protectively to his neck, the ruffles at the end of his shirt flopping. "What an empty threat, Prince. All that to defend your sullied reputation?"

"If you let a word of this breathe out, who else are you implicating?"

A slow light of recognition flickered in Zubov's pretty and vacant eyes. He made a little huffing sound.

"Whom have I had carnal relations with and might also carry the illness?" Grisha pressed.

"The empress . . ."

"If you impugn me, you cast doubt on Catherine's sanity. And perhaps you truly did not consider that part when you concocted this little plan with the grand duke. But I assure you, Paul had it in his head all along and will be more than happy to have those around us believe his mother no longer fit for her duties. They might fashion it a crisis for the empire."

"But . . . ," Zubov sputtered, "anyone with a lick of sense knows Catherine is as clearheaded as ever. She is in her prime."

"And when has the truth ever mattered when shifts of power are readied?" Grisha withdrew his handkerchief and mopped his wet brow. "You said as much yourself. When the Orlovs dispatched Catherine's late husband, they said he had died of hemorrhoids. Everyone believed that story as though angels had drifted down from the heavens to declare it true. If even a few power-hungry fools latch on to your ridiculous tale to have Catherine declared an imbecile, in exchange for a few choice positions granted by her moron of a son . . ."

Grisha paused, drawing in a deep breath, fingers flexing. He knew he took a risk revealing all of this, but on the other hand he knew he was merely collateral damage in this sordid affair. Paul's true target was Catherine. Zubov's talents in the boudoir would be of little interest to Paul—or at least if they were, Paul would need to keep that fact quiet. If Catherine were to go, Zubov could find himself kicked out of the palace with a far less generous pension than Catherine would provide for him should she ever tire of his companionship.

Zubov stomped his black boot on the carpet and made a quick half-turn to hide his expression. Grisha exhaled, feeling the fabric of his waistcoat tight against his bloated stomach. Try as the boy did to hide, even with one good eye Grisha could see everything clicking together in Zubov's mind, how Paul had manipulated him. Paul would never view Zubov as anything other than a pawn. Catherine, on the other hand, adored him.

"I admit I did not consider the matter in this light," Zubov said slowly. "I thought only of the great fear Catherine has of acquiring the illness."

"I will tend to a few last affairs in St. Petersburg and then I will return to the south as the empress has suggested, to negotiate peace with the Turks. That should satisfy Paul for the moment." Grisha loosened a button at his throat. "But it will be on your shoulders to assure he never lets this rumor get out. That Paul is kept in his place."

"If you concede and leave . . . and leave Catherine to me . . . I assure you this rumor will not come to light. I swear it on my life. If I go back on my word, return and cut my throat. And if Paul makes any move to threaten Catherine, I shall cut his throat myself."

It was in the boy's best interest that Catherine remain on the throne, but Zubov also carried a note of true affection in his voice when he spoke of her. Even with the tremendous age difference between them, he supposed Zubov might have developed a measure of passion for Catherine's keen and ever-curious mind, her spirit. It was something they shared, their mutual respect and love for this woman. Zubov's love could never match Grisha's, of course, but the thought left him feeling a bit warmer toward the boy.

"I will do as I'm told," Grisha said, bowing. "But I desire private time with the empress now, so that I may break the news to her. I expect it will take her by surprise."

Zubov's lip twitched. "Of course."

"And you needn't worry," Grisha said casually. "The rumors of the venereal illness are just that. Rumors. It is one scourge I have avoided in this life."

"I was not worried," Zubov said, too quickly.

"Even so," Grisha said, backing away from him so that he might find Catherine, "I thought it would be best to put your mind at ease."

The pasha waited, as Grisha expected he would, even before he detected the chill in the air. He stood right outside the entrance to the room where Catherine and the others were watching the French comedies, laughter still ringing in the halls. From the stern expression on his face, it seemed he had heard every word Zubov uttered.

"They say your woman awarded you a saber covered in diamonds to reward you for your victories over our empire," the pasha said. "Such a prize, crusader. Did you earn every last one of those jewels? Do they each represent a soul slaughtered?"

Grisha turned right and left and then made a full circle to ensure they were alone before he spoke. "You were never awarded such mementos by your superiors? Were there no battles that gave you pause? That made you remember the blood you had spilled rather than the glory? Are your hands so clean you feel compelled to haunt me?"

The pasha bent to stroke the golden fur of the lion crouched at his feet. Grisha cringed and leaned against the wall, sure the lion might leap and sink his teeth in his throat. Both of them seemed corporeal to Grisha, no fuzziness around their edges at all. He kept telling himself these were mere apparitions, visitors in this world. And yet the pasha's presence was no less real.

"I have done all I could," Grisha whispered to the pasha. Stage voices rumbled through the walls along with raucous laughter. He supposed the noises of the audience covered his own voice well enough, but he didn't want to take any chances. "You heard the boy. I must return to the south. It is in God's hands now. My work here is done."

"Your woman will construct the mosque in Moscow?" the pasha said.

"I don't know. I must leave her now. I can stay in St. Petersburg a while longer, but I must withdraw from her affections or these boys will destroy her. She can't fight her favorite and her son when they conspire together, nor can I."

"It would be a terrible thing to leave now when you almost have your woman back in the palm of your hand."

"I will leave to save her. It is the right course of action, even if it comes with regrets."

"I have regrets as well, infidel. We all make mistakes in war." The pasha stared at him intently, even more closely than he had during his past visits.

A powerful sensation washed over Grisha, making his limbs tremble and clouding his vision entirely. He had returned to Ochakov, as though his body had been transported south.

His men wanted vengeance. Whenever they looked toward the fortress, they saw the grotesque and slowly rotting heads mounted along the walls, bruised now with frostbite. The faces of his remaining soldiers grew grim, set with determination. He sympathized with their frustration, felt it gnaw deep in his own soul. Still, he could not give the order. He paced the encampment, biting his inflamed red thumb, already haunted by the number of casualties both sides were sure to incur. There had to be another way. The Ottoman leaders in Constantinople would see the foolishness of their stubborn refusal to relent.

But they did not surrender, not even in the face of a Russian force with far superior numbers. Constantinople was not so far away, merely across the Black Sea. It must have seemed the infidels were closer than ever to triumph in their latest crusade.

He could not turn away. The Turks would only follow and no doubt feel even more emboldened by his cowardice. Even if they did not engage, they would take a few of his men at the very least, stragglers in the back. They would behave as savages, slice off the heads of his men and throw them at Grisha's feet. He must not allow that to happen.

He waited, silently praying he was wrong and the enemy would surrender. He thought he could see their eyes on him, judging, and rightly so.

And so Grisha had given the order to take the fortress, to plunder at will. The fighting commenced. The siege was a success. A massacre, as he knew it would be. He had no choice. The enemy had had ample opportunities to surrender and refused. He did what he had to do.

When Grisha gave the call to charge the fortress, his soldiers were merciless. The bodies of fallen warriors piled on top of one another on the streets, trampled by horses and soldiers. The blue lips and sickly pallid faces of Ochakov's defenders were etched in his memory, constantly accusing him. He had done this. He had given the order. He had destroyed them, had destroyed their world, all for the sake of his New Russia. His version of God, a deity who could allow this destruction, was a cruel being. They hadn't spared the women. They hadn't even spared children. He watched one of his adjutants wander past the remains of the city's mosque with a child gripping his hand. The girl had tangled black hair and blood on her face and the expression of a shocked recruit. When a Russian soldier passed them, the adjutant shielded the child instinctively with his arms. She could not have been more than seven.

The little girl lowered her gaze, afraid even to look at Grisha.

Later, safely inside his own tent, he would vomit into a basin.

Allah would demand retribution, or at least atonement. God would punish him. The Muslims may have called their God by another name, but their deity was one and the same. In the end, he hadn't chosen God. He had let his men run wild. He had chosen war and glory and ambition and blasphemy. God would never allow it to stand.

The Russian mosque was to have been his atonement.

"Make this right," the pasha said, startling Grisha back to the present.

"I'll try," Grisha told him. "But I fear I don't have long left."

"Then you must make the most of your time."

Grisha stared into the eyes of the pasha, vivid and flashing.

"If I fail you," he said, "I have failed you for my empress and my wife."

"Both of whom are below Allah. Even below your God."

"God might punish me for my choices," Grisha said softly. "But I can't ignore the boy's threat and leave Catherine to the wolves. I belong to her. This is my destiny."

As the final performance of the evening drew to a close, Catherine stifled another yawn. The instant the curtain was drawn, Grisha rushed to her side and offered his arm, which she accepted gratefully. She allowed him to drape a warm stole over her Russian gown and watched his reflection in the gilt-framed mirrors on the opposite wall. Grisha tried to smile, but his heart had already compressed into a hard ball. His lips could scarcely part to speak and he loathed the solemn lack of humor in his voice. "Would you see the Winter Garden one last time before you depart?"

She regarded him slyly. "Trying to get me alone?"

He tried to keep his tone formal. "I would be honored by the pleasure of your company."

As they walked to the garden, Catherine noticed the change in him, the stiffness in his shoulders and the stern set of his lips. "What's wrong?"

"Let us wait to speak until we are in private, *matushka*."

The Winter Garden looked as beautiful as he had dreamed, filled with exotic plants, winding paths, and small ponds. A circular temple stood in the center, surrounded by tall pillars and plants native to the Mediterranean climate, with a marble statue of Catherine in the center of it all, as though they had been transported back to ancient Rome and a devoted cult worshipped the empress.

He took a seat at the edge of one of the gurgling fountains, taking in the lush and florid scents. Catherine had been smiling up at her own image on the statue, but as soon as she saw him slump on the bench, she rushed to him and took his hand. "It was too much for you," she said in a low voice. "I should have insisted you not pursue such a lavish celebration. It is my fault."

"I'm fine." One of the trees had been adorned with miniature lemons fashioned from gold topaz. He plucked one of the gems from a low-hanging branch and shifted it from hand to hand, finding comfort in its solidity. "You have seen the night was a tremendous success."

"How could it not be?" she said. "With you at the helm?" She caressed the inside of his wrist, eyes guileless, as though all the time she had been on the throne had fallen away and she was a younger woman once more who had found her true soul mate at last. He had placed that hope in her heart and now he would have to retract it. "You have honored me, husband."

"I have one last . . ." His strength failed. He imagined again, as he had so many times over the years, a retreat to Nevsky Monastery, an escape from the world. He fell to his knees, wobbling. Catherine gasped, but Grisha kept himself upright. "I know you have seen the weakness in my body, wife. But you still believe I am of sound mind, do you not?"

She nodded uncertainly. "Why would I think any differently?"

"And that is why I beg you to grant me these last favors. And then I'll return to the south to negotiate the final peace with the Turks. Our conflict will end once and for all."

"Hush now," she said. "You must stay here and get well. Besides, I thought . . . the matters we had spoken of before . . ." Her lips slanted into a frown. Her tone formalized. "Have I deceived myself once more, Grigory Alexandrovich? Has your heart not truly returned to St. Petersburg? To me? When we last spoke I was under the impression that you wanted to try life as man and wife once more."

"As I have had time to reflect, I wonder if it wasn't impetuous." He stumbled on the words, hating every one of them, hating himself for destroying his one remaining dream in this world. "We have tried before. We have tried to live together as man and wife. It never worked."

Catherine's expression remained stoic, the carefully practiced and diplomatic neutrality she had honed over decades of reign. Her heart might have been torn to pieces, but she would never betray her feelings to the outside world. Not even to him. He was but her subject, after all. A husband in name only.

She removed her gloves and placed her soft hand on his, trying to still its tremors. He could not look at her face any longer but only stared at her small hand, still youthful and smooth. He caught the scent of her perfume, unchanged over the years, floral with an undertone of musk. "What are you saying?" she asked.

"It was but a whimsy on my part, Your Majesty. The whimsy of a deluded man."

"I had not thought it whimsy."

"You asked me to return to the south, to New Russia," he told her. "You wished me to negotiate the final peace with the Turks.

You said I was the only man who could do so. It was wrong of me to question your wisdom in this matter. You are the empress of all the Russias. You have always known best. I am but your servant. It is our fate."

"Then perhaps it is I who am deluded. A deluded old woman."

He grasped her hand tightly. "You are the most perfect woman to have ever walked this earth. But you were right. My place is in the south. I must see to the peace. But promise me, *matushka*. You must be careful. Your son . . ." He still didn't dare speak Zubov's name. He didn't want her to get defensive. And deep inside he began to wonder if Zubov might not be her ally after all. "Consider handing the throne to Alexander. He is a kind boy. He will grow to be a tolerant ruler."

Catherine gave a hoarse laugh. "What a dream," she said. "But passing over Paul? The stir such a move would cause. Could I survive it?"

"You survive anything you set your mind to surviving. I have seen this with my own eye . . ." He gestured to his useless eye, no longer strong enough to hide the defect from her view. At least his humor remained.

Catherine smiled sadly. "I might survive such a momentous decision were you at my side to guide me, husband."

"I wish that could be so. But, *matushka*, I don't know that I will see you again."

Catherine took his arm and tried to make him rise. Summoning every last reserve of his strength, he resisted. His weight was too much for her to handle and he remained in his submissive pose. He wanted her to understand the seriousness of the moment, the significance of his final words. "You are scaring me," she said.

"I need to speak plainly." His breathing came with difficulty, his chest and enormous stomach rising and falling only with great effort. His body could not last forever.

"But why? Why won't you rest and have some peace? Why must you always push me?"

"I won't see you again," he said.

A few tears slipped from her eyes. She was not above playing such tricks, manipulating his emotions, but it was different this time around. He sensed she could not control the tears, only the rest of her expression. "Don't say this, my little dove."

"You know it as well," he told her. "I will not live to see your reign come to an end. It is best I leave. That we let the past be the past so that you might have your happiness here. I have no part in that anymore. I shouldn't have tried to distract you."

"I thought . . . I thought perhaps your feelings were . . ."

"I cannot do it. I cannot return to that place in our lives."

She bowed her head and he had to turn away. But better this than to be taken down by a cruel rumor planted by her own son. He thought of the pasha, of his own horrific memories, and considered mentioning the mosque one last time. But when he saw the crushed look on her face, he could not do it. He could not let her think their entire relationship boiled down to political favors. That must not be her final memory of him. He would need to find another path to atonement.

"You always make the just decisions," he told her. "The difficult decisions. The decisions that have created an enlightened Russia." She tried to pull him up again, but again he resisted. "Promise me you will continue to do so."

"I promise," she whispered. "Only please, husband, rise and let me hold you again."

At last, he pulled himself up. She fell into his arms, weeping. As he held her soft and pliable body in his arms, he began to cry as well. The courtiers had gathered at the perimeter of the Winter Garden, pretending an interest in the exotic plants and their jeweled fruits. Grisha wasn't fooled. He glared at them over Catherine's shoulder. They knew what was happening and wanted to witness the final farewell, get a glimpse of how matters stood between the empress and her old favorite. Grisha didn't see the grand duke but had no doubt Paul's spies were among the courtiers.

Reluctantly, Catherine pulled away and straightened her back. She was a head shorter than Grisha and yet at that moment she seemed to tower above him. This is why she was the empress and he a mere subject. She could survive anything.

"Hot tea," she said. "Rest. I command you attend to your health."

Grisha bowed low. "As you say." He looked up to see her one last time. "Farewell, wife."

She turned and slanted her fan in his direction. "*Au revoir*, husband. Take care of yourself. I will see you again. I cannot bear to think otherwise."

A few guests lingered still in the main hall of the palace, faces he didn't recognize or that were disguised under colorful Venetian masks. His servants in their blue and yellow livery cleared the remains of the feast. Oleg had put the jewel-encrusted hat away for safekeeping and now sampled one of the last of the sugared pears, licking the sweetness from his fingers. Anton stood by the door, frowning at the other boy.

Grisha was so happy to see Anton he could have fallen into his arms. Instead, he settled for a quick click of his heels and a little military salute.

Now his thoughts raced with more he could have said to Catherine, words he could not manage in her presence. But he was so tired he did not know if he could take his quill to vellum. "Do you have time for a letter? I have a few words to commit to paper tonight."

"I can manage it, Your Highness."

Grisha had planned fireworks for the culmination of the night, but they had been late in starting, as the servants waited for the rainstorm to pass. He heard them pop from the courtyard now. The scent of gunpowder seeped through the windowpanes. Blue and silver spirals of light illuminated the dark sky and wispy gray clouds, eclipsing the stars and even the moon itself in honor of the empress.

She said she could not bear life without him. Grisha knew better. Catherine could bear anything. God had ordained her as empress. He might serve her better from a distance. It was God's will.

Anton approached timidly and Grisha beckoned for him to join him at the window.

"Have you any desire to see the southern lands of our empire?" he asked the boy. "Our New Russia. It is my legacy here on this earth."

Anton pulled on the tail ends of his new jacket and frowned. He knew Grisha's moods well now, sensed the melancholy's descent. "Is everything all right, Your Highness?"

"It will be," Grisha said. "In the end I have faith it will be."

Eighteen

FOR IMMEDIATE RELEASE *(FIRST DRAFT)*

ROMANOV HEIRESS TO LEAD BOYCOTT OF VODKA PRODUCTS
ST. PETERSBURG, RUSSIA

Dmitry Potemkin, spokesperson for the Russian Monarchist Society, can now confirm that Romanov heiress Dr. Veronica Herrera has called for a boycott of Russian vodka. The honorary tsarina hopes this action will bring greater attention to the pending imprisonment of Reb Volkov and other issues facing the gay community in Russia.

ST. PETERSBURG
PRESENT DAY

When she saw Veronica in the doorway, Irina pressed her lips tight and smoothed her silky blouse. She tilted the phone away from Veronica and glared, recovering her composure quickly enough. "You should have let me know you were here. How rude."

"You had Michael arrested. How could you?"

"How could you?" Irina glanced behind her in the corridor and then pushed her way into the office, not actually shoving Veronica back but forcing her to move abruptly to avoid Irina's smacking right into her. "We had everything arranged for your visit. Dmitry even created that ridiculous itinerary." She gestured to the red leather binder behind Veronica on the desk. "Everything was in place. And then you had to ruin it by turning your presence in our country into a controversy. Reb, Reb, Reb. I am so sick of that name!"

"I want to help him. I never kept that a secret."

"Do you understand how close we are? We have the votes we need in the Duma for restoration of property to rightful owners. Do you know how much Sasha could inherit?"

Veronica didn't know the exact number, but since Sasha was an heir to the Yusupov fortune, she imagined it was no small amount.

"Our supporters in the Duma are the same people who supported the propaganda law. They count on the Society to support their social views and they don't approve of the homosexual lifestyle. They believe Moscow is the third Rome, an example of true faith for the rest of the world. Your support for Reb and this ridiculous boycott will turn them against us."

"I don't care. I don't want to have anything to do with those people."

"This is the problem when Americans get involved in other nations. You are so sure you have the moral upper hand. You want to impose your worldview on everyone else."

"I'm not trying to impose my worldview on anyone, but that doesn't mean I can't speak my mind."

"You're the heiress to the Romanov throne. When Dmitry suggested we find you and bring you here, of course I went along with that plan. But Dmitry . . . and then you . . ." She put her hands on her head as though trying to contain her frustration. "Neither of you truly understands. The Russian people believe Reb's lifestyle is immoral. No one can help how they feel. That is their imperative. It's none of our concern. Certainly none of yours."

"When something is wrong, it's everyone's problem," Veronica said. "It's not just about how they 'feel.'"

"Reb broke the law."

"With his paintings? Come on. And why did you have Michael arrested? I just heard you say they would hold him as long as you want. This is under your control. You know someone who will keep him there for you. Do you know what they're doing to him?" Veronica heard the tremor in her voice. "He has a black eye. They beat him."

"It is a Russian jail. One black eye is nothing."

"That's all you have to say for yourself? A black eye is nothing? You did this to him."

Irina fiddled with the slender diamond tennis bracelet on her wrist. "You have some sort of proof?"

"I heard you on the phone. I think you planted pamphlets in his coat and told the police to search him. Why? What do you expect me to do?"

"I expect you to be reasonable," Irina snapped.

"You expect me to be your puppet."

"First you meddle in Reb's case. Then you call for a boycott of a major Russian export and insult Vasily Turgekov, one of our strongest allies and a beloved figure in our community." Irina moved closer to Veronica and lowered her voice. "You are a traitor to the true Russian cause. The new Russia. I want you out."

"I'm the Romanov heiress. I'm here to help Reb."

"I understand that. I'm not a monster. I'm not opposed to projects with political implications. For example, the mosque that Dmitry included in your dossier? Grigory Potemkin's old ambition? You could focus your energies on that as a show of goodwill to our Islamic residents. Isn't that worthy of your attention?"

"You only support the mosque because it will smooth out the transition of property to the old families in Muslim regions."

Irina took a step back. The shift in her movement was subtle enough, chin tilted defiantly upward, index finger slowly tapping against her hip. But her features hardened and her voice remained perfectly crisp. "You know, we always had our doubts about you, even if you were a clear descendant of the last family."

Veronica's shoulders tensed. "Because I'm American? Because I support Reb?"

Irina looked her up and down. "No."

"I don't 'look' Russian enough for you?"

"Oh, of course. The backward Russians must all be racists," Irina said sarcastically. "No, we had a much deeper concern. Not only me. Dmitry as well."

Veronica drew in a sharp breath.

"We worried about you because you're not a mother. Both Dmitry and I wondered if Russians would ever truly accept a woman who wasn't a mother. After all, you would be a mother to the people. Their *matushka*."

Veronica focused on the wall behind Irina, at the portraits of Catherine and Potemkin, but the words hit their mark and wounded a tender spot in her heart, all the more painful because deep down she believed them to be true.

"I see how you look at that picture of Catherine, as though somehow she will give you inspiration. But remember she was a mother. You're not."

The dry aching sensation, the hopeless longing, seized Veronica's heart, the same pain she felt when she saw small children. It was a part of life that had passed her by; her miscarriage had brought that chapter of her own story to a close. She tried to accept it gracefully, but the ache was still palpable, throbbing, worse than ever.

Her voice sounded small to her own ears. "I have a right to be here. I belong here."

"You have been away from this country too long. I know you probably have some perverted Western feminist notions and think it is fine to choose not to have children. But Russians are traditional. They are true to the church and to the natural order. Russians will wonder if you are a real woman. How can they trust someone who isn't real?"

Stumbling away from Irina, Veronica tried to engage her brain, to remember that she said this only to hurt her. But the words were too powerful to ignore.

"I think your entire life, you've made a mess of things," Irina said. "That's my sense of you now. I will pray for you."

Veronica looked away, hating Irina and her version of God. "Please don't."

"I should have known. A blasphemer as well, just like your precious Reb Volkov. You're not an Orthodox Christian. But I thought you had a love for this country. For Russian ways. For the Russian soul. I know better now. You shouldn't have come here. We should make other plans and have someone else in line as our honorary tsar."

And what if Veronica hadn't come? She would still be back in Bakersfield, no children, no career, and no prospects. Likely still keeping Michael at arm's length. This was where she was meant to be and now it would all be taken away. "So you have some alternate person in mind?" The words felt broken as they came out of her mouth, dulled by pain.

"Perhaps Sasha can be traced to the Romanovs. I believe he has a more pragmatic view of these matters."

Veronica doubted Sasha's Yusupov bloodline gave him any claim to the throne whatsoever. She also doubted, given how excited the paparazzi had been to follow her, anyone would care if his claim was legitimate. He would smile and look tall and rugged and masculine and date glamorous women. That would be enough for the papers to start calling him the second coming of Peter the Great.

Irina checked her phone. "Consider everything I said. I have a donor meeting this evening. Let me know by morning. I'll make all of the necessary arrangements and ensure your Mikhail is released safely. And I can get you a flight back to America quickly. I think now that I was wrong about you moving to St. Petersburg. You will be happiest back in California."

Veronica felt like she had to say the words, even though she knew the answer. "And if I don't agree?"

Irina looked up at Veronica once more, gaze steady.

"Then I can't promise what will happen to your friend Mikhail," Irina said. "But I know Russian prisons can be dangerous places."

After Irina left, Veronica stumbled back into the leather chair, staring blankly at the itinerary. Her last day in Russia was to have been spent touring landmarks and visiting different bars around the city, trying to convince the owners to participate in the boycott. But of course Dmitry hadn't added that to the official itinerary. Veronica remembered what Irina had just told her, that Dmitry had doubts about her because she wasn't a mother, and then she rubbed the sides of her head until her skin chafed. For all she knew Irina was lying about that, just trying to get deeper under her skin. And Veronica was letting her do it.

She forced her hands back down on the desk and then gazed once more at the portraits of Catherine and Potemkin, their clever eyes and steady gazes. Well, perhaps Prince Potemkin's gaze wasn't particularly steady. You could tell he had commissioned the portrait to be drawn as a three-quarters profile, his bad eye hidden. And narrow cracks split the oil around the corners of the painting. Still, he looked formidable.

Veronica wanted to forget everything, even her reasons for coming here and wanting more out of life in the first place. She wanted to retreat to her hotel room, hide under a blanket, and cover her eyes, the way she used to when she was a child, thinking that if she couldn't see anyone perhaps no one could see her either.

Instead, she stared at Prince Potemkin. As she looked at his portrait, it occurred to her that he had no children, no direct descendants. Dmitry was related to him through one of his nieces, and Sasha was an even more distant relation than that.

Veronica rose to her feet, still eying Potemkin, her heart beating fiercely now. For all she knew, he felt the same way she did about not having children. Perhaps he had regrets. But she bet no one had ever told the prince he couldn't lead because he didn't have children, or that somehow other Russians wouldn't find him "real" enough.

Still standing, Veronica flipped to the back of the binder and withdrew the letter she'd tucked away there earlier. In her previous academic life, she never would have handled such a delicate document with bare hands. She would have used latex gloves and the long tweezers archives provided to turn pages. Fortunately, she was no longer an academic, and she needed to know what Grigory Potemkin, Dmitry's Grisha, had told Catherine. She needed to know right now.

His handwriting in the first two paragraphs was shaky and she struggled to read and translate. But his hand seemed to have steadied somewhat as he finished the letter.

Matushka,

I can't believe we are separated this one final time, especially when I feel the end is so near. I want to be near to hold your little hand and help you with the hundreds of small tasks that occupy your day. But this time, darling wife, even from afar, I must ask you to grant me one last favor to make our legacy to this great empire complete.

We spoke of empire and expansion and absorbing the continent into an enlightened and prosperous whole. I know my project to build the mosque may seem a minor part of this grand vision, but think of the implications. We are rulers who do not need to impose their wills on the people of this land. You, the empress of the greatest land on earth, do not need to rule with an iron fist, but can merely lead by gentle and intelligent example.

I believe you were put on this earth to do just that.

Forgive me for our petty squabbles and shouting matches. Forgive me for my arrogance and all the times I let my ego stand in the way of true communion with you. Forgive my anxieties. Know that I love you for both your beguiling womanhood and your holy destiny as our tsarina. I feel my end drawing near. I know whatever happens, your legacy for this world is greatness and compassion. I wish you were here with me at the end, but I take comfort in the memory of your small hand in mine and the certainty that you will soldier on, as you always do, and many will have been blessed and enriched by your courage and your destiny. You may be the greatest woman who has ever walked this earth. I was honored to even have been near you, let alone allowed to treasure and love you and aid in your mission. I love you.

Your devoted husband as ever,

G

Below that, Potemkin had added curving arabesques, elegant Arabic figures scrawled along the bottom of the page. Veronica didn't believe they were actual letters. They looked more like symbols, a secret code between Potemkin and Catherine.

Veronica stared at the letter, so precarious in her hand. If she had tugged too hard when she pulled it from its hiding place in the frame, the paper would have crumpled to dust between her fingers. She wished she could break the code at the bottom of the page, draw some wisdom from it. Potemkin must have had something monumental to say to Catherine to bother with a code at all. How fragile the message and how many circumstances could have prevented her from receiving it. And yet, this simple letter from Grisha Potemkin, his final letter from the sound of it, had made it into Veronica's hands.

Veronica's academic impulse lingered still. She always liked to play the "what if" game, guessing how figures from history might respond to present-day problems. It was an exercise her colleagues found pointless. Academic history had become the realm of data and statistics and cold analysis. Their loss. History was a connection to the past, spiritual and transcendent. She was connected to a country that prized those two traits, whose Orthodox Christian religion was built on them. And yet the religion had been twisted into a hard political doctrine and the result was hate.

Veronica reread the letter and carefully returned it to the plastic sheeting in her binder.

She picked up her phone and texted Dmitry.

Veronica huddled over the heavy desk with Dmitry and Anya. She had opened the curtains wider and thin moonlight and street lamps cut through the haze outside. Dmitry and Anya both remained stoic, their mouths set in grim lines. Anya's floral *hijab* was slightly askew, and shadows fanned in half circles beneath Dmitry's eyes.

"How is Reb?" Veronica asked.

"He has had death threats before." Dmitry picked up one of the little jade frogs on the desk. His fingers trembled, but he kept his voice steady. "So, unfortunately, he is used to such a tense situation. He will be fine for now, but he is anxious. He is scheduled for transport to Siberia day after tomorrow." Dmitry looked over his shoulder, at the portraits of Catherine and Potemkin, and then back at Veronica. "So you said Grisha now inspires you? Because of this letter. I don't understand. Tell us how this is so?"

"I feel as though I was meant to find this letter. I felt hopeless and then it inspired me." Veronica explained the situation, what she had overheard. She told them Irina was responsible for Michael's arrest, that she had planted pamphlets in his pocket. It was how she intended to manipulate Veronica.

"She wants you to relinquish your claim?" Dmitry said slowly.

"Right," Veronica said. "It caught me off guard. I knew she supported restoration of property to noble families. But I never realized how strongly she saw my involvement with Reb's case as an impediment to this. She's a true believer. She honestly thinks my viewpoint is anti-Russian, that I'm an interloper."

"Does she think the same of me?" Anya said, adjusting her *hijab*. "Or Dmitry?"

"I might be a meddling American, but I think she sees us all as traitors."

At that, Dmitry cringed.

"Irina always had strong opinions," he said in Russian, pensive, catching Anya's gaze. "I thought ultimately she was the best means to get someone like Dr. Herrera in a position to change things. I should have known better. I am sorry."

"If I have to relinquish my title to get Michael out of that hell, I'll do it," Veronica said.

"I only ask that you consider the ramifications," Dmitry said quickly. "You said she wants you to step down, but what will that mean for Reb? I do not think Grisha would approve of anyone forfeiting so easily. He would want you to fight."

"She still wants a ceremonial tsar. She even has a replacement in mind. She thinks Sasha should take my place."

Anya gnawed on her lip and said, "You think this is a good idea?"

"Not exactly," Veronica replied. "I think someone should take my place. But I have someone different in mind." She rapped on the desk with her knuckles and looked once more at the letter, at the scrawl of Grisha Potemkin's handwriting, and then at the portrait of him on the back wall. The cracks in the oil gleamed in the moonlight. "I will ask Sasha to take my place. But only temporarily. Only long enough for Irina to think I've caved."

"Why would he do that?" Anya cut in.

"I don't think he feels the same way Irina does. And I don't think he's as desperate for money or his rightful title or whatever it is Irina thinks. I've asked him to come here to talk it out."

"And then who will take your place?" Dmitry asked.

Veronica straightened her back, tried once more to project a regal air. "My father. Laurent Marchand. He's in St. Petersburg. My *abuela* told me. He wants to see me."

"What?" Dmitry cried. "He has never taken an interest in us before."

"He's tried to contact me. Michael was looking into it before . . ." She felt a catch in her throat. "Well, before what happened. My grandmother gave me his number. We've agreed to meet. I think he will help us."

"Nika . . ." Dmitry leaned forward on the desk, hands flat, holding her gaze. "I understand how difficult this is for you."

Veronica didn't want to hear any platitudes. Not even from Dmitry. "You can't possibly understand what it was like to see Michael in that jail cell."

"Of course I can," he said firmly. "I am thinking about what will happen to Reb."

Veronica lowered her gaze. She hadn't meant to force that image to Dmitry's mind.

"But you must consider the greater good," Dmitry said. "Mikhail is American. He will be released. Reb . . ." His voice started to break, his steady composure finally melting. "He will die in the *gulag*. You know that. Please don't do this to him. Please don't do it to me. You can't throw away everything we've worked toward."

"Dmitry . . ." The tears were starting to form, the dam threatening to burst. She needed to keep it together. She took Dmitry's hand. It felt like ice. He was so frightened. How could she not have seen it before? "I'm not throwing anything away," Veronica insisted. "Laurent can take my place. We can make this work."

"How do you know he will do the right thing for Reb? Support him?"

"I will make sure," Veronica said. "I promise."

Dmitry turned slowly to Anya. "What do you think?"

"I believe Nika," Anya said, nodding. "I believe she will get her father to help. But I have another concern." Anya crossed the room, to the sketch of the mosque, and bit her lip thoughtfully. "Irina wanted to work with the Muslim community. Maybe not for the right reasons, but she wanted to build Grisha Potemkin's mosque. I don't want to lose sight of this."

"The Islamic community has prejudices as well," Dmitry said. "Same as the Orthodox Christian community. If we are supporting Reb, we may have to let go of the mosque."

Anya touched her head scarf thoughtfully. "So the tsarina can call herself a believer and be tolerant. And yet I cannot?"

"I didn't say that," Dmitry told her. "I only said we might need to choose."

"Not necessarily." Veronica pressed Dmitry's hand one last time before releasing it. "Anya, I think you can help. You said you have contacts in the Muslim community. Perhaps we can bargain with them. We support the mosque, same as Irina did. She wanted help restoring property. We ask for something different in return. We ask them specifically not to interfere when it comes to Reb." She glanced at Dmitry. "We shouldn't have to choose."

Dmitry placed his hand on Veronica's arm. "I have to admit, I am impressed with what you have come up with here," he said with a slow smile. "Perhaps Grisha did inspire you after all. But are you sure about this? Meeting with your father."

Veronica stiffened, even at Dmitry's gentle touch. "It's the only way."

"But he has never tried to talk to you before? He never wants to talk to us. Why now?"

"I don't know for certain. But I need to trust that he will help us."

Dmitry tapped his chin thoughtfully. "If he does agree, Anya and I can get him in front of reporters." He hesitated. "Do you want me to come with you to see Laurent?"

"No," she told him. "I need to do this alone."

Dmitry nodded once more and there was a moment of silence, broken by the thud of heavy male footsteps in the hall.

"What's going on?" Sasha peeked his head inside the door. For once, he wasn't smiling. His beard was fuller now. On the one hand he looked like a typical California hipster, but the beard also gave him the trim bearing of Nicholas II. As Irina might have said, Sasha would play very well on Russian television.

"Thank you for coming," Veronica said. "We need to talk."

Sasha stepped inside. His brows pinched as he surveyed their faces. He must have heard at least part of what they'd said. A deeper understanding of the situation began to register in his expression. "What has my stepmother done now?"

Veronica shook her head but didn't explain anything further. She was sure he had heard and simply needed a few minutes to process the information. Somewhere in his heart, he knew what Irina might do to other people when she didn't get her way. She only hoped Sasha hadn't fallen so in love with the idea of reclaiming his fortune that he would go along with anything she told him to do.

"You know what happened to Michael Karstadt?" Dmitry said, switching to English and exuding confidence once more with his rich baritone.

Sasha's gaze landed on Veronica. "I know what happened to your friend Michael. And I heard what you said about my stepmother. I'm sorry. I know she's stubborn, but I never expected anything like this. I don't know what to say."

"Do you want to help us?" Anya said in tentative English.

Sasha hesitated. "What she did to Michael blows."

Dmitry frowned, misunderstanding what Sasha meant. "He doesn't agree with what she did," Veronica said quickly.

"I didn't know anything about it," Sasha said "And I don't agree with her politics. I don't think my dad would have either."

Veronica glanced backward at the picture of pretty Felix Yusupov on the wall. "Your father was proud of his family's heritage."

"Of course. *Konechno*," he added, trying out the Russian word and not completely mangling the pronunciation.

"And as a Yusupov," Dmitry said, "he would have been proud of connection to the Potemkin family." Dmitry gestured to the portrait on the wall. "To the prince."

Sasha gave Dmitry a guarded look. "Yes."

"I can't believe your father would have wanted you to pursue any kind of claim to the throne under these circumstances," Veronica said.

"If you will help," Dmitry said, "I promise we will remember when we review property claims." He opened his arms expansively. "Remember, you and I are family as well."

Sasha exhaled slowly and then glanced at the painting of Prince Potemkin. "I think I can help," he told Dmitry.

"Are you sure you want to cross your stepmother?" Veronica asked. "She thinks she can make you rich."

"Hey, I won't lie, I still want that to happen," Sasha said. "But you're right. It shouldn't happen this way. Who's to say I won't piss her off later and then next thing I know I'm in jail? I know what she's like. I got a taste for it growing up. She cares about herself. That's it."

"So you'll help us?" Veronica said. "Behind Irina's back?"

He gave her one of his easy smiles. "Just tell me what you need me to do."

Veronica returned to her hotel for the night. She was too worried about Michael to get any sleep, but she needed to at least close her eyes for a bit. When she checked in with the floor attendant, the woman grasped her hand and let out a string of exclamations about the lateness of the hour. Veronica gave her a reassuring smile, wishing her *abuela* were there.

"I want to show you something." The attendant reached into her desk drawer and pulled out a T-shirt. She unfolded it on the desk before her. It was the same shirt Veronica had worn at the press conference earlier. Free the Wolf.

"It is too small," the woman said, clearly perturbed and gesturing at the simple cotton item as though it had a mind of its own. "Otherwise I would wear. I bought it on the street from a young man."

Veronica stared at the logo, and the old woman's hands, spotted with brown freckles, curled around her own hand. Memories of the evening rushed through her mind: what Irina had said to her about not having children, the sad look on Dmitry's face when he related his concerns for Reb's safety, and Michael with his bruised eye, trapped and alone in that tiny cell.

She felt the tears coming and tried to push them back. "Thank you for supporting Reb. It means so much to me," she told the woman in Russian.

"Pffft." The woman released Veronica's hand. "I am believer." She reached under the collar of her lumpy sweater and withdrew an Orthodox cross hanging from a chain as proof. She kissed the cross and then tucked it back under her sweater. "Who is anyone to tell us what to think?"

This was the third time she'd heard something like this from a Russian, first the woman at the ticket counter at LAX, and then the policeman at the rally, and now her floor attendant.

"Thank you," Veronica told her. "Thank you. I agree."

"One of my grandsons . . . he is . . . well, he was never quite like the other boys. I think he will appreciate. I love him. I don't want anything to happen to him. What else could a grandmother do? I must show support."

At that moment, Veronica knew she was exactly where she was meant to be. "I am going to do everything I can for him. I promise."

The woman shrugged. "And maybe tomorrow I find shirt in bigger size so I can wear," she said. "We all will do our part."

Veronica waited patiently on a bench, glad for the solitude and peace. The day was cold, but the hazy morning fog had cleared and pale sunlight sparkled on the crisp Neva. The bells of Peter and Paul Cathedral chimed in a sharp, clear rhythm across the water. Nearby, a man in a sagging beret and a thickly lined jacket buttoned against the cold had set up an easel and started to paint a bright orange Rostral Column, focusing on the ship prows hanging from the thick base. Grim vendors bundled in winter coats sold fur hats, old Soviet military medals, and coffee mugs featuring shirtless pictures of the Russian president. Veronica scanned the goods but didn't see any more postcards of Grand Duchess Charlotte. She wondered if the card in her purse was one of a kind.

She checked her phone for the time, strangely calm. She wished Michael could have been there for a chat beforehand, to boost her confidence, but she knew she needed to face Laurent alone.

Even though she had never met him, she recognized him instantly.

Laurent Marchand approached her bench slowly, walking with the aid of a cane. Even though he was bent over, she could tell he was tall. That surprised her; she supposed he'd inherited his height from Alexandra rather than Nicholas. He was handsome too, silver-haired and dignified, with a soft hint of Charlotte's sister Grand Duchess Tatiana in his gracefully aging features. He wore nice gray slacks and dress shoes and a dapper woolen coat. He had the monarchist ribbon on the lapel of his coat as well, the Russian flag with the double-headed eagle.

Laurent had to stop and lean on his cane as he caught his breath. She rose to her feet.

He looked up again. Now he was close enough to catch Veronica's gaze. His coloring was fairer, but she saw the shape of her eyes and the contours of her own face. He approached faster now, at least as fast as he could manage with his cane, and then stopped before her, eyes tender.

Her stomach knotted, the calm receding. She refused to cry. He needed to earn her tears.

"It's true," he said softly in Spanish, the language they shared. "You're as beautiful as your picture. I knew you would be."

"Do I look like my mother?" The words felt awkward, but she needed something to say.

His odd accent combined perfect Spanish with a native French lilt. "Oh yes. I knew that would be the case as well. Of course she was much younger when I knew her." He hesitated. "I hope you don't mind me saying this."

"I'm sixteen years older than she was when she died. I know."

"May I hug you?"

"I'd rather wait on that."

He nodded sadly. "I understand. I'm grateful you agreed to meet with me."

Only because I need your help. But she said: "Why do you want to see me now? Why did you contact my grandmother? After all these years?"

"You were coming to Petersburg to work with the Monarchist Society. I was concerned."

"Concerned? Why? I know next to nothing about you. I grew up without you. You never contacted me." She hadn't planned to get into this. Not here. Not now. She needed Laurent's help. But after nearly forty years of frustration, she couldn't help herself. Veronica's sentences came out in short, staccato bursts that would have been better suited to English, although she spat them out in Spanish to make sure he understood. "All I knew was that you were my mother's professor. Oh! And that you left her alone."

"She wanted to be alone. What happened between us was never meant to be permanent."

"It was a fling? I'm a random accident."

"A fling, yes," Laurent said. "I don't know how else to put it. But I don't believe anyone on this earth is a random accident."

"You weren't curious about me at all?"

"I thought of you all the time, Veronica." He lifted his thin hands, pale and blue-veined and more fragile than the rest of his body. "I kept a picture on my mirror from when you were a toddler. Your grandmother sent it to me. As time passed, I wondered what you looked like as you grew older. What you were doing with your life. But after my experiences and my mother's experiences during the war, I needed to make your safety my first priority."

"It would have been better to let me know."

"My family didn't see it this way. Lena and her family agreed . . ." He looked down at his feet. "Even Lena's grandson, your friend Michael. The one you're so worried about now?" Veronica looked up sharply. He continued, "I'm sorry, I heard what happened. Michael agreed with us. Now more than ever he probably understands. Everyone wanted to keep you safe."

Veronica thought about what had happened yesterday, the way Michael gave one slight shake of his head before he was sped away from her. Her heart made a quick, panicked jump.

"But it wasn't just that," Laurent continued. "I have never been good for women. I've hurt them. I thought I would hurt you. But I guess I did anyway." He put his head in his fragile hands. "It's difficult to explain. Sometimes I hear voices in my head, nagging me, berating me. *Who do you think you are? You do not matter. You*

have never mattered. Every time something good happens, you ruin it."
He shook his head and looked at her again. "I honestly thought
you would be better off without me in your life."

Michael was alone in his cell, staring at the ceiling, face throbbing, no clue what would happen to him next. Perhaps he would
have been better off without her in his life. "Look, Michael was
arrested because of me. It's my fault. That's why I'm talking to you
now. I need to make it right. I have to relinquish my claim, and you
must make yours."

He nodded. "I understand. And now that the secret is out, I
can't see the point in staying away. I want to get to know you, Veronica." A thin shaft of sunlight played on his silver hair. "I noticed you published a paper on my grandmother Alexandra a few
months back."

Veronica's bottom lip twitched. "You read that?"

"I tried to follow you as much as I could from afar."

Her shoulders relaxed slightly, the tension flowing down the
back of her arms and away from her, like a bad memory fading. "It
was meant to be a book originally. But all that is over now. I didn't
make tenure. I'm a failed academic. I'm done."

"I thought it was very good. You can still write and research
and do whatever you want to do. Who can stop you? Where do
you want to live? Go there. Find a job you like and don't worry
about tenure. Enjoy your life. Don't settle for less."

"How European of you."

"And what's wrong with thinking like a European?"

"I'm American," she said. "Americans have steady jobs with
health insurance and kids and houses."

"That's why you came here?" Laurent asked. "You didn't feel
right in California?"

"I don't feel right anywhere. All of the things people do to
make something of their life, a family or a strong career, I don't
have those. I'm always an outsider."

"People on the outside are the most interesting, don't you think? They pay more attention. They keep everyone else from growing complacent."

Veronica bit her dry lips. She had to admit, hearing him say this made her feel a little better. "I suppose that's true. But it can get lonely."

"You want an ordinary life? Why? There are many forms of happiness. I hope you come to see this." Laurent's features remained serene, but he grinned. "You sound introspective, which makes you European enough."

"Perhaps." Veronica fiddled with the strap of her purse, avoiding Laurent's gaze. "When you said you're not good for women—what did you mean?"

His grin disappeared. "It is difficult for me to say. I know you probably have more romantic notions, but your mother was not the love of my life, it was a woman who came before her. I'm sorry. She probably wasn't the love of my life either, come to think of it, but the relationship had a profound effect. I felt as though I was cursed."

He pulled a monogrammed handkerchief out of his front pocket and began turning it over and over in his hands. Veronica recognized the motion of those hands. She made the same movement often enough herself.

"I'm not explaining this well," he said. "I must sound heartless. I cared for your mother."

"Yet you didn't try to find me. When she died, you pretty much made me an orphan."

"By that point I didn't think it would do any good. Your grandmother had taken over raising you. She is a determined woman and quite capable."

Despite everything, Veronica smiled. That was the least anyone could say about Abuela.

"Maybe you understand a little better now," he said. "At least I hope you do."

Veronica stood up. She still wouldn't look at Laurent but began to pace in front of him.

"You remind me of my mother," he said. "She could never stay still."

"Like Nicholas II."

"Yes. I've read that as well." He hesitated. "So what are you thinking? I don't expect forgiveness. But have I made myself understood? At least a little better?"

"I feel like I've heard this before from men who claim to care about me," Veronica said. "They keep secrets, supposedly for my own good. I don't like it."

Laurent nodded. "I understand. I only hoped you would hear me out."

Veronica needed to get to the heart of the conversation. "Did you hear anything about my press conference?"

"Oh, you don't know? It's been on the news all day." When he laughed, Veronica heard an echo of her own voice and twitched in recognition. "You handled yourself very well. Reporters are asking for comments from the Kremlin. You made an impact already."

Veronica's stomach clenched. *The Kremlin?* But Laurent sounded proud of her. That was a good sign. She needed to make sure they were in agreement. "Do you have a strong opinion on Reb Volkov?"

"Of course!" Laurent said defensively. "I think what is happening to him is wrong. The boycott of vodka is a good idea. It will put pressure on the government. Between that and the Romanov heiress speaking about Reb, it can make a difference."

Relief flooded her chest. "I'm glad to hear you say that."

"If my mother were still alive, she would be proud of you. If your mother were still alive, she would expect me to stand with you. And I want to stand with you. I don't agree with what is happening in this country. I never contacted the Monarchist Society because I thought they were taking Russia backward. But what you are trying to do . . . this is different."

Veronica kicked a random pebble beneath her feet. "Technically you are the heir to the throne," she said carefully. "Not me. Even if you've been a recluse."

"I never wanted a claim for myself. I never even wanted to be found." Laurent's voice trembled. "That is why I had to talk to you. I saw what happened to my mother. A Nazi officer knew of her connection to the Russian throne. He wanted to use her. He killed my father. I saw it. He shot my father and I'm sure the wound killed him. He died because of my mother's claim to the Romanovs."

Veronica stared at Laurent. "I never knew that."

"I barely knew my father. And I'll never know for sure what happened to him. That's how it is in war. And that is our family's legacy. How could I not think you would be better off without it?"

"Your father couldn't go to Spain with you?"

"We parted ways so the Nazis wouldn't follow. We thought it would be better in Spain. I loved it. I returned as an adult. But it was a dictatorship under Franco. I've hated our family's roots. I've hated the idea of monarchy, of absolute rule, of the Romanovs. But now I see that there are positive ways to handle a monarchy. I see what you wish to accomplish here."

Veronica leaned over, fishing in her purse until her fingers clamped around the postcard of Charlotte. "Here," she said, waving it in his direction. "I want you to have it."

Laurent looked at the card and then took it gently, staring at the picture of his mother. His gaze softened. He placed it lovingly in the front pocket of his coat. "A strong likeness. I shall treasure it." He stood up and took Veronica's hand.

"Relinquish your own claim," he said, "if that will help your friend Michael. I certainly don't want anything to happen to Lena and Pavel's grandson. They were so kind to our family. I owe a debt and I am happy to repay the favor. I suppose it's time I accept my own legacy and that of my mother. Consider the throne in good hands now."

Nineteen

THE BESSARABIAN HILLS
OCTOBER 1791

Orange sunlight filtered through the massive branches of the oak tree. Leaves gently swayed in the breeze while squirrels scampered to and fro between the limbs, bushy tails shaking as they ran. The wind kicked dust into Grisha's eyes and tiny insects ran through the grass beneath, finding exposed spots on his moist skin, under the furs and the fine silk of the dressing gown Catherine had sent him. A choir of birdsong echoed from above.

Why had it taken him so long to find such a place again? The natural world where one might commune with God. Where all was stillness and bliss.

"I was meant for the monastic life," he heard himself say aloud. "I was called into the service of the empress. I thought it God's will. But I always missed that simple life."

He closed his eyes and sensed a light pressure as another cool towel was applied to his perspiring brow and then gently wrapped from chin to forehead. The end drew near. He was sure of it. His affairs had been careening downward the past few months until it seemed inevitable. His body had finally grown tired of life's games.

When had it all started going wrong? Was it the money? He

hadn't left St. Petersburg as quickly as Zubov had hoped, and his debts from the ball continued to accrue, higher than even he had imagined possible. For the first time, Grisha was glad he had no direct heirs who might be forced to pay after he had departed from this world. Then again, he had been in debt before. And Catherine had always laughed and covered the expenses.

Perhaps the end truly began when the scribbled notes from Zubov arrived, all flattery and begging for advice, clearly dictated by Catherine to make the two of them friends.

As though Grisha had never redeclared his love for her at all.

In her latest care package, Catherine had sent a fur coat along with a dressing gown. He huddled deeper into the fur now. He could not let the antics of Platon Alexandrovich Zubov annoy him any longer, not when he had so little time left.

Voices murmured, at first muffled, but then as though shouting in his ear, sending searing bolts of pain through his head. All of the members of his makeshift New Russian entourage had gathered: boisterous Cossacks with thick black mustaches alongside taciturn Orthodox bishops, a rabbi with a long gray beard, and a mullah in pantaloons so loose they billowed in the wind. All waiting for him to finally pass from the earth.

"From what I gather, he has suffered from malaria since his service in the Crimean peninsula, nearly ten years ago," he heard one of the voices say, high and sweet above the others, though tinged with pain. One of his nieces had accompanied him on this last trip. "He is too stubborn and refuses the drugs. It is only a matter of time."

If only he could make them understand. His own actions could never lead to his end, for this was God's will alone. Soon the angel of death would descend and he would put this world behind him once and for all. He wasn't sure he was ready but had learned not to fight the inevitable. This was the ultimate test of faith.

Soft hands pressed the cool cloth gently on his eyes and then removed it. Anton's youthful features hovered above him. The boy's lips quivered and his eyelids scrunched in a way Grisha had not observed before. What would happen to the boy after Grisha left this earth? He had distinctly outlined Anton's fate in his will. The boy should remain free and clear of any obligations to his landlord back home. He would not return to serfdom. Instead, Grisha suggested a number of relations who might take the boy into their household. But his preference, carefully worded as a dying request, was for the boy to go to the palace, to Catherine's court. Even with Platon Zubov puttering about and Paul plotting in the background, Grisha knew Anton would thrive. If Zubov knew what was best for him he would watch his back around the boy.

He wished he could explain all of this to Catherine.

Anton tipped Grisha's head and helped him take a few sips of sour soup. The taste of cabbage may not have comforted every-one, but for Grisha it was a delight. It tasted of the earth. When he lowered himself back down onto the blanket, blades of grass beneath tickled his back.

"Some people in Europe think he is already dead," the mullah murmured.

Dead and buried in the ground, a corpse already starting to rot. Perhaps it was only wishful thinking on the part of foreign diplo-mats or a rumor spread by his old enemies at court. He drew in the uncontaminated scent of woodland air, the slight movement caus-ing agony.

Memories of home rushed through his mind, days tramping through fields of long grass, trying to keep up with his older sisters as they played blind man's bluff. He stumbled and hurt his knee. His sisters laughed and he ran home to his nurse, who bundled him in blankets and covered his face with a warm towel. She sang a song about a *troika* lost in the snow.

"Don't they have a custom for the dying . . . ," the rabbi said, "something about coins to send them off to the next world?"

All of his wealth in this world came from Catherine. If someone were to take a look at his financial records, they would see Grisha had not a coin to his name. He tried to laugh at the irony but only ended up wracking his body with another bout of hacking, as though his insides might explode from the effort.

One of the sturdy Cossacks began to make the rounds, picking at the ends of his mustache and asking if anyone had some coins he might use. He was greeted by shrugs and apologies. A bishop protested with a grunt. He said the Cossack shouldn't encourage Grisha, that it was inappropriate for an Orthodox believer to die on the grass. Grisha lifted his head.

"Move me and you'll have to contend with that one." He jerked his head toward Anton. "He won't let you interfere with the final wishes of a dying man."

Anton crossed his arms and the bishop fell silent. Grisha rested his head back on the ground, satisfied. Anton bent over and pulled Grisha's gown tighter around his chest. Catherine had spent the entirety of her last letter to him fussing over his health and imploring him to take care of himself. He had managed to write back to her one last time. He didn't trust the regular couriers with this letter though. He had given the note to Anton and watched him safely tuck it inside a pocket. He patted the pocket in his own gown, where a few of Catherine's love letters were still carefully held together with a velvet ribbon.

"Please forgive me," he repeated to the small crowd assembled before him. "Everything I did was in the interest of Empress Catherine. But if I have caused any suffering to any of you present, let us make our amends now." He looked at the Islamic scholar, but the man had shuffled toward the back of the group.

"We all know, Your Highness." Anton added lavender water to a new towel he wrapped firmly around Grisha's neck. "You can be at peace." The boy wiped a tear from his eye.

"And the letter . . ."

"I will see it gets to Catherine, Your Highness."

"No one else?"

"Directly to her. I promise."

Except that Grisha had not been able to adequately express his final wishes and the strain pushed hard on his heart, the last tendril of melancholia having its way with him, telling him he was nothing, that he had never mattered. "I need to finish. I had a thought for a postscript to better explain my feelings."

"She knows your heart better than anyone in this world. You have often said as much. You have expressed yourself clearly."

"If I had a few more moments . . ."

"You need to rest. She knows your feelings and your true affection."

Grisha felt once more as though he were suffocating, as though an unseen hand wrapped tightly around his throat and refused to let go. He sputtered. He had asked to travel because he thought a pristine natural environment might revive his worn body, perhaps even give him a few more months. But it had been a weak attempt to prolong this life. There was no point in arguing with God. When would he ever learn?

"I found something!" He heard the Cossack speak. The man held up a five-*kopek* coin, not exactly the gold used to send off the great Greeks like Agamemnon, to pay off the ferry captain on the way to the next world. Could a captain refuse him passage for such a light fare? Perhaps he would be sent back to this world and then the entourage would have to further contend with his pleas for forgiveness.

Another round of chills attacked and he shuddered uncontrollably, despite Anton's steady hand on his shoulder. A five-*kopek* coin would probably suffice.

Anton's gentle voice whispered in his ear. "It was a pleasure to serve with you."

"And with you," Grisha replied hoarsely. "Make good use of your life."

"I will. I promise."

Anton was pushed to the back of the crowd. Grisha could just make him out. He had the letter to Catherine in a roll by his side. He pulled it out of the casing and held it high, so that Grisha could see it above the gathering mourners.

The pasha stood to the right of Anton, shimmering and distant, a serene smile softening his harsh features. With great effort, Grisha inclined his head toward the letter for Catherine. The pasha nodded and then slowly faded.

Grisha had thought Catherine would die first. She was older than him, but he should have known better. Catherine might live forever. He could almost see her, hunched over the letter bringing word that he was gone and crying softly to herself, shunning even Zubov's advances as she clung to her grief. She was a strong woman and she would be all right. The empire they had built together would go on as well. Their time on this earth was brief, but it had meant something. He needed to cling to that belief.

All of his desires and ambitions evaporated, and it was as though the fever had broken and he felt himself once more. Perhaps he had been taken down too soon, but he had lived life fully and tried to make things better along the way.

The birdsong grew louder, more exquisite, rising slowly and sweetly to drown out the hustle and voices of the people around him. For a moment, he was once again transported back to the golden fields he had known as a boy, playing with the children from the serf families, stomping through the wheat until his nursemaid called for him to come inside, where she fed him buckwheat and turnips and told him stories of Father Frost and the Snow Maiden, the Firebird, and Prince Igor. The vision in his one good eye shifted, the trees and sky and grass merging into a single orange light.

"*Matushka*," he said quietly.

He couldn't see Catherine, but he sensed her presence, the gentle squeeze on his shoulder, the soft voice in his ear like a caress. *You belong to me. Now you can let go.*

Grisha closed his eyes and felt the earth sink beneath him.

Matushka,

I can't believe we are separated this one final time, especially when I feel the end is so near. I want to be near to hold your little hand and help you with the hundreds of small tasks that occupy your day. But this time, darling wife, even from afar, I must ask you to grant me one last favor to make our legacy to this great empire complete.

Anton read the rest of the letter in the dim light of the dying campfire, careful to keep his head back so his tears would not mar the vellum. The prince's scrawling handwriting stopped abruptly at the end of the second paragraph, and then he had added strange Arabic symbols to the bottom of the page, a code for the empress no doubt.

He had not wanted to travel to the south, despite the prince's ravings on the healthful air and clean living of the place. He detested *kvass* and stinking cabbage soup and all of the other vile Russian remedies the prince insisted on ingesting, as though they somehow held more power than the strongest Western medicines.

When Anton had caught these rancid scents, he had been transported back to the golden fields far outside of Moscow and his sisters bent over shafts of wheat. His mother worked with them, brandishing a curved scythe. Her skin was dotted and wrinkled from the sun and her lips pursed into a perpetual frown, although she would still look at him with loving eyes and sing to him softly at bedtime. Anton was six and deemed old enough to work, but he had pleaded a sore throat that day and his mother feared the grippe. She told him he could play on his blanket and they would cover for him.

One of his sisters tripped in the field and skinned her knee so badly she hobbled when she walked. Anton's mother yelled at her to get back to work.

His father had left for the capital after Anton was born. Every so often, they received a small fold filled with coins and crumpled bills but no summons to join him in St. Petersburg.

At last, six years after his father left, the messenger came from court. Did they have a boy? Prince Potemkin needed him, for his valet was growing sick and weak and wished to finally do right by his family.

Without the prince's intervention, Anton would still have been working the field. Anton had visited the old man once but scarcely recognized him. After that, Anton grew convinced Prince Potemkin had summoned him, not his own father. The prince had probably heard the story of Anton's family somewhere and determined to help make it right.

Anton looked at another letter he had saved. The prince had composed it, but his writing had grown so awful, his hands unable to stop shaking, that Anton could barely decipher the words. Nonetheless, he thought he knew what the prince would want to tell the empress and what she would want to hear. He took pen to paper, careful to emulate the prince's handwriting.

We spoke of empire and expansion and absorbing the continent into an enlightened and prosperous whole. I know my project to build the mosque may seem a minor part of this grand vision, but think of the implications.

He thought on everything the prince had shared and his last few months in St. Petersburg. Anton continued to write.

Platon had retired to another room, exhausted from his attempts to comfort Catherine. She cried still but didn't dare let any of her subjects, no matter how close to her heart, see her true emotions.

It was not appropriate. She had enough concerns about the ways in which her court perceived her sentimentality, especially as she aged. As though her emotions had ever hindered her ability to rule.

When it came to maintaining power, appearances were everything; as a woman and a Romanov by marriage only, she knew this better than anyone. She feared some at court, goaded by Paul, would claim she'd grown senile in her old age. Even after all of these years, after all she had done for her adopted Russian empire, they still doubted her right to the throne.

Her love affair had not helped. Grisha had been correct on that point, though she would never have admitted as much to him. Catherine knew well enough how her relationship with Platon looked, the aging woman and her young favorite, the nonsense whispered behind her back. Let them whisper. Any spirited woman in the twilight of life wanted a chance to feel young once more, joyful and energetic, rather than bitter and done. Why should she give up such bliss? And if by some twist of fate their positions were reversed? If Platon were the aging monarch and she an aspiring young woman? No one would think twice of their union.

Only her husband had truly understood, even if he did object to her dear Platon personally. What a singular marriage it had been.

She had his sword knot still, the gold tassel he had given to her when he was still but Platon's age. She could not sleep. Instead she had wandered to her study, where the tassel hung from the wall, and lit the tapers of a candelabra so she might reread the letter her husband's little valet had handed her earlier. She held her emotions in check until she came to the end.

You may be the greatest woman who has ever walked this earth.
I was honored to even have been near you, let alone allowed to
treasure and love you and aid in your mission. I love you.

Your devoted husband as ever,

G

She could have built the mosque. She could have told Platon to hush. If he pouted, she would only need to find another monkey to distract him, or award him a new title. The mosque would have been such a small gesture really. If only she had known it would be Grisha's last request on this earth. She could still order its construction, but what was the point if he wasn't here to experience it with her? What was the point of anything?

If she looked at the letter again she would break.

And then she saw the arabesques, their secret language. Despite everything, she smiled to herself and her cheeks flushed. Her little kitten could still have that effect on her, even after all of these years, even after he had departed from this earth.

Catherine had the plans he had drawn up for the project framed and hung on her wall. She folded the letter into four parts and tucked it behind the backing of the picture. She didn't want anyone else to find it. She would attend to it herself when the time was right.

Twenty

FOR IMMEDIATE RELEASE *(SECOND DRAFT)*

NEW HEIR SCHEDULED TO SPEAK
ST. PETERSBURG, RUSSIA

Dmitry Potemkin, former spokesperson for the Russian Monarchist Society, has issued an invitation for reporters to meet a new heir to serve as ceremonial tsar after the unexpected withdrawal of Romanov heiress Dr. Veronica Herrera.

ST. PETERSBURG
PRESENT DAY

Veronica stared at the frayed sword tassel that had fallen to the office floor last night. Someone had placed it back on its hook on the wall, alongside the other Potemkin mementos. She tried to imagine what the tassel might have looked like when Potemkin and Catherine first met, on the night Catherine seized the throne, bright gold rather than gray and musty with age. Veronica's gaze shifted to their portraits. Perhaps if she stared long enough, she might somehow conjure the prince to help her get through the next several hours.

"Enjoying your last moments as tsarina?"

Slowly, Veronica turned. Irina sat at the desk, tapping her fingers together, face a patient mask. She smiled placidly in Veronica's direction, her latest gray pantsuit so freshly pressed the fabric practically shimmered.

Sasha had followed Irina into the office but didn't bother to sit, only lingered affably, as he was prone to do, near the portrait of his pretty ancestor Felix Yusupov. Sasha took a moment to appraise Felix's serene, if somewhat arrogant, features, and Veronica worried he was having second thoughts.

"I'll sign papers." Veronica tried to keep her voice flat. "Whatever you need. I'll relinquish my claim. I'm through with all of this. It's not worth it."

Irina widened her eyes in mock surprise. "Giving up that easily?"

"It wasn't easy at all." Veronica's heart thudded. Perhaps she should have put up more of a fight. Acquiescence may have heightened Irina's suspicious nature. She modulated her voice to sound angrier, not that it was difficult. "How do I know you'll keep your end of the bargain? How do I know Michael will be released?"

"I stay true to my word. It is part of the code of the nobility. You relinquish your claim and Michael is released within the hour." She hunched forward and Veronica caught the harsh aroma of Irina's reproduction of Catherine's perfume. "In exchange, I want you out of the country. I do not want this organization associated with a pro-homosexual agenda."

Veronica met her gaze. "And I want Michael out of that hellhole now."

Irina turned to Sasha. "You understand what this means for you?"

"I do." Sasha smiled gamely, same mellow smile under the hipster beard. Veronica had a feeling he was a good poker player. She liked that.

"This is a shame," Irina said, addressing Veronica once more. "I think your tenure as tsarina could have been most successful. But you simply could not grasp the full picture. Success is a compli-cated matter and involves compromise."

"I couldn't make the kind of compromise you wanted."

"So what are you going to do now? Go back to your old job?"

Veronica tried not to think too much about her old job: the dry, artificial office air and the dull spreadsheets. "If necessary."

"You would rather sit in a cramped cubicle than take advantage of your position. And for what? Do you think the government is really going to do anything about Reb?"

"You seemed to think they would if I got involved," Veronica shot back.

She clamped her mouth shut and bent her head, trying to seem pensive once more.

"You have three hours to leave," Irina said testily. "I'll make sure Mikhail's visa is returned to him. Your tickets are ready. I'm even going to make sure Mikhail's personal items are collected. I will escort you to the airport myself."

As promised, Michael was released from jail within the hour. They agreed to meet at the lobby of Veronica's hotel, near the dig-ital signs flashing the meetings scheduled for the day. Veronica exhaled loudly when she saw Michael walk through the lobby doors; Irina was in front of him.

Following them into the hotel were a pair of businessmen in fashionably trim gray suits. Veronica felt certain they were Anya's friends.

She backed up instinctively, knocking against one of the paint-ings on the lobby wall, a copy of a still life from the Hermitage with a fresh lemon, a sprawling crab, and a goblet of wine. One of the men nodded at Veronica as they headed toward the electronic board listing the day's conferences. Veronica glanced at Irina, but she was fussing with Michael's luggage.

"The Birch Room," Veronica said softly, not looking at the men as they passed. "That's where they're meeting you. Dmitry Potem-kin reserved the room last night."

One of the men stopped and tilted his head in her direction, recognition suddenly glinting in his dark brown eyes. He smiled at her. "You are not joining us, tsarina?"

Veronica kept her gaze locked on Michael. She never wanted to let him out of her sight again. But she spared one more glance at Irina, who was taking in the hotel lobby with thinly concealed disdain. They were still safely out of earshot.

"Not this morning," Veronica told him, voice low. "But I be-lieve I will see you again very soon."

The men nodded and moved on.

As she neared Michael, Veronica winced. His eye looked even worse than it had the day before. The bruise had turned dark yel-low, which meant it was healing, but it also stood out more prom-inently. Exhaustion lined his face. At least he didn't appear to have any new injuries.

He looked up at her and his face lit up with a broad smile.

Veronica let out a little cry and ran to embrace him, trying not to press against the sensitive area near his eye.

He wrapped his arms around her, not saying anything, content merely to gently stroke her hair and feel her skin on his. After his time in the jail cell, the scent of his body was heavy, but she took it in, took all of him in. She had missed him so much. The time she had spent away seemed such a waste now, but then perhaps she had needed that time away to appreciate what she had.

He whispered in her ear: "I don't know what you needed to give up, but you didn't have to do it. I would have been all right."

"You would not have been all right." Veronica hugged him tighter and whispered: "Trust me. Follow my lead."

Irina waited behind Michael, tapping her hands on her hip. She indicated Michael's luggage, the bag she had packed for him.

"Sorry to break up this lovely scene, but I believe the two of you have a flight to catch."

In that moment, Veronica truly wanted to leave. She missed her grandmother's cozy home in Bakersfield and comforting hugs. Most of all, she missed Los Angeles. She missed Michael's house. She missed his animals and the trucks rumbling by on Hyperion Boulevard and his vinyl records and the softness in her limbs when he pulled her body to his.

Stepping back, Veronica said: "I'm ready."

Michael's fingers grazed hers and she squeezed them reassuringly.

Irina paid the cab driver and marched them through the howling wind, straight into the terminal at Pulkovo, all sleek lines and skylights that let in the weak sun. A sculpture of a white angel with jet-plane wings hovered over a circular information desk. The airport spoke to Russian aspirations to modernity, to wealth, to high class. But the attempt only made Veronica miss Los Angeles all the more.

They jostled through the bustle of passengers as polite announcements in Russian and English and several other languages boomed over loudspeakers.

"Do you really need to be here?" Michael asked Irina as they headed toward a ticket counter. "I mean, I'm sure you have better things to do with your time, lording it over the peasants and rabble and whatnot."

Veronica smiled to herself, glad to hear the old sarcasm back in Michael's voice. Perhaps he wasn't too much worse for the wear.

"I want to make sure neither one of you has a last-minute change of heart." Irina pulled her fur coat tighter to her chest. "And I have no intention of 'lording it over' anyone. I only want what is best for this country. As any patriot would."

Veronica did her best to look finished, completely depleted. It wasn't hard. She hadn't slept at all last night and sheer adrenaline kept her going at this point. "I just want to get on a plane and go home. That's it."

They moved into line, haggard-looking families in bulging coats and well-dressed Russian, Asian, and Scandinavian businessmen ahead of them in the queue. Once they made it to the front of the line and Irina had engaged in all the proper pleasantries with the ticket agent, a computer spat out their boarding passes: one connection in Moscow and then home to Los Angeles.

The woman behind the counter, suit trim and scarf crisp, smiled. "Safe travels . . ."

Her voice faded and she hesitated, looking closely at Veronica. She tried to return the smile but only bit her lip, expecting a flood of questions. *Aren't you the tsarina? What happened? Why are you leaving?*

But if the ticket agent behind the counter recognized Veronica or had any questions, she kept that to herself. She said nothing more.

"I'm sorry things didn't work out," Irina said briskly, checking the gate information. "But really I wish Americans would learn they are not the policemen of the world."

Once she was satisfied with the information on the boarding passes, she placed them in her purse, saying, "I'll just hold on to these for now." She began to remove her coat and Veronica's shoulders tensed. She had hoped Irina would leave once they had their tickets. If she was taking her coat off, she intended to stick with them longer.

While her purse was open, Irina's phone pinged with a text alert. Her lips curled as she looked down to read the text. Veronica pretended to check her own phone, all the while listening intently for Irina's reaction.

"That boy has been given the greatest opportunity in the world," she heard Irina mutter, "and still he manages to get himself in trouble."

Veronica looked up, trying to keep her features neutral. "Trouble?" she asked innocently.

"What happened?" Michael asked.

"Something about gambling," Irina said. "Something about Sasha and a fight . . . a broken jaw? Someone must have gotten him drunk. Perhaps I should have kept a closer eye on him. I suppose some of his Russian friends might be inclined to take advantage of his situation."

"How so?" Michael asked, facing Irina but casting a curious glance in Veronica's direction.

Irina shook her head. "I don't know exactly, but Sasha has been arrested. He's in a temporary holding cell."

"Does anyone else see the irony here?" Veronica asked.

"I fail to see any humor in this situation," Irina snapped.

"You have connections in the prison system, right?" Veronica said, trying not to sound too eager for Irina to be gone. "You can get him out."

Irina lowered her gaze and adjusted the diamond tennis bracelet on her slim wrist. "I do think at some point that boy needs to grow up and take care of himself."

"You wouldn't want any bad publicity before you announce he's tsar," Veronica said.

"Perhaps it's time he learned a lesson. He can't always rely on me to save him."

"So you'll leave him in jail?" Michael asked.

"A few hours in a jail cell? Over some nonsense at a card table and a brawl with idiots?" Irina flashed Michael one of her arrogant smiles. "That will do nothing but bolster his claim, make him stronger in the eyes of the public, more of a man. You see, he has Russian blood. He can handle this."

"I have Russian blood too." Michael bowed his head but then

cocked it slightly to gauge Irina's reaction. "I still got a black eye. I wouldn't wish time in a Russian jail cell on anyone."

Irina appraised the damage on Michael's face. The corners of her lips tugged down, but the tone of her voice remained defiant. "No true Russian would see a black eye as anything other than a badge of honor."

Veronica rolled her dry tongue over the roof of her mouth. "*I don't care how long Irina lived in America,*" Anya had told Veronica last night. "*Deep down she is still a Russian mama. They spoil their boys rotten. She'll act like a Russian mama if she thinks her boy is in any sort of trouble.*"

"Perhaps." Michael's hand moved subtly toward the bruising around his eye. "But you never know what else can happen."

Irina's phone chimed once more and she checked the next message. Then she frowned and dropped her phone into her purse. "I must go. Sasha needs me. I only wish we could have seen eye to eye on things." Reluctantly, she removed the boarding passes and handed them to Veronica. "I hope you have a safe trip back. No hard feelings." She extended her hand primly in Veronica's direction.

"Right," Veronica muttered. She accepted the boarding passes but then drew her hands to her sides. She didn't want to seem too anxious for Irina to go, only bitter and resigned. But she was not going to shake that woman's hand.

Irina pressed her lips together and pulled her purse closer to her side. Then she turned her back to Veronica and walked away, heels clacking.

It seemed to take Irina forever to get out of their line of vision. And even then Veronica waited, heart pumping rapidly. She wanted Irina out of the airport before they made their move.

Finally she felt a light tap on her back.

"It's okay," Dmitry told her. "I watch her get in taxi. We can go now."

"Thanks for coming." Veronica gave Dmitry a quick hug and

then took Michael's hand again. "Change of plans. We're not going directly back to the United States. I hope that's okay."

Michael looked too tired to fight, even were he so inclined. "Where are we going?"

"Instead of boarding the connecting flight, you will stay in Moscow," Dmitry told him. "For a little while. I am to make sure you make this flight. Anya will see to new tickets and that you board next flight safely."

"Why are we going to Moscow?" Michael asked.

"A quick event for tsarina before you leave for California."

Michael shook his head. "Why are you still calling her that?"

Veronica smiled at Dmitry. "Force of habit?"

"I meant grand duchess," Dmitry replied. "Right title for daughter of tsar."

"And while we're there," Veronica told Michael, "we can watch the new tsar on TV."

"I met him back in Irina's office, remember?" Michael said. "That kid who thinks French is Russian. I don't want to watch him on TV. And you're not his daughter . . ." Michael's voice trailed off and then he quietly added, ". . . you're Laurent Marchand's daughter."

"Sasha found out what Irina did to you," Veronica said. "He's helping us. He's distracting her."

Michael rubbed his forehead. "So Laurent? Your father is calling himself the new tsar now?"

"We are calling him this as well," Dmitry said. "He is the true heir."

Veronica gave a quick nod. "I met with him yesterday. I asked him to do this."

"Are you all right?" Michael touched her arm.

"Actually we have more in common than I expected." Veronica reached down to unzip the side pocket of her carry-on bag. She withdrew her red binder and flipped it open to the letter from

Prince Potemkin, still carefully tucked in the plastic sheeting for protection. "And I've been dying to show this to you. I found this the other night. It was hidden in the sketch of the mosque."

Michael bent closer to see the signature. "Potemkin!" He looked at Dmitry. "Your man."

Dmitry shrugged but looked a bit smug. "It is as though he speaks to grand duchess."

"It's true. The letter inspired me," Veronica said.

"And you just took it from Irina's office?"

"Is not *her* office," Dmitry told him. "I already tell grand duchess to make sure letter gets to an archive in the United States. It is what Grisha would want."

"I only wish I knew what this meant." Veronica pointed to the arabesque symbols on the bottom of the page.

"What is that?" Michael asked.

Dmitry leaned in to take a look. And then he started to laugh. "Oh yes! I remember from last night. The mysterious secret code. This is what inspires you?"

"Well . . . yes . . . the letter."

"I found information last night. You are right. Secret language between Grisha and the empress, but it was . . ." He flashed a smile. "Sexual in nature."

"Oh!" Without thinking, Veronica shut the binder hard. Michael chuckled.

"This is all right," Dmitry said. "Grisha inspired you to act. That is important."

"You think he would be proud of us?" Veronica asked.

"I do," Dmitry said.

"What are you going to do now?" Veronica said. "Wait for news on Reb obviously. But after that?"

Dmitry held her gaze. "I think I want Grisha to feel proud of me as well," he said. "And I think even without tsarina at side there is still much I can do here. I will . . . come out."

"To the public?" Michael said.

Dmitry nodded. "Is only way. Too many people are getting hurt. They need to see who is being hurt. They need to see us."

Veronica's pulse quickened. She wanted to tell him not to do it. He would get hurt. He could get lynched. He was putting himself in danger and she wanted to protect him. But she also knew he was right. Russians were allowing laws to get passed that hurt people: Dmitry, Reb, the grandson of the floor attendant back at the hotel. If no one spoke out, the suffering remained abstract. As long as it remained abstract, it would continue.

"Let me know how it goes," she told him.

"I will." He glanced back at one of the displays with the flight information. "You two go now. Safe travels, Grand Duchess."

She smiled and stepped back so Michael could shake his hand. As they grabbed their luggage and moved toward the security gates, she turned around. Dmitry was still smiling, but the corners of his lips were twitching and his gaze had darkened.

The bar seemed more of a quiet hangout for locals than a place for Moscow's elite to see and be seen. Of course, they were far from the city's center and had arrived in the early evening. The place smelled of cheap beer dried on thin wood. Only a few lone drinkers slumped over the counter, looking over their shoulders to take disinterested stock of Veronica and Michael. The bartender kept busy cleaning a lipstick smudge from a wineglass.

Veronica spotted a television propped behind glittering stacks of bottles and figured it would do as well as any. She found a stool while Michael tapped the bartender's back. At first he didn't look thrilled at the interruption. And then he saw Michael's face.

"You look like you had a rough day," he told Michael gruffly, staring at the damaged eye. He found a remote control under the cash register and handed it over.

The first shot was the foyer of the Hermitage Theater: an empty podium with the Russian flag draped over it flanked by two decorative pine trees. Veronica began to play with one of the napkins the bartender had placed in front of her. She was still thinking of the look on Dmitry's face when they left him at the airport. What happened next could help determine his future.

Camera lights began to flash on-screen.

"There he is," Veronica said, pointing to the television.

Slowly, Laurent approached the same podium Veronica had stood behind two days earlier, handsome and dignified in his dapper three-piece suit and carrying his cane, the Romanov ribbon affixed to his lapel.

A Cyrillic caption read: "Breaking News: True Romanov Heir Laurent Marchand emerges from seclusion."

Veronica watched, transfixed, as the camera zoomed in on his face. In the closer shots, his features seemed more vulnerable, his physical frailty more apparent, and for a moment Veronica thought he might need a chair. Laurent cleared his throat and began to address the crowd in elegant French, his native tongue, as a Russian woman translated for him:

"I am here today because my daughter, Veronica Herrera, for personal reasons, has relinquished her own claim to the Romanov throne. I was disappointed to hear this. However, in light of this news, it only makes sense for me to take her place. My name is Laurent Marchand. My mother, Grand Duchess Charlotte, was the secret fifth daughter of Tsar Nicholas II."

Laurent hesitated and shuffled the note cards in front of him. He reached into the front pocket of his jacket and retrieved a pair of reading glasses. It took him a minute to adjust them. In that moment, as the camera lingered, the soft features of Nicholas and Alexandra became increasingly apparent in his expression. Laurent's face gave some clues as to how they might have appeared if they had lived to reach old age themselves.

"First and foremost, I wish to make it clear that I will pursue the same political agenda as my daughter. I understand Reb Volkov will be sent to prison in Siberia tomorrow. This is unacceptable. This type of oppression has no place in our new Russia."

Again, Laurent paused. Slowly, he began to unbutton his blazer. Flashbulbs went off all around him. Laurent looked so delicate it made Veronica's heart ache. She wished she could have been there to take his hand and help him.

But he managed well enough. He looked up at the camera, pale but with a vibrant grin playing on his thin lips. Underneath his jacket, he wore Reb's T-shirt. Free the Wolf.

"If Reb Volkov is not released by this evening, the boycott of Russian vodka will commence, as my daughter alluded to in her press conference. The Romanov family does not support the current direction of the Russian government on social issues. The Romanov family does not believe the Orthodox Church or any other religious institution should condone the persecution of any group as the Russian government supports persecution of those in the LGBT community. This is the modern House of Romanov. And this is what we believe. I will now take questions."

As Laurent removed his reading glasses, reporters shouted question after question, so many Veronica couldn't make sense of them. Veronica half-expected Irina to materialize and insist that Laurent was just a crazy old man. But when the camera panned the room, Irina was nowhere to be found.

Michael put his hand on Veronica's shoulder and gave a gentle squeeze. "Beautiful," he said. "No one can question Laurent's right to speak for the Romanov family."

"I hope it works."

"I think it will. But I wonder what will happen to that boy Sasha?"

"I'm sure he'll be fine." *Handsome men usually are*, she thought. "Anya texted me. Apparently, once Irina found out about Laurent, she threw a fit and threatened to leave Russia for good." Veronica doubted anyone thought that was a bad thing, even her own step-son. No matter what Irina had offered him, Sasha understood it was not worth it.

On-screen, Laurent pointed to a reporter, smooth as a White House press secretary. He should have done this years ago. She smiled at him. Maybe he couldn't actually return the smile, but she thought he could sense it somehow. She had never in her life felt proud of her father. She'd never even had a father. The sensa-tion was strange, and the resentment still lingered, but she hoped it might fade over time.

"He is the true tsar," Veronica said.

"Laurent just picked up where you left off."

"I'm still proud of him," she said.

"What are you going to do when you return to California?" Michael asked.

Veronica shredded the napkin in her hands. "Beg for my old job back?"

He dipped his head. "Cubicle wasteland?"

"That's the one."

Michael took her hand and turned it over in his, pressing his lips softly against her index finger. Veronica touched his chin. The usual doubts still raced through her head. He would hurt her, or worse yet, she would hurt him. But when he bent closer to her, looking so vulnerable, the doubt evaporated. She brushed her lips on his, part-ing them gently, and she was lost, drowning, never wanting to leave, wondering why she had ever left, why she had ever abandoned this when it felt so right. This was where she belonged.

At least for a moment. And then she grew aware of the bar-tender's disapproving gaze. Reluctantly, she pulled back, heart still racing.

"I think you should move back to Los Angeles," he told her as she caught her breath. "And not just for me . . ."

He ran his hand back through his hair and scratched his head.

She laughed softly. "It's okay," she told him. "Go on. I like what you're saying so far."

"You belong there," he continued, smiling shyly. "The fact that I'm nearby works out well. At least for me." He scratched his head again. "I mean, I hope you feel the same way."

Veronica nodded, also feeling shy. "I agree."

"Losing tenure isn't the end of the world. Make the life you want."

"I can still write. I always wanted to finish my biography of Alexandra . . . and maybe it would be fun to do more research on Prince Potemkin."

"You deserve a meaningful life, Grand Duchess," Michael said. "Don't settle for anything less."

The groundbreaking ceremony took place near one of the outer ring boulevards, far from the Kremlin towers and the luxury apartments of the new oligarchs, in a clearing once repurposed for a frumpy Soviet-era bureaucratic building. It was being repurposed once more . . . and none too soon as far as Veronica was concerned. The world could certainly live with one less dull office complex.

They were far enough from the center of Moscow to be away from the worst of the pollution, and the sun was shining despite the bitter cold. Veronica drew in the woodland scent of the park, feeling revived. She thought the site looked pretty, an open square dusted with white snow. The square was surrounded on all sides by official buildings with classical Greek pillars, interspersed with neat rows of renovated apartment blocks. Grigory Potemkin would have been pleased.

When she spotted them, Anya squealed and ran past the men gathered for the ceremony. She hugged Veronica and then nodded happily at Michael. "Welcome. Welcome to Moscow. The true heart of Russia." She wore a floral *hijab* and a new pair of glasses with rosy frames that matched her lipstick. She steered them to a cleric in a white hat and the businessmen Veronica had seen in the hotel back in St. Petersburg when Michael was first released. They had agreed to work with the Islamic community to help secure support for Laurent Marchand's leadership of the House of Romanov. Veronica hoped it was a step in the direction of unity that encompassed different faiths and different ways of life.

The groundbreaking ceremony was brief and to the point. The imam in attendance referred to Veronica as honorary tsarina. She liked the sound of that, even if it was no longer accurate. He then mentioned Veronica and Laurent's ties to the Romanov family. He did not specifically mention Laurent's speech, or his support for Reb Volkov, but he did refer to Laurent and Veronica as "friends of the community."

As the imam spoke, Veronica thought she saw a familiar face hovering in the back of the crowd. His image was fuzzy, as though somehow he was there and yet he was not.

She closed her eyes. Counted to three in her languages. Opened her eyes again.

He remained, smiling calmly in her direction. She knew him. She recognized his face immediately, along with the eighteenth-century attire and the medallion with Catherine's portrait pinned to his jacket. The auburn hair. The slight tilt to his head, so she couldn't see his bad eye. He may have been a figment of her imagination, but at that moment she didn't care. She was glad he had made it and she returned his smile. Prince Grigory Potemkin knew his mosque would be built at last. He nodded at her and then slowly faded from view.

ACKNOWLEDGMENTS

When considering historical subjects for a companion novel to *The Secret Daughter of the Tsar*, I knew I wanted to visit the time of Catherine the Great. Given what Veronica learns about her Romanov identity, I thought she would feel motivated by Catherine's reign and her accomplishments. A chat with a good friend and fellow history buff led me to Prince Grigory Potemkin. Although Potemkin's dogged pursuit of the mosque is my invention, it was inspired by the portrait of the prince drawn by Simon Sebag Montefiore in *Prince of Princes: The Life of Potemkin*. Potemkin strikes me as a man of the Enlightenment: cosmopolitan and fascinated by the multicultural landscape of his homeland. According to Montefiore's work, the construction of a mosque in Moscow was at least a small part of Potemkin's negotiations with the Turks in 1789–90. The friction between Potemkin and Catherine's final favorite, Platon Zubov, though fictionalized, is based on historical records.

For the story set in the present, I wanted my fictional universe to deal indirectly with the 2012 arrest and imprisonment of members of the punk group Pussy Riot. I wanted to deal in a more direct manner with the escalating homophobia in contemporary Russia, particularly the passage of the so-called gay propaganda law by the Duma in 2013. It is my hope that in the coming years, the situation for the LGBT community in Russia will improve.

I wish to extend heartfelt thanks to my agent, Erin Harris of Folio Literary Management, and my editor, Vicki Lame of St. Martin's Press. I would be lost without the moral support and thoughtful commentary of friends and fellow writers Melissa Jackson and Lou Ann Barnett, as well as my family, who worked so hard to spread the word about my first book. Finally, thank you to Barbara Hom-Escoto for introducing me to Prince Potemkin.

SELECTED BIBLIOGRAPHY

Anthony, Katherine (translator). *Memoirs of Catherine the Great*. New York City: Alfred A. Knopf, 1927.

De Madariaga, Isabel. *Catherine the Great: A Short History*. New York: Yale University Press, 1990.

Goscilo, Helen, and Vlad Strutkov (editors). *Celebrity and Glamour in Contemporary Russia: Shocking Chic*. New York: Routledge Taylor & Francis Group, 2011.

Massie, Robert. *Catherine the Great: Portrait of a Woman*. New York: Random House, 2011.

Montefiore, Simon Sebag. *Prince of Princes: The Life of Potemkin*. London: Phoenix Press, 2001.

Polovtsoff, Alexander. *The Favorites of Catherine the Great*. London: Herbert Jenkins Limited, 1940.

Rounding, Virginia. *Catherine the Great: Love, Sex, and Power*. London: Hutchinson, 2006.

Sergeant, Phillip. *Courtships of Catherine the Great*. New York: Brentano's (year unknown).

Soloveytchik, George. *Potemkin: Soldier, Statesman, Lover and Constant of Catherine of Russia*. New York: W. W. Norton and Co. Inc., 1947.

FIND OUT WHERE IT ALL BEGAN IN

The

Secret Daughter

of the Tsar

AVAILABLE FROM ST. MARTIN'S GRIFFIN

Prologue

The clanging of the old woman's summoning bell echoed across the kitchen. Annika raised her voice higher with the other girls to drown out the sound. She wanted to hear the latest gossip free from interruption.

The laughter soon gave way to intermittent giggles and then ceased altogether. A moon-faced sous chef regarded her with a sly smile, as though Annika's every move was destined for failure. Annika stuffed another bite of herring in her mouth and let the greasy skin slide across her tongue. The glacial stares sank her spirit like a stone. If Annika proved derelict in her duties, she'd be released without pay. Someone else would inherit the unenviable task of gratifying Marie Romanov's every last whim. She passed a linen napkin over her lips and excused herself.

Upstairs, Annika found Marie perched in her favorite flowered armchair. Despite the frigid autumn chill, the exiled dowager empress had ordered her chair moved from its place in the sun to a less conspicuous corner of the room. Annika suspected Marie didn't want the young visitor to count her wrinkles in the fading light.

The visitor was bent over a tarnished silver samovar now, pressing the wolf's head–shaped spout to refresh Marie's tea. "Nicholas and Alexandra encouraged your granddaughters to pursue sports, did they not?" He spoke impeccable Danish, though his thick German accent struck each consonant like a mallet. "I understand that even at the end, while the royal family was held captive in Siberia . . ." When he spotted Annika at the door, he hesitated mid-pour and forced a tight smile.

"There you are," Marie snapped. "What took so long?" She drew her ratty ermine stole closer around her neck and made a flicking motion with two fingers. "Show Herr Krause to the door. His audience with me has quite come to a close."

Annika lowered herself into one of the quick curtsies that sufficiently pleased Marie without making her calf muscles ache terribly. The German visitor scowled at her and Annika responded with a small shrug. Despite his fine-looking features, she found nothing appealing about this grim young man.

Herr Krause turned the crushing weight of his attention back to Marie. "Dowager Empress, I can't leave yet. You haven't finished telling me of your family's holidays along the Baltic Coast, before the troubles began."

Underneath her thick layer of facial powder, Marie's expression softened. She caressed the gilt edges of the leather album on her lap. Her gaze flashed over a discolored photograph of her four granddaughters standing in a row, shortest to tallest, hands clasped together. The girls wore identical white cotton dresses and giant sunhats with long ribbons. Their heads were tilted coyly to the side, flirting with the camera, untroubled by any hint of the difficulties to come.

"Nicky and Alix are excessively fond of tennis." Marie reached for the delicate porcelain cup perched underneath the samovar. Herr Krause pressed the hot water spout once more. The tea emitted a fragrant aroma of cloves and cinnamon. "They have taught the older girls to play, and lament Grand Duchess Tatiana's weak serve."

"I understand your son Tsar Nicholas was an avid athlete," Herr Krause said. "And even in his final days sought comfort in his daily walks and calisthenics."

Marie snatched her cup back. Boiling water splashed Herr Krause's hand. He yelped and fell back into a chair. Annika found Marie's speed astonishing, given her age. Then again the dowager empress always greeted reality with nasty swipes, like a bear disturbed during winter hibernation. "See him to the door," Marie said crisply.

Herr Krause grabbed a linen napkin from atop Marie's china cabinet and pressed it to his hand. His slender backside melded into the faded upholstery of the guest chair until he appeared intractable. "I don't understand."

"The tsar has not suffered through his last days yet." Marie's husky voice rose in pitch. The thin blue veins in her neck strained against her papery skin. Annika shifted her weight and prepared to stand silently for a quarter of an hour at least, while Marie delved into another bewildering account of how the tsar and his family might have escaped the Bolshevik firing squad to live in hiding in Paris or San Francisco or the Siberian wastelands. Annika had heard a hundred scenarios, each more outlandish than the last.

This evening, however, Marie merely patted the fringed bangs cut high on her forehead. "We will rescue Nicky, Alix, and the children. We will find my missing granddaughter." Her voice cracked and dropped an octave. "Alix will forgive me then."

Herr Krause extended his hand toward Marie. She shot him a withering look and he quickly dropped his hand back into his lap. "Forgive you for what?"

Marie pursed her lips and leaned against the windowsill. She drew the silken curtains back and stared at the gravel beach outside. Marie's sorrowful, searching gaze once again reminded Annika of the precarious nature of the old woman's circumstances. Hvidore belonged to Marie, yet since the Russian Revolution she had lived here only at the pleasure of her nephew, King Christian of Denmark.

"You are fatigued. I have stayed too long." Herr Krause tossed his soiled napkin back on the cabinet, rose to his feet, and started across the room. He stopped abruptly at the door, bony knuckles splayed on the loose knob.

"Don't abandon hope, Dowager Empress. Remain steadfast and true." Herr Krause drew back his right leg and placed his left palm over his heart. A welt blistered beet red on the back of his hand. "We will restore your family's throne. I promise you that." He bowed deeply in Marie's direction, and then followed Annika out to the hall.

Most visitors to Hvidore couldn't keep their gaze from wandering to the domed ceiling, the statuary lining the walls, or the silvery crests of Baltic waves visible from the high windows. This opulence seemed misplaced in the otherwise sensible residence, like the furs and pearls Marie wore with her practical housedress and sturdy black shoes. Yet Herr Krause's gaze remained fixed on each step before him. He removed a handkerchief from his jacket pocket and wrapped it around the welt on his hand. "Does the dowager empress not understand what happened to the tsar's family?"

"The poor creature lost everyone in the Revolution." Annika trailed her fingers along the wrought-iron railing as she led him down the central staircase. "She won't speak of them in the past tense and refuses to indulge those who do so."

Herr Krause winced. "Should I return and apologize?"

"I doubt it will do any good. It looks like she's lost to the world for the evening."

He tilted his head to the side. "Did you understand what she said about a missing granddaughter?"

Annika suppressed a shiver. She didn't care for this topic. On the other hand, once Herr Krause left, she would spend the rest of the night in Marie's room with a needle and colored thread, embroidering flowers on dish towels while the old woman rambled on about the old country and the old ways. "She mentioned a missing granddaughter before. Some of the girls think she's talking about Anna Anderson."

He gave an abrupt laugh. Annika didn't care for the harsh sound of it. "The lunatic who claims she's Grand Duchess Anastasia?"

"No one knows. No one dares remind the dowager what happened. Why should we? The truth is too horrible to bear." Annika imagined the Romanov family on that final night, crowded together in the basement of the house in Siberia where they were kept prisoners. By now, she knew the story too well. She could hear the girls' high-pitched screams, the blast of gunfire, and the sickening sound of flesh ripping underneath the curved tip of a bayonet. Sometimes, she felt as though she'd been in the room herself.

"Besides, the dowager empress dismissed Anna Anderson's petition immediately." Annika quickened her pace. "She called her a silly imposter out for money. Of course, the dowager is eighty years old. She can't distinguish the living from the dead anymore, poor woman." Annika stopped just short of the main doors and opened the hall closet. She stood on her tiptoes to retrieve Herr Krause's overcoat and black fedora from the top hooks. "I wouldn't put much stock in anything she says about a missing granddaughter."

Herr Krause grabbed her arm. Annika tried to wriggle out of his grip. It wasn't painful, but he held her fast. "What does she say? What have you heard?"

His icy blue eyes bored into her, reminding Annika of the Romanian hypnotist who sometimes performed at Tivoli Gardens in the summer. She understood now why Marie had allowed this young man into her chambers when she'd shunned so many visitors before. "Late in the afternoon, when her mind is least clear, I hear her calling out: 'Alix. Forgive me. We'll keep her safe. We'll protect your fifth daughter.'"

"I don't understand." Herr Krause dug his fingers deeper into Annika's flesh. "Tsar Nicholas and Empress Alexandra had only four daughters and a son."

"Yet another figment of the dowager's imagination, I'm sure."

"Of course. Clearly, she is an ill woman." Herr Krause released Annika's arm and allowed her to retrieve his hat and coat. "Perhaps I might speak with Dowager Empress Marie again in the morning, when her thoughts are more lucid."

An entire morning free of the dowager's prattling? Annika smiled to herself. "I could tell her you were misinformed about the fate of the tsar and his family. She might agree to see you again then."

Herr Krause bent forward to take her hand. He kissed her fingertips with surprisingly soft lips. "I would like that very much."

Annika opened the front door to a freezing coastal gale. Undeterred, Herr Krause placed his hat on his head, tightened his coat around his chest, and took the steps down to the courtyard two at a time. He looked back one last time and tipped his hat in her direction. She found his sudden burst of energy odd, considering he'd spent the better part of his afternoon dealing with Marie's delusions. Then again Marie often commented on the strange quirks of the German race. Perhaps the old woman was more perceptive than Annika realized.

1. At the beginning of the story, Grisha Potemkin struggles with the appeals of a spiritual life versus a career at Catherine's court. Later, Platon Zubov declares Grisha's devotion to God "merely a different type of ambition." Do you agree with this assessment? Why would a cosmopolitan man of the court simultaneously feel drawn to the life of a monk?

2. Clearly, Grisha views the construction of a mosque as atonement. Are there additional reasons the project appeals to him? What is the nature of Grisha's relationship with other cultures and the pasha who continually appears to him? Is Grisha an imperialist conqueror or is his worldview more nuanced?

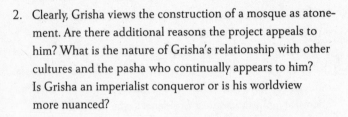

Discussion Questions

3. When Grisha returns to St. Petersburg, Catherine is in the thrall of a much younger lover, Platon Zubov. Grisha then romantically challenges this rival for Catherine's affection. Are we more accustomed to seeing women use their sexuality to curry a monarch's favor? In what ways do Platon and Grisha retain their masculinity while serving under and loving a female ruler?

4. Grisha's attempts to rekindle his romance with Catherine lead to conflict and quarrels between them. Do you think Grisha was more useful to Catherine politically when he kept his distance from her physically? Is this why he remained a trusted friend and advisor even after he ceased to be her lover? Or is it possible he was simply more talented than her other favorites?

5. At one point, Grisha notes that Catherine must hide her emotions from her subjects, even a subject as close to her as himself. As a female monarch, did Catherine need to take special care to control her emotions? What other challenges might she have faced as a result of her gender?

6. In the present day, Veronica comes to Russia to help protest antigay legislation and suppression of free speech. Is the Russian "gay propaganda" law well-known in other countries? Are incidents of violence against LGBT individuals in Russia

St. Martin's Griffin

covered in the West? How do you feel about the news coverage?

7. Veronica finds her connection to the last royal family has already made her something of a celebrity in Russia. Do you think this is realistic, and if so, why are we still fascinated with the last Romanovs? With royalty in general? In what ways can celebrities sway public opinion and affect change?

8. Veronica is continually drawn to both Catherine the Great and Grisha Potemkin, and wonders how they would react to intolerance in present-day Russia. Given what we know of their personalities, how might Catherine and Grisha operate as modern-day politicians? Is it possible to draw inspiration from historical figures to address problems in the present day?

9. Both Veronica and Grisha are childless, but not necessarily by choice. How does this impact each of them? How does it affect the way they are perceived by others? Is it more difficult to navigate the world as a childless woman as opposed to a childless man?

10. Toward the end of the book, Dmitry decides to "come out" in the hope that if Russians know more LGBT individuals personally, it will help turn public opinion against homophobic legislation. In Russia, public figures have been outed without their consent as a means of promoting tolerance. Is the decision to "come out" solely an individual perogative or is it an action that should be taken for the good of an entire community? What are the circumstances under which coming out might become a moral obligation?